# Strange Reality

Darya Kowalski

# STRANGE REALITY

iUniverse books may be ordered through booksellers or by contacting:

iUniverse
1663 Liberty Drive
Bloomington, IN 47403
www.iuniverse.com
1-800-Authors (1-800-288-4677)

ISBN: 978-1-4620-3175-7 (sc)
ISBN: 978-1-4620-3176-4 (hc)
ISBN: 978-1-4620-3177-1 (e)

Library of Congress Control Number: 2015913346

Print information available on the last page.

iUniverse rev. date: 10/30/2015

# Prologue

Carina's relief at seeing the mountains in her rearview mirror and the dark green highway sign with its promise of home in front of her was short-lived as her car hit a patch of glittering black ice.

She automatically steered into the skid but, even though she did everything right, the car's momentum spun her around until it hit the plowed snow at the highway's edge and stopped, facing oncoming traffic.

Her heart in her throat, Carina tried to maneuver the car out of the drift but the wheels spun uselessly. She applied the gas and the brake alternately to get the car rocking enough to clear the drift. A bright light suddenly pierced her car's interior. Too late, she saw the semi bearing down on her. Carina's eyes burned with sudden tears of recognition: Fate had found her.

# The Accident

Off-duty policeman Jackson Dawes saw the semi in front of him swerve and lose control. He slammed on the brakes of his Mustang and slid dangerously, but he managed to maintain control. Dawes heard the screeching of metal-on-metal sheering; he thought he saw a flash of red just before the semi flipped and slid farther down the highway.

He jumped out and dialed 911 as he ran toward the jackknifed semi that sprawled across two lanes, effectively blocking traffic, its cargo slowly seeping onto the highway. The badly shaken driver stepped onto the icy highway just as Dawes approached him on foot. Dawes looked him up and down and saw that he wasn't hurt and told him to get his distance in case the truck exploded. His thoughts quickly turned to the driver of the red vehicle that was only partially visible beneath the truck.

He was horrified by what he thought he might see. Only a miracle could have stopped the truck from crushing the car beneath it. He knew before he looked where the car was jammed, but it was still a shock to see it with a single headlight beaming at the wheels of the huge semi.

Everything that happened after that was surreal and in slow motion like cotton had suddenly packed his brain so full that he could scarcely move—but he did. He turned on the flashlight that he'd had the instinct to grab as he left his car and flashed it at the shorn car beneath the truck. The roof of the car was half curled up like a sardine can lid and the passenger door was partially torn from its hinges. He bent and peered into the interior, expecting to see the worst and saw a woman's body in his flashlight's shaky beam.

He reached forward. "Ma'am? Can you hear me?"

He touched her skin and felt its warmth. A slight flutter of hope flew through his fingers as he brushed them along her neck until he found a juncture to feel for a pulse. He waited without breathing, oblivious to the fact that vehicles were beginning to line up on the other side of the truck. Vague sounds of slamming doors and people shouting didn't break his intense concentration—he felt the slightest whisper of movement pulsing against his fingers and he was suddenly afraid to move, as if his fingers were the only things keeping her alive.

Gasoline fumes permeated the air and Jackson's nose responded immediately. He winced; if he didn't leave now, he could die along with the woman. He quelled his flight-or-fight instinct and assessed the situation. He didn't have time to get to the driver's door and chances were that it would be jammed shut. The sardine can roof revealed the ravaged underside of the truck had no room for escape. The only alternative was to take her out through the passenger door. If he had a few more minutes, he could figure out a way to get her out safely but the smell of smoke quickly dispelled that notion. He fervently prayed to God as he placed his hands beneath her shoulders and began pulling her toward him. For a moment her body didn't move but then, in an agony of slow motion, it began to inch toward him. He felt the placidness of her broken body and prayed he wouldn't kill her with his roughness, but he had no choice. Once her body cleared the seat, he lifted it into his arms and ran.

The force of the explosion threw him and his precious cargo to the ice-covered highway.

# This Doesn't Look Like Home

*My God. What the hell is going on and where is my car? That semi was aimed straight at me.* She checked herself for injuries and then looked around.

Shaking her head in disbelief, she stared at her surroundings—at the numerous buildings disappearing and reappearing in newer versions. *This is freaky.* Even the brick façade of the university college that Carina attended was gone, replaced by an oval-roofed building. A fast-forward film of images flew by as she glanced up and down the streets. Her chocolate-brown eyes seeing one thing, watering and, in a blink, the landscape distorted and changed. Her perceptions altered.

Carina took a few tentative steps into the city of Kamloops and walked along smoking-street after smoking-street of mangled buildings. Bombshell devastation, huge craters, burned debris, and the loose ash of fallen structures littered the once well-known landscape. The skeletal remains of once-familiar shops smouldered sullenly while tall glass and cold metal edifices bloomed in stark contrast to the vast fields of debris.

She covered her nose and mouth against the acrid air that threatened to choke her. *I wasn't out of town long enough for this kind of growth. I left Kamloops to visit a friend and I returned to... this?* She'd only been gone for three days and it no longer looked like a remote, backward town; it seemed urban and modern. *And where did all the snow go? Why am I on this particular street? It leads through the city, obviously, but why are these blocks of buildings being torn down and rebuilt?* She looked at the blackened concrete. *It doesn't need any changes. Since when are buildings left like this?*

The vibrant images of the new buildings, with their brilliant blues, yellows, and reds suddenly appearing before her left her disjointed and shaky. She thought it was another one of her vivid dreams, alive with randomly changing scenes flashing from one strange theme to another, from a downtown stone bench to a sprawling suburban rancher and then a dry and dusty asphalt parking lot. *They were all without logical connections or patterns* she thought as she walked along wide, barren streets that suddenly manifested pink-flowering cherry trees and white picket fences.

One long and narrow street meandered by the side of a stream. *If this is a neighbourhood, it's the most eclectic one I've ever seen. Who'd have a shopping centre beside a stream or barbed-wire fences?* Undeniably, though, beauty hid among the beastly, devastated streets and pristine glass edifices.

She stopped dead in her tracks when a two-story panoramic view of meticulously painted dolphins and whales stood out against an opposing street of buildings that nestled on individual piers.

*Ow!* A blinding stab of pain flared at her temples; she winced. As quickly as the pain seared, it evaporated like a fleeting memory.

*The buildings would soon face destruction.*

*I wonder how I know that.*

The disjointed and sometimes distorted images of her dream changed yet again. A dark wooden doorway materialized out of thin air, wavering like a mirage and then solidifying into a solid brick

4

building. Its appearance, out of a thick haze, startled her and chills tickled her spine as she stepped closer to examine it.

It was an old, decaying building and must have stood on that particular spot for decades. *Then why did it just appear? Maybe I'm fading in and out and everything else is stationary.* She pondered the idea as she discovered the main entrance, overshadowed by two Doric pillars that led to dark, hewn-wood doors. It smelled of damp concrete, age, and decay. A few unidentifiable odours wrinkled her nose in distaste. Sunbaked grass bordered the crumbling walkway. Carina glanced at the brown tangle and saw that there wasn't a bug to be seen crawling anywhere.

*What did I expect? I haven't seen anything moving anywhere and even the lifeless sky holds only the burning sun.*

She stepped forward and discovered that the doors were ajar; she pushed tentatively against them. Peering into the musty interior, she saw an office of some type with dingy desks and dust-laden bookshelves. Mesmerized, she entered the dilapidated building along with three men who'd materialized beside her. Taken aback, yet realizing it was a dream, she stared at their sudden appearance and followed them as they continued past her. She recognized her older brother Matt's blond hair and muscular build first, and then the lankier builds and brunette hair, identical to her own, of her two younger brothers.

"Hey. How'd you guys get here?" she called after them, but they didn't respond. "Why won't you answer me?" She tried to grab Matt's arm, but her hand passed through it. Carina looked at her hand in wonder and looked up at her brothers. They hadn't seen her.

"How can you guys miss me? I'm right here."

*Oh, I know! Now I get it. It's one of those observation dreams where I see what's happening, but I'm not in it. Thank God. I thought I was losing it.*

Not a stranger to lucid dreaming, she followed her brothers, knowing that the only way they could be here was in a dream.

Carina followed them curiously as they filed down a dusty, book-lined passageway. Mathematics, herbal remedies, tarot, witchcraft, and a Bible were just a few of the titles that she glimpsed as she walked by. *What a strange collection.* She continued to glance around as the corridor narrowed even more. *This section looks even older than the first part.* She swallowed nervously as she continued.

She stopped to look at a four-by-five-foot tapestry on the wall. It depicted four scenes: A massive meteor ripping through the Earth's atmosphere and a dragon casting flames in the cities while a phoenix plummeted downward; people living in mountain caves and pictographs of a dormant dragon and a phoenix on the cave walls; people emerging from the Earth and forming communities; the dragon flying high overhead while watching the distant phoenix spiraling up into the sky.

The fourth scene showed a battle with men on foot and horseback. Strangely, the men wore colours of black, navy blue, and dark green. While they fought, a woman walked through the battle, arm upraised and the dragon and phoenix flew above her; threatening immolation. It was a disturbing scene. She read the words embroidered into the tapestry: And the time will come when a stranger to the land will wield the power of the Dragon and Phoenix to end the conflict and bring about peace to the land.

The shelves were cluttered with wooden carvings and stone etchings. She picked up a carved wooden horse and admired its detail. It was so finely detailed that the eyes seemed to follow her as she moved. When she put it down she saw a book about equine management.

She picked up a piece of fool's gold and saw that, like the horse, there were books on geology and metallurgy so she moved on to the next shelf. She saw Anubis and Zeus wedged between an Aztec calendar and a Pegasus with outstretched wings. Her thoughts were interrupted before she could investigate further.

"A new order has begun. The old has been overturned, leaving nothing the same."

"Did you say something?" she asked her brothers just as they came to a full stop in front of a well-placed counter that blocked their movement. A pale, black-haired man stood behind it.

*So, is this a bank or a post office where we have to queue up?* Oddly enough, each one of them waited for his turn before moving to the front to see the pale man who awaited him.

Carina tried to get a glimpse of the counter but a low bar effectively blocked her prying eyes from seeing over it. She wondered what Matt was looking at when he leaned over the counter. *God, it's quiet in here. What are they doing?* Matt straightened up and left the counter without glancing her way. His sudden departure was so abrupt that he was halfway out the door before she had time to react.

She ran after him only to find an empty hallway. *Where'd he go?* She turned around to her other two brothers—they, too, were gone, leaving only her and the man behind the counter. *I know this is only a dream, but I do not want to go to that counter.*

"They've been assigned. They've found positions for them. They're a part of the plan."

She looked at the high-cheek-boned man, "Did you say something?"

When the man didn't respond but continued to look at her expectantly, she forced herself to step in his direction. He'd shown no surprise at her brothers' appearances and he didn't seem disturbed at their disappearance. Compelled by an unspoken command, Carina took another step toward the counter.

*Ow!* The thought and the pain flashed in her head.

*Where do I fit in?* She rubbed her temple absently. *Hey. Dreams aren't supposed to hurt. How did this happen? Where was I when it happened?*

It was obvious that the man behind the counter served a particular purpose and people had to appear before him before being sent elsewhere. Carina moved closer to the counter, anxious to find out why she was having this dream and what it would reveal about her own life. She waited, but the man just stared at her expectantly, *as if he had a secret,* or she realized, *as if I were one of his kind. What a revelation. What is his kind? He looks human, but maybe it's his role that is unique. Has he been specially chosen or preordained? Why would I think of the word "preordained"?* She rubbed her temple unconsciously. She was full of questions but the moment hadn't yet arrived to ask them.

Silence. She realized that no one had spoken except her. Her brothers had ignored her when she spoke to them and she hadn't been able to hear anything they'd said when they walked up to the counter.

She glanced down at his wrist resting on the counter and saw a silver band. The dark-haired man suddenly pushed himself away from the counter. She saw that he'd been sitting and his full height was well over six feet. His black and frenzied eyes held her mesmerized. He moved with an easy step and circled the counter until he stood directly in front of it, holding something carefully between his hands. She saw that it was an intricate metal armband, carved with a dragon and a phoenix locked in combat over an ebony stone in its center. The armband began to pulsate with a crimson glow.

The man deftly settled the armband on her wrist before she could react. *It feels so right.* It started changing, suddenly coming alive, and glimmering once it was on her wrist. A flash of blinding blue light shot out of the stone followed by a crimson-winged, golden bird the approximate size of an eagle. Carina saw a flash of purple and azure as it passed by and headed straight toward the man. A scraping sound like metal on metal distracted her from the phoenix and she turned to see an enormous, red-clawed dragon, at least eighteen feet long, leaping toward the man, who went down under a flurry and flash of claw and talon that devoured him and his armband.

Carina leapt backward and fell screaming onto the hard wooden floor. Her heart raced as she scrambled to her feet and glanced wildly around for the dragon and the phoenix but they'd vanished along with everything else. She had no idea how she knew what was going to happen next, perhaps just intuition, but her dreams never lasted long. Perhaps, she speculated, she wasn't dreaming and she'd somehow crossed over from disjointed images to a clearing glimpse of a strange reality.

# Am I Dreaming?

*Wake up, Carina wake up*, she chanted repeatedly as she asked herself about her perceptions and lack of fear. She wondered why she was accepting the normalcy of her dream. *It was, after all, just a dream wasn't it? What is normal?*

Definitely not the dragon. *Ha. The day I meet a dragon is the day I need my head examined. Okay, I'm in a city that I've known for four years. The landscape keeps changing on me. The only thing that I know for sure is how right this armband feels on my arm. I wonder if my brothers received armbands. They seemed to know their purpose. I haven't a clue about mine.*

She glanced down at the armband; the lifelike dragon and phoenix glimmered. When she looked up, she found herself, once again, at the building's entrance. She drew a deep breath and stepped into the piercing light. She jerked her head when she saw she was now wearing a black, calf-length cloak that completely covered her own clothes. She froze momentarily as she patted the cloak to make sure it was real. It had an unfamiliar coarseness that she couldn't identify.

Looking back, she saw the whole building had disappeared. *Did I just imagine this?* She clenched her eyes shut and covered them with her hands, afraid she was going crazy. She opened her eyes and saw to her horror that she was on an entirely different street, this one congested with buildings.

Carina continued walking toward the core of the city until she eventually heard fires crackling. She discovered shadowed men wearing drab, nondescript clothing, rubbing their hands above the flames. She concealed herself in the shadows when she saw there were no women. At one street opening, she saw a stocky man holding another man by his shirt. He raised his right fist to hit the other man in the face.

She found it strange that no one stopped or questioned her if they saw her. She felt like an experiment allowed to wander randomly around. She couldn't discern the blackness in her brain, couldn't peer beyond the mystery that connected her memories of student and apartment life to what she saw now. She was a stranger in her own city, but it wasn't the same city. *Have I banged my head and now suffer from delusions? Have I somehow crossed into another dimension, an anomaly, or a time shift?* Carina also asked herself if she'd been brainwashed or erased. *I've been watching too many Star Trek programs.* She knew her world wasn't this one and it tormented her by its illogical appearance.

She'd always been logical and followed reason. She had always felt alone, feeling older than she was even though she had several friends. Nothing had prepared her for the present situation.

She caught herself overanalyzing everything. *Maybe that was the dilemma in my time.* The words "my time" sounded strange. Was she accepting the current anomaly? *Those things only exist in science fiction books, movies, and television… and dreams.* She tried to convince herself again, that she was just dreaming until her gnawing stomach got through to her. The relentless hunger pangs were evidence that she wasn't dreaming. *Who feels hunger pangs in a dream?* She was hungry and tired. She had no food or a place to sleep and the sky was getting dark.

She checked her pockets for money, or anything, but they were empty. *What did I expect? And even if I had money, would it be any good here?* Carina forced herself to relax, inhaling and exhaling slowly, until she felt calmer. *I have nothing; therefore, what do I have to lose?* Her thoughts sounded bold and rational but they didn't prevent her from clenching her teeth. She held her breath, exhaling slowly. *How do I find food? By sight, smell, or sound. A store.* Pausing to listen, she heard nothing moving in the dark, empty streets, then a sound like a snake slithering in dry leaves whispered in her ears. It got louder, then quieter, then louder again. She approached the sound cautiously, drawing her dark cloak securely around her for protection.

After a few blocks, she rounded the corner of a tall building and discovered the cause of the rustling. Hundreds of people, all wearing knee-length tunics of brown and white were gathered in long lines. *Where did they come from? Where had they been during the day?* She hadn't seen any of these people on the streets. These were all wearing similar drab clothing. *Did they only come out at night? Had they been hiding?* She couldn't make up her mind whether she should approach the crowd to try to fit in somehow, or stay hidden.

A little girl made the decision for her when she said, "Look, Mama."

Carina looked toward the girl's voice. Her mother glanced up and stared directly at her. Suddenly, there was complete silence. Hundreds of eyes peered at her. Then, as suddenly as the noise had stopped, it began again, a shuffling of feet blending with low, murmuring voices. An old man, white-haired and slightly stooped with age, looked at her warmly with his intelligent blue eyes, and beckoned her to stand behind him in the line.

No one spoke to her. Eventually, she made it to the low building that housed a kitchen and a dining hall. She received a bowl of stew and a hot coffee with milk. She found a wall to lean against and slowly slid to the ground with the bowl on her lap. She savored each tasty mouthful. The old man sat beside her. The too few tables and chairs teemed with people, their conversations bubbling back and forth. She and the old man ate their meals in silence. After savoring the last carrot and spot of gravy, she sighed and put her bowl down. Her coffee had cooled by then and she held the cup in her hands, looking into its depths.

The old man watched her. She guessed him to be in his seventies because of his white hair, grizzled whiskers, and the deeply furrowed brow. He wore a dark-blue tunic that set him apart from the others.

"You're new to the Central Sector, are you not?" he asked.

"Um, yes. What is the Central Sector used for?"

"We process new arrivals and then send them to one of the other four sectors."

"Are the sectors far apart?"

"It would take weeks to get to the Northern sector by horse, which is the closest one, but there are a few outposts along the way."

"How long have you been here?" Carina asked.

"A long time."

"Where did all these people come from? I didn't see them earlier."

"They were here, only hiding and resting. It is safer that way."

"Safer from what?"

"The Banished. They're a nasty bunch of abrasive and backward men who take local residents away when they're unprotected within the sector's perimeter. During the day our posted sentries on every block can see those vermin coming and we hide long before they get close."

"You must have known I was coming, then."

"No, but you were probably under observation, not considered a threat, and permitted to approach."

"What would have happened if I had been a threat?"

"They might have killed you outright, or captured you for interrogation, but probably they would have killed you."

*What? Kill me? What the hell have I gotten myself into?* Her heart tried to break out of her chest in panic. She struggled to control the quaver in her voice before she spoke. "Why... why are the people here in the first place?"

His assessing eyes revealed nothing. "When the Upheaval came many people did not easily change with it. The Leaders are assigning most of us new duties and locations and eventually they will employ everyone. It is taking a fair amount of time as it has to be coordinated among all of the sectors. The individuals here are waiting until they're processed. The cookeries are set up three times a day; we eat together. We're much better protected as a group."

"What do you mean by Upheaval? Who are the Leaders? Is that a new political party?"

He looked at her suspiciously. "You don't know about the Upheaval?"

Alarm bells went off in Carina's head and she could feel the hair on the nape of her neck bristling. She had a flash of insight: She needed to hide her ignorance. "Well, uh, everyone's viewpoint about what happened is different."

He stroked his whiskers. "Quite true."

She changed the subject to steer the focus away from herself. "But where does all the food come from?"

"We grow much of our own food within the sector. In addition, each of the sectors accord extra for reserve, depending on the land usage. You understand the world we know is in flux. Politics are less volatile, as are the countries left after the Upheaval. If we all work together, we will create a better place. It is about time, too. Things have been politically erratic and harmful for too long and change is too slow; several decades to begin again is definitely too slow. Fortunately, the new implementations seem to be better. Enough talk, you must be tired and, if my guess is correct, it is your first day here, is it not?"

"How can you tell?"

"I have not seen you at the cookery before."

"Where did you come from?"

"I am from the Northern Sector initially, but they had use of me here, so I relocated several years ago. We don't get to move once they have allocated us, so I welcomed the commission."

"Has this been going on for a while?"

"Yes, there are ongoing necessary adjustments within each sector. Are you from around here or have you just moved into the area from another sector? It is curious that they would permit someone to move into a new sector without being commissioned, but I suppose they know what they're doing."

Carina had been trying to follow his idiosyncratic speech and didn't have a chance to respond before the conversation ended as the cookery emptied of people. The shuffling and murmuring of voices had receded. The crowds of people in the streets were diminishing, too. "Where are they going?"

"They're returning to their safe places."

"Are the Banished that bad?"

"They used to attack in the middle of the night. They're altering their strong-arm tactics for some reason, perhaps to discourage people from entering the open area for assignment when the committee safely arrives. I hope that they won't change their tactics again. The night is worse, and it is easy to strike fear into people's hearts and minds."

His talk of open areas, committees, and Banished, et cetera, didn't make any sense to Carina. Before she could say anything else, the old man stood up and said a quick goodnight.

"Wait," she called after him. "Where can I sleep?"

"You will have to wait until morning when a proper berth can be found for you. For now, I suggest you sleep in the dining hall."

She woke to the sound of movement—people preparing for the day. Carina's nose wrinkled at the disinfectant smell of the women's washroom she'd found. She wished she could take a shower, but settled for washing her arms and neck in a sink with the edge of the cloak she'd been wearing when she entered the city. The water refreshed her. She hid her conspicuous colourful clothing under the cloak again, which could be thrown back so her arms were free.

The sleeves of her blouse were long and covered the armband; she didn't know why, but she was glad she could cover it. She hadn't seen anyone else wearing one. *Have I been assigned without knowing it? Rather inconvenient not to be told why I'm here.*

The aroma of freshly made coffee wafted invitingly into the room with the next woman, and although Carina wasn't much of a coffee drinker, she smiled and hurried out to receive her own portion of coffee, toast, and scrambled eggs from the side table. She didn't contribute much to the bubbling conversations when room was quickly made for her at one of the tables, but she listened carefully to what everyone said in order to glean more information.

Two days passed during which Carina familiarized herself with the sector's routine and occupants. She wanted to know if other people had experienced what she did—the entrance into the city and its ever-changing surroundings. The people she tried to question ignored her inquiries or looked at her suspiciously; no matter how she asked her questions, she got nothing revealing in return. After a fourth unsuccessful attempt, she realized that she was drawing unwanted attention to herself. The only thing she had learned was that the old man, who helped her the first night, was named Helzion, and he was treated to a great deal of deference, so she knew he was pretty important.

Unable to share her feelings, her concerns, or her hallucinations, or whatever they were, she grew more frustrated and afraid. *What if I'm the only one who is experiencing this? What if this reality is rational now? What is normal? I must be having a nervous breakdown.*

One thing that Carina noticed, whenever she did some exploring, was that there were no sources of entertainment. No movies. No computers. No video games. No sports fields. She couldn't find any books or magazines. She asked one girl if there was a place that they kept or sold books or games.

The girl, who Carina guessed to be around sixteen or seventeen, looked at her strangely but answered her question. "This sector doesn't have any books as it's known as the Sorting Sector. People usually aren't here for a long time. The other sectors have books, but they're restricted."

"Why would books be restricted?"

"The ones that weren't destroyed by the Leaders are valuable."

"Why would they do that? What kind of books did they destroy?"

"To protect people from being negatively influenced by the time before the Upheaval. We're instructed to turn in any books we find. They'll punish us if we read a forbidden book."

"How do you know if it's forbidden?"

"It has to be for learning, like growing gardens or building things." She paused. "I shouldn't be talking about it. If you find any books just turn them in or leave them alone. That's less trouble. The Leaders ask fewer questions then. I have to get back to my chores."

"I'm sorry. I don't want to get you into trouble. You've told me a lot. My name is Carina."

"I'm Kiera."

"Thanks, Kiera. Maybe next time we talk, you can tell me how to pass the time away."

"Kiera grinned. "That's easy. We sometimes get together for history night and then we can hear about the other sectors and sometimes we hear about what it was like before the Upheaval. Sorry, I've really got to leave."

Carina was glad that she had learned a little more about the people, but wondered who "they" were.


Two days later, while enjoying her hot stew, a gnarled old man stood up and began speaking. Conversation ebbed away as people stopped to listen. Carina strained to hear his whispery voice.

"I grew up in the mountains as some of you might know and being an adventurous boy, I always went exploring. I would get in trouble for leaving the safety of the cave but I couldn't resist. I'm glad I did because that's when I discovered that there were more people in the world than I knew. The Southern Sector found me sneaking around some ruins that I'd found and took me in. They re-educated me to be a productive member of society."

He sat down abruptly, his elderly frame shaking from the exertion of standing so long.

"Thank you!" one voice called out.

"We're honoured by your tale," called another.

A woman stood up. "I grew up in the Southern Sector and I miss its flat plains and hills. The Leaders let me learn the ways of plants and I was able to revive the soil and grow food for the sector. I'm being sent elsewhere to share my learning."

Carina couldn't see the woman from where she sat, but she listened along with everyone else. She heard Helzion speaking before she saw him moving to the center of the room.

"Thank you both for sharing your tales. We are honoured."

Everyone murmured in agreement.

"As you know, we have grown as a people. Each sector has grown and thrived from everyone's labour and we continue to grow. It has been slow, children few, but we thrive nonetheless. We still have obstacles to overcome such as the Banished—" People began muttering angrily. He waited a few moments before speaking again. "I understand your anger with the Banished. They cause us a great deal of trouble but we need to remember that eventually we'll catch them all, re-educate them, and they too shall become productive members of our sectors."

Cheering broke out at his words and Carina could see many people at her table nodding in agreement.

"I would like to tell you a tale but it grows late. It's time we all found our beds for the night."

People began dispersing almost immediately. Carina rose along with them and headed to the same room that she had shared with Kiera and the other women until they were assigned. Oddly enough, she still hadn't been questioned and even Helzion hadn't done more than greet her when she ran into him in the hallway.

On the eighth day, Carina heard someone say, in passing, that extra sentries and patrols would be everywhere throughout the sector— the Banished had been silent for too long. Commission Day would be a good time for them to make an appearance.

She wondered what they were talking about and whether Commission Day was coming soon. *Maybe they mean today,* she thought hopefully, *anything to break up the monotony and stagnation. And maybe something will show me why my world has turned upside down.*

Breakfast was hardly finished before a formal-looking meeting occurred. Carina was curious but was kept busy in the cookery where she'd been asked to help prepare the next meal. She'd been working hard in her own world to overcome the blue-collar work of cooking by attending university to get a teaching degree. In fact, her part-time job during university was making pizzas on weekends. *That's all changed,* she thought. *I'm starting all over again and I don't want to do that for the rest of my life.*

She still hadn't figured out how her Mazda had disappeared and why she'd walked into the sector.

Santi, who'd only been in the sector for a few days, ran into the room and happily shared her news, "I've been assigned!"

"What? How?"

"The Leaders have assigned me." The young woman appeared satisfied with her quick explanation. "Maybe you will get assigned, too."

"Did they give you an armband?"

"What are you talking about?"

"I heard that individuals receive an armband when they get commissioned."

"I don't know where you heard that," she snapped and hurried off before Carina could answer.

Santi's abrupt departure only exasperated Carina because, although she'd learned a little more about the sector, she kept running into walls when she tried to glean more information. Santi's commission, however, made Carina hope that she, too, would be called and she returned to the cookery and found that time crawled. When the last of the dishes were cleared away she knew that she was still unassigned.

Later that night two obvious changes emerged: First, the cooking staff didn't move the tables and benches to make space for people to sleep, and there were noticeably fewer people in the sector. The second waited in the dormitories for her to discover.

Gath, the head cook, noticing her perplexed look, said, "It is a pleasant change to have matters back to normal for a week or two. Now that the Leaders have commissioned people, it will be much quieter around here."

"Are you commissioned?"

"Sure, this is my assignment. I have been here for several years. Why. Weren't you?"

"Uh, no, I don't think so."

"Hmm, sounds like they did not know what to do with you or maybe the necessary information from your last sector did not arrive. Don't worry. You will get assigned next time."

"When's that?"

"End of the moon's cycle."

"Thirty more days. What month is it?"

He seemed to not have heard her as he said, "I have to go before my bondmate comes looking for me."

"I didn't know you had a wife. I won't keep you. Goodnight."

Carina returned to the women's dorm, and stepped in quietly. However, her stealth was unnecessary because the room was empty of the thirteen women who'd been there. She saw that someone had come in and piled the mattresses in one corner. *It doesn't make sense.* She pulled a mattress into a corner and curled up on it, using her cloak as a blanket and she fell asleep before she could analyze how she'd remained unassigned.

# Home For 4 Christmas

A loud buzzing roused her from her exhausted sleep. When she groggily sat up, she was in her own bed—in Kamloops, her Kamloops. The alarm had startled her and she didn't remember setting it. She stood and peered around her room.

*What day is it?* She turned on the TV news and learned only one day had passed since her trip to Hope. The only unaccounted time was driving back from Hope to her apartment building, and going to bed, about eight hours. *Was it possible that eight hours were actually eight days in that other place? Was it another dimension? Maybe it really had just been a dream, the longest lucid dream she'd ever had.*

A long pent-up breath whooshed out of her in relief that she'd only dreamed everything. *I sure the hell don't want that to happen again. The first opportunity I get I'm going online to research lucid dreaming.*

Carina quickly realized that it was another school day. She was tempted to skip school just to digest everything she'd dreamed up, but a strong desire for a taste of reality had her preparing for class. She reached for her cloak, a new habit, only to find it absent. However, unlike her cloak, a quick glance at her wrist showed the wristband wasn't gone—and it wouldn't come off.

She twisted it around almost feverishly to find a way to remove it, but it wasn't designed to come off. She was stuck with it. Her heart fluttered in panic and she thought of cutting the band but she was afraid she'd injure herself in the process. She closed her eyes briefly in disbelief and mentally shook herself to wake up because, if the band was real, so was the other reality. She threw on a sweater to dismiss its existence.

She left for her three classes and the remainder of the day passed in a nightmarish, foggy haze. She sat through her classes taking notes while her mind kept reeling in shock and fear that the other-world experience was real. She could no longer blame it on a dream or alcohol, which were plausible excuses.

*What can I blame it on? Maybe it's just stress-related. I spent the Christmas break working late shifts at the pizza place.* Eight in the evening to four in the morning, including New Year's Eve had been her respite from the intensity of her university classes. It wasn't much of a break really, because the only rest came from one glass of champagne generously provided by a customer to ring in the New Year. She'd taken it out to the back alley during a lull in orders. She'd toasted to one and a half years remaining of university courses and the completion of her teaching degree.

Carina remembered throwing the glass down the alley and hearing it break to seal the toast. Her thoughts didn't stop there; they continued to replay the events that led up to her experience. She wanted to tell someone, but dismissed that thought immediately because, if she was having a hard time believing it, it was unlikely that she could convince anyone else it was real. Carina tried to go back to her normal routine—school, work, and study to stave off her terror and panic.

Saturday night finally arrived. It was a rare evening at home. Work was cancelled on Saturday because of the snow that had been falling steadily for two days. The snowfall proved treacherous for one driver who'd lost control of his car and hit the power generator at the bottom of the hill. The entire neighborhood was without power. Carina decided to make the most of this unexpected break by taking a restorative bath by candlelight. Fortunately, the building still had hot water.

She filled the tub with steaming water and added some relaxing cedar oil. A pot of Earl Grey and a book rested beside the tub. Sliding into the fragrant water, she sighed with pleasure but after only a few minutes, the phone rang.

She grabbed a towel and trod barefoot across the kitchen to the phone. She stood talking in the cold, dark kitchen for several minutes before saying goodbye to Joanne, who lived on the first floor of her building, and scurrying back to her hot bath.

Shortly after easing herself down into the steaming water, she started to shiver and her vision grew foggy. At first, she thought some cedar oil had gotten in her eye until she realized she was shivering uncontrollably.

Her first panicked reaction was that she was having an allergic reaction to the cedar oil and the only thing she knew about allergic reactions was that people died from them if not treated in time. She yanked out the bath plug before blowing out all but one of the candles so they wouldn't start a fire; the electricity hadn't been restored yet. She began scrubbing herself vigorously under the shower to wash off the oil. She tried staying calm but the eerie effects of the single candle only heightened the out-of-body feeling, watching herself going through the motions but not really being there. Whether it was the pent-up stress from her lucid dream, the armband, the prolonged exposure to her cold, dark apartment, or an actual allergic reaction to the cedar oil, Carina wasn't thinking, just reacting.

She wrapped a towel around herself, fumbled in the dark through the kitchen to call Joanne back. It took all her concentration and control to force her quaking fingers to push the small buttons on the telephone. There was no response. It never occurred to her to phone 911, as it would be quicker to get assistance in the apartment building. *I have to find the landlord* was her first rational thought. She had no other choice it seemed to her in her panicked state. Lois, who lived across the hallway from her, was away for the weekend and the apartment to the left was vacant.

Carina put on her nightgown and housecoat and took the lit candle, but its feeble light scarcely lit the hallway to the stairs. Each trepid step took her away from the security of her apartment. Silence cloaked the darkness as the candle lit up a minute patch of wall where she ran her hand. The feeling of disembodiment continued to follow her as she navigated the hallway and then the stairs until, four frightening floors later she arrived at the caretaker's apartment. His door flew open just as she was about to knock.

"Could you help me?" she managed to ask the bleary-eyed landlord. "I think I'm having an allergic reaction. Could you take me to the hospital?"

"What did you say? I'm just going to the front to clear the driveway before someone has an accident." He wove drunkenly as he walked and bumped into the wall.

Carina's tears fell unchecked. *What am I going to do now?*

The beam of his flashlight lit up the hallway. "I'll take you to a married couple upstairs who can help you."

She felt his hand on her elbow as he guided her upstairs to the fourth floor.

"Hello, Mrs. Campbell, this is Carina. She thinks she's having an allergic reaction, but I can't watch her right now. Could you keep an eye on her for a bit?"

Carina didn't hear the rest of the conversation as Mrs. Campbell, an elderly, gray-haired woman, led her into the living room which was lit by a large propane lamp.

"Would you like a cup of tea, dear? Max, would you pour some tea? It should still be warm. Now why don't you rest on the sofa? It will be a minute before he brings the tea."

She paced, trying to control her erratic breathing.

"You've got to relax, dear. You're probably feeling anxious with the power being out. Do you live by yourself?"

"Yes."

"Drink some of your tea. It will help calm you."

"Thanks."

"Why don't we take you to the hospital? Max just has to warm up the van. That will give you time to go back to your apartment and get dressed. I'll come with you if you like."

She nodded. The oppressive silence of the building beat down on her. Everything seemed to take forever, but finally they were driving the five minutes to the hospital down the icy hill and snow-covered streets.

The place was full. She'd heard how a full moon always filled emergency wards and, as she scanned the packed waiting room, tonight was no exception. First, she had to explain to the admittance nurse why she was there and then she anxiously waited to see a doctor.

It took two hours before she saw a doctor; by then, she was showing no indication of whatever had struck her. The doctor looked at the chart after listening to her explanation about the cedar oil. "I can't find anything wrong with you. I believe you panicked. Did you think you were going to die from the reaction?"

"Yes, I had a friend whose eldest son was allergic to bee stings and she said he had to carry atropine with him all the time because he'd die without it."

"I think your fear and anxiety were triggered because of the power outage and the period of time you were in the dark, but there's no reason it should occur again. With a good rest, you'll be fine." He left the curtained area without a backward glance.

Embarrassed, she returned to where Mr. and Mrs. Campbell sat. She was at a loss for words as the three of them returned to the apartment building. The electricity had been restored.

"Thank you for helping me."

"You take care of yourself."

"I will." Carina returned to her own dark and silent apartment. She cleaned up the candles, pools of water, and pondered her own strange behavior. At four in the morning, Carina was still wide-eyed and agitated. *What's wrong with me?* Fearful and alone, she felt compelled to write a quick note of explanation of the night's events in her journal when she saw it on the nightstand. Finally, in utter exhaustion, she fell asleep. She didn't dream.

# 5
# Where Are My Shoes?

Sunlight shining through the curtained window fell on Carina. She opened her eyes reluctantly to glance at the clock on the nightstand. It wasn't there, and neither was her nightstand. Bolting upright in shock, she surveyed the mattress and the floor that lay only inches away—they weren't familiar.

The armband glimmered in greeting when she glanced down at it. "I hate you."

Her shoes were missing. *Damn, where are they? How am I going to explain this one?* She moved the mattress, and thoroughly checked the entire room without success. She paced from one side of the room to the other trying to make a decision, until finally she carefully opened the door and peered into the hallway. It was clear. She made her way toward the cookery while trying to remember the last thing she'd done in the sector.

The rotund cook gave her a funny look when he saw her bare feet. "Did you lose something?"

"No, I just couldn't find them."

"Is that why you missed breakfast?"

"I didn't know what else to do."

"Maybe someone picked them up on the way to their assignment. We'll have to arrange for another pair. For now, mind where you put your feet while you're preparing lunch."

"Sure." Carina let her mind wander while working. She'd been cooking for so many years it was automatic. She knew that she hadn't imagined last night because the fear and the panic had been too real. It had been the first time in her life she'd genuinely believed she was dying, and it had terrified her. Now she was back here.

"Onions do that to me, too," Gath's voice cut through her thoughts.

She looked at him blindly.

"There's a trick to cutting onions...."

She let him ramble on as she wiped her eyes on her sleeve.

"We have fewer mouths to feed."

"Oh?"

"Seems that nineteen were left unassigned, but that will be rectified, I'm sure. Strange though, you being the only female left."

The remainder of the day passed by in a blur before she went back to the empty sleeping quarters and found a pair of shoes but nobody else in the room.


During the lunch hour on the eleventh day, a terrible feeling of foreboding seized her. Her pulse raced, and she assumed the nightmare experience from her cedar-oil night was happening again. Gath saw her pale face and told her to go out the back door for some fresh air.

Helzion, who always seemed to be around, followed her out to the alley. "Are you all right?"

"I don't know. I feel horrible."

"Come with me and we will find out what is wrong."

She followed him to another building. They entered a medical office and Lachash, whom Helzion introduced as the healer, asked her what was wrong. He was tall, and his dirty-blond hair and mustache were neatly trimmed. He had a competent air about him and she confided her symptoms once Helzion had left the room. She told him about her quickened pulse, sense of panic, and the unpleasant situation that led up to it in explicit detail because of her anxiety. Caution at revealing too much was forgotten as Lachash kindly asked some pertinent questions.

"Was the water really hot?"

"As hot as I could tolerate it."

"What was the temperature outside the tub?"

"It was considerably cooler. I assumed that I was having an allergic reaction to the cedar oil that I put in the water."

He gave her a surprised and searching look, and then asked, "You know about the properties of plant oils?"

"I have always been interested in plants and their uses."

"It sounds like your body was trying to adjust itself too quickly to the drastic differences in temperature. The additional heat brought on the uncontrollable shivering because your body was trying to maintain its correct body temperature."

It sounded plausible to her. "Then what's going on with me now?" *Besides the simple fact that I go to sleep in one world, wake up in another, and that I'm constantly afraid because of that stupid cedar oil.* She suddenly felt uneasy when she saw him writing down everything she'd said.

"I'm not sure, as I cannot determine anything physically wrong with you. I believe you have been experiencing panic attacks. I'll let Helzion know that you should rest for a few days." As she turned to leave, Lachash added, "You might not want to mention how you learned about plants. Some people might view it with suspicion even though your previous sector permitted it."

"I'll keep that in mind."

Helzion walked with her back to the main building and suggested she lie down for the remainder of the day. It was only later when she woke up in the middle of the night that her escalating fear and anxiety had her pacing the room once again. She kept reliving that horrible night. *When will it stop? If it happens again, and I'm alone, will I die? No one would know until the morning.*

Carina was unfamiliar with panic attacks and did not know they could occur long after the traumatizing event that triggered them. Her trigger seemed to be the darkness of bedtime, just like the darkness of her apartment.

*The healer would be anxious too, if he kept going from one world to another.*

She grabbed her cloak and headed for the cookery. She didn't find anyone there so she decided to make a pot of tea and keep herself busy.

A Defender, a guard, who'd heard the noise, entered the cookery. "What are you doing?"

He was taller than she was, with broad shoulders, and his close-cropped hair further added to his menacing demeanor. She knew the Defenders followed orders given by the Leaders and were responsible for security within the sector. She didn't know how many of them there were but they had their own barracks in the sector.

"I couldn't sleep, so I came to the cookery."

"You're not allowed in here without permission."

"Oh, Gath never said anything."

"Do you work with Gath?"

"Yes, I've been working with him for a few days now."

"I guess that explains why you know your way around here. I guess it is all right for you to be here, then."

"I'm making tea. Would you like some?"

He smiled and no longer seemed as menacing. "Yes, in fact, I would. My name is Elzak. And yours?"

"Carina." She felt the tension seeping out as she sipped the hot tea.

"You have been here a couple of weeks, have you not?"

"Yes, I've been waiting to be assigned. Were you assigned duty as a Defender?"

"Yes, they quickly assigned me to this sector because of the escalating turmoil the Banished are causing."

"Why are these Banished creating problems?"

"They were not happy with the new order of political matters after the Upheaval and they tried to undermine our achievements whenever they had an opportunity. Fortunately, the rebellion was quelled but not before many lives were lost."

"Is that why I saw all those demolished buildings?"

"You saw that?"

"I viewed the destruction when I entered the city."

"Really. What route did you follow?"

"I'm not sure, there was so much debris and things kept changing dramatically."

"Changing?"

"Yeah, it was a really weird experience."

"You were lucky then."

"What do you mean?"

"That route is forbidden."

"Because it's so dangerous?"

Elzak nodded.

Carina, sensing his pensiveness, changed the subject—she was getting good at that. "What were you saying about the rebellion?"

"Hmm? Oh, those who caused the uprising were either killed or disappeared. By now, they have probably rebuilt their ranks by taking people from different sectors. The Banished, as they call themselves, escaped before we could give suitable punishment or recultivate them."

"Recultivate? What do you mean by recultivate?"

"It's where they send misfits and troublemakers for evaluation and correction."

"Oh, like a prison?" She feigned comprehension. She could only assume that it had something to do with rehabilitating criminals.

"Prison? I do no not know what you mean."

"A place to put criminals until they serve their punishment."

"Not just to serve their punishment, but to alter their perceptions so that they definitely desire only to be part of the whole."

"The whole what?"

"The Protectorate."

Carina was busy breaking down the meaning of the word. *Protect. A place to protect.* She didn't know if that was the exact meaning but her ignorance might become more obvious if she didn't figure out what he was saying to her. "Yes, we must preserve the Protectorate."

Elzak smiled in agreement. "Yes, we must. At all costs."

She was glad that her brain had functioned enough to spit out "preserve the Protectorate" as it seemed to please Elzak. His words at first caused a growing sense of alarm over the unknown Banished but, as Elzak elaborated on the expectations of the sector, she felt a sense of understanding about its underlying workings. It made sense in an orderly way but there were an awful lot of expectations and rules to obey. She drank her tea as quickly as possible to make her escape.

The next night brought more anxiety. Instead of letting the solitude and darkness increase her uneasiness, Carina grabbed her cloak and walked briskly to the cookery. Fortunately, nobody was there to see her nervousness while she made herself a cup of tea. The back door opened onto an alley and she sat on the concrete stairs outside the door, concentrating on her breathing to bring her panic down.

She continued this way through exhausting days and dreaded nights. She wasn't getting much sleep and looked drawn.

Helzion commented on her appearance one day. "You do not look well. Are you sick?"

"No, I'm just haven't been getting much sleep. It's lonely with nobody else in the room or hallway."

"Would you feel better if there were someone in the room with you at night?"

She was embarrassed to admit that she would.

"Try not to worry, someone will probably be showing up very shortly and you will have more noise than you care to have."

Carina used part of her free time to do a little exploring around the building. Unfortunately, many areas were off-limits to people. She had access to the cookery, the sleeping area, the childcare facilities, but not the upper or basement floors, nor the long, dark hallways along one wing of the building. She gave up trying to find answers about the sector and decided to go outside. The street in front of the building opened onto a small square where people could gather. However, when she decided to explore behind that area, a Defender quickly rebuffed her. He made a point of reminding her of the rules that she was supposed to know.

It was like being a virtual prisoner. She couldn't leave the designated area and she couldn't explore the building. She decided on leaving the way she'd originally entered this reality in the square, twenty-three days earlier but another Defender ran to her, yelling.

"Where do you suppose you're going?"

"Why? Can't I go for a walk?"

"You're not allowed to leave the sector unless you have been assigned and are moving to another location within the sector."

"I'm sorry. I didn't know."

"That is no justification. You're from this region now and are required to observe all of the rules that apply here."

Carina nodded. "I will from now on. It won't happen again."

Satisfied, his scowl lessened. "Consider this a warning."

She returned to her room where she went over her knowledge of this sector. *What had Elzak said? Leaders assigned individuals jobs and then those people disappeared. They restricted people to the designated area. Rebels, the Banished, were against the current society. They were rebuilding the region.* Carina really didn't know much more after living in the sector for twenty-three days than she did initially.

She calculated the number of days remaining before the next Leader meeting: Nineteen, less than three weeks. What was she going to do for the next three weeks? Carina knew two things: She was going to learn more about this place and she was certainly going to be as unobtrusive as possible.

Later that evening, when she couldn't sleep, she went to the cookery and made some tea. Elzak happened to walk by and, although he couldn't stay, suggested that Carina sit outside on the steps to feel the cool night air.

"The front steps, mind you; it is a well-lit area and much safer." He hurried off before she could thank him. Carina sat outside for a half hour or so before he came by again, suggesting she return to her room.

"Let me know if you wish to go outside again and I'll keep an eye on you."

"Thanks. Goodnight."

"Goodnight."

# A Disturbance

6

It was during one of her nightly outings that she heard someone running and to her left, a scuffling. She stood up, trying to peer past the streetlights. She was ready to retreat into the building, but stopped when the sounds of fighting, shouts, and fist blows echoed in the distance. She ran down the steps and passed two buildings before peering around the corner. Carina's shadow from the streetlight must have startled them because one man, who'd been about to hit the other man on the ground, ran away.

Without thinking, she moved toward the fallen man lying on his stomach.

"Are you all right?" A low mumble came from him, but there was no sign of consciousness. "Where are you hurt?" She moved and saw in the streetlight the blood on the ground. Gingerly, she turned him over and saw his wounded stomach. He'd been stabbed. She ripped his shirt into strips and used it to apply pressure to staunch the bleeding.

"Help!" Carina yelled. "Help!"

A Defender quickly joined her and then another.

"Give me your shirt," she demanded. "He's bleeding and I have to stop it."

The Defender slipped off his shirt, watched as Carina folded it with one hand, and placed it on the other blood-soaked cloth. The second Defender ran to get additional assistance and brought a stretcher. The three men lifted him onto it and carried him to the building just as Helzion opened the door. The bright light from the doorway fell on the wounded man's face.

"It's Malcom!"

Carina heard Helzion's whispered amazement before she walked past him. She continued applying pressure to the wound as they carried him into the cookery. *Of all places,* she thought. The men carefully put him on the wooden counter where food was prepared.

Helzion barked orders to the Defenders. "You! Go to Lachash's home and tell him to get here as soon as possible. Check and secure the perimeters immediately."

"Yes, sir."

"What happened?" Helzion asked Carina.

"I heard a commotion. Two men were fighting and this man fell to the ground. The other man ran away when he saw me. This one's losing blood from a stab wound."

Several minutes passed and Lachash had not arrived.

Helzion muttered, "What is keeping him? I am going to dispatch someone else to check."

Carina was momentarily left alone with the unconscious man in the cookery. She hoped that Gath kept his cookery sterile for the man's sake. She grabbed new cloths and fresh water.

Malcom must have sensed her presence because his powerful hand suddenly grabbed her left wrist. His deep blue eyes bored into hers as he asked, "Are you the Stranger?"

"The stranger?"

"Have you come to help us?"

Her armband slipped a little farther down her wrist. The metal bumped his hand. He turned and saw it. "Yes, you are!" He said joyously despite his injuries. "Thank all that is good. You will deliver us justice and freedom."

"Come in here!" Carina heard Helzion yell. "Hurry!"

Carina turned to look at Malcom.

"Do they know?" he asked, looking at her armband.

"About the armband? No. Why?"

"Wait." He released her wrist just as Helzion entered the room. "Did he speak?"

"I-I didn't understand what he was trying to say to me," she stammered out.

Lachash arrived, quickly assessing the situation. The bleeding from the wound had slowed considerably. "I can clean him up on the outside, but I don't know what type of internal wound he has. If they have damaged his internal organs, his condition may worsen. We can only wait."

"Can't you take an x-ray or do tests? Repair the damage?" Carina asked.

"There is only a clinic in this area. We don't have the necessary equipment, but if you wish to help, you can get a clean cloth and some water."

"That's it? Is that all you can do for him? Can't we take him to a hospital? What kind of place is this?" She knew she'd overstepped her bounds but Malcom was the first person to ask about the armband. If he lived, she could ask him more.

Lachash yelled, "Out! Get her out of here!"

Carina was about to protest, until she noticed a tiny shake of Malcom's head before he started groaning. All eyes turned toward him. She ran to get clean water and cloths. Her indiscretions weren't mentioned again as she helped clean and bind the injury. Lachash gently probed the skin around the wound, trying to determine the extent of the injury and then stitched it up.

Carina, watching from the side and passing Lachash his instruments and cloths, tried not to blurt out when she saw what Lachash was doing. *You damn fool. It's a stab wound. What if an organ has been hit?* She tried to hide her fury at not being able to question Lachash. *He's the healer and he must know what he is doing.*

A Defender arrived. "There is someone to see you, sir. He says it is important."

"Can't it wait?"

Right on cue, a harried-looking man ran down the hall and stood panting outside the room, bleary-eyed and disheveled. "Healer, Healer. My wife has gone into labor. Something is wrong. She has been screaming in pain. You have to come right away, please."

Lachash glanced at Malcom. "Well, I…. First, we need to move him. There is a quiet room down the hall that will work for now. Later, when he stabilizes, we can move him to the clinic. Carina, I need you to watch for any changes in his breathing, coloring, and temperature. If anything changes, send for me. Can you do it?"

She nodded. "Yes, I can."

"We will take turns watching Malcom," Helzion added. "You urgently need to attend to Bondmate Harper and her blessed child. Nothing is more important than the infant, not even Malcom."

Carina saw Lachash's demeanor change: His face beamed as he acknowledged Helzion's words.

"And you, Carina, should go have some tea because it might be a long night."

She left the room behind Lachash and the Defender. The pot of tea she'd made earlier was cold. Carina turned to grab the kettle and saw the dried blood on the wooden table. She moved to get a cloth to clean it up and saw more blood on the floor and a torn bit of fabric. *It looks like the same material that the wounded man wore, but what's this? A map on the other side.* Carina heard footsteps behind her and stuffed the cloth into her skirt pocket.

"Do you need some help?" Elzak asked.

"I just need the mop."

By the time he returned, she'd finished washing the blood off the table.

"Gath would have a fit if he saw this mess," Carina spoke quickly to cover her nervousness.

"Quite the night, wasn't it? Especially with you finding him and all. Weren't you afraid?"

"It all happened so fast. I don't think I had time to be afraid. You left me on the steps and a few minutes later, I heard some strange sounds. When I went to investigate, I saw two men fighting. One ran away and the other fell down."

"Why didn't you call someone when you heard the commotion?"

"I didn't think it was anything important. You know the expression, 'curiosity killed the cat.'"

"No, I've never heard of it. What is it supposed to mean?"

"You know. Sometimes if you're curious, it may get you into trouble."

"You're right about that." He paused, "What is a cat? Never mind, I have to go. I just stopped by before checking the perimeter again."

"Is trouble expected?"

"We don't know what to expect."

"No, I guess not. Be careful. I'm growing fond of our cups of tea."

"I'm not afraid of anything. I'll give those Banished a drubbing that they will never forget if they get in my way," Elzak boasted.

Carina had a cup of tea after Elzak left on his rounds. *I like El. He's kind of sweet. Nerdy but sweet. I guess I've made a friend.*

Helzion's dour face rankled her daydreaming and she gulped down the remaining tea before hurrying to the sickroom to relieve him from his watch.

He was deep in thought when she entered.

"Any change?" she asked him.

"None. I wish he would regain consciousness. We need to know how he got back here. His knowledge of where the Banished are can change everything. We could stop living like hens in a cage." Helzion was almost talking to himself. He looked directly at Carina as if he'd just realized he'd been speaking his thoughts aloud.

"It's my turn to watch him. Why don't you get some rest?"

"Do you require anything before I go?" he asked gruffly.

She saw the sink in the corner. "I need a bowl and cloth to clean him."

Helzion returned a few minutes later with a bowl. She could see that he wasn't used to the late hour and said, "I haven't slept much lately so don't worry if you don't get back right away."

"I'll be back in an hour."


It was early in the morning when Malcom started tossing back and forth feverishly. Carina, half asleep, felt the bed shudder and looked up to see Malcom's forehead beaded with sweat. She wiped his brow with a cool cloth and discovered he was burning up. Carina went to the door and called for a Defender, but nobody heard her.

Malcom was thrashing wildly in his bed. *He'll reopen his wound if I don't do something about it.* She started looking in the cupboard for something to tie his hands with, but there was nothing except a white sheet. She ripped two long strips from it. She managed to tie his muscular legs together but his left arm kept thrashing.

She heard him mumbling the words, "Tell me you're real."

She leaned closer and put her hand on his shoulder. "Of course I'm real. You're certainly going to open your wound if you're not careful," she said softly.

His eyes were shut as he muttered, "Wound be damned. It doesn't matter now that I've seen you."

She wondered if he was aware of what he was saying. "Your eyes are closed," she humoured him.

"Water. Hot. I'm so hot. What's your name?"

"Carina," she whispered.

He opened his fever-glazed eyes. "Beautiful, Carina. Kiss me before you find out who you really are, because then no one may get close to you."

"You have a fever and don't know what you're saying."

"When you find out who you are..." The remainder of the words were mumbled as fever wracked his body.

She ran to the door but couldn't see anyone. *Where is Helzion?*

Carina lost track of the time as she continued to sponge his hot body with the cloth. Blood had begun to ooze from his wound again and she carefully changed the dressing with supplies that Lachash had left on the table.

"Damn. He's still too hot." *Do I cool him or cover him with a blanket and make him sweat to break the fever? Cold, make him cold.* Carina grabbed the remainder of the torn white sheet and went to the small sink where she soaked it in the cold water, wrung it out, and then draped it over him. She fanned the sheet to make it cooler several times through the night.

Each time she laid the sheet over him, she whispered, "Make him well. Break the fever." She didn't realize the intensity of her wish to heal him until her jaw began to ache from clenching her teeth.

Hours later, she touched his forehead and found it much cooler. She bent closer to his face. His breathing was slow and steady. He was sleeping.

Carina sank back into the chair, her forehead on the bed, and sobbed in exhaustion and relief.

Which is how Lachash found them. Malcom with his hands tied to the bed and Carina asleep against it. "Should we wake her?" Lachash whispered to Helzion as they entered the room.

"I must have fallen asleep. I left her alone most of the night. Why is he trussed up like that?"

"I surmise he had a temperature and was in danger of opening his wound. She must have known to tie him up. We can come back later. The cloth is still damp so they haven't been sleeping long."

"Should we try to wake her or move her? That position doesn't look very comfortable."

"She is probably too tired to notice. No, they have earned their sleep. We will give them an hour or two, but first untie his wrists."


Carina woke to Lachash and Helzion's voices coming down the hallway. She jumped up and stood at the window when they walked into the room.

"Ah, good," began Lachash, "you had a long night, I hear."

"He certainly appears to be better."

"Well, I just have to check the wound and make sure that it's not infected."

"Is that you, Lachash?" Malcom rasped.

"So, you are awake. You gave us quite a scare showing up that way after disappearing for two years. We gave up on you a long time ago."

"We will question him later," Helzion interrupted.

Carina glanced at Helzion, hoping to get some knowledge of the sector's machinations.

Helzion saw her expression. "We will talk about last night when we debrief you."

"Yes, you are right, Helzion," Lachash said. "I'll check the wound immediately now that I am here." He gently checked the bandaging. "I see that you have redressed the wound, Carina."

"He was tossing and turning so much the wound began seeping, so I cleaned it as best I could."

"Was that before or after his fever?"

"It was a long night. I don't remember exactly."

"I am sorry, I never came back to relieve you. I fell asleep," Helzion said forthrightly.

"And my apologies for taking so long. Bondmate Harper's adorable baby was reluctant to make his entry into the world. From what I can tell, though, you have done a fine job with Malcom," Lachash conceded.

Both men turned to Malcom. Carina felt like she'd been dismissed and she found herself in the cookery with a steaming cup of hot coffee from Gath before she knew it.

"Did you have a long night?"

"You could say that." Gath left her alone to ponder the previous night. It was a coincidence that she'd been outside in the first place. Carina tried to recall what Malcom had said, something about justice and freedom. *And what's that about the stranger? Weird, he seemed to know the significance of the armband, and that's something I'd love to find out more about. Even though it's hidden beneath my sleeve, he knew it was there. No one else knows about it.*

# Kidnapped

Carina went for a walk to clear her head. She was so lost in thought that she was unaware that she'd walked past the front of the building where she'd originally discovered the sector people; she'd managed to slip by the sentries, who were engaged elsewhere at that very moment. When she realized where she was, she turned and collided with something solid.

She heard a deep voice say, "You be coming with us."

Carina wasn't prepared for the black hood they threw over her head. She forced herself backward against her assailant and kicked hard where she fervently hoped his leg would be, but when she tried to grab the hood off her head, her arms were forced painfully behind her back.

Carina kicked and struggled although she couldn't hear clearly through the hood. All she could think of were the news programs that showed kidnappings, drug crimes, and murders. She wasn't in her world and she didn't know anything about these people. When they grabbed her legs, she jerked her body as much as she could to escape. It was futile and it only exhausted her. They carried her for what seemed like several blocks. The hood smelled of sweat and something else that Carina couldn't distinguish at first, but then

45

realized it was blood. The tremendous pressure on her stomach against the man's shoulder, combined with the smell of the hood, made her gag reflexively until he put her down. After that, they forced her to walk. Sometimes someone would grab her arm and pull her first one way then another, and sometimes they shoved her down to compel her to walk stooped over.

Eventually, after what felt like hours, they stopped and pushed her to the ground. The air grew cooler and Carina surmised it was night. She could hear muted laughter through the hood, but nobody approached her. She tried moving to get more comfortable and even tried to move her hands only to be grabbed and shaken like a wet puppy.

"You better not be thinkin' of escape. I be watchin' you."

The hood lifted and her head forced backward. A wet tube was shoved into her mouth, nearly choking her as the first squirt of water hit the back of her throat. She swallowed greedily, but the tube was ripped out before her thirst was sated. Her parched throat croaked weakly in response. She looked wildly around in the darkness; she couldn't make out her surroundings or her foes. She gasped when a fiery red moon suddenly pierced the darkness.

It was several minutes before she could tear her gaze from its angry surface. She turned to look around her. The terrain was mostly flat, broken by the occasional boulder or rubble. Her captors must have drifted off to sleep. She turned to view them, but the moon disappeared again. She tried to remain alert, hopeful that the moon would come out.

It was still dark when they woke her. They cut her bonds and gave her a minute behind a boulder to take care of her personal needs before they herded her in front of them once again. This time they didn't put the hood on her head. It was too dark to see where she was going anyway. She walked and they pushed her in the right direction if she strayed.

The monotony of the walking, combined with her sharp focus on the ground, numbed her to the passage of time. She scarcely noticed that a scorching sun was now up and didn't spare a glance at her tormentors. Carina began to slow and even the malicious prodding didn't provoke her.

"Look after the merchandise, Barket. We not be wantin' her to arrive damaged."

They pulled her hair backward and water trickled into her throat. She tried to grab the flask and drink more but Barket shoved her to the ground.

"What do you suppose you be doin'?" a voice asked.

"She be tryin' to take the water," Barket supplied.

"Can you not be handlin' a mere wisp of a girl?"

A slight scuffle ensued between her tormentors and Carina used the time to take a long look around her. The water had revived her. She didn't waste her time on her captors; instead, she quickly figured that, if she truly escaped it would be a waste of her time. Barren grey land met her eye in all directions. Her hopes plummeted. The tall sector buildings had vanished.

Her dejection numbed her to the tight grip on her arm when they roughly pulled her to her feet and forced her to march again. It wasn't until they'd walked for a few minutes before she thought to ask, "Where are you taking me?"

"Did I say you could speak?"

"No." Carina gulped uncertainly.

"It not be your business."

"Not knowing my future is my business."

He laughed. "She be havin' gumption that be for sure. We be gettin' a good price for this one."

Carina whipped around and saw her abductor clearly for the first time. He wasn't much taller than she was, but he was much older. He had an oily, grey-and-black scraggly mass of shoulder-length hair. His clothing may once have been dark green, but all of it was dirty, ripped, and food-stained.

She looked into his pale blue, watery eyes, and asked, "You're selling me?"

"Of course. What be you thinkin' we were doin'?"

"You can't be serious. Nobody sells people anymore."

"Ha, ha, ha. I not be laughin' this hard in years. Your sector friends might not sell people, but they be as dirty as the likes of us. Keep yer mouth shut. I not be needin' to be judged by the likes of you, and a woman to boot. Put the hood on her before I hit her."

Carina shot him a glare. "Bastard."

She didn't get the intended reaction. He laughed even more. "You be priceless, girl. The boys be likin' you."

Her heart thumped as she blindly ran toward him, head down, and plowed into his gut while pounding and scratching blindly. She didn't recognize the screeching as hers.

"Get her off me."

She'd drawn blood by then even though his hands were protecting his face. She didn't care. She'd known she didn't stand a chance, but she realized she had to fight and it felt like minutes had passed when only seconds had until Barket pulled her off him. They retied her hands and threw the hood back over her head. Rough hands ran over her body, and she felt faint with fear. She instinctively brought up her only means of protection, her knee, and made contact. The groping hands suddenly released her. She could only hear muffled sounds.

"That be teachin' you not to touch the merchandise."

"You be one to talk, Scar. I only just be pullin' her off you."

"Damn hell-cat." He pulled Carina close to him and lowered his head near her ear. With one hand he raised the side of the hood, and whispered, "The way I be lookin' at it, little girl, I can be sellin' you to one man, or I can be sellin' you to many. You be spendin' the rest of your life on your back. Now I not be wantin' anymore sass. Do you understand me?"

His last words were soft and deadly, and Carina's face was wet with tears as she shook her head.

Scar slowly licked the side of her face in one long, obscene motion. "Yum, salt. I be thinkin' you get the message now."

Carina's tears continued falling. The hood absorbed them after Scar released her. She was pressed forward and ordered to walk. She obeyed.

After several hours, the motley crew stopped once again. They allowed her to see to her needs, this time behind a broken stone wall. There was no red moonlight to show the surroundings, but she knew walls meant habitation. They had to be approaching the end of this trek. They left Carina slumped against the wall. She didn't move from where they pushed her and barely ate the black, leather-like food they gave her even though she hadn't eaten since she'd been in the sector.

Scar, seeing her disdain, asked, "What? You not be likin' the fare of us less civilized folk? Did you not be gettin' served rat in the sector?" Scar asked maliciously.

Carina put her hand to her mouth and retched up the half-chewed food. She ended up wearing what little she had eaten. She heard the two men laughing at her with wicked amusement. Her head felt light and distant, and she moved to lean against the wall where she slumped into oblivion.

Awareness returned when they dumped her unceremoniously onto a hard, dirt-packed floor where Barket whipped the hood off her head and released her arms. She heard the clang of the metal door closing before inky blackness enveloped her.

At first, she didn't dare move because the unknown darkness scared her. When nothing echoed in the endless darkness, after waiting for an indeterminable amount of time, she blindly crawled toward the last sound she had heard, the clang of the door. Her outstretched hand finally touched cold metal. She ran her hand along its edges, stood up, and allowed herself a moment to clear her head. There wasn't any doorknob or latch. She touched one edge and slid her hand on the wall as she traced the shape of the room. It didn't take her long to discover the approximate size of the room once she steeled herself to walk blindly in the darkness. She covered the extent of the four walls, which felt textured like pebbles, and was back at the door within minutes where she kicked an empty bucket that had apparently been set there for her personal needs. Other than the bucket, the windowless, six-by-ten-foot cell was empty.

Carina carefully lowered herself to the dirt-packed floor until her eyes were ground level, but no light shone from beneath the door. Crawling back into a sitting position, she made her way to the nearest wall where she leaned up against it, rocking herself as the coldness seeped into her bones. In her exhausted state, she slid in and out of consciousness until the clang of the door sounded and a bright light pierced the cell. Somebody held something to her mouth.

"Drink," a voice whispered.

She moved her hands up instinctively to grasp the container and it was ripped from her hands as a result. Something soft was put into her hands, but she never had time to adjust her eyes before the door clanged closed and she was left alone. "Wait!" she yelled too late. She stuffed the food into her mouth, too hungry to worry about its identity. It was bread.

She listened for any sounds from the door but could hear nothing. She thought of the voice that had whispered. It was a woman's voice and that was important. It meant that she'd arrived at her destination and she'd find out what was going to happen to her. She pondered her fate as she waited in the dark.


Carina got very cold and very hungry. She paced around the room endlessly, trying to distract herself. When her hunger pangs tormented her, she paced even faster until she tripped and fell. She didn't bother to get up; she just lay there and wept.

When the door clanged open once again, Carina raised startled eyes to the bright light, but had little time to do more than grasp the bread and the small flask that were pressed into her hands before the darkness swallowed her again, but not before she had heard the whispered words, "Be strong." It wasn't until later that she discovered a rough blanket near the door and she wrapped it around her shoulders. It didn't do much to stave off the cold, but it was a comfort, a touch of sanity in an insane time.

Time blurred as the darkness pressed relentlessly against her brain. She'd gone from reliving a happy family life with her brothers to pondering the sector and how she had no explanations as to how or why she was experiencing two realities. She'd sung until her voice cracked from overuse and thirst. Nightmares kept jumping out at her as her imagination ran unchecked. She moaned in pain as her hunger ate away at her self-confidence and strength. The days ran into each other. Each opening of the door brought a new flask and a piece of bread but nothing else. Carina found herself considering that even a worthless bit of dried rat would taste good. *Oh, how far I've fallen to actually want rat meat.*

Carina began withdrawing into herself increasingly with each passing day. She thought she heard voices telling her to wait, to be patient, to ignore her gaoler, to pretend to be weaker than she appeared. She assumed it was the woman who brought her food. *Why did she whisper? Was she also afraid? Was she a captive, too?* She was vaguely aware that underneath her blanket the armband was pulsing, sending pleasant warmth through her body. Carina had forgotten all about it. She fell restfully asleep.

She didn't know what had changed as she opened her eyes to the darkness. She felt rested and alert. She found herself humming, "The House of The Rising Sun," but switched to, "You Don't Know You're Beautiful," when she didn't know all the words. Several tunes later, she heard what she'd been waiting for, she'd already knocked over the waste basket as she threw the blanket as far as she could away from her and turned so that, when the door opened she was facing the farthest corner from the door rocking and grinning to herself as she hummed tunelessly.

A hand touched her shoulder and Carina smiled foolishly. "My Precious. Where's my Precious?" she asked and then started to laugh when her croaking voice came out Gollum-like. She didn't stop laughing even when her gaoler harshly told her to shut up. She laughed harder, holding onto the bread tightly.

It was then that she heard the harsh voice, "It looks like she be finally ready. Clean her up for sales. She stinks."

"Yup, Yup. I be stinkin'." She tried her best piratey voice, just like his, and then started laughing once again. She heard a harrumph behind her but didn't turn around. She didn't hear the clang of the door this time.

The woman behind her was trying to pull Carina to her feet but Carina wasn't cooperating. "You be makin' him mad. Get up before he comes," she whispered urgently.

"Stand back," the gaoler ordered.

The woman released her abruptly and Carina sat down with a thump just as a cold bucket of water was thrown on her.

She gasped in shock. She was hoisted onto her feet, roughly towel-dried and then dragged unceremoniously out of the cell and pushed onto a hard wooden bench. Carina blinked her eyes rapidly and tried to focus them in the dim room. She was in a cramped cell with iron bars all around her. It was a relief to be sitting on a wooden bench and not the cold floor. She tried standing but only managed a few steps before she collapsed weakly onto the bench once again. She didn't know how much time had passed in the cell. She felt torpid and her clothes hung loosely on her. She discovered she still grasped the bread, and ate it slowly, methodically.

She looked up, startled, at the sound of voices. Within a few moments the room began to fill with dirty, foul-mouthed men. Their coarse language grated against Carina's ears, and she winced against the onslaught of noise.

"Come on, pretty lady, stand up so we be gettin' a good look at your wares."

Carina leaped off the bench as she felt a hand grab at her shoulder. She stood, swaying on her feet in the middle of the cell to avoid the long, reaching arms from all sides.

"Look at that hair; she definitely be fresh meat."

"Yeah, look at the length, must be one of them breeders." Turning to Carina, "Be you one of them breeders?"

The question was aimed at Carina but another voice cut in, "Maybe she be a wild one who be comin' out of the ground for the first time."

*Damn. This is a nightmare.* Carina didn't respond to the taunts that flew around her. She had to stay focused for an opportunity to use what she learned now for her escape in the future because she knew that, provided the opportunity, she'd make a run for it. *God only knows when that'll be.* She hummed tunelessly and looked everywhere but at the men around her.

"See, boys? She be broken and ready to train."

The furor rose at the gaoler's loud claim. The men were openly discussing, arguing, bargaining, and passing things she supposed might be money. The clamour in the small room was deafening. Carina was pulled from her cell and shoved through the throng until finally she was standing in front of a grizzled, silver-haired man who might be in his late fifties.

"What do you want to do with her, Trator?" the gaoler asked, grinning from ear to ear.

"Truss her up. I be takin' her back to my place."

"She might not be ready to travel."

"Not my concern."

The gaoler tied Carina's hands in front of her. "The hood, too," Trator said. "That way she won't know where she be. Less chance to escape until I be breakin' her into my way of thinkin'."

Carina never had time to react before she felt herself pulled roughly forward. She could hear the men's laughter behind her and the loud voice of the gaoler as he brought out a new prisoner. Trator pulled her onward. He'd laugh spitefully whenever she banged into a wall or tripped. He taunted her cruelly by saying, "Did your lovin' mother not be teachin' you to walk?" Or, "Oops, I be forgettin' to say duck," after she'd already banged her head. She heard only a few of his snide remarks because of the thick hood. She was only aware of the rhythmic twisting and turning of her body as it was pulled every which way. Her shoulders and arms would relax briefly only to be pulled viciously forward in the next instant. Her only company beneath the hood was the hammering of her heart and the whooshing of blood in her ears.

The trek ended with a final yank that tripped her and left her gasping for breath on her hands and knees.

Trator yanked hood and hair. "Welcome to your new home, my pet." He cackled. "All you need to be rememberin' is I be ownin' you and when I be tellin' you to do something, you be doin' it. Understand?"

"Yes," Carina managed to croak out. Her throat was dry and sore. She found his manner of speaking, along with the other men she'd run into here, difficult to understand.

"I not be hearin' you," he said as he pulled her hair even harder.

"Yes, I understand!" she spat out.

"Make me some supper."

Carina didn't move quickly enough and received a painful kick in the ribs that sent tears to her eyes, but she was too exhausted to move. The days in the cell with meager rations had weakened her. Trator kicked her again, this time harder, more viciously, and pain shot through her. She realized she had to move and tried awkwardly to rise but couldn't get up without assistance.

"I be thinkin' I be payin' too much for your carcass."

"Maybe it will be easier if you untie my hands."

"No sass," he said as he kicked her again but, after watching her clumsy actions, he relented and cut her bonds.

Carina winced in pain and bit her lip to stop from crying out. She looked around for something to grab onto and then crawled toward the wall. It took her a moment, but she managed to stand and then turned to look at him.

"Everything be near the fireplace."

Carina was scared and the panic threatened to overwhelm her. *Breathe. Calm down. I can't lose control now.* It took her several deep breaths before she could coherently piece together her thoughts. *He really isn't that smart if he's going to let me be around knives. Then again, he'll be expecting me to do something.* As it turned out, there weren't any knives to be had, or utensils of any kind, for that matter. She had to arrange the stones and stoke a flame in the fireplace before she could cook on it. Carina was dirty and burnt her hand by the time the meat and potato stew was ready.

Trator grunted at her and called the food slop, but he ate all of it. She was looking at him expectantly, hungrily. He looked up at her sneering as he wiped up the last of the grease with his bread.

"Hungry, be you?"

"Yes, I am."

"Well, you be havin' to earn it, maybe tomorrow."

"What?"

Slapping her, he said, "Do not ever be questionin' what I be sayin'."

Her cheek stung where he slapped her. She began to dread what could happen next.

"Take off your clothes," he commanded.

She froze where she stood and then, what seemed like minutes later, she tried to run past him, but he'd been ready for that and managed to grab her around her waist, lifting her up off the floor as she struggled to get away.

"Put me down, damn you! Get your filthy paws off me!"

He threw her to the ground. He knelt down beside her, and before Carina could even scream, he'd grabbed the collar of her shirt, ripped it down the front, and shook her violently until her teeth rattled. He pinched and poked her until tears ran down her face in shame and humiliation. When he started to laugh, Carina looked up at him. Her tear-ravaged face betrayed her fear.

"Now you be afraid of me. You be a bit scrawny to my likin', but I be takin' you where you lie, if I be whole. You should be afraid. The last piece of trash I be havin' cut me up. That be why you be here, to replace her. She got a little cut up in return." He backhanded her. "Now I need a new housekeeper and worker in the shop. Someone not too homely to be scarin' away the customers, yet not too beautiful that she be decidin' to up and leave me when she be left alone, and," he said meaningfully, "someone who not be liftin' her skirts for anyone else and cause fightin'. So you listen carefully to me," he said with a slap across her face. "You be preparin' my meals." Slap. "Takin' care of the house,"—slap—"and whatever else I tell you. If you cross me, I be sellin' you to the highest bidder and you be makin' me some money in a different, less appealin' way, if you catch my meaning. And," he paused for effect, "you not be mentionin' my manhood to anyone, or I might be considered weak and someone might be decidin' to challenge me."

"I'll do what you want," Carina sputtered, "give me a chance." Her heart, she was sure, had ceased its steady beating and swapped itself for a whirlwind, instead. Her cheeks stung and her eyes watered. Since being in the sector, Carina had known doubts and discomfort when confronted with the unknown. This had her hands trembling violently and she tasted the deep fear she'd faced in her apartment and the darkness of the cell... Except this fear was different: It was tangible, and it made her angry.

"Clean up the cookery," he said as he dumped the dishes onto the floor.

She swiftly moved to pick up the dishes, but he tripped her and, as she fell, the grease smeared across her stomach, onto the skirt that she still wore. She nearly hit the wall in the process except for her outstretched hands.

"When you be done, you be sleepin' under the table out of my sight."

"Yes," she said meekly while fighting for domination over her hatred and violent thoughts. Carina tried to cover herself with her shredded shirt. He'd ripped the shirt badly, and the sleeves dangled at her wrists.

"You not be needin' that because you be stayin' dressed like you be until I say otherwise. That way, if you plan to escape from my pleasant company, you be less likely to be runnin' around half-dressed. Put it this way: If a less generous soul than me be findin' you, he might not be as kind and might be enticed to taste your wares. This way, I don't 'ave to tether you. Move it."

Fueled by her anger, she hurried to comply after his threat of rape, spinning around the room trying to do what he asked. Later, she crawled under the table, a niche cut into the wall, silently swearing to herself.

# 8
# Broken Bones

She awoke under a broken cement ledge that was part of a parking lot outside the downtown Safeway store in Kamloops. The swirling snowflakes fell eerily onto the silent streets. Carina looked down, and knew, even before she looked, that her chest was bare—the shirt she'd been wearing had long since fallen apart and Trator had ripped it off; only the cuffs remained of the once fine material.

Carina was scared to find herself back in Kamloops in the middle of a frigid snowstorm. *What's happening to me?* She screamed the question in her head as her shaking arms reached under her skirt for her black slip. She pulled it down and off and then pulled it on over her head until it covered her chest.

She cringed to think someone might see her in this disheveled state. She had to get home as quickly as possible before anyone saw her or she froze to death. Suddenly, she remembered she had no keys to open her apartment.

"God, it's so far, and it's so cold, and... I'm barefoot," she sobbed.

In her crazed state she imagined she saw Trator's gleaming yellow eyes piercing her where she stood and, when he grabbed her, she screamed and pushed him backward. She could feel his eyes watching her as she walked unsteadily away, wincing each time she put a bare foot forward.

Trator came at her again. This time she heard him say he was a taxi driver. *That doesn't make sense.*

Disjointed voices reached out to her as she kept walking.

"Miss," said one voice. "Are you all right?"

*No, it's only one voice. It's not Trator.*

Again the voice spoke through her haze. "I'm a police officer and I'm here to help you."

His soft voice made her turn blindly toward him but she was crying so hard she couldn't see anything more than a disembodied shape. She leapt back when he tried to touch her.

"Shh, it's all right, I won't hurt you. I only want to help you. Here's my badge, I'm a police officer. You're safe now." He pushed a cold object into her hand.

She managed to focus long enough to see the badge. She didn't struggle when a warm blanket was placed over her shoulders and she was pushed back gently onto a bed. *A bed in the middle of the street, that's weird,* she thought.

"Shh, lie down. You're safe now."

She had a moment of dizzying panic when she felt a mask of some sort placed over her nose and mouth. She quickly passed into the black darkness that had been threatening to overtake her, but she was warm.

"She's lucky not to have frostbite or hypothermia after being outside in this weather. God only knows how long she was out there. Whoever did this to her is sick. Her face and eyes will be swollen for a while. The split lip will heal with minimal scarring, if any. Her broken finger and cracked rib will heal in time. We have her on fluids to get her electrolytes up, particularly the potassium and magnesium. How she'll fair mentally is another matter altogether.

What happened to her?" Dr. Montgomery asked Detective Jackson Dawes who'd been assigned to the case.

"From the bruises and injuries, I'd ask *who* happened to her. When can she answer some questions? Was she drunk or using?"

"No, her blood work clearly showed no form of drug in her body, but she is suffering from mild malnutrition."

"So, what you're saying is she was starved and beaten."

"We won't have those answers until she wakes up. By the time she's awake, her fluids will be up but right now, I suggest we let her sleep for a while longer. I don't think she'll be ready to answer questions for a day or two. Meanwhile, I can keep you posted on her condition and, if there are any changes, I'll call you. Do you know who she is yet?"

"No, not yet. We're still investigating. Thanks, Montgomery, I appreciate your cooperation. Oh, was there any indication of rape?"

"No, although there are rope burns around her wrists and bruises on her knees, there is no indication of rape."

Dawes's eyebrow went up a notch before he said, "Thank God for that." Just then, his partner for the last five years, Alec Granger, entered the room and hurried toward him.

"What's up, Jackson? Was our Jane Doe able to talk?"

"No, they have her sedated. This whole thing stinks. I can feel it."

"Any clues that might help us identify her?"

"Not yet. We got some prints despite her broken finger, bandaged hands and wrists. Her face is swollen from multiple contusions and we can't get a clear picture of what she looks like until the swelling goes down. She isn't wearing a wedding ring."

"If she isn't married and lives alone, she'll be more difficult to trace."

"As if it isn't complicated enough, she's obviously been beaten over a period of time and some of the lacerations are already healing. Her cracked rib is a few days old, and I just found out that she was starved."

"Here is a woman found at five oh-seven in the morning on a minus-twenty-three-Celsius day, barefoot, wearing a skirt and a black slip to cover her torso. Whatever happened here makes me sick thinking about it. This is Kamloops, for Christ's sake. I moved from Vancouver to get away from this stuff. What about drugs or alcohol?"

"No, nothing. She's clean. Her prints aren't in the system and no one has come forward about a missing person. What did the taxi driver say?"

"Not much. He was on his way home when he spotted her. He said she was walking in the middle of the street when he found her, or she found him."

"What do you mean?"

"He said she appeared out of nowhere, right out of the storm."

"With the kind of weather we've been having that doesn't surprise me, but it doesn't explain where she came from."

"Maybe she's not from here. We get so many people from the lower mainland during the ski season. She could have come up for a holiday."

"Good point. Let's head back to the station. We'll have to phone the hotels and resorts and see if there's anyone who has gone missing."

"That's not reliable. You know how those ski parties last for all hours."

Jackson grimaced. "It's a start, and I'm putting you in charge of it."

Alec rolled his eyes. "Thanks for the vote of confidence."

A brief smile lit Jackson's face. "While you're at it, get in touch with your contacts in Vancouver and find out if anyone's been reported missing that matches Jane Doe's description."

"Sure thing." He glanced at Carina. "Are you going to stay here?"

"Just a little longer."

"I'll contact you if something comes up."

When Jackson phoned the hospital later that afternoon, Dr. Montgomery told him that there were no changes in Jane Doe's condition. Jackson said he'd drop by in the morning. When he arrived at the hospital the next day he ran into Dr. Montgomery just as the doctor was leaving Jane Doe's room.

"Jackson, just the man I hoped to see."

"Why? How's the girl this morning?"

"She hasn't regained consciousness yet and that's not a bad thing under the circumstances. Her vitals have improved and we've taken her off the meds."

"May I go in for a few minutes?"

"Sure, but don't wake her. We'll let nature do that. If there are any drastic changes, I'll give you a call."

"Thanks." He moved toward Carina. The pallor of yesterday had lessened and the hollows under her eyes weren't as pronounced. "So, Jane Doe," he whispered, "who did this and why?" He lingered a little longer until he felt the vibration of his cell phone. He moved into the corridor. "Dawes."

"Hey, Jackson. I just wanted to fill you in what we found out, or lack of them. We haven't had any hits from the hotels or ski resorts. We're still checking into the bed-and-breakfasts. Trickier, you know, since some people run them under the table."

"Thanks, Alec. Do you have any news from Vancouver?"

"Yeah, they checked the records and sent up a pic of a missing girl, but she's Asian so she can't be our girl."

"Damn, I was hoping to receive some good news."

"It's only been twenty-four hours; maybe no one has noticed that she's missing yet."

"Thanks for the info." Dawes hung up the phone.


Jackson returned later that afternoon and waited impatiently inside Carina's room. Montgomery had assured him that she'd be waking up about now.

It was his day off. He paced restlessly for an hour and then he decided to head for home. He knew Montgomery would call him when Jane Doe woke up. He headed to his car. The snow was still drifting down but not as fiercely as it had been earlier in the week. Still, it delayed his departure as he took time to brush off the accumulated snow from the windshield. Finally, he was finished and was just about to shut the car door when he heard his name called.

"Jackson! Hey, Jackson!"

It was Alec, bundled up against the cold. "I've been trying to reach you, but you weren't answering your phone."

Jackson grimaced. "It's in the car. Did something happen?"

"I believe we might have a lead. There was a call from a university student named Brad Masters. I heard dispatch speaking to him. He was asking whether it was possible to file a missing person report even if he wasn't the next of kin. I took the call. He described his friend as a brunette, divorced, lives alone, and doesn't have any immediate family in the province that he knows about. He said she never misses class, but she missed Monday, Tuesday, and now it's Wednesday. I got her phone number but no one answers the phone. She lives in a secure building so he couldn't gain admittance when he dropped by, and the apartment manager wouldn't let him in. I should have checked with you first before I asked him to meet us at the hospital to look at Jane Doe."

"No, that's all right. It would save us some time if his friend is Jane Doe."

# Finding A Friend

When they arrived at the hospital a blond-haired man was pacing at the entrance. They approached him, "Brad?" Alec asked.

Brad nodded. "Are you the officer I spoke with on the phone?"

"Yes, I'm Detective Granger and this is my partner, Detective Dawes."

"Why did you ask me to meet you here?"

"We have a Jane Doe in the hospital we haven't been able to identify, and no one has reported a missing person except you."

"My God. You can't be serious. It can't be her. She doesn't drink, and she's the gentlest soul I know."

"I'm not saying it's her, but you have a missing friend and we have a Jane Doe.

"And you think it's Carina. I'll be able to tell right away, once I see her."

"Well." Jackson paused for a moment. "It might be difficult to identify her."

"Why. Is she hurt?"

"Our Jane Doe has been beaten and her face is swollen." Seeing Brad's white face, Jackson squeezed his shoulder. "We need your help, Brad. Do you think you're up to it?"

Brad held his mouth tightly closed and nodded.

Jackson looked at him squarely in the eye as he said, "When you see her, you're certainly going to be shocked, but the doctor says she has been recovering steadily and should be regaining consciousness sometime today."

"She's unconscious?" His voice wavered slightly.

"Yes, they kept her sedated for the first while, but now she's on her own."

Dawes went to the nurse's desk and asked for Dr. Montgomery. It took several minutes, but he was rewarded for his patience when he saw him coming down the hall, clipboard in hand, speaking with a nurse. Dr. Montgomery shook Brad's hand when Jackson introduced him.

"This is Brad Masters. We believe he knows our Jane Doe. Would it be all right to take him in and have a look at her?"

"She was sleeping when I last looked, but"—he looked at Brad— "if you can identify her, that will help us all." Montgomery had a quiet yet strong voice that carried his concern to Brad.

Dawes took Brad into the hospital room and Brad approached the bed silently until he was right beside it. He looked at the bruised face and bandaged hands. "What the heck happened to her? My God, who did this to her? This was no accident," Brad blurted out as he ran his hand nervously through his hair.

"Is this Carina?"

"The wavy hair is the right color and those eyebrows look like hers but with all that swelling and bandaging, I'm not sure."

"You have to be sure." This was the moment to push Brad. "Your friend is depending on you, Brad. Do you recognize her?"

A slight movement caught Dr. Montgomery's complete attention. "Gentlemen, please." Montgomery's voice rang out authoritatively.

They turned to look at him in surprise. He was staring at his patient's lips and then he leaned closer.

"Brad? Is that you?"

Montgomery turned to Brad, "She's asking for you."

Brad gulped. "Carina? Are you all right?"

"Where am I?" Carina asked in slow, painful breaths.

"You're in the Royal Inland Hospital."

"How much school have I missed?"

"Don't worry. I'll take care of it for you, Carina."

"I can't miss anything. It's time for our final exams."

"Shh, don't worry."

Dawes interrupted, "Thanks, Brad, I really appreciate your help, and I'll be in contact with you later but right now I'd like you to remain outside. Alec is downstairs. He can give you a ride home as soon as I'm done."

"I have to get to work and it's not too far to walk from here." Brad glanced at Carina once more, patted her arm, and said, "I'll be back to see you later."

"Does he have to go?" she rasped.

"It would be best." Jackson turned to Montgomery, and asked, "Is it all right if I ask her a few questions?"

"Well, all right, but try not to upset her," he admonished. The stern look he gave Dawes brooked no argument.

"Miss Douglas? I'm Detective Dawes. I'm going to ask you a couple of questions. Do you know who did this to you?"

"No," Carina whispered.

"Did you see anyone?" He hadn't meant to be harsh, but he immediately saw the effect of his questioning.

"Yes," Carina said, tears rolling out of the corners of her eyes.

"What happened?" He spoke softly, less insistently.

"They s-s-sold me like I was c-cattle."

His mouth dropped in disbelief. "I'm sorry, would you repeat that?"

"They sold me like I was cattle!" she said angrily and then clamped her mouth shut.

Dr. Montgomery interrupted briskly. "Enough of the questions; she's getting agitated. There will be more than enough time for questions later. I need to ask a few questions of my own," he said, shouldering Dawes aside. "Please give me a few minutes while I check her responses."

Carina gasped in pain. Her hand felt like it was on fire. She tried raising her left hand to look at it, but couldn't. "What's wrong with me?"

"Shh, it's all right. I'll describe your condition to you, so there's no need to worry. Your hands are scraped from what appears to have been a fall, maybe you tripped, and your left index finger is broken."

"What else?" she whispered.

"Well, you have the beginnings of two black eyes, but they will heal and your split lip will have a negligible scar."

"My chest hurts when I breathe."

"That's your fractured rib. Fortunately, it will heal quickly. The best thing for you right now is to rest. You're safe here."

*Maybe I am*, Carina thought, *because I'm with people. I seem to go to the sector when I'm alone.*

She drifted off into sleep and Montgomery breathed a sigh of relief. He motioned for Jackson to follow him into the hall.

"Did she say anything else? Will she be all right?"

"What did you ask her that upset her so much?"

"I asked her what happened and she said they 'sold her like cattle.'"

"Are you serious?"

"Those were her exact words."

# Looking For Answers 10

Jackson spent the next three days speaking to different people who knew Carina, building a profile of her usual habits and haunts. He had checked her work schedule over the weekend she went missing and discovered that she'd left the restaurant at 5:30 AM Saturday morning. She'd had a late and hectic Friday at work and, according to one waiter, headed immediately toward her car. From her landlord and her neighbours, the Campbells, he learned that she'd had an allergic reaction on Saturday evening and they'd taken her to the emergency room and later they'd arrived home around midnight. She appeared the following Tuesday morning when the call came into the station. That left two unaccounted days.

Jackson reviewed his precise notes. He was able to piece together Carina's history since she'd been in Kamloops. She was twenty-seven years old, divorced from a marriage of six years, currently in her fourth of five years of university study. In another year, she would graduate with a well-earned teaching degree. From speaking to people who knew her, they described her as a reserved woman who they liked and respected. Her friends and acquaintances all agreed that she led a quiet life now that she was divorced and seemingly spent a lot of her time alone. He speculated about her being married until he heard about the odd living arrangements between herself and her husband and how she lived apart from him for a year while he worked in another province. He wondered what kind of relationship they'd had together but didn't dwell on the possible implications.

Living apart from her husband made her life routine. She'd traveled forty-five minutes from Sun Peaks to school, five days a week, and then came home to an empty house with only an occasional phone call from her husband to chase away the lonely nights. A year later, her husband had returned home after his employer laid him off. However, when he arrived from Saskatchewan, not intending to remain for more than a day or two, he had shown up on the doorstep of their home with three suitcases, a duffle bag, and a plane ticket in his pocket. While Carina had been living her studious frugal life, he'd been making plans about his own future. He wanted to leave the country for three years to find new business opportunities for himself and left Carina to eventually complete her education.

"And then," he'd said, "we'll get back together." Jennifer, a friend of Carina's had shared that piece of information with Dawes in case it would be useful.

Carina's ex left four days later for Malaysia. He wanted her to wait without financial support until she finished university and then they would get back together. Waiting three years, remaining married but living in separate countries was a hell of a request. She would have had to work full time or go on welfare in order to survive and to heck with her education. *What kind of man could do that?*

She'd entered her third year of university officially divorced, a year later.

Brad Masters had been a close friend of Carina's long before he'd married Maria. They had worked on two term papers together and Brad admitted that his interest in Carina, a woman who seemed ordinary, had been piqued when he discovered that she read fantasy novels. She'd occasionally played a few games of Dungeons and Dragons with their group.

Dawes discovered that she'd never dated anyone after her divorce became final and that Carina worked Friday and Saturday nights and sometimes Sunday afternoons. She'd been cooking full-time at Boston Pizza since August but switched to weekends only while she went to school full-time. She worked a brutal shift, Friday and Saturday from 8:00PM to 4:00AM sometimes 5:00AM.

The turnover rate at the pizza place was incredible. When Dawes questioned the staff and a former employee, he came across an ex-waiter who'd asked Carina why she continued to work there with low wages, rotten management, and dirty conditions. She'd replied, "This is the best damn motivator for finishing my education."

Dawes had to laugh. He admired her spirit. All the people who knew her commented on how she could overcome whatever life threw her way. *She'll get through this, too, I bet,* he thought.

Jackson went to the hospital to interview Carina. The swelling had gone down although both of her eyes had shiners and a small bandage covered a cut above her lip. "Hello, Miss Douglas, I'm Detective Dawes. Do you remember me from a few days ago when you were found?"

"I'm sorry, I don't remember much."

"Do you remember saying that you had seen your assailant?"

She shook her head. "No, I'm afraid not."

"Do you recall saying that they had sold you like cattle?"

"Really?" she asked in surprise.

"You were missing for two days. We didn't know your identity until your friend Brad came to us, concerned for your whereabouts."

"I didn't know. How? Where was I found?"

"Downtown on Seymour, not far from where you work. You were barefoot and..."

Her eyes searched his. "Yes?"

"You were wearing your black slip to cover yourself. You didn't have a blouse on over your skirt, just shirt cuffs."

"Was I...? Was I raped?" Carina whispered.

"No, you weren't. You have rope burns around your wrists from being tied and, I assume, escaping from whoever confined you."

She glanced at her wrists but only saw bandages. "It doesn't hurt. Did they give me a shot for pain?" She kept looking at her wrists as if something else should be there.

"Doctor Montgomery probably gave you something for the pain. Do you remember what happened to you?"

"It was cold. I woke up under a ledge of some type. Were you the one who found me?"

"No, it was a cabdriver who saw you on the street. He tried to help, but you ran away from him."

"He tried to grab me and I assumed he was one of them."

"Them?"

"Yes, I forget exactly, but there was more than one person."

"Can you describe them?"

"It's too vague. I can't remember. I want to remember but, when I think about it, it slips away."

"That's okay, don't try to push yourself. It will come to you. Is there anything else you can remember?"

"No, not right now. I'm sorry."

"Don't apologize, Miss Douglas." He caught himself taking a personal interest in her instead of a professional one and he chided himself for not sticking straight to procedure.

"The doctors said I could go home in a day or two. Brad reminded me that I have some major projects due in the next two weeks of school."

He pulled up a chair and leaned over to speak. "Are you up to them?"

"I have come too far to give up now."

"Yes, I know you have."

Her eyes widened. "You do?"

"You were married for more than six years?"

"Yes, I was married but now I'm divorced and that's part of the past. I'm leading rather a studious life at the moment."

71

"Did you and your husband part on good terms?"

"Ha! Do you mean did I drive him to the Vancouver airport and wish him luck? Or did I take him to the cleaners?"

Her sarcasm wasn't lost on Jackson. "This is obviously a sensitive issue. I meant, would he come after you?"

"I must admit that I was afraid when I heard he was returning from Saskatchewan. I had friends watching out for me."

"Why were they watching?"

"My ex-husband had a lot of anger and resentment from his first marriage and toward women in general. I dreaded, feared, that I would set him off. He was a little unstable the last time I saw him."

Jackson looked at her again.

"Sorry, I was being sarcastic. It's my defense mechanism."

"Did you fear for your life? Is that why you told the lawyer to make the divorce as uncomplicated as possible?"

"You're thorough," Carina murmured. "Yes, I remember him saying once that if anyone did what his previous wife had done to him, he'd hunt them down to the ends of the earth."

"Your ex-husband actually said that?"

"It's amazing what some people say when they love you."

Dawes raised an eyebrow questioningly.

Carina sighed. "I wish I was being sarcastic but it was one of those situations where love wasn't enough."

There was silence for a few moments.

"Where is your ex-husband now?"

"The last I heard, he was still in Kuala Lumpur, Malaysia. I don't know if he has returned to Canada."

"Do you believe he'd come after you?"

"I hope not, that's why I tried to have the lawyer not take him to the cleaners although my acquaintances and the lawyer thought I was a fool. I don't know, maybe if Malaysia didn't turn out and he became unbalanced...."

"Do you mean he seemed unbalanced when he left?"

"He was acting out of character when I last dealt with him. If he's in Canada, you could find out very easily, couldn't you?"

"I'll check it out, Carina, but it might not be that easy."

"I don't think he did this to me or I'd remember it. He understands right from wrong and he was always striving to be above the sweaty and uneducated masses. I know he sounds like a nut. He was older than I was. He was close to turning forty and believed he had nothing to show for his life. He was confused and misguided yes, but not what I would call a nut."

"I have one more question to ask you. Douglas is your maiden name, isn't it?"

"Yes. I don't want Crandall on my degree when I graduate. Are there any more questions?" she asked, looking into Dawes's startled face.

She didn't seem angry at her ex-husband and that surprised him. He tried to imagine the kind of relationship that they had had to instill such loyalty. He faltered at her last question, surprised by her openness. "Yes, just one more." He paused, reluctant to continue. "Tell me about your relationship with your husband."

"We had a good relationship until he left. We were friends."

Dawes grimaced. "That's not what I mean."

Carina looked directly at him, "What do you mean?"

"I don't want to embarrass you but I have to ask."

She leaned closer.

"Were you and your husband intimate?"

A perplexed look crossed her face. "What do you mean by that? Of course we were intimate. Exactly what are you implying?"

"It's just a question, Ms. Douglas. Looking for connections, motives."

She moved away. "Are we done here?"

He nodded. "Yes, that's all for now. I'll do some checking on your ex-husband and then I'll get back to you."

Detective Dawes left, but he wasn't as confident about her ex-husband as she seemed to be. He'd have to verify Mr. Crandall's whereabouts. Even if he were in Malaysia, he decided that it didn't mean Crandall had not arranged Carina's abduction and that made him an official suspect.

Dawes went back to Crandall's previous employer in Kamloops. The office of Economic Development was located on Tranquille Street and it catered to potential new business owners and businesses relocating into the surrounding area. He found out that the city had downsized the office and laid Crandall off. The only other information he could discover was that Crandall was quite talented, but his aspirations in economic development were too visionary for the small businesses that were typical of Kamloops. Crandall had been encouraged to pursue employment elsewhere, thus the move to the city of Regina where the job also only lasted for about a year.

"So, that's two failed jobs, two moves, turning forty, and getting divorced. That explains the motivation behind the third drastic move and, perhaps, the possible motivator for retaliation against his wife after she filed for divorce."

He shared his discoveries with his boss and then headed home for the evening.

He visited Carina's hospital room two days later and discovered she'd already checked out. He went to find Dr. Montgomery.

"Where is she? Why have they released her? Why wasn't I told?" he demanded.

Dr. Montgomery met Dawes's browbeating calmly. "When Ms. Douglas asked if she could go home, I said yes but not until she assured me that she would make an appointment with my office in two days. I want to monitor her progress. She needs to take it easy, but she has been stable for two days and we need the beds."

"Do you genuinely believe she's well enough to leave? What about her memory?"

"I gave her the name of a counsellor she can make an appointment with. I discharged her only because she assured me that she wasn't going to be on her own. She phoned someone to pick her up and the nurse said a woman came for her about a half hour ago."

"What about Davis? He was supposed to be on duty here."

"He went with her to her apartment."

"Thanks, Montgomery, I'll let you know how things are going."

"Ms. Douglas will be fine. She'll heal with time."


Carina stepped out of her friend's car. "Thanks for bringing me home, Jennifer."

"You're welcome." She patted her coifed hair. "I'm glad you have decided to stay with us for a few days. My husband and I will feel better knowing that you're not alone."

Carina turned to speak with Officer Davis when he followed her and Jennifer to the entrance of the building. "I'll be fine, Officer. I just need to get the manager to let me into my apartment."

"I'll wait with you then."

"That's not necessary."

"I have my duties, ma'am."

Chagrined, she managed to smile and thank him. The apartment manager opened the door and led the way to her apartment. He tried to start a conversation with her but one nervous glance at Officer Davis stopped him mid-sentence.

"Thank you for letting me in. My spare keys are inside, so I'll be fine."

He nodded and left.

Officer Davis held up a hand. "I just want to check that your apartment is clear."

"Is it really necessary?" Carina asked. "I didn't expect you to follow us all the way from the hospital. You've done more than enough."

He smiled. "I've been asked to not let you out of my sight. We've just changed locations." He turned and stepped inside the apartment and returned a moment later. He motioned them to enter.

"Thank you again. Come in, Jen. I'll just grab a few things from my apartment—especially makeup and dark glasses."

"Don't worry, Carina. The bruising will heal and I'll do your makeup so nobody will see anything but your nice smile."

She looked at Jennifer's manicured nails and makeup. "I'm going to hate having everyone stare at me."

"Is there any way of avoiding it? Maybe they'd let you hand in your course work and you could get the lecture notes from a classmate. That's the advantage of a small campus: They can be more flexible in special circumstances."

Carina nodded. "You're right and maybe if I explained things to them, they could make an exception." She walked around her apartment until she found her keys and purse and laid them on the table. "Why don't you two have a seat? I need to get a few things from the bedroom." She went to the bedroom and closed the door. She looked at her unmade bed and moved to the closet where she selected some clothing and discarded the sweater that Jennifer had brought to the hospital. As she turned to put the clothing into an overnight bag, she saw the note that she'd written on the nightstand. Her hand trembled as she read it.

Carina heard knocking at the door and stuffed the note into one of her textbooks. She heard Detective Dawes talking with Officer Davis but didn't leave the bedroom. Instead, she sat down on the end of the bed and stared at her pillow, not really seeing it as mental images flashed through her head of the other place. She didn't remember everything, just disjointed images that had been popping into her head ever since she woke up in the hospital. She'd let it slip about her abduction but nothing else. Nobody would believe her if she told them. She looked at the brown envelope that she still carried from the hospital and emptied its contents on to the bed. She recognized her watch and earrings, but the bracelet was foreign.

She picked up the bracelet and turned it over in her hand. The dragon and phoenix carved in the metal seemed to stare at her. The inlaid gem seemed to whisper across her mind but Carina shook her head, frustrated that she couldn't recall it. She stuffed it back into the envelope and noticed a small scrap of cloth. Peering at it closely, she could see lines and curves on it. *Damned if I know what it means.* She returned it to the envelope and then went to her cedar trunk and buried it beneath her clothes.

She left the bedroom, but only after she'd garnered enough self-control to face everyone. She saw Jennifer talking with the detective at the front door.

"Mrs. Bertrell was just telling me that you're going to stay with her a few days."

Caught by surprise, Carina asked, "Do you know him, Jen?"

"Yes. Detective Dawes was at our house; we were so concerned about you."

He turned to Jennifer. "May we have a few minutes, Mrs. Bertrell?"

Jennifer smoothed her tan slacks as she stood up. "Sure, I'll be in the living room."

"Why did you leave the hospital? Don't you know it might be dangerous?"

"Dr. Montgomery said I could check out of the hospital if I felt up to it and if there was someone with me for the first few days. Of course I know it could be dangerous, but," her voice turned to a husky whisper. "I can't live by being afraid of everything. Besides, I'm not alone. I'll be staying at Jennifer's home for a couple of days."

"You'll have to come up with a better plan than that. What will happen if we don't catch the guy who beat you up?"

"Well, I can't stay at Jennifer's place that long. She has her family to take care of and doesn't need me as an added complication. I'll come back here and keep in touch with my family and friends."

"Who's going to look out for you?"

"I have friends to keep an eye on me and besides, I'm paying rent and I may as well live here."

Dawes was running out of ammunition and decided to switch his tactics. "You're not going back to work right away, are you? Your late shift leaves you vulnerable."

Carina grimaced and held up her hand. "No, my broken finger nixes that idea for a while and my ribs are still tender. I can't do much pizza flipping now."

"Well, that's one good thing."

"What's so great about it? That job pays my rent. My student loans only provide enough for the basics, not extra expenses."

"Maybe you can get a roommate," he advised her.

"I like my privacy."

"You're being very stubborn, Ms. Douglas, and not making my job any easier."

Carina's bold façade crumbled.

His voice softened. "My apologies, I know the effort it must be taking for you to keep calm and relaxed after all that has happened. I'm usually not such a heel. I'm glad you're going to Mrs. Bertrell's house and we'll come up with something after your time runs out there."

He called Jennifer back.

She said, "I'll take your bags to the car."

"Thanks, Jen."

"Sure, sweetheart. I'll be right back."

Carina heard Dawes offer to help and she was glad for the reprieve. She stared morosely out the balcony windows until they returned. She turned and realized she ought to water the plants before she left.

"I'm ready to go," Jennifer told her.

"I just need a minute to water the plants."

"I can help."

"No, that's all right." After assuring herself that she hadn't missed anything Carina grabbed her purse and keys, and said, "Okay, let's go." She locked her apartment under their supervision.

"I need to talk with the manager before I go, so I'll say goodbye," Dawes said. "I would like you to come to the police station tomorrow and look at some photographs. Maybe one of them will help you remember."

"What time should I be there?"

"I'll pick you up from Mrs. Bertrell's house at ten if that's all right."

"I'll be ready."

"You will take good care of her won't you, Mrs. Bertrell?" Carina ignored the glance that passed between them, but wondered what they'd talked about when she wasn't there.

"She's in good hands."

# Transitions

Carina wore her dark sunglasses when Detective Dawes picked her up the next day. She'd tried unsuccessfully to cover the bruises. If he noticed as she got into his car, he didn't say anything. He greeted her amiably and took her to his office where he placed several mug shot books on the desk in front of her.

She looked through the books for at least forty-five minutes without recognizing anyone. She excused herself to go to the washroom and Dawes offered her a cup of coffee when she returned. She moved to sit once again but froze mid-stride when she saw a grizzled-looking, white-haired man in faded clothing at the police counter. From a distance, his voice sounded gravelly. She was concentrating so hard that the Styrofoam cup of scalding hot coffee exploded in her hand. She glanced down in surprise, just as Jackson grabbed her by the arm and led her to the nearest water fountain where he placed her scalded hand under the cold water, then toweled it dry.

She looked at her hand. "Boy that was a dumb thing to do." For a moment, she'd thought the old man looked like someone she knew but she couldn't quite place him.

"Is everything all right?" a detective asked.

"Did you see that old white-haired man at the counter?" Dawes responded.

Detective Granger went to the counter while Jackson wrapped a clean, soft cloth around her hand. "We'll bandage this later."

"There wasn't anyone at the counter, Jackson," his partner reported when he returned.

"Are you all right, Carina?" Jackson asked as he led her back into his office. He motioned Granger to shut the door and then he lowered his voice to say, "That old man.... Did you know him? Did he look like the man who abducted you?"

She stared off into space. "Yes, he looked like the man who abducted me. I'm not sure. It could have been him. He looked like the man who bought me. I don't know, maybe I'm just imagining things."

Granger raised his eyebrows. "You're saying that someone bought you? Here in Kamloops? Jackson mentioned that you said something about being sold like cattle when you first woke up in the hospital."

She couldn't answer the second question without revealing the extent of her memory. The snatches of memory she had didn't make sense. "I don't know what I'm saying." She turned. "Are we done here?"

Granger admonished her, "That's a very serious accusation."

Seeing the old man had caught her off guard and she had reacted. *I don't know why I reacted so strongly to that man or how my brief memories are connected, but maybe there is a connection. I'll have to be careful with how much I reveal in the future until I understand what is going on.* "Maybe you're right. That man triggered a response for some reason, and maybe I just overreacted. Forget what I said."

"Thanks, Alec," Jackson said, exasperated.

"I'm sorry, Jackson."

"*Something* happened to her."

"Hey, I'm sorry."

"I'll take you to Mrs. Bertrell's home," Dawes offered.

She looked at him. "Actually, I'd appreciate it if you would take me to my apartment building so I can pick up my car."

It looked like Dawes was about to say something, but he nodded. "Yes, that's a good idea. I was wondering if you were surprised to find your car in its stall."

"No. Should I have been?"

"I don't know. I had originally thought you'd been abducted at work but when we found your car parked in its stall we were surprised.

"I'm sorry but I don't remember."

Dawes glanced at her speculatively but didn't say anything else.

As Carina put packing tape around the last of her boxes destined for storage, she reflected on what had happened since she'd woken up in the hospital. She'd commuted from Jennifer's home to the university and finished her reports along with her classmates over the next two weeks—her professors had more than understood about her need to remain unseen so that her work wouldn't suffer from being stared at constantly. The only person from school she spoke to was Brad. His continued encouragement helped her immensely. Brad had tried to ask her about her abduction but she'd told him that she didn't remember anything. He said he could still see her, lying in the hospital with her face swollen and her hands bandaged. His protectiveness warmed her heart and she'd tried to assuage his frustration because he'd felt he couldn't do anything to help her. He and his wife had offered their support if she needed it.

Detective Dawes had called Carina every few days to see if she'd remembered anything else. She found him to be a very caring and professional man who treated individuals with fairness and respect. She told him that she would spend the last month of school at a friend's home, a family with one child. *Jackson's not going to be thrilled when I tell him the extent of my plans.*

After labeling the last box, Carina looked at the phone and hesitated to call him. She dialed and then made small talk with him before she said, "I wanted to let you that that I'm putting everything into storage and staying with friends until the semester ends. After that, I'm going to Calgary to stay with my mother for the summer. I have to do my teaching practicum in Barriere when school restarts in September. I'll have to live in Barriere for three months and it's easier to live there than commuting back and forth from Kamloops."

"I'm glad you won't be alone for the next few weeks, but I'm deeply concerned about you leaving the province."

"Dr. Montgomery told me that I'm doing fine and he did already refer me to a counsellor."

"What if you begin remembering something from your abduction? The case hasn't been suitably resolved, Carina. We weren't able to confirm your ex-husband's whereabouts."

"Is he a suspect?"

"We don't have many leads about your abduction and I don't want to dismiss any possibility if it will solve the case."

"I appreciate your concern, but so far you and my mother are the only ones who will know where I'll be for the summer."

"Does he know where your mother lives?"

"My ex? How would he know I was there?"

"Now isn't the time to put your safety in jeopardy."

"He's very good at finding out pertinent information, but I truly don't believe he had anything to do with my abduction."

"How will you get there?"

"My mother is coming by train and then we'll drive my car to Calgary. I have exams in four more weeks and then I can leave. I won't be alone."

Dawes was running out of things to say. "I'm only concerned for your safety. Do you know what happened with the last abduction in Kamloops?"

"I'm very aware of the similarity. That one happened after midnight as she was leaving work to go home, but you don't have to worry, I don't have my job anymore and I spend all of my nights studying."

"You overlooked one thing, Carina." Dawes's voice dropped to a whisper. "You can identify the ones who abducted you, and the other girl can't because she's dead. If I were your abductor, I'd be very concerned that I could be identified."

She shuddered at his words. "Not one day goes by where I don't have to remind myself that I was abducted and my fate could have been a lot worse than a couple of broken bones and a split lip. I believe leaving here is a good idea."

"I agree with you. I feel like I can breathe a little better now that I know someone is with you all the time."

The phone call ended with Carina's reassurance that she'd be careful.


Dawes tried to put the situation out of his mind until he learned that Carina stored her belongings and ensconced herself, with her suitcases and textbooks, at her friend's place. "I don't know what it is about this particular case, Alec. I can't help thinking that there's more going on than we know about."

"You always take your work too seriously, Jackson. You're a good cop."

"That's the crucial thing, am I taking this case so seriously because our reputations will increase if we solve the previous abduction with its murder, along with the Douglas case, or am I—"

Alec finished, "Or have you developed a personal interest in Ms. Douglas?"

Jackson looked at Alec. "I'll have to be more careful in the future. Until Carina's memory returns, the case is at a complete standstill; there are neither clues nor leads to follow."


Once her exams were finished, Carina said her goodbyes to her close friends. Only Dr. Montgomery, Brad and Maria, Detective Dawes, and the Bertrells knew where she was going for the summer. Her mother, who'd taken the train from Calgary to Kamloops, waited while Dawes gave Carina last-minute instructions for the summer.

"Be cautious in Calgary."

She sighed. "I'll be careful."

He put his hand on her arm. "I don't want you to take any unnecessary risks."

"I won't be doing much as I don't know anyone else in Calgary. My mother's only been living there since my dad passed away."

"Well, if something or someone comes up, I want you to call this number." He handed her a piece of paper with contact numbers for the Calgary Police.

She fingered the paper. "Really, that's not necessary."

"You may be leaving the province but that doesn't mean you're safe. If the perpetrators believe you can identify them, they'll come after you."

Carina's smile wavered momentarily. "I'll be careful," she said quietly. "If anyone out of the ordinary shows up—"

"Or your ex-husband."

"We've been over this."

"Promise me you'll phone."

She smiled. His concern was touching. "I promise and thank you for being so supportive."

# Graduation 12

Carina's summer away from Kamloops allowed for an interval of quiet before what would prove to be a very busy university semester. All too soon, she had to return to reality from her brief idyll in Calgary. Living by herself was sometimes an ordeal because of the panic attacks, but fortunately, she could always drive into Barriere and stay with friends. The farm owners came by daily from their other property to feed the horses and ducks, which gave her a sense of security.

Except for infrequent panic attacks at night and fear of being alone, Carina mused that the past events in Kamloops were an occurrence of accumulated stresses that had overloaded her mind and her imagination went wild. What with a divorce, work, three-hour classes, and many early morning study sessions, something had to give. It bothered her that she couldn't recall the beating but she assumed there was some rational explanation and she still couldn't control her bouts of panic, but she was learning to recognize the signs.

When her practicum was over in December, she moved back into Kamloops and found affordable accommodations in a basement suite. She worked like a whirlwind to complete the eight-course workload that each education student had to go through. She figured that the degree should be embossed in gold after all the blood, sweat, and tears she'd paid for the formal education.

The panic attacks had lessened to a trickle. She sometimes reflected on the past and figured that she'd imagined it all as she no longer recalled the past images that had haunted her. She remembered the abduction but didn't recall any details. Detective Dawes had no leads to follow and wanted to leave the case open but Carina had been insistent that they close the case as she did not want to pursue it. She recalled his words, "You mean it?"

"Yes, I do. It's time to leave it in the past. I'm graduating soon and I have my whole future ahead. I'm definitely going to move away from Kamloops as soon as I can if I can't get a teaching position here. It's a chance to start over."

"Fine, I'll discuss it with my superior and if he agrees, I'll close it, but not before then. If another similar case does come up and is connected to this one, I'll reopen your case and you may have to be questioned."


Carina's friend Katie had arranged a small party at her house for after the grad ceremony. Her mom and close friends all came to wish her well. She appreciated the recognition. She considered getting a formal education the hardest thing she'd ever done. Receiving the degree was a milestone and the conclusion of a long journey.

Carina applied at schools in and around Kamloops unsuccessfully. Brad was hired in Merritt and they got together for a barbecue or two over the summer.

"Congratulations, Brad."

"Thanks, I'm glad I got a job near Kamloops. Maria still has two years to go in her program."

"You'll have to commute."

"What about you? Where have you applied?"

She sipped her Diet Coke. "All over British Columbia. I don't really care where I end up. I even applied in Prince George. They're sending someone from human resources to do formal interviews next week. I feel positive that I'll get a teaching position, but I don't know where yet. I'll keep watching the papers. Are you still working at the group home?"

"For another week at least and then we're traveling up to Fort St. John. How about you? You're working at that stationery warehouse, aren't you?"

She harrumphed. "I was lucky to get the temporary job. A few interviews I had wouldn't hire me because I was overeducated or they didn't want someone for temporary employment."

"We'll certainly keep our fingers crossed for you." Brad surprised her again. "What about Jackson?"

"What about him?"

"You've seen a lot of him."

"In a professional capacity."

Brad nodded knowingly. "The case is closed now so why don't you hook up with him?"

"Since when have you been a matchmaker, Brad?"

Brad laughed. "Hey, gotta try finding you someone as you don't seem to be doing any dating."

"You're worse than my mom." Carina smiled. "He is kinda cute."

Maria arrived on the scene. "Who's cute?"

"Brad is trying to set me up."

"What's wrong with that?"

"I've got to find a job first before I can even think of getting together with anyone."

Brad said, "Well, you know who to call when the dust clears."

"Yeah, Brad, I think I smell smoke and it's not just from the barbecue."

During the last week of August, she phoned Brad to let him know that she'd found a position.

"Where is it?"

"Surrey, someplace called Surrey. I never heard of it until I went there for an interview over the weekend. It's near Vancouver."

"You've only been to Vancouver a few times. You're not expected to know everything."

"It's a private school," she explained.

"It's a beginning," Brad reassured her.

"It's a huge city."

"I forgot you grew up in a small Alberta town. You'll get used to it."

"I'm having a garage sale tomorrow and I've already got a moving truck booked. Can you come help load up the truck? I'm going to drive to Surrey on Sunday."

"I'd be glad to help. Have you found a place to live?"

"I phoned ads in the Province newspaper and tracked down a place, living with three other people."

"Roommates." He teased.

"I like my privacy so it will be a new experience for me."

Carina soon became so engrossed in her first teaching job that she didn't have time to worry about anything but work. She often stayed past five before heading home and, because her employers paid their teachers poorly, saying teachers were a dime a dozen, she began working for a small tutoring service that sent her to Vancouver and White Rock.

White Rock was usually a rushed trip as she'd arrive, do her two hours of tutoring English as a Second Language to international students, and then return home.

She was fortunate to keep tutoring once her school closed for the summer. The beautiful weather and the extra time on her hands led Carina to use her weekly trips to explore the town of White Rock.

Once she took a different route that led to the ocean. She laughed when she saw a huge white rock sitting alongside the railroad track, thinking, *that's where they got the town's name.* Later she found a small plaque that told about the legend of the son of a Salish sea god who fell in love with a mortal Cowichan princess. When their parents objected, the young son threw a huge boulder across the water and took his bride with him to the opposite shore.

Carina learned of another, sandier beach with shops and a larger population surrounding it and decided to go explore it. *This place looks fabulous. I can't wait to get to the beach.* It was more difficult finding an available parking spot at Crescent Beach than she realized, and she circled several blocks surrounding the beachfront. *Where's the parking? I have to go around the block again. Maybe someone vacated a spot. Oh my God.* Carina slammed on her brakes as she nearly hit the car in front of her. The street contained several small shops in two-story buildings but one building shone like a beacon. *Oh my God. I have to be imagining this. It's the same building. Those whales and dolphins, I've seen them before. This is the same place I remember from the sector. This can't be a coincidence.* The two-story structure that had grabbed Carina's attention was painted entirely on one side with blues, blacks, and greys, depicting three grey whales and four dolphins swimming in an ocean.

She still hadn't taken her foot off the brake as she stared, eyes swimming in tears at the memory of what the wall meant, at the memory of everything that she'd buried subconsciously. It came back to her in a rush of memory and emotion: The Leaders, the Banished, being sold, not being fed for days on end, tied to a steel ring with limited distance to move.

A honk from the car behind her broke her reverie and forced Carina to continue driving. She wiped her eyes but didn't stop as she speedily left White Rock. *I have to get home.* She thought her dream and reality were somehow connecting. *I dreamed it, didn't I? I dreamed it. It's not real.*

Carina was so dazed, she didn't realize how quickly she got home. She parked her car, entered the house, went to the bathroom, and vomited.

She touched her ribs. Words flashed through her head. "How many times do I have to be tellin' you to move?" A kick coming at her... ducking. Slap. Slap. Carina touched her lip, wincing as she remembered the beating. She collapsed on the laminate floor, shaking.

Some time passed before Carina got up and washed her face and hands. She went to her room on the top floor, undressed, and crawled into bed. For the first time in several months, Carina found herself fearful and panicky when bedtime came. Sleep eluded her until she finally got up and made her way downstairs into the living room. Her three roommates were in bed sleeping, but she felt better knowing that if something happened, someone would find her. It was that buried fear of dying alone that had invaded her psyche in Kamloops.

The next day, Carina rummaged through piles of papers to find Jackson Dawes' business card so she could tell him to close the police file. I have to tell Brad. I don't know why I've waited so long. He's interested in fantasy stories. Maybe he'd believe me—if not for his imagination, then at least in the name of friendship...but he likes to talk. What if he tells someone else? How can he keep it from his wife? I can't tell Jackson. He'd never believe me. He's a cop. Damn you, Andy. If I trusted you and you left me, how can I trust someone else? She cursed her ex-husband for taking away her ability to trust anyone. Why'd you have to leave like that? She thought a few more moments and then decided. I have to get Jackson to keep the case closed permanently. There's no way I want anyone else finding out about this.

She dialed Jackson's office because he'd repeatedly asked her to phone if she remembered anything about her abduction. His recorded message greeted her, "Hello, this is Detective Dawes. I'm not in the office at the moment but you may leave a message or push the star button to be transferred to the front desk where someone can help you immediately. Thank you for calling." Beeeeeep.

"Hello, Jackson, I mean, Detective Dawes, this is Carina Douglas. You asked me to call you if I ever remembered anything. Well, I've remembered everything, absolutely everything, and I just wanted to let you know that it isn't connected to any other case. I don't think you can do anything more. Thank you for being there when I needed you."

Jackson, who'd just entered his office, heard only the last four words and, although he grabbed the phone before the sentence ended, he only heard the dial tone through the receiver. "That voice sounds familiar." He rewound his messages, tapping impatiently on his worn wooden desk as he waited for the last message to play. When Jackson heard her soft, familiar voice, he smiled. "It is you, Carina."

His mind raced back to the first time he saw her.

In the first few weeks, then months, he had watched her eventual recovery. She had never acted like the victim. Instead, she'd met adversity with quiet resignation, her strength coming from some unknown inner source he couldn't fathom. He had been frustrated at not solving her case. This woman made him feel that he owed it to her to find whoever had beaten her. He admired her. Maybe he even loved her.

"Alec would laugh at me for admitting that possibility."

Jackson was relieved, yet disturbed that she had her memory back. He dialed the number displayed on the phone and then waited patiently for her to answer.

"Hello?"

"Carina? This is Detective Dawes."

"Oh, hi." They exchanged a few more words and then Carina said, "I guess you're calling because of my message."

"Your message mentioned that you remembered everything. That's great. Now we can catch those crooks who abducted you."

"No. That's not why I called you. I owed it to you to let you know that I have remembered everything, but I don't feel that you can help me."

"Are you sure you don't want me to reopen the case?"

"Yes, I'm sure."

"I don't agree with your decision but I understand it. Is there anything else I can help you with?"

"Thank you, no. I'm glad you called back." But Carina didn't want to reveal any more than she had so she stated the first thing that came to mind, "Yes, now that the matter is closed, I can ask you out on a date." Carina could only imagine Jackson's stunned expression.

"You could have called me anytime, Carina. You didn't need a reason."

"I didn't know if you were allowed."

"Allowed to date?"

"I know you couldn't when the case was open, but I thought...." Her reason for calling was quickly disappearing and Carina was beginning to wish she hadn't called. *He's only going to say no. What am I doing? I'm not sure I want to date.*

"When you put it that way, sure, I'd love to go out on a date with you."

"Really? I mean, great."

"How about today? I can get my neighbour to watch Casimir, my dog, and I can be in Surrey in less than four hours."

"Today? You'd come all that way just for a date?" She teased him for the first time. "I thought there were a lot of girls in Kamloops."

"Yes, girls. Not women, not like you," he said huskily.

"Tonight?" She thought of how her roommates' would react if Jackson showed up. "How about a restaurant, Detective?"

"Jackson. You don't have to call me detective anymore."

"Jackson." She thought of his trim form. "Will you be in uniform?"

"No, I'll come in my civvies."

Carina, who'd been feeling rather lost in the city of Surrey, said, "That would be nice. I have missed having a familiar face around. When should I expect you?"

"How does six sound?"

"That sounds great."

"I'll see you then."

"Sure."

"Oh, Carina, another thing."

"Yes?"

"Do you like Greek food?"

She laughed. "Love it."

"Greek, it is. I'll see you at six."

She could hear Jackson chuckling as he hung up the phone on the other end. She felt better after the phone call. *Maybe I should just tell someone what happened and let the chips fall where they may. If he thinks I'm crazy then I'll just have to live with it; at least I'll have tried.*

She felt better, almost lighthearted, after she hung up the phone. She dialed Brad's number and talked with Maria a moment or two before Brad came on the line.

"Hi, Carina. How's Surrey treating you?"

"It has its defining moments. It's sure strange living in such a big city."

"You'll be a city girl before you know it."

"How about you? How's the tutoring?"

"It isn't what I expected." The conversation carried on for several minutes before Brad asked her how she was feeling.

"Yesterday, I remembered everything that happened to me," Carina blurted out before she could change her mind.

"Really? You mean about your abduction? Do you want to talk about it?"

"Well, Brad, you've known me for about four years now and I think you'd probably believe the wild story I want to tell you, but I'm not ready to tell you everything right now."

"What made you remember?"

"A building. I was tutoring in White Rock and heading toward Crescent Beach when I saw a painted building. That building was in a dream I had, but it wasn't a dream. It seems to connect what I remember with my current reality." She knew it sounded weird the moment she said it.

"What do you mean, current reality?"

"Brad, take the most amazing fiction you've read and apply it to reality as you know it." Her voice quavered.

"What does this have to do with your abduction?"

"Everything. I'm sorry, Brad, I can't tell you on the phone. I thought I could, but—" Her voice broke.

"Are you crying, Carina?"

The doorbell rang.

"I've got to go Brad, someone's at the door. Forget I phoned."

"Wait, you can't hang up. Tell me what's wrong."

The doorbell rang again.

"I'll try you later. I've got to go."

Carina leaned against the doorway in her room, unable to move. The doorbell went unanswered as Carina tried to regain control of her emotions. *What was I thinking? I can't tell anyone. They'll assume I've lost my mind. I think I've lost my mind.*

# The Date

Carina dressed meticulously. She was nervous about seeing Jackson again, partly because of her phone call earlier and partly because of him. He'd been professional, but nice to her in Kamloops.

Jackson arrived promptly at six and Carina quickly grabbed her coat and purse and went to meet him before he had an opportunity to come to the front door. She stopped at the end of the walkway, suddenly overcome by shyness. *Wow, I forgot how he looked,* she mused, as he closed the door of his car, and moved toward her. He had a panther-like grace when he walked. She'd never noticed it before. His cropped chestnut hair suited him.

His hazel eyes twinkled as they met her own. "Hello, Carina, it's really great to see you." He moved toward Carina and kissed her on the cheek.

"Detective Dawes," she admonished and he was about to step back when he saw her smile.

He hugged her and Carina found herself hugging him back. "I've always wanted to do that."

Carina didn't know what to say. "I think I did, too, but I didn't realize it until now."

An awkward silence passed until Carina broke it. "Have you ever been to the restaurant called Minos? It's on Scott Road."

"No, I haven't been there."

They arrived at the Greek restaurant and Carina scanned the walls as they sat down; a serene blue covered them and white pillars hung with plants all around the room between the tables. They both admired the paintings before ordering from the many authentic Greek dishes.

Jackson was the first to speak. "What else have you been up to?"

"Well, you know I worked at the private school this year and they paid so poorly that I started tutoring on weekends, usually after church. Once the school year ended, I kept tutoring. It's easier now because I can tutor during the week."

"Oh? Where do you do your tutoring?"

"In White Rock."

"White Rock is beautiful, isn't it? Have you gone to any of the beaches?"

"Yes, I have. They have two main beach areas and I went to the one called Crescent Beach."

"How did you like it?"

She twirled her water glass. "I, uh, actually, I didn't see it."

"Why, was it closed?"

"No, well, because I saw something else."

If Jackson noticed that Carina was speaking more softly and was fighting some kind of deep emotion, he didn't say anything, which relieved her.

"I...."

"What did you see?" He spoke just as softly.

"There was a building that I recognized."

"What kind of building?"

"I don't know. I was too upset to check. I didn't go back."

"Why not?" When she didn't answer, he asked, "Have you spoken to anyone else?"

"I phoned Brad right after I called you this morning."

"Carina?"

"Yes?"

"Why did your message on the answering machine say that I should close the case because there wasn't any more that I could do? Do you know who abducted you?"

"Yes, I do."

"Then why won't you tell me? It's your ex-husband, isn't it?"

The glass shook as she carried it to her mouth. Swallowing hard, she said, "No. It's a little more complicated than that."

"Then who?"

"His name's Trator. Actually, he wasn't the one who grabbed me. Two men grabbed and carried me away."

Jackson put his hand around hers as she fiddled with the now empty glass. She gave him a shaky smile and continued speaking.

"They put a black hood on my head so that I wouldn't see where we were going. They brought me to a building with a jail cell in it and then men came and bid on me. *He doesn't need to know how they treated me before I was sold.* "Trator was the one who bought me and beat me."

The waitress interrupted the conversation as she refilled the water glass. Carina was glad for the temporary reprieve and used the moment to regain power over her emotions.

As soon as the waitress turned away, Jackson asked, "They drove you to White Rock and sold you? How did you get abducted and then arrive beaten and starved back in Kamloops three days later?"

"No, they didn't drive."

Jackson's head swiveled toward Carina. "They flew you to White Rock? Without an airport they'd have had to use a small plane that could land on water or a helicopter."

"They didn't fly. They walked."

He kept on talking and missed her words. "I don't see how they could have done it. They'd have had to fly over the mountains. It would have been a small airplane or a helicopter."

Exasperated, she interrupted him, "I didn't say they took me to White Rock. I said that a building triggered my memory in White Rock."

"So, you were sold in Kamloops then?"

Carina rubbed her forehead before continuing. She'd expected him not to believe in the other place but she didn't realize how adept Jackson's questioning techniques would be. She didn't want to blurt out her words bluntly and let the repercussions begin. She didn't want to see the cold calculating look in Jackson's eyes that she'd seen whenever he spoke of criminals and how he was going to catch them. She wanted to make a connection.

Carina hadn't allowed herself an unguarded moment since her husband had abandoned her. The craving she had for the slightest touch from another person even in friendship magnified her loneliness. She sighed, recognizing her efforts with Jackson would be futile. Remorse flooded through her. "I shouldn't have called you."

A guarded look came into his eyes. "What do you mean by that?"

She faltered. "I-I-I should have thought it through before I called you. I saw a building and overreacted. I shouldn't have dragged you away from your work."

His calming words filtered through her turmoil. "What kind of man would I be if I didn't take the time for a friend?"

"I'm sorry."

"Quit apologizing. I just want to get to the bottom of this."

Carina's resolve strengthened at his words. "That's just it, Jackson. I don't want to find the underlying cause of this. I wanted to make sure the case would remain closed permanently. Look, I know I've handled it the wrong way. I did phone about the case, but...."

Jackson studied Carina. "You didn't phone me for a date, did you?"

"No—I—maybe I did."

"Now that we have that cleared up." He laughed.

Carina smiled shyly. "Was it the no or the maybe?"

A broad grin lit his face and her body reacted. It had been a long time since a man had looked at her with such warmth.

"And here I am interrogating you."

"You were only doing your job."

He looked at her intensely. "It's never been a job helping you."

Silence fell between them. The restaurant patrons and the clatter of dishes faded away as Carina absorbed his words. She was afraid to breathe.

"Carina?"

Jackson's query brought her out of her reverie. "Shall we go?"

She reached for her purse.

"I already paid."

"I'm sorry. I didn't notice. Let me give you some money."

"You can buy me breakfast."

"Breakfast?" What is that supposed to mean?

"I mean, you can buy me breakfast when we go to White Rock tomorrow."

Carina had already pushed open the glass door and left the restaurant ahead of Jackson. She flinched when he grabbed her arm.

"I wasn't hitting on you. That came out the wrong way." Jackson tried to apologize.

"No, you're just doing your job. You're on the job. I'm not a business you can run."

"I should have asked you first if you wanted to come to White Rock."

"And it's just a coincidence that you want to go there."

Jackson didn't reply. He led her to his car and seated her inside. Several minutes flew by while he maneuvered through the traffic toward Carina's place.

Carina waited, feeling like a shrew. She could already feel rejection stealing over her. Jackson must have sensed it because, after one look at her face, he pulled his car over to safe place on the side of the road. He turned off the engine and turned to her. "You're doing the same thing you always do."

"What do you mean?" The words came out in a twisted whisper.

"You're blocking me out, everyone out. You always seem isolated, even when you're with people. You have to allow people to help you more often. Why try to constantly solve all the problems yourself?" He turned toward her, his thumb caressing her cheek and feeling the wetness. "Oh, Carina, I'm a heel."

"Please take me home, Jackson," she pleaded.

Carina heard his tormented sigh as Jackson started the engine and re-entered traffic. Carina didn't speak. *I feel like such an idiot. Oh, what he must think of me.*

Moments later, Jackson pulled the car up in her driveway and waited. Carina raised the palm of her right hand and touched his cheek as she tentatively kissed him on the mouth. The electricity in their kiss surprised her. "Goodnight, Jackson."

Jackson got out of the car and was at Carina's side before her door had closed. They walked up the sidewalk and Carina turned at the front door. "One more thing, I know that you're a detective but I think the only way you can help both of us understand this is if you approach going to White Rock as an unbiased observer, as a friend. Try to forget for a while that you're a cop."

"I'll try," Jackson grinned at the turn of events. "Goodnight," he said and then quickly kissed her cheek and left.

After she saw his car drive away, Carina sat outside on the front steps reflecting on the wisdom of involving Jackson. Although she'd known him for over a year, it hadn't been on a personal level. Why *do* I always isolate myself? I have friends, acquaintances, but I don't reveal much about my inner thoughts. She knew the answer: I can't get hurt. Nobody really wants to know. She assumed from her experiences that this was true. She'd moved around too much in her youth and adulthood with her parents and then her ex-husband to make more than a smattering of close friends and those friendships changed as she moved.

*Romance? Am I ready for romance? I don't know if I can trust enough to love again.* Thoughts of her ex-husband and the closeness they'd shared drifted, as they often did, through her mind. Her heart ached as she wept.

At seven the next morning, Carina realized that she had two more hours to wait before Jackson would arrive. She dressed carefully, her comfortable flared jean skirt followed by a black turtleneck and a maroon jacket. Her hand twitched when she pulled her black slip up until it rested on her hips beneath her skirt. She paused briefly but the memory receded. She decided she needed to finish one more thing before she left to exorcise her fear of going to White Rock. She put her dad's Swiss army knife, a lighter, some money, and a mirror in her skirt pocket. She hid her identification within the hem of her skirt. She felt foolish carrying them. *They might come in useful if I end up back in the sector.* She could only recall that the sector was somewhere else. The remaining details were an elusive fog in the swirling background of her memories. *Should I tie up loose ends here? What if I don't come back? What if I get stuck there?* Her thoughts were mixed, unsure.

She went to her battle-scarred cedar trunk. With the bed, the table, and the trunk in the same room, there was almost no space for moving around. She opened the lid carefully and began rummaging until she reached the bottom. A brown manila envelope with her name and the Royal Inland Hospital stamped clearly on it lay inside. The envelope contained the items from that fateful wintry morning in Kamloops when she'd been found. She'd forgotten about the envelope. She dumped its contents on the bed and studied their mysterious presence. *I guess I don't remember everything. Maybe I don't want to remember.* Her intuition wouldn't let her discard them.

If she were entering another dimension, like some of her memories suggested, they might be the key.

She fingered a smaller white envelope, her will. The information in it still named her ex-husband as the executor because she'd never gotten around to making the change. She placed it on the table. *If it is meant to be it will be.* Her grandmother's face swam before her as she recalled how her grandmother used to apply those words to everything, from winning at a bingo game to who'd become the next pope. Somehow, the memory of her beloved grandmother eased the tension that had enveloped her all morning.

She grimaced as she glanced around her room. The room was very different from the house, situated on half an acre that she and her husband had shared. She closed the bedroom door with quiet resolve and went down the copper-coloured stairwell to the kitchen to wait for Jackson's arrival.

It wasn't long before she heard the crunch of tires on the driveway. She walked down the sidewalk before Jackson had even closed the door to his car. She looked at him appreciatively. He had a great physique and his short chestnut hair emphasized his lean face.

"And how are you this morning?"

She roused from her daydreaming. "Hmm? Fine, and you?"

"What were you thinking just now?"

Carina blushed and then grinned. "I was thinking about California boys."

Jackson looked at her but she didn't elaborate. "I can't take you to California but I can take you to the Pantry."

Carina laughed. "Sounds pretty good to me."

"Which one is closest?"

"There's one in White Rock." She could have named two others located in Surrey.

"Are you sure?"

He wasn't asking whether she knew where the restaurant was but whether she wanted to go to White Rock first thing. "It's on our way."

Jackson didn't ask her about the envelope she'd been clutching until they took their seats in the restaurant and ordered.

"It's the envelope from the Royal Inland Hospital. This is what I was wearing when I was brought into the hospital."

"Was everything accounted for?"

"Yes, my watch and earrings were there but, even though I've looked at it several times, I didn't recognize this until Sunday." An armband clunked onto the table when Carina emptied the envelope.

Jackson picked it up and examined it closely. "It looks intricate. Is this a ruby? It's huge. It must be worth a fortune."

Carina shrugged her shoulders indifferently. "It was given to me."

He held it toward her. "It looks too big for you. Why don't you put it on?"

"I'd rather not."

"Why not?"

"Because of what it might do."

"What it might do? It's just a fine piece of metal."

A memory niggled through her thoughts. "It comes alive."

Jackson blinked twice. "Excuse me?"

"You heard me."

"Metal comes alive in science fiction movies."

"That's what I thought, too."

"Would you mind explaining things to me?"

She drew a deep breath and exhaled slowly. "Before I was in Kamloops, I was in Boston Bar and Hope."

"The towns?"

She nodded as the food arrived but she kept talking. "I remember the trip, but it gets foggy once I got to Kamloops. I entered the city, what I thought was Kamloops, but it wasn't. I thought I was hallucinating or dreaming because of the way the scenery changed wherever I looked. There were buildings being torn down alongside newly built ones." Her words flowed out as she finally recalled what had happened. "There was a black-haired man standing in one brick building. I think his job was to give new people assignments but he didn't give me one, just this armband. Maybe I'm wrong saying it comes alive. Maybe it just appeared that way at the time."

"You don't remember driving home once you got to Kamloops?"

"Basically."

"What does your dream have to do with your drive from Boston Bar?"

"Because," she paused and inhaled deeply to calm herself, "it wasn't a dream. I ended up somewhere else that was Kamloops but not Kamloops."

Jackson looked at her skeptically, but didn't speak until the waitress bustled by. "Carina, I believe you're talking about repressed memories from your abduction. Maybe you should talk to someone professional like a hypnotist or a psychiatrist."

"I don't need a shrink and I'm not crazy. I experienced it."

He leaned forward. "I'm not saying you didn't but you're not recalling it as it really happened."

She nodded. "Maybe you're right. I hadn't thought of that." She didn't speak for several minutes.

Finally, Jackson spoke again, "Did anyone else have an armband?"

"Just the man who gave me mine but no one else."

He studied the intricately carved dragon and phoenix on the armband. "These are mythical, aren't they?"

"Yes."

"This place that you were in, was it within driving distance of Kamloops?"

"You misunderstand; I think it was Kamloops, but an entirely different one with entirely different people. I didn't recognize anyone and they dressed and acted differently."

"Did that include the ones who abducted you?"

"Including them."

"Are we talking about a different time?" Jackson was in full interrogation mode.

"I don't know."

"A different dimension like out of science fiction?"

"I don't know."

"Help me out here, Carina. I'm trying to digest all of this. What does the building you saw in White Rock have to do with Kamloops?"

"I don't know. Maybe it was White Rock and not Kamloops that I was in. I don't know which one."

"I'd like to get to the bottom of this but I'm not sure you're up to it. Maybe talking to a professional will help you cope with the shocks it might bring. I don't want to trigger a bad memory."

She knew she'd lost him. It was as if a thick blanket of disbelief had settled over him. Her eyes hardened from his rejection but she spoke anyway. "You mean you don't want to be the cause of a breakdown, don't you? So," she said as she fingered the armband, "this particular piece of metal with its dragon and phoenix is just an armband and I'm afraid of it for no reason? And," she continued, "if I put it on," she slipped the armband with its blood red stone onto her wrist and watched as it self-adjusted to her wrist so that it wouldn't slip off, "nothing will—"

Carina felt a rush of fire course through her body as the blood-red stone began to shimmer. She tried grabbing onto the table in an attempt to steady herself. The last thing she saw was Jackson's bulging eyes before he disappeared.

# Amnesia... Again?

14

"She's coming around."

Carina opened her eyes to the sound of the voice and found startling blue eyes looking anxiously into her own.

Helzion demanded, "What do you think you were doing outside of the sector's security perimeter?"

She shook her head to clear it. "Who are you?"

"Stop playing games. You know damn well who I am." Helzion's eyes flashed angrily.

"Where am I?"

"Look at me," Lachash said. "You're in the complex now, my dear."

She turned to face the source of the gentle voice. The round face and salt and pepper hair seemed vaguely familiar.

"How are you feeling, Carina? Do you remember me, Lachash, or where you are?"

"I think so. What happened?"

"Well, you have been missing for about forty-eight days and today you were found on the ground just outside the perimeter. Do you know how you got there?"

"The last thing I remember," she said truthfully, "was feeling intense heat rush from my feet to my head and the next thing I'm here." *I don't know how I got here.*

"Where were you all this time?" Helzion asked.

She rubbed her hand across her eyes, suddenly very weary.

"Are you all right?" Helzion's voice immediately softened.

"I was just dizzy for a second or two."

"Helzion, I want to check her out. Could you come back in about half an hour?" Lachash said.

Immediately, she started to tremble.

Helzion reluctantly nodded and Lachash turned back to Carina. "Do you hurt anywhere?"

"No, yes," she said in apparent surprise as her hand went to her rib cage. "I feel a dull ache when I breathe deeply."

"What happened to your lip?"

Her hand flew to her upper lip where she touched the rough scab. At that exact moment, she saw her scraped and bruised hands. Her eyes widened in surprise.

Lachash took her arm. "Did you fall?"

"I don't know."

"What is this around your wrist?" He peered closely, unaware that Carina's heart started thumping crazily in response to his proximity. "If I didn't know better, I would say these were rope burns. Who did this to you?"

Her eyes filled with tears as she looked at him. "I don't know. I can't remember."

Lachash tried to calm her when he saw her distress. "Shh, it is all right. From the condition of your injuries, this happened a while ago. I need to do some tests and figure out why your ribs hurt. Lie down and let me have a look." His eyes widened in disbelief at the large purplish blue bruise that covered the left side of her rib cage. "Does this hurt?" he asked as he gently pressed on the yellowing edge of the bruise.

"No."

The examination took only seconds. "I don't feel anything broken," Lachash said. "I can do some further testing. Your wounds are healing. Which injury is older is harder to tell. I would have to say the freshest wounds are on your wrists because of their rawness."

"Will I be all right?"

"I'll have you mended in no time," Lachash said reassuringly. "Why not relax, close your eyes, and I'll be right back."

He met Helzion at the door.

Carina heard his angry demand.

"May I speak to her now? I've been waiting long enough and she has a lot of explaining to do."

"You will have to wait. She is in no shape for an interrogation."

"What is that supposed to mean? What did you find out?"

"I examined her. She's been beaten repeatedly from the looks of the scab on her lip. Her scraped hands and knees are healing. She has a bruised rib. Her wrists, once I rolled up her sleeves, have raw rope burns. They're the most recent wounds. What concerns me is that she doesn't remember how she got this way."

Tears rolled down Carina's eyes as she heard his words.

# In Denial

Jackson stared disbelievingly at the vacant seat across the table where Carina had just been sitting. He immediately looked under the dining table and began searching the restaurant, his mind denying what his eyes had seen. When the waitress came to the table, he asked her if she had seen the woman, he had been sitting with.

"I'm sorry sir, but I haven't seen her."

"Would you mind checking the washroom for me?"

The waitress looked at him strangely but complied and returned a few minutes later. "I'm sorry, sir. There was no one in the ladies' room. Will that be all?"

"Yes, thank you." His mind was trying to catch up with reality. He had just seen a woman disappear before his eyes. "People didn't vanish. It's the twenty-first century and people don't disappear by putting on a bracelet."

What the hell am I supposed to do now? Put out an All-Points Bulletin? That will have them laughing at the station. "Detective Dawes puts out APB for a young woman who vanished before his eyes." Nothing even shows she was sitting here. *Except*, he thought, and picked up the brown envelope from the Royal Inland Hospital that lay on the seat of the bench. He found a scrap of torn material inside. He pulled it out of the envelope. It had scribbling on it. A map? Of what? He paid the bill, leaving a generous tip for the waitress. He carried the envelope with the bit of material to his car and decided to return to Carina's place and asked to see her rooms.

One of Carina's roommates was in the open garage with a German shepherd on her grooming table, when Jackson entered her shop. She turned off the clippers before speaking. "Did you have a good breakfast?"

"Yes. May I have a moment of your time to speak privately? I need to talk to you, but it can't be repeated to anyone."

She tossed him a questioning look, said, "Okay."

"Carina has disappeared."

"What? How? Weren't you with her?"

"Yes, I was. Did you know that she was abducted over a year ago?"

"No way. Carina would have mentioned it."

"I assume she would have preferred to keep it to herself because she wasn't able to remember anything about the event until recently. I drove here from Kamloops when she phoned and said she'd remembered."

"Wow."

"I need to find out if she's been back to her rooms. May I look?"

"I'll show you her rooms," Kelly offered helpfully. She put the dog in a travel kennel and then showed Jackson to Carina's rooms. Kelly led him through the ramshackle house, then the upper rooms. Carina's three rooms consisted of two bedrooms and a full bathroom. The first and smaller room was on the right side of the hall. It had three bookshelves that lined the walls; there was also a trunk and several boxes. The second bedroom was larger and it contained two tall bookshelves, a table, a television, a stereo, and her bed.

"She is a pack rat," Kelly explained.

"I see that. She sure loves books, doesn't she? Would you mind if I look around?"

"Are you sure that she would want you looking around in her rooms?"

"I came from Kamloops to help her. I've known her for over a year, and I've been trying to find her abductors since then."

"You're a cop?"

"RCMP." He showed his badge which he carried even when he was off duty, and although he was here as a friend for Carina, he'd quickly up the police involvement if he believed it were necessary.

"I'm not surprised."

"Why's that?"

"Carina is the type of person to have a cop for a friend, so I guess that means I can trust you. If you have any questions, just ask me."

"Actually, if you want, I can ask you questions while you're working with your dogs so you don't fall behind with your work."

"No problem."

They returned to the garage.

He took out his notebook. "How long has Carina lived here?"

"Since August of last year."

"Does she get many visitors?"

"Every now and then a whole bunch of her coworkers swoop down on this place and do a movie night. I usually leave because who wants to hang around with teachers?"

"You don't like teachers?"

"When I was younger, I didn't like teachers just because they were teachers and now it just feels weird being around them. They did a Mel Gibson night, when they watched *Braveheart*, and they all dressed in theme clothing."

Jackson smiled. "That must have been interesting," he said as he tried to picture what Carina might have looked like.

"The guys' kilts weren't too bad."

"How many of them were there?"

"Seven, eight, I think."

"Other than movie nights, did she get many visitors?"

"No, just the teachers."

"Did she go out much?"

"Not that much. She usually had a lot of school work to do."

"What about the other room upstairs?"

"That belongs to Oleg. He's older and drives a bus, and works odd hours. They avoid each other."

"Oh, why is that?" Jackson asked curiously.

"Carina and I confronted him about his attitude."

"What kind of attitude?"

"Oleg knows everything. He knows how to do everything better than anyone can possibly do even when they have the training. He likes controlling people and situations."

"He didn't like your confrontation?"

"Carina was quite blunt and he took offense. Now they avoid each other even though Carina apologized."

"Would he harm her?"

"I don't think so. He's been here for about two years, but I really don't know him. He'll disappear in his room and not come out for two or three days. Kind of weird."

"Thanks, Kelly. I'll be in her rooms. If you can think of anything else, just let me know. I'll let myself out when I'm done. Here is my card, if you need to contact me. I have my cell phone with me while I'm in the lower mainland, so you can call anytime."

"I'll let you know."

Jackson returned to Carina's rooms. The large room where she slept and probably did most of her work, might reveal something of her whereabouts. Glancing around, he saw that her tastes in music included soft rock and classical. The narrow table was covered with stacks of papers, bills, assignments to mark, and a couple of books.

He recognized the collage of pictures on the white wall. It had once hung on her living room wall in Kamloops, but now he knew each individual. Carina had changed a lot since then. The young girl, in the picture with her brothers, had grown into a lovely and talented young woman. He glanced at her university photograph and reflected on how she'd earned that degree. Everything in the room had a place. The room felt cozy, comfortable, like Carina. He went into the bathroom, giving it only a cursory glance, nothing seemed out of place.

The smaller room with the bookshelves and plants didn't appear to be used for more than a storage area for several boxes and pieces of furniture. The shelves were lined with schoolbooks, science fiction, and fantasy books. He recognized Tolkien, and Brooks, but he didn't know many of the other authors. Although the rest of the shelves covered every topic from religion and history, to mathematics, a large concentration was in fantasy and fiction. This intrigued Jackson because it was another side to Carina that he had not known about. The serious and often wise front that Carina presented to the world didn't even hint of her interests.

He chose one book off the shelf, *Rusalka*. "I think I'd like to borrow this to see what type of writing Carina's interested in, but that will have to wait."

Jackson left the house after he said goodbye to Kelly. He had found nothing that would give him a clue as to Carina's whereabouts. He was still reluctant to give much credence to Carina disappearing before his eyes. *It had to have been a trick, but then again, why would Carina want to trick me?*

# Reenactment 16

Four days later, Carina returned to the small room that served as sleeping quarters. A cot had been set up for her and she was given strict orders not to do any strenuous work. She left the empty room and made her way to the cookery.

Malcom intercepted her. "Hello, Carina. Do you remember me?"

She glanced at his short iron-grey hair and beard. She shook her head. "No, sorry."

"You saved my life."

"I did?"

"Yes. Let's find some warm food and talk this over, maybe I can help you to remember a few things. That bump on your head seems to have made you forget the last few weeks."

They sat at a wooden table to one side of the dining room with their trays.

"Let's see. I'll tell you what I remember about that night and maybe it will prompt your memory. I was in a dark alley about a block away, fighting with a man. He must have seen you because he finally let go and ran off. Unfortunately, he had already stabbed me."

Her eyes widened. "Stabbed you?"

"Yes. Do you remember the fight and how you found me on the ground?"

"I'm sorry. I don't remember any of it." Ever since she'd been found, different people kept trying to question her, albeit unsuccessfully. Carina felt overwhelmed at all the questions. *I don't remember. Why don't they leave me alone?*

"Would you be interested in seeing the alley where it occurred? It might help if you saw where it happened. I'll ask Lachash what he thinks."

"I do hope to remember things. If he agrees, then I guess I would be willing to go to the alley. I haven't been allowed outside ever since they found me."

"It has been for your safety."

"Oh." She squirmed uncomfortably.

Later in the evening, Carina received a message from Malcom to meet him at the front door.

Once there, the Defender greeted her. "Hello, Carina. Are you out for some night air? I have to go do my rounds but I'll be back in a few minutes to check on you. Don't wander off."

She sat pensively on the stairs while trying to remember her identity. Everyone seemed to know her, even the Defender. A noise came from a distance. It sounded like men arguing and then sounds of fighting just like Malcom had mentioned. She looked around for the Defender but there was no sign of him. Suddenly she heard a faint call for help and ran toward the sound. She found two men struggling with something. One man looked her way and ran off in the other direction, but not before his arm jabbed forward and the remaining man fell to the ground. It was Malcom. He was bleeding from a stomach wound. Carina couldn't speak until a Defender came running up to her and asked her what had happened.

"I don't know. He's been stabbed, get help." The Defender ran off and quickly returned with a stretcher and someone else to help him carry it. It was several seconds before Carina realized that someone was whispering her name and shaking her shoulder, as she stood there immobile.

"Carina, are you all right?" Lachash asked.

"Continue applying pressure on his wound while we carry him into the main building."

As they entered, Helzion came and looked down, "My God, it is Malcom."

Carina stepped back and dazedly put her hand to her head. Unseen hands helped her as she slumped onto the step.

Lachash sat beside her, "Carina, what's going on? Do you recall this night taking place before? Do you remember witnessing the knife attack? You took care of Malcom by yourself that night; you changed his bandages and kept him cool. It was a very a long night. You tied him to the bed because his wound might have opened."

"Yes, he was thrashing around, and I was afraid for him," she said tonelessly.

"You did well. He is all right now."

"But he just got stabbed," she said in disbelief.

"No, he did not get stabbed tonight but he did a few weeks ago. Can you remember that night when he was injured and carried from the alley to the cookery? You took care of him when he ran a fever. You helped him when he was tossing and turning in the bed. You must have been under a lot of stress staying up all night."

"It was a long night. Neither you nor Helzion returned to help me."

"I had to go help deliver Bondmate Hunter's baby. Do you recall how her bondmate rushed in while we were treating Malcom?"

She considered a moment. "Yes, I remember that he was anxious."

"In the morning we came in and told you to go and rest. However, you must have been feeling a little upset because you did not go to your room right away. Do you remember going outside for some fresh air?"

She nodded, "I was trying to clear my head."

"Yes, and did you walk around?"

"I suppose so. I was distracted and not paying attention."

"Did you come back inside?"

Her brow furrowed deeply. "No, I don't think so. I assume I walked to the perimeter of the block, I'm not sure, but I didn't go any farther when I realized where I was. I didn't mean to go farther."

"Of course not. Did someone make you go farther?"

"I tried to back up but there was someone behind me."

"Did you see who it was?"

Carina's eyes were tightly shut. "No, they put something over my head so that I couldn't see."

"Then what happened?"

She cried softly. "I was in a room where men were yelling."

Lachash put his arm comfortingly around her shoulders, "You're safe with us now, Carina. You do not have to be afraid because you're only remembering something that has already happened to you in the past. They cannot hurt you any longer."

"A man bought me. I—"

She saw Lachash look at Helzion, who'd been sitting quietly in the dark corner. "A man bought you?"

"Trator. He was dirty. Everyone there was dirty. He beat me repeatedly. Sometimes he wouldn't let me eat for days in a row. Day after day, I thought I was going crazy. Then one day, he forgot to chain me and, when he left, I ran away as far as I could. I don't know how I got out; it was such a maze. I just sat down in confusion. Then I woke up here." She paused, still a bit confused. "Tonight wasn't real, was it?"

Lachash reassured her, "No, it wasn't. I am sorry if it has upset you, but when Malcom suggested showing you the alley. I believed that we could spark your memory."

Carina sighed deeply. "It was a shocking way to do it, but at least I can recall things more clearly now. If you don't mind, I would like to get some sleep."

He smiled at her. "We'll see you in the morning."

She didn't fall asleep immediately. She recalled the countless days in the dark cell, had they been so many? *Forty-eight days they tell me I've been missing. Forty-eight days. Did Trator let me go? I don't remember. I remember the sector. How did I get here?* She was relieved to be in the sector because it meant she didn't have to endure Trator's punishments. *I hate that bastard. Those Banished ought to be punished for what they did to me, for what they do to all their prisoners.* Hatred burned in her; it had an unfamiliar, rancid taste. Her forgotten armband flared and pulsed darkly in response. Ever since she'd begun wearing it, it had sat on her arm, hidden. *Why have I been hiding it? I don't remember that, either. Maybe I've had so many difficulties because I've been hiding it*, she speculated. She moved the armband from her upper arm to her wrist and it became smaller and impossible to remove. She left it there and glared at it as if it were alive. *I must be tired. I'm seeing things.* She closed her eyes wearily.


"Good morning, Carina," Malcom said as he met her outside the dining hall. "I hope that we did not scare you too much with last night's events."

Her eyes assessed him. "It served a purpose, thanks."

He nodded. "You're taking things calmly. Are you on your way to Lachash? I'll walk with you." They left the building and headed toward another. "Did your memory come back? I was wondering," Malcom began, "if you remember when I asked if you were the one?"

She feigned knowledge. "It was a while ago."

"Yes, it certainly was a while ago, but I haven't forgotten anything about it. I've been under Lachash's scrutiny until just recently. I feel bad that you received these wounds because of me. I mean, if it wasn't for you staying up all night and nursing me, you might have been concentrating more on your surroundings and not have walked outside the perimeter into a trap."

"What did you mean when you asked if I was the one?"

"Your armband is what gave you away. Do you still wear it?"

"You mean this thing? Is it supposed to change size?" She held out her wrist. "It won't let me take it off." She spoke of the armband as if it were alive.

"It is much more than an armband and you urgently need to keep it hidden."

"Why?"

"The time isn't right yet."

She wanted to know more. "Right for what?"

"In time you will learn more. Right now, you're our liberator, the one sent to free us from the Leaders."

"I don't understand, what do you mean from the Leaders? Aren't you one of them?"

"I used to be, but I know the fundamental truth now."

"Are you telling me that you're a Banished?"

"Does that shock you? If you give me time to explain, you will see our side and understand why I'm one of them."

"Keep away from me. I know your kind, terrorizing women and treating them like slaves. Don't touch me."

"Keep your voice down," Malcom said in a sharp whisper as he looked across the street.

"Why, so you can fool these people? You're a traitor."

He grabbed her wrist in a vise-like grip, "Listen to me. I have spent two years with the Banished and I have learned hidden truths. The so-called Leaders are out to create a perfect world and anyone who doesn't fit is recultivated or eliminated."

Her words flew at him. "Oh, yeah? And you're selling and abusing people is preferable to the Leaders?"

"I don't know what you're talking about."

"Well, these rope burns come from being tied up like a piece of cattle, put on an auction block, and sold to the highest bidder. Here's the broken finger and bruised rib. I was starved and treated like garbage." Her voice quavered in the retelling of her experience. "Now, I don't care who you're pretending to be. I'll keep your identity secret only because I don't know my own. Once I have my memory back of how I got to the sector—"

"You don't know your identity before you came to the sector?"

"That's not relevant to you."

"It may be relevant to us all."

"I was dragged from the sector, locked in a cell while they attempted to break me, and then I was sold. Sold like an animal and then treated like one. If you're a Banished like them, nothing will keep me silent," she said vehemently. "Stay away from me. Don't come near me or talk to me. I want you to keep your distance."

They both saw Helzion approaching on the street. Malcom used the moment to grab Carina and forcefully kiss her. When the expected slap across his face came, he shook her, and shouted, "Calm down, you're upset. Just because I'm a man doesn't mean I'm evil like the Banished. Helzion, help me. She's irrational."

Her actions confirmed his words. The slap pushed her beyond endurance. Traitor! She blindly launched herself at him.

"Defenders! Lachash!"

Carina managed to trip Malcom and leaped on top of him, hitting him. When he tried to grab her, she moved onto her back as he rolled above her. She managed to bring her knee up and he moaned as she made contact with his groin. She pushed him off and got up. "Leave me alone."

Helzion motioned for the two Defenders, who'd shown up, to grab her. Her stance shifted as her fists came up. Her actions momentarily stunned them until Helzion yelled, "Stop her."

They approached her from two different directions and she only managed to swing at one of them before the other grabbed her.

"Let me go. He's the traitor." She struggled, trying to catch her breath from her exertion.

"Trator? He was the man you said bought you. You have confused things. Take her to Lachash and have him sedate her."

Carina struggled futilely. The Defenders dragged her with them as they left.

Helzion turned on Malcom. "What did you say to her? Are you making passes at women again?"

"I was accompanying her to Lachash. I asked her if she'd remembered anything else about her abduction. She got upset and when I touched her arm she got irrational just like you saw," he lied calmly, watching Helzion's eyes. "Where did she learn to fight like that?"

"Yes, where did she? We cannot have violence in our women." His eyes flashed. "She may need to be retrained."

"It must have been the Banished. After all, she was with them for forty-eight days."

"Did you see such fighting when you were with them?"

"It wasn't uncommon."

Helzion changed the subject before Malcom said anything more. "Your debriefing session is today. You have two years' worth of crucial information to share from your spying on the Banished. Are you ready?"

"Yes, let's get on with it."

"I have asked Daric to join us."

"Daric? Why him?"

"He was against sending you to infiltrate the Banished and I wish to show him that the decision to send you was a good one."

Malcom ground his teeth at the mention of Daric. He was the youngest of all the Leaders, groomed from birth to play a major role in the progressive development and control of the sectors. He was well trained in everything from military tactics to hydroponics. He had been away when the Leaders had planned to have one of their own infiltrate the Banished as a spy. He didn't want to risk having a Leader, one of their own, turned against them. It was too dangerous: A Leader, with his silver-tipped staff of power and knowledge could destroy the entire foundation of the known world. Helzion and the others had gone ahead with their plan and sent Malcom despite Daric's warning.

They re-entered the main building and went toward a restricted area. The room was a small auditorium. Two tiers of tables and chairs formed a horseshoe around one long table and it was to this table that Helzion led Malcom.

"Hello."

"Daric," Malcom said as he sized him up. Two years had toughened his appearance. He wasn't the youth he remembered. He was tall, almost 6' 3" and broad-shouldered.

"So, Malcom, what have you been doing for the last two years?"

"You're straight to the point, aren't you? Will the others be attending this meeting?"

Daric held up his staff and Malcom recognized it immediately. He carried his black staff of power like a lethal weapon. Malcom had given up his staff when he had left two years before, the price he'd had to pay. He didn't regret it. He'd learned too much during his time away to turn him away from the Leaders and the staff. He had no desire to retake the required oath of binding that the Leaders took.

"I see you've been busy. You speak for all of the Leaders. How did you manage to earn the high staff?"

"A lot has happened since you left. A Leader was needed and the staff chose me."

"I've been at a Choosing. I hope it will lead you in your tasks."

"It might have chosen you but you elected to be elsewhere." His choice of words wasn't lost on Malcom. "You have always been hotheaded, but giving up your staff to become a Banished was your brashest move. If the Banished had learned of your identity, they could have undermined and destroyed us. You swore an oath to preserve the sectors. We need to maintain control over the people. Guide them into executing their tasks. The Banished haven't learned of your identity, have they?"

"No, of course not, and I have the scars to prove it. The initiation rites of the Banished are a little harrowing, to say the least. It took over a year to get past the outer echelon of rank. This group is cautious. I had always thought them to be roughly organized, but they run it democratically."

"What? Don't they have one individual who acts as their leader?" Helzion asked. He'd been waiting for Malcom and Daric to finish their verbal fencing before he spoke. They'd always competed against each other.

"Well, there was a recognized leader, greatly admired and capable of having his men do anything for their cause. His name was Andzej."

"You use the past tense when you talk of this man."

"His sudden untimely demise is part of the reason I'm here. He met with an accident between my knife and his throat. The fool had grown quite fond of me and told me that I was like an elder brother."

"You killed him?" Helzion asked in surprise. "Why?"

"Because those were my official orders. Eliminate the cause of the Banished's insurrection and create chaos in their ranks. He was the principle cause and I have wreaked havoc on the rest by eliminating him."

"What happened then?"

Malcom shrugged. "Well, I'm afraid I offended a few people by assassinating him and they wanted my head. I had other ideas. I had to leave, but not before I verified that he was the hub of their wheel. They're in such chaos right now. Choosing a new leader is causing dissension and the men are dividing into factions. They're vulnerable and we could easily take them with a divide-and-conquer strategy. We could eliminate them once and for all."

"Your manner of speech is different; you must have picked it up while living with the Banished. I hope that is all that you picked up," Daric warned. "Did you have any more questions for Malcom, Helzion?"

Helzion turned to Malcom. "I do not know if that explanation totally summarizes your two-year absence but I suppose it will suffice for now. I trust that you'll make yourself available if we need you."

Malcom narrowed his eyes at his dismissal. He gave Daric a tight smile and a nod before he turned and walked slowly to the door. He overheard Daric ask about Carina.

"I heard you had an altercation with the woman, Carina. She was the one reported missing for forty-eight days. The Leaders are disturbed that the Banished are becoming bolder in their attempts to undermine us."

"Yes, they grow bolder. She became distraught when Malcom triggered a memory of her abduction," Helzion explained.

"Is that what it's called? Distraught? Hitting a man. You know no woman may rise up against a man. It's part of the laws. Why hasn't she been assigned?"

"We do not know where she came from because of her memory loss and she was in the sector only a short time before she was abducted. We haven't received a file yet."

"I want a report sent to me as soon as possible."

"You're leaving?"

"Yes. I was on my way to the Northern Protectorate when word reached me of Malcom's return."

"Good journey."

Malcom held his breath as he closed the door behind him.

# The Interrogation

Carina held her head in her hands, sedated and sitting slumped in a chair. She was aware that the two Defenders stood behind her watching her every move. Her anger had subsided, leaving clarity in its wake. She knew she shouldn't have attacked Malcom. She had only been a handy tool for his deception. *Just like a man. Where are all the women? They'd understand.* She heard a rustling behind her and heard footsteps approaching her. When she looked up, she saw Helzion talking with Lachash. It gave her time to think. She'd noticed how Helzion commanded attention even on her first day in the sector. *Why didn't I think of that before? Only men were in charge.*

Despite the confusion in her head from the drug, Carina heard everything that Helzion said to Lachash. Her mouth was dry and she felt weary, shaky, and uncertain. She closed her eyes briefly. *Why am I always so tired?*

"Carina?"

"Hmm?"

"Why don't you come and sit over here?"

Hands graciously helped her stand and she floated across the room. "I'm dreaming."

"That's the drug," Lachash said. "She'll find it hard to resist us at this point. We can send the Defenders outside."

"Why aren't there any women here?" She gave voice to her disjointed thoughts.

"There are some women here, mates to the men."

"Why don't they live here? Do they have other homes?"

"Yes, but let us speak about you."

Helzion wavered in front of her eyes.

"About me? Am I in trouble?"

"You did hit a man and that is forbidden."

"He wasn't being very nice to me. Traitor," she mumbled, thinking of Malcom.

"You've mentioned this Trator before. He bought you. Did he mistreat you?"

"He was cruel. He beat and starved me. He always slapped me when he talked to me. I could never move fast enough." She rambled on. "I don't know which was worse, him or the cell."

"The cell?"

"They made me walk for days, with a hood over my head. I only saw the moon once. I miss the moon."

"Focus, Carina. What happened then?"

"Ruins, lots of ruins. Underground, they took me underground. It was like a gopher hole, dark and long and then they locked me in a cell and left me for a long time."

"How long?"

"Days of darkness… bread… and water." She yawned as she spoke.

"How much longer can she go, Lachash?"

"A couple of questions maybe."

"Carina? You've been through many hardships. I need to ask a couple more questions. Do you think you can answer them?"

"My mouth tastes funny. I can try."

"Which sector did you come from?"

She looked at him, uncomprehending.

"Where did you come from before we met?"

She sat a few moments as images floated through her thoughts. "A city with water and mountains. I worked there."

"Worked where?" Helzion asked. He shook her when he saw her sleeping and then stormed away in frustration.

The Defenders returned and carried her to her room in the complex where one of them stood guard outside her door. Lachash, who'd seen to it that she was sleeping comfortably, pulled the blanket to cover her.

In her sleep, she mumbled, "I was a schoolteacher. It was a nice job."

"Did you say something?"

As he closed the door behind him, he said to the Defender, "Make sure she sees me tomorrow morning."

"Yes, I will. Goodnight."


Carina woke with a nagging headache and a feeling that she'd let something slip but couldn't quite place where her uneasiness came from. She was startled to find a Defender outside her door. "Oh," she grabbed her head, "it wasn't a dream."

The Defender turned. "Lachash asked me to take you to his office this morning."

"Ow, please, don't talk so loud. I'll follow you; I get lost in all these hallways and rooms."

"I have often thought the same thing. I'll show you the direction because it is in a different building."

"Are you sure? I don't want to get you into trouble."

"I am sure. It is not often that I get to escort a beautiful woman."

She laughed, embarrassed. "You're very kind."

"No, you are very beautiful."

She turned to look at his face and saw his sincerity. Her recent experiences made the Defender's remark an immense pleasure to receive.

"There is nothing wrong, is there?"

"Were you on duty yesterday when I-I…."

"Attacked Malcom?" he asked without preamble.

"I'm sorry you had to witness that."

"No need to explain. I'm Zach Gallager."

"Thanks for escorting me, Zach."

"No problem, Miss Carina. I'll leave you here and get back to my duties."

She pushed open the door and heard Lachash, "Hello, Carina. Come in and have a seat. How are you feeling after last night?"

"I have a headache, but that's all."

"Do you remember what happened yesterday?"

"Some of it. It gets foggy after they brought me here. Did I do anything wrong?"

"No, not at all. I just wanted to make sure there were not any residual effects from the medication."

"What medication?"

"You were hysterical when they brought you in yesterday and I had to give you something to calm you."

"Is that why I have a headache?"

"Possibly. I need to ask you a few routine questions. Are you allergic to anything?"

"Not that I know of."

He made a notation in his file, "Are there any health problems in your family? There should not be if you were bred properly, but we do like to check."

*Bred properly? Who talks like that?* "I don't remember."

"Last night you could not remember where you came from before you entered this sector."

"I said that?"

"Yes. Do you remember mentioning a city by water where you worked?"

Carina looked at him. "What was my work? Maybe I could do the same thing here."

"No, that will not be possible."

She apologized. "I'm sorry, but I don't seem to remember anything at all from before I came to this sector."

"Hmm, I assumed your memory was fully restored, but apparently not." He checked her pupils, ears, reflexes, but there were no obvious reasons for her continued memory loss.

"I cannot find anything physically wrong with you. Maybe something happened during your abduction that your mind does not want to remember. It is possible that something will cause you to remember. Perhaps, once your file arrives from your old sector, something in it will help us find a simple solution. Do not worry. We will find out."

"I hope you're right, Lachash."

"Let us finish the examination. Do you plan to have children?"

His question startled her when she realized he wasn't finished. "I suppose so, eventually."

"You have good hips for it."

*Where the heck is this leading?* "When I get married, I'll think about having children but I'm not planning to have them yet."

"I could recommend you for the Carrier Program if you qualify."

"The what?"

"Maybe they called the Carrier Program something else in your sector. You get special privileges and of course respect from everyone because of your role in the continued growth of our society. After all, we want our society to thrive. They could assign you there; the Leaders must have your file by now and will probably assign you soon. You missed the last assignment day while you were absent and you will have to wait twenty-three more days until the next assignment day."

"Couldn't I choose what I want to do in the sector, something that I'm good at?"

Lachash turned on her. "You know we're all assigned, some from birth. No one chooses their future, especially women—surely you know how valuable women are to everyone. Women should have only one job, and that is having children. Our population needs to be rebuilt and that cannot be done if there aren't any children." He paused at her silence. "I have no doubt that is what will happen to you. In fact, I can speed up the process by doing a few other tests."

"What other tests?"

"The internal examination, to check if you have any abnormalities that we may need to be concerned about."

Carina leapt to her feet. "NO!" Seeing his surprise, she hesitated. "I mean, uh, couldn't we wait until the Leaders assign me?"

"It might be too busy then to do a thorough examination, especially with the influx of people we usually get at that time."

She didn't know why she balked at what he had suggested. *Is that my role? Why doesn't it feel right? I keep saying the wrong thing because I don't remember my past.* "I guess you're right," she began, her head swimming with what words to say next, "but I'm not ready. I feel nervous after the abduction and then what happened yesterday."

Lachash mistook her uncertainty for shyness. "It isn't that bad, Carina, and it does not take too long." He wondered what made her react the way she did.

She wouldn't meet his eyes and pursed her lips in agitation and beat a furious tattoo with her toes on the floor.

"Carina?"

She glanced up.

"You have been with a man before, have you not? I mean, at your age, surely you are not without experience."

Her face suffused with color. It wasn't something she openly talked about. *I'd remember that, wouldn't I?* An image of a brown-haired hazel-eyed man popped into her head.

"When you were taken from the sector, did they...?"

She looked at the floor and recalled Trator's brutality.

"You can tell me," Lachash urged.

Her words were quiet. "No, I wasn't raped."

"I am glad. I wouldn't want you to have fear of a man's touch. Women are carefully protected and raised to be docile so they aren't prepared for violence." He looked at her and asked again, "I know you have had amnesia, but do you remember being with a man?"

Her forehead furrowed and her eyes narrowed as she tried to discover the answer in her memory. She couldn't remember having close relations with any man. "I don't think so," she finally said.

"You mean you do not remember."

"No, I don't remember."

"Then this test is all the more important to do."

"Please, no, I'm not ready. I need time." She looked directly at him then. "Please give me time so I can get used to the idea."

Lachash read the uncertainty in her eyes and relented. "Fine, for now. I'll give you time to think about it. Perhaps I could arrange for you to speak to another woman, and she can prepare you as to what to expect."

"That would be good. Thank you."

"But I'll do the test in two weeks whether you're ready or not."

Carina looked at him doubtfully and murmured her thanks as she brushed past him in a hurry to leave his office.

He called after her, "You have been helping in the cookery, have you not?"

His question totally threw her for a moment before she could reply. "Yes, odd jobs in the cookery, and wherever else I've been needed."

"I know you're supposed to take it easy for a few days, but I think that you need not return to the cookery. How would you like to help in my office until then? I do not have a lot of patients, but there is office work that needs to be done."

"That would be a pleasant change from the cookery." Carina thought it was a great suggestion but didn't realize that Lachash had so much power that he could assign her to a particular task.

"I have been muddling through the office work myself ever since my last secretary married one of my patients. Their physical characteristics were compatible and offspring desirable; they would have been disappointed otherwise. We do keep a tight control on the population of our city, especially genetic flaws and inbreeding. My secretary was in her breeding prime, as you are. We need strong bloodlines to build a strong foundation for our city. We can discuss this later. Right now, I have another appointment. Get dressed, go back to your room, and I'll see you tomorrow morning at nine."

Carina returned to her assigned room simply because she had no other place to go. She pondered Lachash's words, especially that last one about her being in her breeding prime. *I can't wait until this is all behind me, and I know what my role is.* Unconsciously, Carina unclenched her fists.

## New Arrivals

When Carina opened the door to the women's sleeping quarters, she found that she had three new roommates. A petite, copper-haired woman was sitting on a mattress, along with her two daughters.

"Hello."

"Hi, I'm Carina."

"My name is Chenaanah and these are my daughters, Loriia." She pointed to the younger, dark haired girl, "and Liisa." The long-limbed, red-headed girl.

She smiled in return. "Hi."

"We're from the Northern sector. They told me that my bondmate is alive. The Banished took him."

Carina flinched at the mention of the Banished. "What is your bondmate's name?"

"Malcom Graer."

Carina successfully hid her surprise. "How long was he missing?"

Chenaanah's voice was wistful. "Two years."

*Malcom?* "It must have been very hard for you."

"Well, he was a Leader, and they take care of their own."

*So he was the same Malcom.* She hid her shock. "They didn't reassign you?"

"I was in charge of the Carrier Program in that sector. It was a very rewarding position, and I suppose I will probably miss it."

"Will you be doing the same thing here?"

"That will depend on Malcom and what he would like to do. How about you? What are you doing?"

"I'm going to be working with Lachash, the healer, in his office for a few days. Will you be returning to the Northern Sector?"

"I do not know what I will be doing yet. I cannot wait to see Malcom; it has been so long since I last saw him. They are debriefing him now. They want to be sure he is ready to take his old job back as a Leader."

The woman spoke in a gushing manner that made Carina want to change the subject. "It's almost lunch, and you must be hungry. If you like, I'll take you to the dining area with me as I'm on my way there."

Carina asked more questions on the way. "Your bondmate was a Leader. What did he do?"

"He was in charge of overseeing the defenses for all the sectors. He had to travel a lot back and forth to the different sectors. He said he did it because he liked the horses. He sure is lucky to ride a horse as most of us have to travel on foot or by wagon. That is how I got here, by wagon, but they would not let us near the horses."

"Where do they keep the horses? I haven't seen any here."

"They usually do not bring them this close to the sector, so we had to walk a bit. The Defenders escorted us. They can't have women wandering loose in the sector can they?"

"No, that is dangerous. They might get abducted like I was."

Chenaanah's mouth dropped. "You were abducted? That is horrible. Are you all right? Did they hurt you? You're so lucky to survive. Malcom says that only a handful of people ever return once they have been abducted."

Carina averted her eyes. "It's not something I want to talk about right now."

"I understand, you poor thing. I sincerely hope things will get better for you. Once you get assigned you will be taken care of and nothing like that will ever happen again."

"Will you be living with your bondmate?"

For the first time, Chenaanah's composure altered. "That will depend on Malcom. He may not choose to continue our joining. He has been away a long time and the Leaders might keep us apart."

"Why would they do that?"

"I will know more after his debriefing. He was a Leader and chose me. If he is not a Leader, then he cannot choose his mate."

Loriia interrupted. "I am hungry. Can we eat now?"

Chenaanah looked at her daughter and smiled. "You girls must be starving by now. Those travel rations cannot beat a hot, cooked meal. Will you come with us, Carina?"

"Thank you, I will."


One characteristic of this world was the lack of solitude. She hadn't given it much thought during the days that she had the room to herself. She only wanted to sort out the tangled web that surrounded her. She looked down at the armband that she'd been unconsciously rubbing. Images of the tapestry flowed through her mind of the dragon and phoenix. *Somehow that tapestry is linked to this armband. What were the words I read? I don't remember. The world was in peril and the people went underground. When they came up—they are the people here! They've got to be. That would explain a few things. The blue tunics of the Leaders, they are one of the groups of men in the tapestry—*

"Carina?"

"Yes?" She was drawn into making small talk with Chenaanah and her two daughters. She couldn't understand why the Leaders wouldn't reunite Chenaanah and Malcom. Carina was prepared to be critical of Chenaanah's job and bondmate, but she found that Chenaanah was very sincere and likeable.

Fortunately, Chenaanah's bondmate didn't join them during lunch. *I am lucky I didn't get into more trouble than I did.* Chenaanah and her children monopolized her time for the rest of the day. Carina didn't mind the girls' playfulness because it kept her mind off her lapses in memory. For now, she had to settle for the few things she remembered. *I hope that my file from the Leaders will fill in the blanks when it arrives from my old sector—wherever that is.*

Later, when Carina returned to the women's dorm alone she used the time to reflect on Malcom's words. *What had Malcom meant about the Leaders creating the perfect world and recultivation for anyone who didn't fit in? If he was a Leader, then two years among the Banished were bound to have changed Malcom's loyalties. What would happen if he resumes his duties as a Leader? Don't they even consider the possibility that he may have changed over? Damn, what do I do with this information? Do I tell someone? Would they believe me? From what I have experienced with the Banished, they're abhorrent. I have to be careful who I talk to.*

Carina woke up early the next morning, surprised to find that she was still dressed. Wow, I must have been tired. She checked the rest of the room, but the Graers were still sleeping. She changed her clothes and put on the same drab clothing given her. Carina tried to take off the armband; she couldn't get it over her wrist. She unconsciously pulled her sleeve down when she heard noises behind her.

She smiled and greeted Loriia and Liisa. "Good morning. How are you doing? Did the dinner with your father go well?"

The girls bubbled with excitement. "Yes, we sure have missed him."

"He must have missed you a lot, too." She looked at Chenaanah wondering if her meeting with her bondmate went well. Carina remembered Malcom kissing her and wondered why he had done it. She would have a word with him about that.

Loriia's dark hair swirled angrily when her words burst out. "I hate those Banished for taking Daddy away. I hope they get caught."

Chenaanah gathered Loriia in her arms. "Do not worry, honey, Daddy is safe with us now."

Carina turned to leave. "I'll let you get dressed. I'm off to the cookery for breakfast, I'll see you later," she said as she closed the door.


"Well, if it isn't the lovely Carina."

Carina knew, without looking up from her breakfast, that it was Malcom. "Morning."

"May I join you?"

"If I said no, would it make a difference?" she asked as she glanced up.

"My. Aren't we being charming this morning?"

Carina changed the subject. "You must have been happy to see your wife and two lovely daughters last night."

"Yes, my lovely daughters who are almost total strangers to me, and my wife, so proud of her role in the Carrier facility. I used to believe in all that, but now the mere mention of it makes me sick to my stomach." He spoke quietly, careful not to draw attention.

"Why are you telling me all this? If you're trying to find an excuse to explain why you're a traitor, then don't bother."

Before Malcom could say any more, his family arrived.

"Hi, Daddy." Loriia hugged him.

"Hi, Sweetling."

"Carina, I didn't know that you knew each other," Chenaanah said.

"I'm here thanks to Carina, she was the one who found me in the alley and helped the healer take care of me. She nursed me through the fever that could have killed me. I owe her my sincerest gratitude for saving my life."

"Oh, Carina, thank you for helping him," Liisa said as she engulfed Carina in a warm hug.

"I'm glad I could help." She returned her hug and looked up. "I don't mean to be rude, but I must rush off to work."

"What is this about work?" Malcom asked.

"I'm going to be helping Lachash out for a while in his office until I'm assigned."

"I'll see you there later. He wants to check my wound. He says that I'm stubborn for not staying in bed like a proper invalid."

Carina entered Lachash's office where he greeted her with a pleasant hello and a warm smile. He went over the files and routines with her. "I usually do several home visits in the afternoons, so I get many people coming to the office in the morning. In the afternoon, you will be on your own most of the time. If there isn't any work to do, you will probably have a few early days. I am sure that you will soon understand the procedures in the office."

It was quite hectic for the first hour or two. When Malcom showed up, it got worse.

"Hello, Carina."

Carina tried to remain businesslike. "Good morning, Master Graer."

"Call me Malcom. Master Graer sounds foreign to me. Besides, you saved my life, and that makes us old friends by now, wouldn't you agree?" When Carina continued to ignore him, he spoke quietly, "Eventually, Carina, you will listen to what I have to say about your presence here, but for now, you need to read a few medical files. When you do, check for testing, abnormalities, and check your own file."

"I won't know what the particular tests mean as I don't have any medical training."

"Check for notations that have been made in those files, and your own. You will notice similarities, and I can tell you what that means."

"Why should I compare them?"

"Because you don't trust me, and you need to see the evidence for yourself. Please listen to me. I want to tell you about the sector."

Carina was curious. Finally! Information! She nodded and led him to an empty examining room. When she turned to face him, he quickly began speaking.

"I realize that you don't trust me. I don't blame you. Let me tell you about me and why I'm a Banished." He paused briefly. "I'm not worried about my assignment because my loyalties are with the Banished. Ever since the Upheaval—" He stopped speaking when he saw Carina's confused look. "The Upheaval occurred when the layers of the sky were destroyed. The earth became unprotected from the heavens. The effects weren't obvious at first until decades later when people were dying by the millions from decaying diseases caused by the sun. In order to survive, people went underground. They went into the mountains and lived in caves or other shelters deep below the earth. Decades passed. It was hard to imagine that there was any life left, but there was, and the survivors eventually resurfaced."

Carina was shocked to her core as she made the connection between his words and the story the tapestry told her.

Malcom saw her stricken look. "You didn't know? I'm sorry. We survived, that's what is important. People returned to the surface and were united as a community under the group we call the Leaders who were, at first, chosen by the people but now are bred and taught from a young age to assume the role of Leader when a Leader dies. Those who surfaced came under their control and have been dupes for the Leaders' teachings, which are nothing more than a complex set of rules which define jobs, homes, relationships, and the right to have children. I have two children because the Leaders allowed me—because I was a Leader—to have them. There are many who will never know the joy of child-rearing because they have no choice. The tight control wielded by the Leaders, along with their recultivation program, ensures blind and ignorant adherence to the sectors' rules. The Leaders are leading the people to believe that the society is concerned about each individual. The fundamental truth is they are only concerned with what each particular individual can contribute to the society. They are expendable if they don't conform. I intend to set a trap, but not for the Banished. I want Leader control over the people to end, and I want to play an integral role in making sure that happens. I believe that people should have the right to choose their own destinies, their own roles in life." He didn't let Carina speak. "If I had doubts about my choice to become a Banished, they disappeared when I saw your armband. I've tried several times to approach you about your armband but you've avoided talking with me. I need to know whether you were given the armband or only found it. I know I've told you too much, but I have to trust you. I'd like to tell you more, but Lachash will be looking for his next appointment, and you." He gently touched Carina's arm. "Please consider my words."

Carina had a dozen questions but moved to the door of the examining room. She looked at Malcom. "I'll consider them."

They'd only just returned to the waiting room when Lachash came out and motioned for Malcom to follow him. Malcom glanced at Carina one last time. She nodded to him and whispered, "I was given the armband." She could see his Adam's apple quiver as he seemed to fight an unknown emotion. She saw his eyes tear, and then his joyous smile.

"Thank you, Carina." He turned and entered Lachash's office.

Malcom's emotion touched a chord in Carina. She believed him.

Later, when Lachash left to make house calls, Carina looked for her file because Malcolm had said there was one, and she recalled the minor tests that Lachash had already done, but couldn't find it. She looked through the other patient files but didn't understand much of the medical terminology in some of them. Carina recognized some information: chromosomes, DNA, RNA, blood disorders, but didn't understand the medical jargon that accompanied them. There were physical descriptions of each person; hair and eye color, height, and racial background. She still didn't know what Malcom was trying to prove to her by telling her to read them. Carina carefully returned the files.

A pattern developed in Carina's life in the next two weeks. She'd have breakfast, go to the office until mid-afternoon, play games with Chenaanah's daughters and help with any new arrivals. The numbers had been slowly building. First Chenaanah and her daughters, then two elderly ladies, and now there were fifteen women in total.

She met them all in the healer's office as they came in for the physicals. She wondered why some of them had the same tests done. Lachash had said that each new person in a sector was checked out for health problems or any infectious diseases. Carina didn't know enough about medicine to question the process, but it did seem rather odd to her that younger women were given different tests than older ones. In addition, some older men and women received no testing. She assumed that infectious diseases could happen in anyone, so why exempt certain people?

Malcom couldn't show up to question her because he'd been sent to the Northern Sector to take over a new patrol. Chenaanah told her that his reassignment included some new duties and that he was in charge of a force of men who were planning to attack the Banished in their hideouts.

Carina was aware of how the number of men in the sector had grown. They didn't come through the healer's office for physicals, and they avoided each other as if the other had rabies. She had seen them avert their eyes after giving discreet nods to each other moments before. Something unusual was going on. Two days before the Leaders were due to arrive, Carina asked Lachash if everyone, including new men to the area, had to have physicals.

"Yes, unless their files arrive before that, why?"

"There are many more men around lately, and so few women. I can't recall seeing those men in the office."

"That's usually what happens. Fewer women are officially allowed to travel because of their value for childbearing. Most women could not bear children after the Upheaval. Now, women are treated as rare and valuable commodities and quickly assigned. That reminds me, your file must have arrived in this sector by now and that means you will probably be assigned tomorrow."

"Tomorrow. I'll be nervous all day."

He looked at her seriously. "Do you like working here, Carina?"

"Yes, I do. I'm learning all the time and people are so kind."

"Would you like me to put in a word for you to be assigned here? I could speak to the Leaders."

"Would you? That would be nice. At least I'll know what I'm doing."

"I'll speak to Helzion first thing tomorrow."


Zach approached Carina after she finished breakfast.

"Carina, Helzion wants to see you this morning. I'll take you to him."

"Could you let Lachash know that I'll be late?"

"He already knows."

Carina accompanied Zach to Helzion's dark, wood-paneled office.

"Lachash mentioned that you might be interested in staying on in his office," Helzion said.

"I like the work, the people, and I would feel very useful in the sector."

"I am sure you would be useful in other ways. Lachash says you would be a good candidate for child-bearing."

"But I'm not bonded."

"We could arrange it so you become bonded. We could impregnate you with a genetically compatible male and then find an appropriate mate for a foster father who'd make sure you had everything you'd need during your pregnancy and you would be assigned to a permanent sector."

"Is *that* how it's done? I'm not ready for children."

Helzion looked at her with calculating eyes. "Having children is a gift in our society that women freely give."

Carina didn't know what to say. "Then I guess I'm fortunate to be considered. I have to get back to work now. Is that all right?"

Helzion waved her away so she left his office. *If Helzion has seen my file then it* must *be in Lachash's office. I'll have to wait until he goes out on his calls and search for it. No one is going to use me as a brood mare.*

Carina finally found her file in Lachash's personal office. It was filed under Carrier Program along with several others. It gave a run down on her vital statistics plus test results and recommendations. At the bottom of the form were several boxes.

The one checked off said she was a candidate.

Helzion walked in.

Carina shoved the file back in with the others before she turned around. Her eyes widened. "Helzion, Lachash isn't here. May I help you?"

If Helzion had seen anything, he didn't mention it. "Yes, you left my office before I could ask you a question. I was talking to Lachash earlier, and he mentioned that you had seen several men who might not have had physicals."

"I just wondered why so many men didn't get physicals, but Lachash explained that they might have had files with them already in the office or they were destined to arrive from their previous sectors. There seemed to be more women having physicals than men. I have a habit of asking questions sometimes, but I hope I didn't cause any difficulties."

"You do ask the strangest questions sometimes, Carina. Which sector did you say you came from?"

Ignoring his question, she said, "Those men that I saw over the last few days, there were at least thirty of them."

"That many?" Helzion asked, beginning to be alarmed. "Did you see them doing anything suspicious?"

"I don't know, they seemed to go out of their way to avoid each other, but they seemed to know each other. Maybe I was mistaken."

"I have been so busy that I have not been noticing anything unusual. It is good that we have such an observant person working with us. Thank you for mentioning it, Carina. Which sector are you from originally? You did not say."

"I still don't know where I'm from. I was hoping that when my file arrived it could fill in my memory lapses."

"What has the healer said to you about that? I assumed that you remembered everything after you recalled the episode in the alley with Malcom."

"It didn't. He said that he hoped it would come back totally over time."


Zach Gallager came into the healer's office early in the afternoon, with Lachash leaning heavily against him. His face was cut and bleeding and his left eye swollen shut.

"The Banished are here, and we're fighting them, but we're outnumbered," Zach warned.

Carina was stunned, "Oh, no! What can I do?"

"You can either run or stay and take care of the wounded. I'll not force you to stay because it could be dangerous," Lachash said earnestly. "I know how afraid you are of the Banished. I could ask Zach to take you to another sector."

Carina looked down to see a drop of blood fall to the floor from Lachash's hand. "What's wrong with your hand?"

"I have a nasty cut from a knife I tried to avoid."

"Let me look at it." Carina put a sterile absorbent pad into the palm of his hand and told him to apply pressure until the bleeding stopped. "Have they sent for help yet?" she asked him.

"Yes."

"Zach, are you going to stay?" Carina asked quietly without looking up from her task.

"If you are, Miss, then surely I will also."

"Good, I want you to help Lachash into the examining room. We'll look at him. You're limping, too. What happened out there?"

"Those men you saw, they're the Banished," Lachash explained.

"What about the Leaders? What happened to them?"

"I do not know but I am sure they would have ridden out of the sector immediately to seek reinforcements."

Carina put a new bandage over the other. When the bleeding slowed, Lachash looked at the wound. A long slash had cut deeply into his hand. "It is my right hand, so I cannot do much, you will have to close the wound. How fine a stitch can you sew?"

She looked at him to see if he were serious. When she saw his grim face, she put on a brave front. "It won't be pretty to look at, but it will be done, anyway. Is there something that I can give you to numb the area? This is going to hurt."

"I should be fine. It's not across the palm." He began describing what she needed to do.

She washed her hands and then threaded the needle. Her hands were shaking so it took a few attempts before she succeeded. She felt queasy as she held the ragged flesh between her fingers and passed the needle through the edges of skin. She flinched each time the needle poked through the flesh. *Sewing a piece of material and sewing flesh are two entirely different things. I hope I don't get sick on him while I'm doing this.*

She spoke nervously. "Is the fighting over?"

"No, and there are too many Banished out there and very few of our men."

"Why?"

"The majority of our men were deployed elsewhere."

When she was done, Lachash looked at her work. "That will do." There was a hint of a smile on his face and Carina suspected that he was trying hard not to laugh.

"Am I doing something wrong?"

"No, my dear. It's just that your face is all scrunched up and you are wincing more than I am." He smiled again and Carina blushed when she realized that she had been wincing because of her appalling task.

"If I can smile, Carina, it is because I have faith that the sector will prevail."

She nodded and changed the subject. "Tell me why you're limping."

"I think I did something to my ankle."

"Zach, grab some long bandages. I'll wrap it. You will be on the sidelines, but you can help if more people come in. I'll give you something for the pain if you tell me what would be appropriate."

"That isn't necessary."

"I strongly believe it is. What if someone comes in with something I don't know how to treat? I'll need your help."

Lachash acquiesced. "The cabinet at the bottom is where I keep the medications. Here is the key. Have you ever given someone a needle?"

Carina looked at him, saw the hopefulness in his eyes but had to say, "No, but I gather I'm going to be learning how."

Despite the pain, he grinned. "I don't know who needs help more, you or me. Are you sure you want to do this?"

"No, but I'll do it anyway. Why don't you have oral medications?" Carina was tense and shuddered as she carefully filled the needle and tapped it as Lachash had directed, before giving it to him.

Lachash was watching her face as she pulled out the needle. "You did a nice job," he commented.

By the time Carina had finished injecting him more people had trickled into the office. One was suffering from a minor head wound, and another had a knife wound. Carina knew first aid, but she'd never had to use it. "I don't know how to help these people," she blurted out.

Lachash calmed her. He observed everything she did and told her what else she needed to do. Zach was able to take care of minor wounds and his level-headedness was also a calming force.

"Isn't there a hospital?"

"We have never needed one because this sector doesn't have many permanent residents. I've been able to handle injuries whenever any altercations occurred between the Banished."

"Is there another room we can use for patients?"

"Yes, there is a meeting room across the hall that can hold several people," Lachash responded.

"Zach, can you check on the meeting room?"

Zach first looked startled and then shot a look at Lachash. "Are you sure we want to use that room?"

"We have no choice. Cover the center to make room for emergency cases."

He nodded. "I'll be right back, Miss Carina."

*What was that all about?* "Is there some reason that room might not work?"

"That room is kept for recalcitrant people."

She looked at him with eyebrows raised.

"It is for recultivation."

She froze briefly as she felt fingers walking slowly down her spine at his words.


It was two or three hours later when silence settled over the sector. No one inside the clinic knew the outcome of the battle, but the amazing sight of two Banished entering and carrying a severely wounded man seemed to indicate that the battle was over and the Defenders had lost. Carina knew that they were Banished because of their rough clothing and fearfully moved away from them.

"Where's the healer?" A grey-eyed man who stood at least six feet tall looked down into Carina's eyes. "Tell him to look at this man," he ordered.

"And who are you to be giving orders?" Lachash demanded.

The grey-eyed man grabbed Carina by the waist and pulled her against him and held a knife against her throat.

"You're holding the only person who can help you," Lachash stated calmly, but his mouth was tightly drawn and his anger was almost palpable.

"Why her?" The grey-eyed man asked without releasing her.

"I am injured so she will have to follow my instructions to help your friend."

Carina didn't dare breathe as the feel of the cold steel brushed her skin.

Lachash glared at him. Carina will do what I think needs to get done," Lachash said in a steely voice. "And first, I need you to move so that I can see the wound." He looked at Carina and saw how shaken she was by the man. "It's all right, Carina. They won't hurt you because you're the only person who can help them right now."

Carina glanced at Lachash and drew in a shaky breath as the man released her. Her voice shook but she finally spoke. "Tell me what to do." She bent to examine the wound and saw that it contained what looked like a slim piece of steel that was slimy with blood.

"What is it, Carina?"

"It is some kind of thin metal thing about six or seven inches long."

"A knife?"

"If it's a knife, it has no handle."

Lachash ran his good hand through his hair. "Do you two have any idea what it is?"

"He was coming out of the long alley, I don't know. What is down there?" One of the Banished asked.

"Which alley?"

"It's the alley that's beside the huge brown brick complex near the main street."

The description of the brown brick complex made Carina immediately think of the alley behind the cookery.

The wounded man, barely conscious, mumbled, "B-boning k-knife."

"Yeah. Yeah," said a bristle-faced Banished, "just help him."

"We cannot just pull it out. It might be lodged in an organ. He could have internal bleeding. My hands aren't going to be any help to him and we don't have anyone else who is skilled enough to aid your friend," Lachash said.

"What about the girl? She seems to be helping people," Grey-Eyes said as he eyed the blood on her apron.

"She is my assistant and has only been helping me with the minor wounds. This is major surgery."

"Do it," Grey-Eyes ordered.

Lachash glared at him before he told Carina to pull it out.

"It's slippery, and I haven't anything to pull it out with."

"Try the forceps."

"Take it out," the injured man muttered.

She placed her hand on his shoulder. "I don't know if you're bleeding inside."

"Everyone out of the room," the wounded man began, "including the healer but I want the girl to stay here with me. Move it."

"You can't order me out," Lachash sputtered.

"We can carry you outside. Until your reinforcements show up, we're in control. We know that the majority of sector guards are in other sectors or at the outposts. It's only a matter of time before they show up, of course. We want to be gone by then," Grey-Eyes said.

Lachash confronted him. "You have taken the sector?"

"That's not your concern." Grey-Eyes grabbed Lachash and dragged him out of the room. Lachash glanced worriedly in Carina's direction.

Carina turned to face her patient, but before she could do anything, he said, "Malcom told us that you were the one sent to help us overcome the Leaders, but he has his doubts about you." The wounded man showed surprising strength when he grabbed her wrist. "You're the one, aren't you?"

"I don't know what you mean."

"Show me the armband," he demanded brusquely.

"The armband?" Carina feigned ignorance and was amazed that this wounded man suddenly contained such energy.

"Don't play dumb, I know that you have it," he rasped. "I'm the Cleric, Ritik, and I know your man Malcom and he described you in detail. You don't think I came up with this wound just for the fun of it, do you?"

"You're calling me dumb when you're the one who got himself skewered just to see me?"

"You have spirit, even though you pretend to be docile like all sector women are expected to be, I'll give you that. Just show me." He fell back wearily.

*Obviously he knows about it and perhaps he can give me more information so I can figure out how to use it, do whatever it is that needs to be done in this reality, and then go back to my reality.* Carina pulled up her left sleeve to reveal the armband with its glimmering blood-colored stone.

His eyes lit up when he saw the stone. "Did you find it?"

"No."

"Where did you get it, then?"

"It was given to me. Who are you to question me?"

His grip tightened. "Who gave it to you?"

"A man who also had an armband."

"Do you know anything else about it? Have you seen the man who gave it to you again?"

"No, I haven't seen anyone else with one, so I was afraid to show it. I assumed people received them when they were assigned. The man who gave it to me was killed, I think."

"What do you mean?"

*Damn! How does a person just say, "Oh, there was this eighteen-foot-long dragon and a phoenix and they pounced on him?"* Instead, she said, "There was an accident."

"Nobody has them, not even the Leaders, and they must not know about the armband for as long as possible." His voice had begun to waver.

"I don't understand."

"You are the only one who can wield the power of the armband and until you know how and why to use that power, your life, everyone's life, is forfeit."

"What do you mean everyone's life is forfeit? I didn't ask to be here. I didn't ask for the armband. I was just in the wrong place and time." Her voice got louder. "Why don't you tell me why this place exists and why I've been brought here from my world to this backward male hierarchy where I don't even dare to be more than just a passive female?"

He grabbed her wrist. "I'm running out of time. There is so much that I want to tell you, no time. Later." His energy was faltering. "You have the power to heal me. You can do whatever you want, but you must want it." His last words faded before he passed out.

Carina stared at the unconscious man. *I can heal him? He is a Banished. I think they're despicable.* Her conscience pricked her. She couldn't leave him to die. *If I want it.* She closed her eyes, *I don't know whether it's right or wrong, but I have to try.*

Unconsciously, her left hand hovered above the man and stayed there as Carina began concentrating on the knife and visualized it exiting without damaging the inner organs. The blade shimmered with a white light and slowly began to wiggle and then suddenly it flew up and into Carina's outstretched palm. Carina opened her eyes in surprise at the blade and the silent man. Her hands shook as she soaked up the slight ooze of blood around the wound with bandages. She knew that she would have to close the wound, but she didn't know how. She worried that the blade had done internal damage.

There was a knock on the door and Zach peered around it. "I heard shouting. Are you all right and how is he?"

"Quickly, I need Lachash, I have the knife out, but now I need to close the wound."

Lachash entered the room, limping between the two Banished men. "Good job, Carina. How did you manage to get it out? Zach is getting the sterile materials as we speak."

"How do we know if he's bleeding inside?"

"How is his abdomen? Has it become rigid or enlarged?"

Carina touched the man's abdomen. "No, nothing's changed."

"He is breathing normally. Maybe we've been lucky."

The grey-eyed man's eyes pierced hers knowingly. "Maybe we have been."

She averted her eyes but then Lachash gave her instructions on how to close the wound. When it was over, the room's occupants let out a collective sigh of pent-up tension.

"The wound has to be kept clean. That man must get a lot of rest. Now, would you mind telling me why you Banished are here?" Lachash asked querulously.

"I've said before, it's not your concern, Healer."

"You have been lucky the sector's men have not burst in here."

"They've been occupied elsewhere."

The door flew open as another Banished came in.

"Jairus," Grey-Eyes acknowledged him.

"Varun, how's Ritik?"

"The blade is out and he is resting now," Lachash replied.

"Can the cleric travel, Varun?" Jairus asked.

Lachash interrupted. "I would not advise it because of his loss of blood and we don't know if any of his internal organs were damaged."

"We might have to leave shortly if the reinforcements arrive," Jairus said.

# An Unexpected Find

Varun asked Jairus, his leader, "What should we do now, sir?"

"We're lucky to have suffered only a few losses so far. It is unfortunate that we lost our chance at grabbing the Leaders. More than likely reinforcements will be showing up soon. Malcom did a good job of keeping the majority of the men away. I wonder how our presence was given away."

"Did the girl say anything?" Jairus asked. "She isn't a healer as far as I can tell."

Varun paused for a moment. "The girl was the one who pulled the knife out of Ritik."

"What do you mean the girl took out the knife? You let some amateur pull a knife out of Ritik? Take me to them," Jairus demanded.

Varun jumped to his orders. He knew better than to get in the way of Jairus' infamous temper. They burst into the healer's office at the same time.

Varun took Jairus to the examining room where he had last seen Ritik lying on the stretcher.

He saw Ritik sleeping. "Close the door, Varun." Jairus grabbed Carina by the shoulder. "No, you stay here." Jairus scanned her and she met his eyes. She tried to shrug off his grasp, but he pulled her tightly against him. She struggled and kicked.

He spoke authoritatively, his voice a deep baritone. "Stand still; I'm not going to hurt you." It wasn't until Jairus felt the tension begin seeping from Carina that he released his grip on her left arm. He slid her long sleeve up her arm, stopping when he saw the armband.

Carina pulled her other arm free to cover it up. She didn't do any more than that, just stood there like stone.

"Take off the armband so that I can look at it," he demanded.

"It won't let me."

He caught her arm and reached under her sleeve to pull on the armband. It slid down to her wrist but was too small to remove.

"If it fits your arm, it should fit over your wrist," Jairus said. He slid the armband up her arm and down to her wrist again.

She tried to pull her arm free. "I told you it can't come off."

"Then how did you get it on?" He held her gaze and then released her when he heard Ritik moving. "How are you, Ritik?"

"A little tender. It's her. You saw the armband?"

"Yes, I saw it."

"Jairus, it's really her. She took out the knife just by thinking about doing it. I came to just long enough to see the knife as it flew out of me and into her outstretched hand." Ritik's tone was full of the excitement he felt, but barely above a whisper.

"Did she heal you completely?"

"I don't hurt too badly. She had to sew me up afterward. I don't think she knew that she had the power to do it. It was the armband."

Jairus' voice rose. "It was a damn fool thing you did getting wounded like that. What were you thinking? You could have been killed."

"But I wasn't killed and now there is no doubt about who she is. What are we going to do about her? She assumed they provided the armband to individuals when they were assigned."

"So you're saying that she's untrained and of no use to us?" Jairus asked.

There was a startling knock, and Varun stuck his head in. "I've just received a report that the Leaders' forces were seen not even twenty minutes from here. The men are waiting for further orders, sir; what should I tell them?"

"Tell them to get ready to pull out after they finish getting the supplies from the list. We'll be leaving in ten minutes."

"What about her?" Varun asked.

"We take her with us," Jairus said.

"Why the fuss over her?" Varun asked.

"She may be untrained," Ritik said, "but she also happens to wear the armband of the prophecy. We have very specific orders about her."

Jairus' looked at him. "How could your brother Andzej give orders when he didn't know she existed?"

"I told him."

Jairus looked at him disbelievingly. "Another one of your dreams, Ritik?"

"Yes. Even if she doesn't yet know who and what she is, we can't let anything happen to her."

Carina had been moving away as they spoke and upset a small stand of equipment when she ran out the door and past the Banished, who were anxiously waiting in the outer room, and out the main door.

"After her. She must not get away!" Jairus shouted to Varun.

Varun yelled to his three men who were standing guard, "Catch her!"

The three men nodded and ran off.

Carina knew they'd seen her when she heard them yell, "After her!" She ran on, not looking back as the streets flew by in a blur, blindly changing her route until she was breathless. She paused at the corner of a building to listen for any sounds of pursuit: Nothing. She hoped she'd lost them. She took off, but at a walk, still panting for breath. It was harder to see; daylight was fading. She tried to figure out the importance of both the Banished and the Leaders but she didn't have enough information. If she had been paying more attention, she would have seen the figure that loomed out of the dark.

"Hey, my beauty, thought you be leavin' old Trator, did ya? I be havin' to teach you a lesson."

"Damn! Is there anybody who *can't* get into this sector?" She retorted in frustration.

He yanked her head back and Carina yelped in pain. "Hey, boys"—he turned to a group of motley dressed men—"look what I be findin'. She not be likin' my hospitality, so I guess I be havin' to sell her to the highest bidder." When Carina struggled futilely, he licked her face with his tongue.

His men cheered wildly at his suggestion before he silenced them. Trator grinned as he pulled Carina's face toward his, but before he could follow through, a cold, steely voice resonated behind him.

"Let her go, Trator."

"Jairus. Good to be seein' you again after such a long time, but this be none of your affair."

Jairus' eyes didn't leave Trator's face as he spoke. "You Scavs have been selling people for too long now, and we're going to stop you once and for all."

Trator scanned the terrain around him. "You be alone. How are you going to stop me? By yourself?"

Varun and another twenty men appeared.

"This be provin' interestin'," Trator remarked snidely although his eleven men were outnumbered.

They ranged themselves behind him, waiting for the signal.

"Let her go."

"It not be like you to be interferin' in Scav business. We were just foraging, and we found her."

"You and your outlaws have been terrorizing people for too long, and it's going to stop."

"Look at who be callin' us outlaws. It be you and your crew that the Leaders be lookin' for, not us."

"They don't even know your group exists."

"We wreak havoc, and you Banished get hunted. I be likin' that kind of deal. It be benefittin' us."

"You're not only scavengers, you're parasites."

Trator's men leapt forward and attacked at his nod. Knives flashed and fists flew as they ignited the fires that fueled old hatreds and battled over possession of Carina. For a few minutes, it looked like Trator's men would overcome the Banished but Jairus couldn't allow them to take Carina away. He knocked his opponent to the ground, jumped over him, and used the momentum to plow into Trator. Jairus smashed his fist into his face and Trator retaliated by slamming his foot into Jairus' chest.

Carina used the confusion to scramble away from them but tripped when another man smashed into her.

Varun saw her fall but didn't move. Carina looked behind her to see why he wasn't watching her: more men.

"Enough!" He roared.

A few men looked at him, and they, too, saw the line of Defender forces advancing on them with their knives drawn.

Jairus pushed Trator away as he wiped the blood from the corner of his mouth. "We've got bigger problems than the girl."

Trator nodded and grinned. "Looks like we be havin' to fight together if we be wantin' to get out of this one."

Jairus scowled at him. "Varun!" Jairus shouted. Varun disarmed his opponent and ran toward Jairus. "Get the woman and Ritik, get them to safety and get them to Andzej as quick as you can before we run into any more of those blasted Scavengers or Defenders. Send a signal when you've done that." He glanced at Trator. "No offense."

"You be owin' me for the girl."

"We'll bargain later, but right now we have some Defenders to take care of."

Carina heard the word bargain, and fled, but Varun soon caught up with her.

"Let go of me!" Carina screamed, clawed, and kicked at him.

Varun pulled her arm painfully behind her and she stopped struggling. "Damn it woman. I'm trying to help you."

"If you're trying to help me, then let me go."

"I can't do that."

"Let me *go*."

"No, I'd rather die than do that."

His statement shocked her. "So what do you want me to do? Thank you for chasing after me when this has been my first chance to escape from the lot of you?"

"Where are you going to run?"

"Anywhere but here."

"You plan to chase after the Scavengers?"

"Of course not."

"Well, then, talk some sense."

"Then leave me here and I'll go back to where I work and forget about everything I saw. If anyone asks me about you, I'll say I don't know anything."

"I can't do that. You're going to have to come with us one way or another. It's for your own good."

"And who are you to say what's for my own good?"

"Listen, girl, we can go on like this all day until we're caught by either the Scavs or the Leaders' men. Just listen to me. I'll let you go your own way if you can answer one question: You seem so anxious to run back to the Leaders and away from us, but can you honestly say, without a doubt, you know who your real enemies are?"

It had been confusing to hear Trator admit they were the ones kidnapping people from the sector. If Trator was a Scav, then whose side was Malcom on? Their rough language and clothing made her think that she'd misjudged the Banished by confusing them with the Scavengers. Still, why should she trust them? *Why can't I remember who I am so that I can decide? Would it matter even if I remembered?*

Varun waited. He could hear the fighting and knew he was running out of time. He also knew that everything depended on getting Ritik and Carina to safety.

She shook her head. "I-I don't know."

"Listen to me," Varun began, "I know you don't know what to do or who to trust. Before you make any foolish decision, you need to know us better and then you will understand. We're running out of time, and we have to get to safety. I swear on my life that if you decide to leave us, then you will be free to go."

"What if your Jairus won't let me go?"

"Then I'll help you escape," and with those words he took out his knife, cut his hand and squeezed until blood dripped onto the dirt at his feet. "Here is my blood oath, I'll keep my word and keep you safe."

Carina couldn't doubt the sincerity of his words or actions. "I don't trust any of you, but I'll go with you only because of your oath. I hope it means something."

"Good girl. We have to help Ritik. Andzej will flog me if anything happens to his brother. What is the shortest route to the healer's office?"

"Turn to the left once you're out the doors and it's straight down the street."

Varun saw that Ritik was still in the examining room, sitting on a chair talking with another Banished.

"Ritik, we have to get to safety. Do you think you are able to travel?" Varun asked.

"I'll manage."

"Are you all right, Carina?" Lachash asked when he saw her.

She went to talk to Lachash; Varun stood behind her. "I'm all right, but I have to go with these men."

Lachash tried to grab her arm and glared at Varun. "You're not taking her or anyone else."

"We need a hostage or two to guarantee our safe passage out of here." He nodded toward Zach, who'd been talking with Lachash and a Banished. Varun quickly held a knife to Zach's back. "We'll take these two, but we'll leave the remainder of the people in your care."

Carina spoke up. "It is all right, Lachash, and we don't need any more trouble. I'll be fine, don't worry."

Varun turned to her. "I want you to collect some antibiotics and painkillers. Here is a bag to put them in."

She shot Lachash a glance, which he returned with a glare, and then retrieved as many pharmaceuticals as she could.

"I want you to help Ritik," Varun said to a Banished standing near him. "You two"—he pointed, indicating Carina and Zach— "move in front where I can keep my eye on you."

They circled around the main building and out of the yard. This happened to be the square where Carina had found the people milling around, waiting for their meals when she first arrived. Varun took out a horn and blew two long, piercing blasts.

"Carina," Zach whispered, "I have a plan to escape."

Varun's voice boomed out almost in his ear. Zach jumped. "I've been watching you. She isn't going to be safe here. We're taking her to a place where she will be. You can come with us and guarantee her safety, or you can return to the sector. We won't force you, boy. We don't take prisoners like the Scavengers do."

Zach looked at Carina. "The Scavengers?"

Carina swallowed, glanced at Varun. If what she'd heard was true, then there were three organizations with differing agendas in this world: the Leaders with their guards, the Scavengers, and the Banished. Who were the good guys and who were the bad? "It's up to you, Zach."

Zach nodded. "Fine, if Miss Carina says it is all right, then I guess it must be true."

Carina didn't know why Zach was so compliant. She assumed all sector people hated and distrusted the Banished.

Varun clapped Zach on the shoulder. "Good lad. How about giving my man, A'dor, a hand with Ritik? After we've left this place well behind, we'll stop and rest."

Jairus heard Varun's signals from a half-mile radius; even the fighting men heard. The fighting between the Banished and the Leaders was still intense but Jairus' men were well-trained. The men pulled up their scarves when the street began to fill with thick smoke from tossed canisters. The Leaders' men were thrown into confusion. They couldn't see anything as they coughed and rubbed their burning eyes. By the time it cleared, the Banished had melted away, along with their injured men.

Helzion, who'd been in the rear guard of the sector forces, came to the front and joined a man on a horse.

"We'll need to see what damage has been done and then do a head count and find out who's missing."

"Damn those Banished," Helzion said. "They've probably taken prisoners like they always do."

"At least we were forewarned and had time to make sure the Committee Leaders were kept safe," Daric murmured.

"Thanks to Carina."

His black eyes glittered. "I'll be curious to meet this young woman."

# Missing

By the time the Leaders' forces re-entered the square after the battle, the sun was red in the west and dropping. The waning day created an urgency to find everyone hurt or hiding. Sentries kept a constant watch in case the Banished came back.

Gath had recovered from his attack and was preparing supper in the cookery. His wife, who'd heard how he had stabbed a Banished, was working at his side, determined to stay close. She'd been given to Gath several years prior. At first, she had withdrawn from the big bear of a man. Slowly she'd learned to accept her assigned position and came to love her bondmate fiercely. By the time the meal was finished, everyone was accounted for except Carina and Zach, who Lachash had reported taken.

"I don't understand it at all," Helzion began, "why would they attack and only take Carina and Zach as hostages?"

"We will call it a night for now. We have had more than enough happenings today and we do not need to deal with anything further without some rest. I want to meet with Lachash first thing in the morning. For now, we all need to calm down," Daric ordered.

"Good idea. We will change the sleeping arrangements just for tonight so we can utilize our few sentries," Helzion said. "I hope we will have a quiet night. The Banished are known to strike only once in an area."

"I hope you're right, Helzion, Goodnight."

"Goodnight, Daric."


It was shortly after two in the morning when Scavengers removed and replaced each of the eight sentries with their own men in front of the complex.

Trator and Scar gave directions to twenty other Scavengers who had joined them, on the best way to infiltrate the building:

"If our man inside has done his job, the door will be open. We need to look at the layout of the interior." He knelt down and sketched a rough layout of the building. "This be the cookery off to the left of the main entrance. Two large doors lead into it, usually unlocked. If there be too many people quartered in the sector, the excess will sleep in the dining area. This be the first place that we be checkin'," Trator's grim smile was a mere slash on his face. "There be a back door to the cookery, but our inside man said that it not be likely to be left open. It be havin' a steel bar across it, which be meanin' no access through that entrance. Once we be reachin' the dining area, we start a blaze in the cookery. We raise the alarm and let people come to us outside where we be waitin' for them.

"We 'ave only three exits out of this building to watch for and one of them be blocked by the fire and the other, the front doors, accessible only for a short time until the smoke pours out. The rest of the people be comin' out of the side door. I want ten men at the side entrance, and five remainin' at the front entrance. Once the fire starts, we be rejoinin' you at this entrance."

Trator now watched his four men slip into the main foyer of the building and waited until the Scavs dressed as Defenders left to make their rounds. Trator then opened one of the doors to the dining room and held his breath as it squeaked on its rusty hinges.

There were no running footsteps so the rest of the men entered behind Trator.

"Barket, I be wantin' you to hold the door so that it stays open. We not be wantin' another noise to give us away."

Gath, who'd been drinking a cup of coffee in the cookery and thinking of how he'd attacked the Banished, heard the grating of the door and stood up to investigate. He opened the door between the cookery and the dining room and something hit him on the skull from behind. He slumped unconscious to the floor.

"I be wantin' one of you to secure the hall, and the other to be stayin' here, we be movin' this sap once we be lightin' the fire."

"He be lookin' awful heavy," a Scavenger observed.

"Then we be leavin' him here," Trator snorted.

Trator and his accomplice set to work at gathering combustibles. When the fire burned fiercely, they left the cookery and retreated into the foyer. Trator was feeling bold and yelled, "Fire! Fire!" before he stepped outside.

Meanwhile, Marta, Gath's bondmate, who'd come to check on him, entered quietly through the cookery's backdoor.

"Gath? Gath? Oh, my God!" she exclaimed as she hastily pulled the cord that turned on the water and propped the back door open. Concerned for her bondmate, she hurried into the dining room and saw him lying on the floor. "Gath, Gath, say something!" She shook him roughly. She ran her hands through his hair and until she found the swelling lump. "Who hit you Gath?"

Gath groaned as his eyelids fluttered open. "Go tell Helzion, he is in the other complex, but be careful. Tell him that I believe we're under attack. Quickly," he groaned weakly.

She kissed him on the forehead. "Will you be all right?"

"I'll be all right. You send for the reinforcements. I need to watch the door."

Gath got shakily to his feet, waiting for his head to clear. He looked in the cookery and saw the still-smoking pile of rubble. If Marta had entered through the back door without difficulty, then whoever hit him was either in the building or at the entrance. If they were, they had been expecting to hear mayhem. He went to the foyer and could hear the sound of people running toward him. "They were thorough," he muttered. "They've already sounded the alarm."

He met the first two people in the hallway. "It's a trap; the fire was set on purpose. Do not go out the doors. Stay inside."

"What be goin' on here?" asked a Defender in a deep voice; he was Trator's planted man.

"The fire was set on purpose and I think that whoever started it is waiting outside the exits. My bondmate went to get reinforcements," Gath explained to the two disguised Scavengers.

"The cookery door be open?" the Scavengers asked.

"Yes, they did not check it."

"Sounds like they probably be at the other entrances, if it be a trap. Barket, go and make sure nobody be goin' out the side door."

Gath did not know that the two men were Scavengers, although he wondered at their strange speech but had little time to ponder before being shoved back into the dining room.

The false Defender's order came too late because he heard a woman's scream.

When Trator heard the scream, he snickered slightly. "Here they come."

Fighting began in earnest as several real Defenders ran out the side door and fought their attackers, who they assumed were Banished.

"Get the women to safety!" Gath yelled.

Trator decided to open the main door. He looked inside, but there was no smoke. "Damn," he swore, "someone be puttin' out the fire. Come on, boys, let us be creatin' a bottleneck." He rushed inside. He could hear the loud sounds of fighting in the distance. When two young girls ran down the hall toward him, he grabbed them and shoved them toward one of his men. "Take them outside."

Chenaanah's daughters were forced outside the main doors and into the arms of the men who'd replaced the sentries. "Take them and put them with the other prisoners."

Reinforcements began arriving, entering through the cookery entrance, and joining in the fighting. Trator found himself fighting in two different directions. The Scavengers, who were at the side entrance, soon found themselves attacked from behind, and they quickly retreated down the stairs. They held their prisoners in front of them as shields.

"Trator! This way."

Trator and his men heard the shout and put up another show of strength before they withdrew from the hall. All the Scavengers escaped by pushing the prisoners toward the soldiers and running in all directions. Trator held onto Liisa, not wanting to lose his prize. Defenders soon surrounded him.

"One step closer," he said, "and she be dyin'."

Face red with suppressed fury, Helzion ordered, "Let her go."

"I not be thinkin' so. She be my ticket away from the likes of you."

Helzion lunged forward to grab her. A knife slashed towards his arm before he was shoved off his feet. Soldiers moved to help him, and in the minute-long diversion, Trator and his hostage disappeared.

"I thought you said they did not strike twice in one day," Daric roared after chasing a Scavenger down the street. "They will pay for this. I want a thorough search begun immediately!"

Just then, Chenaanah came running out of the building, "My daughters! They have my daughters!"

Helzion moved to comfort her as he looked at Gath, and asked, "Who else is missing?"

"They have taken the eight sentries."

"Cora and Lizbet are also missing," Chenaanah added between sobs.

"They have taken Aadam and Dan, too," a shrill voice spoke up.

"I want a messenger sent to the Northern sector immediately. Tell Graer to get here immediately. I want twenty men sent in each direction from the main complex. I want every building in this sector searched. The Banished have gone too far, and they're going to pay for this," Daric swore.

The Scavengers scurried away and crept through the streets that led back to their underground headquarters. Several hours later, eight prisoners were given away to pay debts and the others were force-marched until they were packed tightly in a cell, the same cell block that had once held Carina prisoner.

Meanwhile, Carina followed the Banished more than two hours through broken terrain until they came to a deserted building they could take refuge in. The only reason they stopped was that Ritik showed signs of exhaustion. They were all near collapse. Carina was breathless from the pace and her muscles vibrated in exhaustion.

"We ought to be safe enough while we rest. I'll take the first watch," Varun told the others.

Carina's stomach growled and Ritik looked at her. "I haven't eaten since this morning."

"Do we have any rations?" Ritik asked.

"I have some dried meat," a Banished offered.

"We weren't expecting to run into the Scavengers," Varun said.

"So how was this supposed to turn out?" Carina demanded.

"It is complicated."

"What is so complicated about attacking innocent people and abducting them?"

"There is more going on here than you know," Ritik said. "We've been planning this for a long time. We were hoping to get the Leaders to listen to us and come up with an end to the turmoil.

We wanted to get them to aid us in getting rid of the continuous problems caused by the Scavengers."

"But someone let them know we were there. You," Varun said pointedly.

"I guess I'm an observant person," Carina said. "I noticed that the number of men had grown. As far as I was concerned, if they were Banished, we were in trouble."

"Yeah. Leader propaganda," Varun snorted. "Everyone's been led to believe everything the Leaders say without question."

"Do they know that there are people called Scavengers? Don't you think it is possible that they only know about the Banished?" she asked naively. "If I believed them, then that's because they abducted me from this sector, took me to God knows where, and then sold me to the highest bidder. That man in the square, he was the one who beat me, starved me, and humiliated me. I can't remember who I was before I arrived at the stupid complex because of him." She turned away and stood at the window, looking out at nothing.

"I can see we're all tired. Let's get some sleep. We can discuss this later," Ritik said.

Early morning light seeped in through the windows. "There is someone in the area," Varun alerted them.

One of his men replied, "I'll check it out." He opened the door, but quickly closed it. "They're the Leaders' men. How did they find us and why would they come after us? Sir, there are men in the streets outside."

Varun spoke with Ritik quietly. "What are we going to do?"

"Maybe they know about Carina."

"No. If she didn't know who she was, it isn't likely that the Leaders know, either."

"A'dor and I could create a diversion and then Carina, you, and Zach could head into a building they've already searched," Varun suggested.

"How many of them are there?" Ritik asked.

"I've seen six men, two to each building."

"We could ambush the two that come here."

"I have been watching them," Zach spoke up. "They go to a building, search it, and then meet together before they head out again. If we ambush them, we'll be giving our location away." Zach paused. "There are two more, so that makes eight."

"What if there are even more?" Jairus frowned.

Carina bit her lip nervously. "What happens to Banished when they're caught?"

"They're sent for recultivation. Why?" Varun sent her a piercing glare.

"I have another idea. Zach and I can go outside where they're meeting. We'll say that we escaped about eight hours ago while you were helping Ritik and we saw you head west."

"No." Varun said adamantly. "That would mean we've wasted all of our efforts."

Ritik spoke from his viewpoint at the window. "I've counted twelve of them so far. Our building is only two away from where they're currently searching."

"Then let them take us all."

Carina retorted, "No, that's foolish."

"May I speak with you, Ritik?" Varun pointed to a secluded corner of the room and they walked away to talk. "Any suggestions? I promised Jairus to keep her safe."

"Let me have a brief word with her. Carina, would you come here? Listen carefully." He glanced at Zach and lowered his voice. "Your idea is a good one, and I know you will be safe for a time in the sector now that the Scavengers are gone. We're going to help you but you must keep the existence of the armband a secret. Once they find out about it, your life will change and they might even decide to protect their interests by stopping you, recultivating you, killing you, if they can't manipulate you. You've been lucky to keep it hidden so far, but you'll have to be even more diligent."

Chagrinned, Carina asked, "Stopping me from what? Thanks for sharing your concerns but you haven't told me anything that I can understand. I don't want to be involved in any of this."

"But you are involved because you wear the armband and are a part of the foretelling."

"What do you mean I'm a part of the foretelling?"

"The Cleric has visions and has seen that someone would come wearing the sign of the Dragon and Phoenix and lead us to freedom. You don't have a choice. You need to join us. Our lives are harsh, but we're free from the dictates of the Leaders. I am not happy with your plan, but it's all we have at the moment. Zach will have to remain with us."

"Whatever for?" Carina demanded.

He lowered his voice so that only she would hear him. "You've shown your colours and we know that we can trust you because of the armband and what you did for the Cleric. Zach, on the other hand, has no reason to keep quiet and he could give us away. He could betray you. Do you want that?"

Carina digested his words. It behooved her to abandon Zach, but Varun did have a point, there wasn't any reason for Zach to be loyal to them. "You should have left him at the sector. Now he has no choice, does he? If you tell him now, he could call out and betray us all."

"So could you."

"Like you said, I have too much at risk." She paused. "You'll treat him well?"

"He'll be safe with us and, hopefully, want to join us once he sees what we're all about."

She nodded even though she had no idea what they were "all about," and spoke a little louder, "I'll go when it's clear outside."

Zach moved to join her. Varun came up and hit him on the side of the head. "Sorry Carina. It's for the best. He'll be out long enough for you to leave."

"I'll hold you to your word."

171

"Hold on, Carina. Varun, give Jairus and Andzej a message: Tell them that Carina needed a guide; I had to go with her."

"No, I can't let you."

"You will, Varun. I had a dream that our success depends on many things. One of those things requires that I make the journey with her." He knew his brother Andzej would be furious when he learned that he was still in the sector and that he had wanted to remain here, but it had to be done.

"If it weren't for the fact that your dreams have a habit of coming true, I'd never agree."

"Thanks, Varun." Ritik turned to Carina. "I'll be right behind you."

They went through the door and crept down the alley.

"I need you to pretend I'm still ill and you're helping me."

"We can't go any farther. The Defenders are coming," Carina whispered under her breath.

"Quickly, into the street so that they don't see where we came from."

They hurried into the middle of the rubble-strewn street so that the remaining Banished could escape when the sector's men began coming toward them.

"Who goes there?" a voice called.

"Elzak!" she called when she recognized his voice.

"Carina, is that you? We thought we would never see you again. Who is this?" he asked, turning to assess Ritik.

"This is Ritik. He helped me escape from the other two men. He said the Banished abducted him more than seven years ago." Because of Carina's healing, Ritik was almost fully recovered but he acted as if he were still severely wounded. "He was hurt at the sector, but the Banished forced him to come with us anyway. He's still too weak to walk, and that's why we're still here." Her voice changed. "I'm so glad to see you, Elzak. I have been so dreadfully afraid. I don't want to be a Banished prisoner again," Carina simpered.

Elzak glowed. "Do not worry about anything, Carina. I'll take you back. Did you see where they went?"

"I saw them go west last evening, sir," Ritik supplied.

"Is there any food and water?" Carina begged. "We're very thirsty and hungry. I don't think I've eaten since yesterday morning."

Elzak began yelling orders to return to the sector while Carina and Ritik were given some bread, dried meat, and water on the way.


The group didn't arrive at the main complex until three hours later than expected. Helzion and Daric came out to hear how they'd been found.

"Ritik? I don't know you, but you remind me of someone… but who?" Daric murmured. "How long have you been with the Banished?"

"Seven years, I think, I was only a boy when I was captured."

"The Banished won't be too happy that you have escaped."

"They'll be furious with me. I couldn't stay there anymore; I was just waiting for the right moment to escape."

"We have a lot to talk about, but I see you're still somewhat weak from your wound. How did that happen?"

"I was stabbed by someone when I was running away from the Banished."

Daric spoke again, this time to two Defenders. "Take him to the infirmary and have Lachash check his wound. I want someone with him constantly."

"Yes, sir."

As Ritik was led away, he stole a quick glance at Carina's flushed face.

Daric turned to Carina. "I have already spoken with Lachash about what happened at the infirmary. I have heard many things about you. You have been quite useful to Lachash, and until he is better, you will continue your duties there. Helzion has told me that you came from another sector, although your file has not arrived.

Perhaps you didn't come from one of the other sectors. Maybe you're a wild one who recently surfaced from underground or," his voice lowered, "you're an illegal. If you've been born from an illegal union, then we'll have to recultivate you. Where did you come from?"

"I don't know."

Helzion whispered in Daric's ear.

From the look on Daric's face he wasn't pleased, but he said, "You're a mystery to be solved. Until then, my apologies, I hope your memory will be fully restored."

I hope so, too. I want to be assigned like everyone else."

"I am sure we can arrange that. How well do you know Bondmate Graer?"

"Chenaanah? I have spent some time with her and her daughters, but I don't know them that well."

"She is going to need support until Malcom returns."

"Why? Did something happen?"

"The Banished attacked at around two this morning, taking ten men and four women. Two of them were Chenaanah's daughters."

"How did that happen?"

"They started a fire in the cookery. Fortunately, Marta put it out and went for help."

"I don't believe it," Carina said incredulously.

"The Banished finished what they failed at earlier." Helzion grimaced. His face was hard and shadowed with inner turmoil.

"No, not them. It must have been the Scavengers."

"What are you talking about?" Daric asked.

"That's why the Banished came the first time. They wanted to let you know that there is another group calling themselves the Scavengers, and that they're responsible for the kidnapping and the raiding."

"That is just another one of their lies."

"No, before your forces arrived, the Scavengers and Banished were confronting each other. I heard one Scavenger admit it."

"Quiet!" Daric ordered. "We'll discuss this later at your debriefing."

Carina's dark eyes glittered, but she held her tongue.

Daric continued, "I want you to help Chenaanah and Lachash after you have eaten and rested."

Carina entered the building and turned left into the dining room. The door squeaked and she met Gath's startled look.

Relief flooded his face when he saw her. "Carina, you're back."

"I managed to escape from those men." The lie came easier the second time.

"You must be famished."

"Definitely."

Carina sat in the cookery and ate the scrambled eggs and toast while Gath worked.

"Gath, who is the man with Helzion?"

"He is one of the Leaders from the Southern Sector. Everyone watches out for him because he expects everyone to follow the policies and rules. He is a military expert."

"What is his name?"

"Daric."

"Just Daric?"

"Yes, the Leaders don't reveal their last names that I know of, or at least, I have never heard it."

"Does that mean Helzion is a Leader like I assume he is, and Malcom is no longer a Leader?"

"Yes, Helzion is, and Malcom gave it up when he infiltrated the Banished."

"How many of them are there?"

"Ten. They say you have memory loss. I imagine that must be hard on you. I will tell you what you may have forgotten. There are usually two Leaders in each sector. Two are in the northern hills where the wild ones first came out of the ground after the Upheaval, and two are where the land meets the vast water to the south. Then there are two near the Deadlands and the final two are not far from the Wastelands in the west. The first two are permanent locations but the Deadlands and Wastelands sometimes need to relocate if there are signs of sun disease. We now have three Leaders with Daric here."

Carina tried to laugh while processing the details he'd revealed. "You know, it isn't often we meet a Leader."

"I think that is preferable. Minding one's own business is better," Gath agreed gruffly.

Carina thought she heard a note of derision in his voice. "What happened here last night?"

He related how the Banished entered the cookery, knocked him out, started the fire, and the fight in the hall. "They got fourteen people, too. Daric is riled and he has sent for extra forces."

"Really?"

"They got Graer's daughters and, because he used to be a Leader, they're determined to catch them. Maybe they can escape as you did. It is rare to have someone escape."

"Graer did," Carina said.

Gath nodded. "So he did."

# The 21 New Healer

Chenaanah wasn't doing very well when Carina visited her. She was sitting listlessly on the bed and her face was as pale as fallen snow. Her eyes were red from crying and, as Carina began to talk to her, she ripped the tissue she was holding into shreds.

"Here's a glass of water, drink some."

"I am not thirsty," Chenaanah said tonelessly.

"Are you hungry? I can bring you something from the cookery. I'm sure Gath wouldn't mind."

Chenaanah continued staring bleakly into space.

"Do you want to talk about it?" She put her hand on Chenaanah's shoulder.

As if a dam broke inside of her, Chenaanah began talking without pausing and didn't stop. She recounted Loriia's first tooth, Liisa's first words. She talked on and on, reliving the highlights of her daughters' lives and dredging up tiny details that made each girl dear to her.

Carina listened as Chenaanah talked and leaned forward when she heard her mention Malcom's name. "I'm sorry, what did you say about Malcom?"

"He might reject me now."

"Why would he do that?"

"It is the law. When a woman is given to a Leader, he is responsible for her for as long as the children need nurturing, but if anything happens to them, he can reject her for another who can give him children. I am too old to have any more children."

"But he loves you, doesn't he?"

"We have been apart for more than two years and even now he manages to be assigned to duties that take him elsewhere."

"Do you want me to talk to him?"

Chenaanah pushed Carina away. "Of course not. If I must accept his rejection, then I will. I would honour him by accepting his decision."

"It won't come to that. The searchers will find your daughters."

"I hope you're right."


Carina went to Lachash's office. He was ensconced in bed, resting. Carina approached him and he, as if sensing her presence, opened his eyes.

"Carina," he whispered.

"Are you thirsty?"

"Yes."

Carina poured him some water. "How are you feeling?"

"I have been better."

"I hear the Leaders are sending you help until you're feeling better."

"Yes, they found somebody very quickly, and he'll be arriving shortly."

"You don't sound too impressed, why?"

"They will probably send some young inexperienced, wet-behind-the-ears lad who calls himself a healer."

"I'm sure they'll send someone who is as well trained as you are."

"Humph."

"You can still advise him with the patients."

Lachash considered Carina's words. "Yes, you're right."

"You will feel better once you're on your feet again."

"Is it true that the Banished attacked last night? Were many people taken?"

"It wasn't the Banished that took them. It was the Scavengers."

"Who are the Scavengers? Of course it was the Banished. What are you talking about?"

"Yes, what are you talking about?" a harsh-sounding voice asked.

Carina turned around and saw the Leader called Daric. "I told you there are two groups out there. The Banished and another group called the Scavengers. I think *they're* the ones who are responsible for all the abductions."

"You do, do you?" Daric arched a black brow. "Maybe you would like to elaborate on that? It isn't often a woman so boldly states her opinion. Perhaps it's time we found you a bondmate."

"Uh, my apologies," Carina stammered. "It all happened so quickly that I probably got my details mixed up."

"No harm done, but you might want to remember your place as a woman."

Carina looked at the floor. "Yes, sir. Please excuse me as I have duties to attend to here. There is a new healer covering for Lachash and I have to find him."

Daric grinned. "You have found him."

"You?" Lachash blurted out.

"Yes, I don't have the experience that you have, but I assure you I am qualified. I'm a military man; all my Defenders are important so I received training as a healer so that I could help them in the field if necessary."

Carina said nothing while Lachash talked, but then she said, "I'll return to my duties."

"Actually," Daric said, "I would like you to show me around and stand by as I check the patients."

"As you wish, Healer."

"Call me Daric," he said with a broad grin at Carina's obvious discomfort. "Let us start with you, Scott."

Carina looked at Lachash—she'd always thought his first name was Lachash.

Daric turned to look at Lachash. "How are you feeling?"

"Not bad, considering."

"Yes, you managed to be in the fray right at the beginning."

They had wrapped Lachash's ankle in a cloth bandage once things were less hectic. It wasn't broken, just twisted. His wrist had a fracture and had been immobilized to prevent movement.

"How did you get hurt?" Daric asked.

"I wasn't in the fight. I fell down a flight of stairs when two of the Banished suddenly burst out of the main building door and knocked me aside."

"You will be mobile in a few days, but your wrist will prevent you from doing any complex hand work."

"I'll manage with you and Carina assisting."

Daric turned to look at her.

Lachash continued, "Both Carina and Zach were quite helpful during the conflict."

"Yes, from what I have heard, both were kept quite busy. Is it true that you pulled a knife out of one of the Banished?" Daric asked.

Carina nodded.

"Were you scared?"

"Terrified."

"Did you tell her how to do it?" Daric asked Lachash.

"No, the Banished ordered us out of the room, but I came back and watched her sew up the wound."

"Let us look at the patient that she worked on, then. Try to sleep, Scott, and you will feel better in no time."

"Sure," Lachash said reluctantly. Lachash preferred to be in charge of his own office and patients, but there wasn't anything he could do when faced with Daric's assumption that he was in charge.

He didn't like Daric's familiarity with his first name and, as he watched Carina and Daric leave the room, he wondered how Carina would bear up to Daric's blunt and insensitive ways.

Ritik heard footsteps in the hallway. He saw Carina and the Leader Daric approaching him and quickly closed his eyes to feign sleep.

Carina scanned Ritik, worry etched on her face.

"How did you know that his injury wasn't serious?" Daric asked.

"I think a knife wound is serious," Carina replied.

Ritik opened his eyes.

"Hello, how are you feeling? Ritik, isn't it?"

"Yes, sir. I'm still having pain, but it's not as bad as before."

"Weren't you a little bit nervous or concerned at having an untrained person pulling out the knife that was in you?"

"I don't see that I had much choice and neither did she, because the healer told her to do it."

Daric poked around the stitched wound. "You did this?" He asked Carina and she nodded. "It looks very good."

"Thank you, Healer."

"You have done it before?"

"No, not at all." Carina scrunched up her face. "I've sewn cloth, but there's no comparison between that and human flesh."

"It is a bit puffy, and we will watch it closely for the next day or two. Watch for any liquid discharge and monitor his temperature. Report to me immediately if anything changes. Was he given any shots?"

"I gave him an antibiotic and a painkiller."

"You gave him the injection?"

"I gave him the needle after Lachash explained the dosage and where to put the needle. He was the second person I have given an injection."

"You know you scrunched your face when you mentioned the sewing and the needles. I gather that they're not your favorite activities."

"No." Carina smiled. "Nevertheless, it had to be done and now I know how to do it if the demand arises again."

"Hopefully, we'll eliminate the Banished and you will never be in that position again." He turned to Ritik. "We're going to have to send you for debriefing, and possibly you will go through recultivation once you're feeling better."

"Recultivation?" Ritik asked.

"You have not heard of it? Well, you have been exposed to the dissident Banished and their antisocial functions, and we will need to discover whether you will be a beneficial addition to our society." He turned to Carina. "We will need to take some blood tests. I'll get you to draw some blood samples from Ritik."

"I'm sorry, but I have never done that before. Lachash always did that for the new patients."

"I guess you will have a chance to learn."

"No!" Carina blurted out. "I would rather not. I'm neither trained, nor qualified to do that and I don't think I could stomach it. I mean I might get sick. Why don't you get Bondmate Graer to do it? I believe she was in charge of the Carrier Program in her old sector. Wouldn't she know how to take samples? Besides, she needs something to keep her busy and take her attention away from her missing daughters. She isn't feeling very confident right now."

Daric gave Carina an appraising glance before he spoke. "I believe you're right about Bondmate Graer. Why don't you get her and tell her that she's been temporarily assigned to this office? Continue with your duties until you've shown her all she needs to know about Lachash's office. We'll find you something to keep you busy. I think that I know the perfect thing, but I'll check your temporary file first to check the tests Lachash probably did when you arrived."

"Oh, I just thought those were meant to check to see if we were in good health."

"That is true, but for the women there are additional purposes."

"Which are?"

"To check if they are candidates for the Carrier Program."

"Wouldn't the previous sector have done those tests?"

"Only the Northern and Southern sectors do those tests because they have the equipment."

"Oh."

"I'll check your file and let you know what its implications are."

Carina didn't like the sound of "implications." It inferred something sinister. Maybe she was just reading too much into his words. "I should return to my duties. I'll go find Bondmate Graer."

Carina found Chenaanah exactly where she'd left her in the sleeping quarters. "Chenaanah? When you were in charge of the Carrier Program, did you have to take blood tests?"

"Yes. Why?"

"The Leader Daric needs your help to take some tests. Lachash is injured, and I guess Daric is too busy. He says that you're temporarily assigned there."

"Really? How did he know about me?"

"I suggested that he pick you to do the tests because I didn't know how to take a patient's blood or how to do tests. I'm not particularly fond of giving needles." She winced squeamishly.

Chenaanah's countenance brightened considerably when she heard about Daric's medical request. "When does he need me?"

"Now, but why don't you and I have lunch first?"

Chenaanah gave Carina a quick hug. "I'll just wash up first."


The atmosphere in the dining room was subdued. People whispered among themselves. Carina chose a dining table away from the whispering because she didn't want Chenaanah to hear anything that might upset her. After the meal, Chenaanah excused herself. Carina, who'd seen Elzak, the Defender, at another table, walked up to him.

He looked up. "Hello, Carina. You're looking well."

"Thank you, yes, I'm feeling fine. I'm, however, a little concerned about Bondmate Graer and the way she has been reacting about the abduction of her daughters. Has there been any success in tracking them?"

"No." Elzak sighed. "We've finished checking the surrounding area where we found you and Ritik, but did not find anything else that indicated that the fourteen missing people had gone that way. The other search parties haven't been successful in their search, either. It is as if they have disappeared."

"Will the search continue?"

"Of course it will. It is one thing to take people, but Leader children have never been taken."

Carina saw Chenaanah walking down the hallway and quickly whispered, "Bondmate Graer is coming. Try to be positive if she asks you anything, all right?"

Elzak nodded.

"Sorry to interrupt," Chenaanah said.

"That's all right, Chenaanah. This is Elzak; he's one of the many men looking for your daughters."

"Really? Do you have any news?"

"I am sure that they are well and it is only a matter of time before we find them."

"Thank you. I guess everyone is doing all they can."

"My pleasure, Bondmate Graer."

"Thank you, Elzak."

They said their goodbyes and then Carina took Chenaanah to the cookery where Gath had prepared healthy lunches for the patients.

# The Examination

Carina hurried to deliver Lachash's meal and was surprised to see Daric sitting beside him, deep in conversation.

Daric looked up. "Carina, we were just talking about you."

"About what?" she asked suspiciously.

"Why don't we leave Scott to his meal and you and I can have a talk in the office for a few minutes?"

Lachash studiously avoided her look and studied his food, instead.

"Your first name is Scott?" she asked. She saw the anger in his eyes, and thought, *I've hit a nerve.* "I've only known you as Lachash. I hope you don't mind if I keep calling you that." She winked at him and received a smile in return.

"You, my dear, may call me anything you like."

Daric muttered under his breath as he left the room and she followed him to Lachash's private office where he grabbed a file before sitting down.

"I have your medical file here and the results of several of the tests that Lachash took. There is one test, however, that seems to be missing. I spoke to Lachash and he said you had refused the internal examination."

"He wanted to see if I'd be a good brood mare and I didn't know that the test would be required in a new sector."

"It will, especially with women. Surely Lachash enlightened you about the value of women in any sector."

"Yes, he also said my missing memory was the problem, and he was going to send a woman to talk to me before he did any more tests."

"It's imperative that those last tests are done."

"Lachash said he'd give me two weeks."

"We need the relevant information now in order to process you."

"But—"

"No buts, Carina, it has to be done as soon as possible. Today, in fact."

"Today? But Lachash can't do it."

"We have other qualified personnel."

"Like who?"

"I can do the test as I have assisted in the Carrier Program several times just to familiarize myself with the workings of that department."

Carina almost leapt through her skin at the mere thought of this Leader touching her in such a way. Fortunately for her, Daric was only toying with her and gauging her reaction before he spoke. "Lucky for you, I spoke to Lachash and he filled me in on all the details, so I've asked Bondmate Graer to assist me. I'm sure you'd agree that she, under the circumstances, would be perfectly qualified to do your tests today."

"Do you have to be here when she does the tests?"

"As I mentioned, I'll be assisting her."

Carina didn't speak for several minutes and when she did, she licked her lips before she spoke, "Could you stand so you don't see anything? You're a stranger to me and I'd be embarrassed."

Daric prolonged her uncertainty. Carina realized he had more control over her, a control that hadn't been totally there before.

Finally, he said, "I could do that if it would make things easier for you, Carina."

"Yes, if you would, I'd feel more comfortable."

"On one condition."

"Yes?"

Daric, a master at manipulating people, lowered his voice. "Don't resist it. I want you to go to the examination room and undress immediately. I'll ask Bondmate Graer to bring you a gown."

Carina sighed. "I will do as you ask."

"Good girl." Daric smiled at her. We will join you in the examining room in five minutes. That should give you enough time to get there and change before we arrive." He limited the minutes of her freedom so she wouldn't have time to dwell on it. "Now go. I'm timing exactly five minutes."

She turned to leave.

"Carina?"

"Yes?"

"We'll examine you whether you're ready or not." The steel tone that Carina had heard before in his low voice was back, and she nodded before she fled from the room. Carina had just enough time to get to the examination room, strip her clothes off and put on the gown before she heard Daric and Bondmate Graer's voice outside the door. Carina was flustered and looked to see if she were totally covered. Just as the door opened, Carina spotted the armband and hurriedly pushed it up to the highest possible position on her arm, hidden just below the short sleeve of the blue gown. She froze, her hand still on her arm, when both Daric and Bondmate Graer entered and looked at her. She smiled and nonchalantly lowered her hand. It was then that she noticed the tray of equipment that Daric carried.

Bondmate Graer was all business when she entered the room. Back in her role as Director of the Program, she was no longer the weepy Chenaanah that Carina knew; instead, she was a stranger.

"I'd like you to lie down, Carina. Good girl. Now, if you'd open your mouth for me so that I can take a look inside."

Carina thought that was easy enough to do and quickly opened her mouth. Bondmate Graer stuck in a tongue swab and asked her to say ahhh. "Ahhh." The next thing she knew Carina was coughing as Bondmate Graer had put the stick in with one hand and then dropped in a pellet that she had been concealing with the other. "Water." She reached out her hand behind her and Daric quickly placed a small cup in her outstretched hand. She placed it to Carina's mouth. She'd forcefully kept her hand pressed against Carina's shoulder so that she couldn't rise even while she coughed. "Swallow."

Given that she was lying down, Carina couldn't do anything else, so she swallowed the water as it was poured into her mouth in slow but steady increments. Bondmate Graer handed the cup back to Daric, still keeping her hand on Carina's shoulder. Once he'd taken the cup, she slowly stroked Carina's throat to ensure that the pellet and water stayed down. A few seconds later, she released Carina's shoulder and continued talking. "I'm going to do a pelvic examination. I know you feel uncomfortable about the whole thing, so I suggest that you just breathe deeply with me. Inhale one, two, exhale three, four, inhale five, six, exhale seven, eight."

By the count of ten Carina felt a lot more relaxed, even sleepy. She yawned. Briefly, she opened her eyes and focused on Bondmate Graer before she closed them again.

Graer exchanged a triumphant look with Daric and nodded to him with the prearranged signal.

He moved to examine Carina before the drug wore off. "Good, we've got about ten minutes before she's alert again, so let's do all that we need to do. Put her feet in the supports and we'll begin," Daric ordered.

Graer quickly moved Carina's legs while Daric grasped the first implement, raised the blanket below Carina's waist and put out his hand to receive the individual items that Graer handed him. His expectations were instantly confirmed. "There are no tumors or scarring, which most women have had after the Upheaval altered them but she could be sterile like so many women have been for the last several years." After a moment or two, he said, "If we're lucky she will be fertile and she can be impregnated. I am done. You clean up, and I'll hold the tray and appear not to be looking at what you're doing; she won't suspect that it wasn't you who did the examination."

Their timing was perfect. Carina opened her eyes and saw Bondmate Graer standing near her legs, and she could feel something cold brush her inner thigh. "Well, that is done, Carina. Now tell me that wasn't so bad, was it?"

Carina eyed Daric out of the corner of her eye, but he hadn't moved. *Maybe I was daydreaming*, she thought, in an effort to account for her sudden lapse of awareness. "You're done so soon? I didn't feel anything."

"Wonderful. There was nothing to worry about after all, was there?"

"No, I guess not. I'm sorry if I caused any trouble."

"Do not worry about it. Daric, I am just about done. Why don't you return the tray so that it can be sterilized, and I'll finish up with Carina so that she can get dressed and continue with her day? Thanks for assisting me."

"You're welcome, Bondmate Graer. I would not have interfered with such an expert as you." He left the examining room and returned the tray. He had the file and made notes in it before he returned to Lachash's office.

She turned to Carina, "I noticed that you did not eat much at lunch time. Are you eating enough food to sustain you?" Graer asked.

"Yes, I am. Gath makes sure I don't miss a meal."

"That is good to hear. Gath has a way of making sure everyone is fed, and we do want to make sure that everyone has proper sustenance in this sector. We're finished and you can get dressed. I'm sure you'll be relieved to know that all the tests are over."

"Thanks, Bondmate Graer."

"I was only doing my job, Carina, and after this examination, you may go back to calling me Chenaanah."

"Thanks, Bondmate Chenaanah."

Chenaanah smiled on her way out. She'd had to deal with the odd difficult girl over the years, especially when it came to wild ones which is what Daric had suggested Carina might be, so she knew exactly what to do to help the patient. Daric was more than capable of handling it himself but his subterfuge had made the difference in gaining Carina's trust.

Carina, unaware of the exact details of her examination, slowly got dressed. *It wasn't so bad after all. I closed my eyes and didn't feel a thing. Chenaanah is sure good at her job. Thank goodness, maybe she can take over all of the duties and I won't have to give any more needles or anything.*

Carina admonished herself for thinking negative of the Leaders. It seemed to her that they did indeed have the best interests of everyone in the sector. She could understand the importance of checking everyone's health within a sector. Daric had acted in an unexpected manner by showing kindness. She hadn't expected that from the previous interactions that she'd had with him. *Maybe he wasn't such a bad guy after all.*

# Daric Has Other Plans

Amazing what a little bit of crushed Caroweed can do to an unsuspecting person. Chenaanah knew it as an effective tool and one that she'd used successfully in the past. She had followed Daric's instructions precisely. She'd twinged with remorse for duping the only person she'd gotten to know in the sector, but she'd stuffed that away with the relief she felt doing something productive again—especially since she genuinely believed that she'd lost her position entirely by moving to this sector with her daughters.

It hadn't bothered her to be without a position when she'd first arrived in the sector, since she had Loriia and Liisa to keep her busy and she was their teacher as well as their mother. That all changed instantly when her daughters were kidnapped. Now it seemed that all she had on her hands and mind was time, lots of it. Her opportunity to participate in the Carrier Program once again pleased her. She'd been raised to believe her role as a woman was exactly what it was. She thought Carina was kind, but quite untrained for the duties of a healer's aide. It actually wasn't necessary that she regain her memory. If her file arrived, if it existed—and if it didn't exist, that would confirm her as a wild one, someone from the caves or mountains who had never been processed at any sector—it would enable the Leaders to categorize Carina and her assignment would be straightforward if she were found to be fertile instead of sterile like ninety-eight percent of the population. Then, it would only be a matter of choosing a compatible bondmate once Carina had been impregnated at the centre. Bondmate Graer had other duties to attend to in her reinstated role and needed to get on with her duties. She pushed the examination and her role in it out of her mind. She'd done her job on behalf of the Leaders and that was a reward within itself.


The actual tests done in the district were very limited; it didn't have the necessary equipment and tools required to analyze blood, fluids, or DNA. Daric originally thought he'd take it to the Northern Sector to be analyzed. Instead, he decided to attend to two problems at the same time and called Bondmate Graer into his office, well, Scott Lachash's office.

Knock. Knock.

"Come in." Daric looked up as Bondmate Graer entered the room. "Thank you for your earlier help. The Leaders appreciate your dedication to duty and the society."

Bondmate Graer blushed. "I am glad I could serve the Leaders."

"I called you in to ask you to perform a duty that you performed expertly in your last sector. I need someone who is knowledgeable with the tests that we require of both men and women, someone who knows the correct tests to request to confirm sterility or fertility. We have a backlog of tests that haven't been thoroughly analyzed and they need to be taken to the Northern Sector for immediate processing. You, of all people, can appreciate the utmost importance of these tests."

"Yes, I know how important all testing is. It is due to that testing that my two daughters were born in the first place."

"I think Carina may be a true candidate. Even if she is around thirty, she can still have babies."

"A breeder?" It had been more than three years since she'd seen a breeder. "That is good news, indeed. I hope I can assist in this case, if it is true."

"I was hoping you would say that, Bondmate Graer. I would like you to take all the testing done in this sector to the north and I would like you to be ready to leave within a half hour from now. I have selected eight reliable men who will see to your comfort and safety on your trip there."

"How can I possibly leave? The testing will take a few weeks to process. What if my daughters arrive back and I'm not here? I can't just leave without telling Malcom."

"I know you would not normally question an order from a Leader but I will be lenient because of your recent loss. Lachash is under orders to rest, there are no new patients, and there won't be for several days. I really want you to do this," he said as he placed his hand on her shoulder. "I understand that you want to be here and the sooner you leave, the sooner you can return. Malcom will be here soon. He'll be searching non-stop for your daughters. I truly believe you will benefit from being away from this sector. I want you to go back to the Northern Sector and revisit places that you went with your daughters so that when you come back and find them here, you will have all that you want."

Chenaanah's face lit up. "Really? You truly believe they will be here when I come back?"

"I have no doubt about it." Daric looked sincerely into her eyes as if he believed that he was omnipotent and had the power to do anything he wanted. "Now, I have taken more than enough of your time and I am afraid that the men might already be waiting for you outside in the square. They will enable you to do your duties. Why don't you check there before you do anything else?"

"But my duty is to be here for my daughters."

"You know your duty is to the sector and you know how important a breeder is, or have you forgotten what your life was like before you became a bondmate?"

"No, I have not forgotten." She lowered her head submissively. "Thank you for bringing me back to my senses. I will perform my duties immediately."

"Thank you, Bondmate Graer. I look forward to seeing you and your daughters soon."

Bondmate Graer left the room and hurried out. Reminded of her important role in finding a breeder was exciting but the tests were secondary to the excitement of seeing her daughters again. She knew Daric's reputation and felt confidence, once again, that her daughters would be found, and within a week or two she would be hugging them to her and never letting them out of her sight.


Daric did his job effectively while Bondmate Graer was absent; he oversaw all of the aspects of the sector, including security and processing. He made sure that everyone, including Carina, was busy preparing for the next assignment date. He took Carina with him on personal medical visits, if he found them necessary.

Daric knew that Carina probably wondered what happened to Bondmate Graer, so he thanked Carina for suggesting that Graer take over some of the nursing duties and explained where she was. "I know it helped take her mind off her daughters, but I thought that she might benefit from a few days away from here; about a month, actually. Give her distance and time to recover from her loss. We are still looking for her daughters and the other twelve missing people, but we have not had any success."

"I'm sorry you haven't found them."

"Yes, so am I." He grit his teeth. "But it isn't over yet. Those Banished will be learning a thing or two about attacking us."

Carina didn't respond to his comment about the Banished, just nodded, and then left the room.

Chenaanah Graer returned to the district over a month later. The tests themselves took only six days. She'd spent the first evening quietly in her room and begun the related work the next day. She had quickly attended to any file assigned to her, motivated by being back in the Northern Sector where she'd happily spent the last several years with her daughters. She'd even worked late into the evenings to speed her return to the Central Sector and, hopefully, her daughters. When the time dragged out because she was given other cases to work on, she became anxious.

Finally, arrangements were made and the two-week return trip passed by in a blur of worry and excitement. When she neared the Central Sector, her hopes rose. She entered the square where Helzion met her.

"Bondmate Graer. It is wonderful to have you back. I see colour in your cheeks. Good to see you doing so well."

Being as polite as possible, as was expected when speaking with a Leader, she didn't immediately ask about her daughters. "Yes, it has been a recuperative journey."

"Good, I am glad to hear that especially after—well, you know what I mean. Oh, look here, Carina has also arrived to greet you."

"Chenaanah. You're back. I'm so glad. I've managed to postpone all of those yucky tests for you."

Chenaanah laughed. "It is not that bad, Carina, you will see."

"I just saw Daric and he said that he'd like to speak with you as soon as you're refreshed from your journey."

"I think I will see him now. I have some work that I need to return to him and he might have some good news for me." While she was speaking, Chenaanah kept glancing around, as if hoping to see her daughters hiding and waiting to surprise her. She knew they probably were in class and there were strict rules applied when classes were in session. "It is good to see all of you. Perhaps I'll see you later for meals?"

"Definitely Bondmate Graer," Helzion said. "I will let you be on your way. I believe you will find Daric in his own offices. Do you know where to go?"

"Yes, everyone knows where the Leaders meet," she said as she hurried off.

Chenaanah quickly made her way to the low building that housed the Leaders' meeting place and their many separate rooms. She asked a Defender where Daric was and the Defender pointed out the direction. "He is expecting you, Bondmate Graer."

Daric had heard the horses and knew their significance. He didn't go out directly to meet Bondmate Graer when she arrived, as he needed a few extra minutes to prepare for their meeting. When he heard her footsteps, he stood behind his desk to say, "Bondmate Graer, welcome back."

"It is good to be back. Did you—?"

"No, we have not been successful in finding your daughters. I am very sorry."

She swallowed hard. "I brought the information that you asked for."

"That is great news. You have been very helpful and I am deeply grateful." He paused. "We won't give up our search."

"Thank you for trying. I appreciate it. If that is all, it has been a tiring journey and I would like to rest a bit." She didn't wait to share in any of the information that the files revealed, an indication of the depth of her disappointment at not finding her daughters waiting for her, as Daric had said would happen.

Daric didn't dwell on Bondmate Graer's sudden desire to return to her quarters. He was quickly lost in the files, delving into the information they contained. He just gave most a cursory glance until he found the one he was looking for. He quickly scanned the contents of the file and smiled.

# An Honour

Daric looked up from the desk. "Carina, I am glad that you were so prompt in getting here. I hope I wasn't interrupting anything. Have a seat so that we may talk."

Carina glanced around Lachash's office until her eyes settled on a file that lay on top of the desk. It had her name on it.

Daric saw where her eyes were focused. "Yes, it is your file, not the one from your previous sector, but the one containing the results of those tests Bondmate Graer took a month ago. The good news is that the tests show that you're a prime candidate for the Carrier Program."

"Lachash said the same thing. I told him that I wasn't ready to get bonded and settle down."

"Yes, he mentioned that, but it is an honour to be fertile."

"What does this honour entitle me to?"

"You will be bred with someone who is physically compatible, and then we will find you a suitable bondmate."

Carina stood up in shock. "I'll do no such thing."

"You know the law. You do not have any choice."

"No damn way. This is my body and no one is going to do anything to it. I'm not from here and your laws don't apply to me."

"Exactly where are you from?"

"I forget," Carina said a little more slowly.

"Well, I will overlook your backtalk because of your lack of memory, but I warn you, you're here in this sector and our laws apply."

"What other choices do I have?"

"You do not have any choices. You're a woman. If you are lucky, however, there is another option."

"And what is that?"

"It is possible that a Leader might choose you as his bondmate and you could have children with him."

"There aren't many Leaders to choose from, and it isn't likely I'll meet that many in the near future."

"I already know someone who is interested." Daric had stood up while he talked and walked up very close to Carina.

"Who?" She didn't look up, suddenly afraid of the answer.

"Me."

Carina spat out the words, "You? You're kidding. I don't remember who I am and I barely know you."

"Most women do not know their bondmates before they are bonded."

"I-I don't love you."

"Love, my dear Carina, has nothing to do with it, but…" He pulled Carina towards him; his arm around her low back prevented her from running. He looked deep into her eyes and then he kissed her.

Carina's eyes flew up to look at him in shock and surprise. She hadn't expected this.

"You have such a beautiful body, Carina, made for loving."

She didn't have time to react to his comment as a sharp knock on the door interrupted them.

"Come in." He released Carina reluctantly.

Helzion and Malcom entered. If Helzion was surprised to see Daric and Carina together, he didn't show it. Malcom's face, on the other hand, was a rigid mask.

"Daric, Carina," Helzion said.

Daric shook both their hands. They grasped each other's wrists in a firm grip and then released it, followed by touching the right fist to the left side of their chest.

"I have been looking at Carina's medical file and I have decided that she would make me the perfect bondmate."

Helzion beamed. "Congratulations on your wise choice. I think you have chosen well. Her features and personality are a plus for you. I believe the other Leaders will agree when we next meet. Congratulations, Carina," he said as he kissed her on both cheeks.

Malcom did likewise but an unreadable emotion flickered in his eyes when he looked at her. He then shook Daric's hand again.

Daric's revelation stunned Carina, and she could only smile mutely.

"Please go and finish your duties, Carina. I would like to speak to Helzion and Malcom. I'll expect to see you at supper time," he added.

Carina nodded and turned to leave the office; her insides were screaming. She saw Chenaanah in Lachash's room and went directly to Ritik's room after she nodded at the Defender outside his door. "Hello, Ritik."

"Hello, Carina."

"Do you know anything about the Carrier Program?" she asked without preamble.

"Yes, it is another word for selective breeding, trying to ensure that the best of the society will survive."

"Why?"

"We have no way of knowing if there is anyone else left in the world because the sectors are cut off from it. We have tried endless times to find a way beyond our borders but there is no protection from the sun. Many have died exploring the land. For us the rest of the world no longer exists and it is their responsibility to create a new world order."

Carina's mind reeled with his words. They made her realize her limitations. She was trapped and she would be forced to have children because there was nowhere else to go.

"This program, is that why everyone gets tested?"

"Yes. If you have what the Leaders want, they will go to any length and they will coerce you, if necessary."

"I suppose if you're a man, it must be quite good."

"No, you get assigned to whatever the Leaders choose, and some aren't allowed to marry. You're just a tool used to meet their ends. The women are chattel and even their bodies aren't their own if they can bear children."

Both heard the door click shut. "Do you have any idea what would happen to you if anyone heard you?" Malcom demanded. "Ritik, you should know better."

"I'm sorry, Malcom. I wasn't thinking."

"Damn right, you weren't thinking. I just left Daric and Helzion in the office. What if they'd walked in on your discussion? Of anyone to watch out for at any given moment, it's Daric, and he is at the top of the list." He turned to Carina. "Have you told him?"

"Told me what?" Ritik's eyes lit up curiously.

"I have been picked for the Program. Daric chose me."

"What do you mean?"

"He wants her for his bondmate," Malcom said.

"My word."

"I have to go out, but we'll talk about this later." Malcom left the room as abruptly as he had entered it.

Carina quickly followed him and nearly ran into Chenaanah as she was coming down the hall. "I'm sorry. I wasn't watching where I was going."

"No problem. Is something wrong?"

"Uh, no, I was just rushing to collect the trays from our patients."

Later in the afternoon, Carina made her excuses to Chenaanah. "I am feeling really tired so I think I will miss supper this evening. I ate too much at lunch. Would you mind telling anyone who asks that I'm resting?"

"You know, I wouldn't mind avoiding everyone right now, too."

"Maybe Gath can give us a tray to tide us over until morning. You go back to the sleeping room, and I'll see what he says."


Carina entered the cookery. "Gath?"

"Yes?"

"Bondmate Graer is feeling under the weather. I guess she's taking the loss of her daughters harder than we thought. She doesn't want to go to the dining room to eat tonight. I have convinced her to rest and I'll bring her a meal. I said I would eat with her. Would you mind making up a tray?"

"My pleasure, it will be only a moment."


Carina and Chenaanah had an uninterrupted evening. They talked quietly together.

"Did Malcom choose you?"

"Yes, we met while I was working in the Carrier Program. Malcom was a little shy back then and we almost didn't meet but when we did, we fell in love almost immediately."

Carina smiled. "Sounds romantic."

"Yes, Malcom was a charmer back then, once he got over his shyness with women, and I was more than willing to be his bondmate."

"What do you think of the Program? Do you truly believe that what they're doing is right?"

"It isn't my place to judge."

"Do you think it is fair that women don't have control over their own bodies and that their lives are determined by others?"

Women have existed under this system for a long time and it works," she said robotically.

"Nevertheless, women should have the right to have control of their own lives and that includes procreation."

"No one really has control of their own lives." Chenaanah spoke to Carina as if she were a child. "The Leaders provide the structure and cohesion that keeps our society together. Now, I am a bit tired so I think I'll go to bed."

"Goodnight." Carina didn't know what to make of Chenaanah's response, but wished her a pleasant sleep.


A sound awoke Carina in the middle of the night. She listened carefully and heard sobbing. It was Chenaanah. Carina got out of bed and walked over to her bed. "Chenaanah?" she whispered.

"I-I am sorry," she hiccupped, "I did not mean to wake you. I began thinking about Loriia and Liisa, and I couldn't help myself."

"Shhhh," Carina said as she hugged Chenaanah, "you don't have to make apologies. Not knowing where your daughters are and how they're doing must be a horrible feeling for you to be going through."

Chenaanah cried softly until, as Carina sat beside her, finally she quieted, and Carina realized that she'd fallen asleep. Carina lay her down and covered her with a warm blanket. *I'll talk to Malcom tomorrow.*


The dining room was quiet when Carina and Chenaanah entered to eat their breakfasts.

"Where is everyone?" Carina asked Marta.

"They left early for a scheduled meeting of some sort and they left with an armed escort of Defenders."

The unexpected reprieve from the Leaders enabled Carina to think about her situation. She used the afternoon to visit the patients briefly and then a prolonged visit with Ritik.

"Hello, Ritik."

"Hello, Carina."

"I have come to check your wound and change the bandaging. I desperately need to talk to you about yesterday."

"You left so quickly that I wasn't sure that I'd heard correctly. Daric has chosen you for his bondmate?"

"Your stomach is wounded but not your hearing," Carina said shortly. "You should have been out of this bed already but they seem to be keeping you here."

"I'm sorry, but I am just stunned, that's all. I'm surprised to hear that Daric wants you for his wife. We sure didn't expect that. He's a very shrewd character and I'm sure he has his own reasons."

"You're stunned. How do you think I feel? I've just become chattel."

"This isn't something we considered. This could change everything."

"What do you mean?"

"Has your memory returned yet?"

"No."

"I didn't want to go on until you had your memory back."

"Go where?"

"You, Carina," Ritik paused, "have been sent to us. We genuinely assumed it was a legend, not reality, that a visitor wearing the armband depicting the battle between the underworld and the heavens would lead us into a new time."

Carina thought of the dragon and the phoenix, and a picture blossomed in her mind: The dragon was attached to the underworld and all manner of bad things, while the phoenix showed goodness, light, and the promise of continuing life.

"You mean me?" Carina asked incredulously.

"Yes, you. Malcom said he saw the armband. Let me see it. There is the legend: 'And the time will come when a stranger to the land will wield the power of the Dragon and Phoenix to end the conflict and bring peace to the land.'"

"I remember now! I know that legend!" she said in surprise. "I saw a tapestry with those words on it the first day I got to this sector, only I had no idea where I was. You think I'm that person?"

Carina pulled her blouse down just enough to reveal her shoulder and upper arm. Ritik stared at the armband. Carina's eyes dropped to the once-dormant stone as it began pulsing. Mesmerized, she stared at the dragon and the phoenix as they circled the armband. A piercing red light flashed out and caught Carina in its intense glow. The two watched the characters revolve until Chenaanah's voice broke the spell. "Where are you?"

"In here," she called. "I'm just changing Ritik's bandaging."

"Oh, good. He is the patient that I want to see. I have to prepare him for recultivation."

"Recultivation?" Ritik responded. "I assumed that was no longer needed after my debriefing was completed. I'm not a threat to the sector!"

Carina could feel the tension in Ritik's rigid body.

"It is not my place to say. They are preparing the pit now." She looked at Carina. "I need your assistance preparing him."

Carina glanced at Ritik's eyes and saw raw and naked fear. It chilled her and her heart thumped hard against her ribs. Her arm suddenly felt warm and she quickly covered the armband.

Ritik caught the movement and his fear turned into something else. "Relax," he whispered, "or you'll endanger us both."

Somehow her emotional response and the armband were linked together. *Why didn't I notice this before?* Her mind reeled with the idea that she was the glowing girl in the tapestry. She strove for control and managed to sound nonchalant as she spoke. "I saw that Lachash somehow managed to soak his cast and it needs to be replaced. You know how demanding a patient he can be. Would you change the bandage?"

Chenaanah laughed. "Tell me about it. He gave me a stern lecture on the importance of serving meals on time to the patients. Good for their disposition. I'll tend to him and then I will return."

As soon as she heard the door click behind her, Carina demanded, "What's going on? What's the pit? What's recultivation? Why are you so afraid?" The armband flashed beneath her blouse and Ritik reached up to cover the blue flash that it was emitting.

"This is an unexpected complication. If you can't control it, you'll be discovered."

Irritation showed on her face. "I can't control it."

He gripped her arm tightly. "You can and you have to. Now isn't the time to lose control of yourself and do something ludicrous. If they recultivate you, we're doomed."

"Then tell me what's going on. What are they going to do to you?"

"Not until you calm down. You're not going to like what I'm going to tell you and your reaction is going to get worse."

She forced herself to hold her breath while she mustered up visions of flowers and pussycats. "Calm, smelling flowers, soft pussycats purring. Soft pussy cats purring." Her breath gushed out. "I'm better. I'm not glowing in the dark anymore."

Ritik looked at her strangely.

At his perplexed look, she said, "The armband isn't flashing."

"I don't know how much time we have, so I'm going to talk as quickly as possible. Don't interrupt and stay calm."

"Whenever someone says to stay calm, I know something bad is about to happen."

"It was a risk coming here. I had to ascertain if you were the one we've been waiting for. If you are, you're going to have to make decisions, repercussive decisions that will forever alter everyone."

Carina's opened her mouth to speak but closed it as his hand covered it.

"I wanted to bring you to my brother, to teach you everything you're going to need to know to survive but now there's no time. The only thing I've accomplished is learning that you and the armband are united. Your emotions trigger a response. If you can control your reactions and learn to use the armband's power, you can alter the world."

"You're insane," she blurted out as she pushed him away.

"Control yourself!" He ordered harshly and then softly, "Insanity is the least of our worries. If I am recultivated, I could give away all of my secrets. I'll betray my brother, and the hundreds of men whose lives will be threatened as a result. And you—I'll betray you." He broke off in anguish.

She leaned forward. "How can you betray them? Haven't you learned some kind of technique or knowledge to repel them?"

His eyes met hers and beckoned. "Sit down and listen carefully."

She sat on the side of the bed. Her eyes focused intensely on his face.

"There's a locked room here called the Pit. It's used for remaking people."

"What?"

"The Leaders bury people up to their necks before they're forced to swallow a seed."

"What kind—"

"The seed absorbs them and sends out shoots, but they don't bear fruit. The 'fruit' is the victim—remade. Every memory forgotten, wiped clean, and then they re-teach them to be perfect members of society." He spat out the last words as if they were poison.

"Good God!" Carina sat back, rubbing her face nervously.

"It's a fact. You've heard mention of it, I'm sure."

Pasty-faced, she nearly wept in realization. "Why didn't I figure it out? Cultivate: Plant. Recultivate: Replant."

"Are you all right?"

"Am I all right? Hell, no! Are you all right? You've just told me the most horrific thing I've ever heard, and you ask me if I'm all right." She stopped her frenzied pacing. "I won't have any part of this horror."

"Keep your voice down," he admonished, "or I won't be able to finish what I have to say."

She kept running her hand through her hair repeatedly; if she'd seen herself at the moment, she wouldn't have recognized the scared banshee she looked like. *Focus, Carina, focus. Pretty flowers, lilacs, my favourite, soft pussycats, Siamese pussycats, pussycats, pussycats. His fear, he was terrified when he heard about recultivation.*

They froze when they heard noises in the hall. Carina jumped off the bed. "It's Chenaanah. How am I to explain why I've taken so long?" She ran to the sink to wash her hands. "I'll say I just finished."

The expected interruption didn't happen. She gingerly stepped toward the bed while eyeing the door nervously. She forced herself to meet Ritik's eyes, "If they recult"—she cut the word in half as the word stuck in her mouth distastefully—"remake you, what happens to you then?"

"Me? I won't care about anything. I'll be oblivious to everything except what the Leaders teach me, mold me into, but I'll be killing everyone I know, have known, and love. Mass contamination means mass recultivation."

"The Leaders win no matter what then?"

"If they recultivate you, Carina, then nothing can stop them." He paused. His face lit up enigmatically.

She saw it. "What is it? Have you found a way to stop this?"

"Yes." He licked his dry lips. "I know exactly what we need to do."

Her stomach tightened manically when, in a rush, he told her his epiphany.

# The Ceremony

## 25

If Chenaanah noticed Carina's paleness when she entered Lachash's room, she didn't comment on it. "I was delayed preparing the Pit. The men had to remove the wooden boards and stretchers that we used during that fight a couple months ago," Chenaanah explained.

"Yes, it must have been a mess. I had completely forgotten about it."

"It is ready for the ceremony."

"The ceremony?" Carina managed to ask.

Lachash looked at her with concern. "Are you feeling all right?"

She lowered her eyes. "It has been a surprising day."

"I heard your test results were in. What did Daric tell you?" Chenaanah asked.

"Do you mean did he tell me I had two possible futures?"

Chenaanah looked at Carina, cocked her head.

Carina, seeing her look, replied, "He said I was a good candidate for the Carrier Program and he'd find a bondmate for me after I'd been impregnated, and then he said the alternative was to marry a Leader—and he wants to be that Leader."

"What an honour," Chenaanah said.

"You're a very fortunate young woman," Lachash said.

"You must be excited." Chenaanah gushed.

"Excited isn't the exact word I would use," Carina said warily.

"Don't tell me you still believe in love and such nonsense," Lachash reproached her.

"Lachash, I won't marry someone I neither know nor love. Please excuse me; I have other duties to attend to."

Carina bustled out of the room before Chenaanah or Lachash could say anything else.


Chenaanah found Carina in the sleeping quarters later that evening. "Is that why you were asking all those questions last night? Because Daric wants you for his bondmate? That explains the rush to have the full results of the testing that was done."

"I don't even know the man," Carina said, exasperated.

"It will feel strange but you will accept him eventually."

"What if I don't? I'll be trapped with a man who I might detest, or who might detest me. I don't think I could stand to be trapped in a marriage."

"No one could detest you, Carina."

"I think I should have the right to choose my own bondmate."

"This is the established law in all of the sectors and you can't do anything about it. You will just have to accept it."

"I won't accept it." Carina stood up as she spoke and turned to leave the room. She couldn't go anywhere to be alone except the front stairs. She went and sat there until night was well under way and then returned to her room.

She hadn't been there long before she heard a knock at the door. When she opened it, she saw Elzak standing there.

"Yes?"

"The Leaders Daric and Helzion request your attendance."

"My attendance? For what?"

"The Ceremony of Rebirth."

She stood there open-mouthed.

"Here, put this on."

She looked down at the white robe he thrust at her. "What is it?"

Elzak was close-mouthed, "It's required."

"Why aren't you wearing one?"

"I wasn't chosen to attend. I'll wait here while you change." He turned away before she could ask anything else.

Carina turned, closed the door, and leaned heavily against it. Already her arm was flashing hotly. *Oh, God. They* are *going to make me watch. How can I do this?* She touched the armband and heard Ritik's words, "You can do it. You can close your eyes so that you don't have to watch."

"Miss Carina," Elzak's voice broke her concentration. "We have to go now without delay."

"I'm coming." *Close my eyes. Pussy willows and kitty cats....*

Two Defenders joined them at the main door.

Elzak nodded to them and left. She felt herself led forward. They crossed the open square to the clinic that lay in utter darkness, belying its latent threat.

"Why is it so dark?"

Her escort quelled her words, "You must not speak."

They led her through the dark halls and knocked at the door they'd brought her to.

Helzion opened it. "Be welcome, Seed-Bearer."

The Defenders thrust her forward and Carina heard the soft yet solid click of the door as it sealed her escape behind her. The dimly lit room appeared ghostly in the cloying candle smoke and incense that clung in the air. She coughed as her sudden inhalation carried the sickly sweet smoke down her throat.

"This is your first time at a rebirth, Carina. You have been honoured to attend. Follow me."

Helzion left her standing frozen against the door. He turned after a few steps, a flash of annoyance crossing his face.

Carina stepped forward and reluctantly followed him, expecting to sit on the outskirts of the room.

She saw a square of darkness that lay unlit by the candles—the pit. *Where is Ritik?*

Helzion didn't stop until he reached it. Light flared and, for a moment, Carina thought it was her armband because her stomach lurched when she saw Ritik buried in the pit with only his head showing above the earth. Then she saw Daric. Loathing pushed away her fear as she was brought directly before him.

His face was eerily ecstatic as he saw her, but he didn't pause in the words he was intoning. Unknown words curled from his mouth as the pitch of his voice rose and fell. He went on for several minutes, simultaneously tracing intricate patterns around Ritik's head with his black oak staff.

Carina felt something pushed into her hand, but she was too enthralled at the hypnotizing words and patterns to take much notice.

Abruptly, Daric's words cut into her fugue. "Seed-Bearer, step forward."

She looked up and saw his arrogant eyes challenging her to disobey. She stepped forward without volition and found herself uttering words in a language she didn't know but understood. "I am the Seed-Bearer—the life-giver. Destroying but not desecrating the sanctity of this man." She swayed rhythmically to the words, stepping barefoot into the pit. Awareness of another presence filled her when her feet touched the earth there.

Daric led her hand to Ritik's face and nodded.

Even in her heady trance, tears welled up as she slowly took the seed and placed it in Ritik's mouth.

\*

She avoided Chenaanah as much as she could during the next few days. Even Gath was unsuccessful in drawing her out of the wall she'd built around herself. Lachash had returned to his duties and was giving commands left, right, and center. Chenaanah and Carina were kept busy sterilizing the rooms and everything in them. Carina didn't complain as it kept her too busy to think.

Chenaanah wisely didn't mention Daric or the Carrier Program when she talked with Carina. But after getting the cold shoulder for three days, she figured that she had to make amends.

Carina came into the waiting room.

"Carina," Chenaanah called, "we have been so busy ever since Lachash started walking around again that I have not had a chance to talk to you. I am going to be taking blood samples today; did you want to watch and see how it is done?"

"I'll watch what you're doing but don't ask me to take anybody's blood."

"Three people need to be done, so I'll get the equipment and we can get started."

"Sure."

"First we pick an arm that shows the most promising vein. I have this rubber tubing that I tie around the upper arm. See, the vein is more prominent now."

"Do you have to give us detail by detail description?" the patient asked. "I really don't want to know."

"Carina is learning how to do this task, and you will just have to be still while I do the test. No need to worry, she's only watching," Chenaanah explained. "Lachash said that you have given a couple of injections to him already."

"Yes, but aren't those different types of needles? Thicker?"

Chenaanah continued to name the appropriate steps of the procedure. "Taking the blood is easier than watching."

Carina winced as she watched the slim-looking needle slide under the skin and into the vein. "I think I'll just watch if you don't mind."

"Sure." Chenaanah grinned.

After their rounds, Chenaanah and Carina were both nervous about going to eat in the dining room, although they had different reasons. Chenaanah knew Malcom was back and was nervous about seeing him, and Carina wanted to avoid Daric. They both walked into the dining room as if waiting for someone to jump out at them, and sat at one of the smaller tables. They were already eating when Malcom and Daric entered the room and joined the women at their table.

"Hello, ladies. It is a pleasure to see you again after so many days," Daric said, but his eyes lingered on Carina. "It is a shame we're running late, and we could not join you sooner. Had I known how much your presence lit up the room, I would have made sure we arrived sooner." He bent and kissed Carina on her cheek, startling her.

She tried not to jerk away in repulsion. The night of the ceremony was hazy, but she remembered Daric's eyes. "Hello, Daric, won't you have a seat?"

She also remembered Ritik's blank, soulless eyes as she slipped the seed into his mouth and watched as they glazed over. She pushed the horrifying memory away and forced a smile on her face. "Did anything new happen while we were away?"

"It has been really quiet since you left the sector after the ceremony. Lachash is back on his feet."

"Yes, Helzion went to see him."

"How about you two? Where were you off to?"

"Well, that is the good news. We met with the other Leaders, and they approved our bonding and they want to formalize it at the next month end meeting."

Everyone at the table was silent for their own reasons.

"What is this I hear about bonding?" Lachash, who'd just arrived, asked.

"Carina is going to be my bondmate."

"Congratulations."

"Congratulations," Helzion echoed.

A few minutes later Chenaanah asked, "Have you found out anything that will lead us to my daughters?"

The table's occupants went silent. "This isn't the appropriate place to be discussing such matters," Daric reprimanded her.

Wild-eyed, Chenaanah retorted, "Well, where is the appropriate place?"

"Carina, would you please take Bondmate Graer back to her room. I can see that her loss still upsets her."

Carina was going to make a comment but there was something in the set of their faces that broached no questions. "Yes, I will. Come with me, Chenaanah."

"No!" Chenaanah shouted. "I want my daughters."

"Malcom, look to your bondmate," Helzion ordered.

Malcom got up and, between them, they led Chenaanah out of the dining room away from all the eyes that were following their movements.

"Let's take her to the healer's examining room," Malcom commented. "She can lie down in one room and then you can go to get the healer from the dining room. Maybe he can give her a Caroweed draught."

Carina went in search of Lachash and told him what Malcom had asked her to do. "Malcom has taken Chenaanah to the examining room until you arrive."

Lachash nodded and left the dining room. Helzion had already departed. Carina had intended to go with Lachash, but Daric asked her to wait. He stood up and took her by her arm. Carina looked around, besides noises from the cookery, the dining room had mysteriously emptied. Swiftly before Carina could react, Daric pulled her into his arms and kissed her.

She pushed him away. "This is happening too fast for me, Daric. I don't even know you."

"We have a lifetime to get to know each other."

"You mean until you can cast me aside?" She blurted out the first thing that came to mind.

"Where did you hear that?"

"Why do you suppose that Bondmate Graer is so upset? She no longer has her daughters and believes that Malcom will soon choose another bondmate."

"I assure you that won't happen to you."

"You don't know the future."

Daric's grip on Carina's arm tightened.

"Ow. You're hurting me."

"We have had to talk to Malcom about her. We need him to return fully to his duties without having any kind of distraction. That is why I made a bid for you."

"What does that mean?"

"Malcom is enamored with you. Lachash said that it sometimes happens that a sick or injured person forms a personal attachment for his caregiver. I had to put a halt to it at once. I need Malcom for other things."

"So, your bid for me is just a scam to get him back into line?"

"I am sure it will be a profitable situation. Once I checked your file, I figured that having you for a bondmate would be good for me—and, a good way to keep Malcom and Chenaanah together."

"I'm being used to manipulate Malcom and Chenaanah into compliance?"

"Essentially, but you sound offended. There is no reason to be offended. You have a wonderful opportunity and can only benefit by it."

Carina tore her arm free. "I have no intention of being your bondmate or anyone else's until I'm ready and until I choose my own bondmate." She understood the futility of her words but had to say them.

Daric laughed deeply. "That is preposterous. Women don't choose anything unless we let them."

Carina stormed out of the dining room, seething. *What the hell am I going to do now?* She hurried to see if Chenaanah was all right and met Malcom just as he was leaving the healer's office.

"Malcom, before you go, may I have a word with you? How is Chenaanah?"

"Lachash gave her some Caroweed potion. I had not realized that she was taking this so seriously."

"Of course she's been taking the abduction of her daughters seriously. And she's afraid you'll reject her and choose another bondmate. Sometimes she cries at night."

"She should know better."

"Know better? What else can she think? You've been absent for two years and now that you're back, you manage to be too busy to see her. She's had to deal with the loss of her daughters by herself because you haven't even acknowledged her feelings or comforted her. No wonder she assumes you're rejecting her for someone else." Carina looked into his eyes and saw that there was some merit to Chenaanah's fears. "You were considering it, weren't you?" Carina accused him.

"It isn't what you think."

"What do I think? I think that you came back here, didn't feel particularly close to her, and your missing daughters gave you a perfect excuse to abandon her. You even found a replacement for her, didn't you? But that has backfired now that Daric has made a bid for me."

"No, it isn't what you think. I don't believe in what she does for a job."

"Why don't you talk to her?"

"It's no use."

"Are you saying this as a Banished or as a Leader? Either way, you have an excuse to cover your actions."

Malcom winced at Carina's harsh words but didn't deny them.

"Look, Malcom, I'm flattered that you'd want me for a bondmate, and that does explain your behaviour in the past, but you have a wife and two lovely daughters, who we all hope will be found. Your wife has committed herself to you. You have a history together. If you're a Leader, you will reject her and take another bondmate. If you're a

Banished like you claim, then you will make it work. From what I understand, Banished don't like the way the Leaders run this society. Which philosophy is yours?"

"It is complicated, Carina. What if she doesn't understand what has happened and she reports me?"

"Then you deal with it. I think you owe it to her and to yourself."

After a few moments, Malcom said, "You're right. I don't like what she does, but it's not her fault; she knows nothing else. I do still have feelings for her; I'm not insensitive, I've just been preoccupied."

"Then you need to find out, don't you?"

"Telling her will jeopardize everything if she won't join me."

"Wasn't it you who said: Be discreet? Don't rush anything. You have two years to make up for. Take your time with her and help her cope with the loss of your daughters. I think she's strong enough to deal with their loss, but not your loss, too."

"I guess I have a lot of work to do. About choosing you, what sane man wouldn't? Daric has grown into a powerful man and I have been gone too long to challenge him. I supposed I could protect you by marrying you."

"That's very gallant, but protecting me at the expense of your wife would never agree with me. I could never fully trust in someone who could be so calculating."

"Like Daric?"

"Especially like Daric. He said that he made a bid for me only to bring you back in line. I told him that I would never marry someone I didn't know or love."

"How did he react? He could imprison you. Send you for recultivation to make you more compliant."

Her hand, of its own volition, slapped Malcom across the face. "How dare you repeat their threats of recultivation especially after what I saw, after what they made me do to Ritik?"

"I detest recultivation with every fibre of my being. They believe it was an honour they bestowed on you. I can understand why Daric manipulated the situation to choose you now that you're betrothed."

"An honour?" Her voice rose. "I demolished a man and had a monster take his place."

"He isn't a monster. He is exactly what he was before, physically, right down to the cleft on his chin. The only difference is that he does not recollect his life before the rebirth."

A flash of insight stopped her tirade midstride. She almost kissed Malcom as revelations filled her. She could scarcely contain her excitement as she forced herself to speak calmly. "You're right, I'm overreacting. I don't know what came over me. About Daric, what do you suggest I do? Marry him?"

"If need be."

His reply surprised her. "What?"

"You're supposed to be here to bring an end to this society and deliver freedom to the people. So far, I haven't seen that. You don't have your memory. You don't know where you're from. If you don't know where you're from, how can you figure out where you're supposed to go or why you're here? If you're just an ordinary person, marry Daric, and have a respectable life as a Leader's bondmate. He can do many things for you. The only reason I haven't given up on you is that Ritik swears you're the one because you removed the broken knife blade from him by some unknown power. You have to get your memory back. Who knows, maybe you're meant to marry him."

"The last time you walked in on Ritik and me, a bright red light had just come out of the bracelet and begun circling me."

"Then what happened?"

"You came into the room and it was gone."

"Show me the bracelet."

Carina moved to comply.

"No wait, turn here, down the alley, no, there's too much light and one of the Defenders might mention that he saw us together."

And indeed just then Elzak came walking down the street in their direction.

"Malcom, I think that you should come with me and see your bondmate immediately. She's very upset about her missing daughters and you will have to comfort her before she becomes even more distraught."

Elzak heard Carina's last sentence.

Malcom nodded. "Yes, you're right. I'll go there right now."

"Wait," Carina called. "I'll go with you. I have to check on another patient."

They moved off toward the building and Elzak walked by, continuing his patrol.

They went into one of the examining rooms. "Let me see the armband."

"Excuse me," she said, "it won't move." She pulled the material down over her shoulder and revealed the armband.

"You have a beautiful shoulder."

"We're here to look at the armband."

"Of course. You said that it began to send out a light?"

"Ritik had just told me that I had been sent to help."

"Then it happened?"

"No, uh, I'm not sure. I think so. Nothing is happening now."

Carina looked down at the armband.

"I have to check in on Chenaanah. Thank you for telling me about her and…" he paused, "reminding me of my duties."


Malcom searched for Chenaanah and saw Lachash with her.

When he saw Malcom, he motioned for him to enter. "She is much calmer now. Try talking to her."

"Chenaanah? It's Malcom. How are you feeling?"

She opened her eyes.

"I just came by to see that you were all right. I can't have my girl getting sick on me."

Tears came to her eyes. "You haven't called me that in a very long time."

"I know. I should have said it sooner. A lot happened while I was away." He stroked her cheek. "But I'm still the man you fell in love with and you are still the only love for me."

Chenaanah sighed as her eyes teared up.

"Don't cry." He pulled her close and kissed her gently on the lips. "I love you and I always will."

She returned his kiss. "Oh, Malcom."

He lowered her back onto the pillow. "I know. A lot has changed since we were a close family." He paused uncertainly. "I don't just mean Loriia and Liisa. I'm going to tell you something that's extremely dangerous to know, and because I want you and me and yes, our daughters to be a family, I'm going to tell you."

"What is it, Malcom?"

"I think, I'm a Banished, I mean, I am a Banished," he blurted out.

"You're a what? You mean those scum who took my daughters?"

"Light of my life, trust me. I love you and I need you to believe in me. Can you do that? That's why there is such conflict everywhere; there aren't just two groups. Yes, it has been the Leaders versus the Banished but there is another group, the Scavengers. They're the ones who have been taking people. They're very dangerous."

"I love you, Malcom, but it's a shock to hear you declare yourself a Banished."

"I know, but it means I can and will get our daughters back."

She hugged him fiercely. "Oh, Malcom."

He held her to him and stroked her hair. "It will be all right."

Chenaanah's arms relaxed their hold and Malcom saw that the Caroweed had done its work and she'd fallen asleep.

Carina brought breakfast to the patients early the next morning. Chenaanah was in the office waiting for her and helped her deliver the food.

Surprised to find her calm and efficient, Carina caught Chenaanah's eye. "You look like you are feeling better this morning?"

"I am better, thank you."

"You're sure?"

"Malcom came to visit me last night."

"How did that go?"

Chenaanah's voice dropped to a whisper. "He said that you weren't abducted by the Banished."

"True. It was another bunch called the Scavengers. When the fighting was going on there seemed to be only the Banished and the Leaders, but when I tried to escape from the Banished another group tried to grab me. They called themselves the Scavengers."

"So you do not know if you believe fully in the Leaders?"

"Chenaanah, my memories are only of this current sector. I don't know where I came from, who I was before I came here, or anything about either group. I don't know the laws, and I keep saying the wrong things. It is very frustrating."

"I'm sorry, I understand now."

"Does this have anything to do with what Malcom said to you last night?"

"He said that if the group called the Banished or the Leaders don't have my daughters, the Scavengers might."

"But the Banished and Leaders are on opposite sides. I've mentioned the Scavengers but no one has listened."

"I think that sometimes it's good not to be heard."

Carina raised an eyebrow but didn't say anything more when she saw Lachash walking toward them.

"Ladies. You both are busy today. I saw that everyone already has their breakfasts. Chenaanah, I'll need your help with Marta; she's burned herself in the cookery. Carina, I think our Banished patient can have his bandages permanently removed."

Everyone hurried off to do their duties.

There was only one Banished with bandages: Ritik. Carina rushed to his room. There he lay, just as she'd left him before the ceremony.

"Ritik, are you awake?" she whispered as she gently touched his arm.

Ritik opened his eyes.

She gushed at his response. "I'm so glad you're all right."

"Why do you call me Ritik? My name is Rysh."

"Rysh?" Carina faltered. "You don't remember me?"

Confused, he asked, "Should I?"

"It's me, Carina."

"Ah, Carina. Daric spoke of you, his betrothed. You have been greatly honoured to be a Leader's Chosen. You're here to remove my bandages. Daric told me that I was wounded in a fierce battle with the Banished and that's why I can't remember my past."

Reminded of her task, she asked, "May I look at them?" Her hands shook as she slowly removed the bandaging until she saw his skin beneath them. "What the—? They're gone?" She scanned his stomach.

"Amazing, isn't it?"

Carina jumped as Malcom's voice broke the quiet. "The scars are gone."

"He's been remade."

"He doesn't remember who he is."

"He'll remember his duties," he paused meaningfully, "as a Defender."

Carina looked at Malcom. The bleakness in his eyes ravished her soul. He returned her look and whispered, "He's lost."

"I still have the armband."

"A pretty piece, but until you learn how to use it, your only choice might be to wed Daric or—"

"I can't."

"Or be remade like Ritik." His last words fell like an irrefutable judgment.

Suddenly frightened, Carina left and went into the nearest empty examining room. She kept her eyes downcast as she closed the door and then leaned heavily against it, her breath exploding from her. Carina remained in the examining room for several minutes, huddling in one corner with her arms and head resting on her bent knees. *How can I escape this madness?*

# Where Is She? 26

Detective Dawes was unsuccessful in tracking Carina down after she disappeared from the restaurant. He drove through White Rock several times, approaching Crescent Beach from several different directions. He had walked from one end of the sandy beach to the other. One entrance had a restaurant at one corner and the road dead-ended beside the restaurant. There were only a few other stops before the beach.

*Which building is it?*

*God, how long have I been searching here?*

The sky was already beginning to darken into shades of navy blue as the sun began its descent. He turned his car around and began to drive away slowly. He had not gone far when he glanced though his side mirror. Someone must have bumped it, he thought because the mirror was turned to the side. He manipulated it into place and, as he did, a blue building flashed briefly in the mirror's reflection. He turned the mirror. It wasn't a blue building. It was a painting on the building. He didn't know why, but he brought the vehicle to a quick stop, got out, and turned to examine the painted wall.

"Wow," he breathed.

The artist who'd rendered this drawing had depicted a marine vista, frolicking dolphins, and whales. He saw the scrawled artist's signature: Wyland.

"Could this be the building?" He asked himself. "It has to be. Carina said she saw the building as she approached Crescent Beach. I know that if I saw this huge mural, I would pause. It's too bad they're building beside it; no one is going to see this painting anymore."

The small restaurant was closed; it was already 7:00 PM. Carina had been missing for almost nine hours. He peered into the small coffee shop. "I'll have to come back tomorrow and see the interior."

He woke at home at five the following morning and the lights were still on. He'd read until sleep claimed him. He decided that he'd drive to White Rock for breakfast at the restaurant with the painted whales.

He arrived in White Rock and headed toward Crescent Beach. It was 6:30 AM. He used the time to study and photograph the side of the building. He went inside when the restaurant opened. There were six tables that sat two people and then four booths that sat four people, inside. He chose a booth, ordered breakfast, and read the *Vancouver Sun* while waiting.

There was a steady stream of people for the first hour and a half and then, around eight in the morning, there was only one other customer left in the restaurant. Jackson glanced up briefly as the customer, an elderly lady, leaning heavily on her cane, went by his table and opened the door to the restroom.

Carina, however, looked up as she heard the door open. She was shocked to find herself sitting on a cold, tiled floor in the corner of a wheelchair-access bathroom cubicle. She got shakily to her feet and left. She went to one sink and stared at her image—unchanged, it seemed.

Carina stiffened as the other cubicle door opened. Carina exhaled when she didn't recognize the older woman.

"Good morning," the woman greeted her.

"Good morning," she uttered automatically.

"It's going to be beautiful today. I wish Calgary had the same beautiful weather and scenery that White Rock has."

Carina couldn't speak for a moment as her memories flooded back, and then replied, "Yes, Calgary is very dry compared to here. However, it does have the mountains in the distance."

"You've been there?"

"My mom lives there."

"Oh, how nice. You have a pleasant day, dear."

"Thank you. You, too."

Carina ran the water, cupping some in her hands and splashing her face repeatedly. The cold water refreshed her and made her jump from one train of thought to another. *Great,* she thought, *I have managed to jump from one reality to another. How did I get to White Rock? I was in Surrey when I left. God, Jackson must have had a bird to see me disappear. I hope my car is outside or I'll be hitch-hiking home. Maybe I can phone Kelly to pick me up.* She straightened her jean skirt, which changed to a lighter colour when she was in the sector, and inhaled deeply for fortitude before opening the restroom door. She found herself in what appeared to be a small restaurant.

Jackson didn't look up as the older woman returned from the restrooms but, when he heard the second set of footsteps, he looked up, expecting to see the waitress so he could ask for a refill of coffee. It was his croak of surprise that caused Carina to look in his direction.

"Jackson?"

"Carina?" He stood up, put a hand on each of her shoulders, and asked, "Where the hell have you been? I've been looking everywhere for you. How did you get here?"

*That answers one of my questions.* She said nothing, but stepped closer to him. His arms slipped down her back and he hugged her to him. Carina could smell his aftershave, Brut, she loved that smell. She rested her head on his shoulder for only a moment.

"Why don't we sit down?" she asked at last.

"Of course. Where are my manners? Would you like anything? Coffee?"

"I would really like a hot chocolate and a chocolate muffin." She wanted chocolate, a pleasure unknown in the other reality. She'd just realized she'd been craving it for the last two weeks. "What time is it?"

"Just after eight."

"What day is it?"

"It's Wednesday. You've been missing for more than nineteen hours."

Out loud she said, "Over nineteen hours? Really?" but in her head she was calculating the number of days she'd been in the sector and came to the conclusion that one hour in her reality equaled one day in the sector. *Yet,* she thought, *when I went back there it was the same, as if I had only been gone for a while. Weird.*

"Is something wrong, Carina?"

Carina started laughing until she almost cried. Carina couldn't stop laughing and it was several minutes before she regained her composure. "I'm sorry, but I couldn't help myself. That question seems so bizarre and out of place after everything that has happened in the last while. What can possibly be wrong with a person who can experience two realities? Who can pull a broken knife blade out of a wounded man, get abducted in one reality, and then zap back home in time for coffee?"

"Carina? You're not making any sense."

"Nothing makes sense to me, so why should it make sense to you? I just opened my eyes to find myself on a bathroom floor in White Rock. Tell me how you dealt with my disappearing before your eyes."

"I guess I've been in denial. I figured you were playing a joke."

The hot chocolate and muffin arrived at the table.

"Hmm, I missed that. They only had coffee or tea."

"Where you were?"

227

She looked at him over the rim of the cup. "What will it take for you to believe me?"

"So, you're still claiming that you were in a different reality?"

"Do you want me to go into detail about each day that I was gone?"

"You were only gone for nineteen hours."

She showed him the napkin she'd written on. "Well, according to my calculations, each hour here is one day there, more or less."

"Carina, I can't just believe that you were in another reality."

"Jackson, you saw what happened when I put on the armband."

"I don't know what I saw."

"How did I get to White Rock?"

"I don't know why you didn't take your car. Maybe you're going out of your way to elaborate this hoax."

Her brown eyes narrowed. The firm set of her jaw betrayed her reaction to his comments, but Jackson didn't recognize the subtle signs of her anger. "A hoax? I was abducted a year ago, but I decide to play a hoax now? Did I beat myself up to make it look good? Did I risk hypothermia in the middle of a cold winter night to make it more realistic? Ha! I don't believe this, I should have known better than to mention this to you in the first place. Do you know what I believe your problem is? You don't have any sort of imagination whatsoever. Everything has to be logical and have a fundamental reason for happening. Some things just refuse to fall into a nice little category. I thought I was going crazy when this first occurred but too much has happened and I have had to accept the impossible, the improbable. This is a mind-boggling situation, and I needed someone to confide in. I genuinely thought I could share it with you, but I see that I made a grave mistake in judgement. I should have told Brad, at least, he's more understanding than you are. Oh, by the way, thanks for the muffin, but I have to be going."

Jackson called after her, "Carina, wait. I'll give you a ride."

Carina, who was no fool, swallowed her pride and waited outside for Jackson. They drove most of the way in silence. Jackson tried to start a conversation. "I stopped by your place and talked with Kelly. She showed me your rooms."

"What? You were in my rooms?"

"When you disappeared, I went to your place."

"Kelly let you in?" She was not sure what to make of his intrusion.

"Yes."

"Great, now I have to deal with her questions. If I'm going to be labeled as crazy, I would prefer that the whole world doesn't know."

Jackson didn't say anything for a minute. "I only had the brown envelope that you left at the table. It's in my briefcase. There was only a scrap of material in it."

She stuffed the scrap into her jean skirt's pocket. "I'll look at it later. Maybe it will make some sense to me."

The rest of the drive was completed in utter silence.

Jackson was the first to speak when they pulled up in the driveway. "I guess I don't get a chance at a second date."

"I don't think that's a good idea. Until everything is resolved with this mystery, I don't think I should be getting romantically involved with anyone."

"I guess this is goodbye."

She didn't look at him. "I'm afraid so."

"What are you going to do now?"

"Although you don't believe the situation exists, I do have a few issues to work out. I want to do some research online and see if I can find information on the significance of the dragon and phoenix on the bracelet. Maybe I can find some old legends."

"That's a good idea."

"I think I'll go to Kamloops for a few days."

"I can drive you there, if you like."

"That's nice, but I'll have to come back on the bus. I think I'll take my fishing gear and do some fishing."

"If you come with me, I'll guarantee to return you to Surrey whenever you choose. When did you want to leave?"

"As a friend?"

He nodded. "As a friend."

She assessed his offer although he was being stubborn by not recognizing that she was telling him the truth. "Is tomorrow too early?"

"No, tomorrow is fine. That will give me time to check out of the hotel. What time?"

"We can leave early in the morning, if you like, seven or eight. We'll miss the afternoon heat that way."

"I'll pick you up at eight."

"I'll be ready."

She went to her rooms and dialed. "Hello, Katie, it's Carina."

"Carina. How are you? When are you coming up for a visit?"

"How does tomorrow sound?"

Carina packed enough of her clothing for one week, including good hiking boots. One of her biggest concerns was of what might occur while she was absent in the other city. She wondered if she should prepare for the possibility that she might never come back to this reality.

*What do I do? Start packing?* Carina sat down to pay her outstanding bills, and then she went to her closet and dug around until she found her fireproof safe. She pulled it out from its hiding place, opened it, and pulled out her Last Will and Testament. She wrote an additional sheet for the Last Will and Testament that designated specific personal items to family members. She would have to get the additional page witnessed.

Jackson arrived at 7:45. "Where is your fishing gear?"

"It's in the back of my car. I'll get it."

Jackson found it difficult to believe that a woman could like fishing. He was even more surprised when he saw a tackle box, a rod and reel, a fly fishing rod, and a pair of green waders in the trunk.

"Fly fishing?"

"Yeah, I've been teaching myself how to fly fish, but I prefer the rod and reel."

"I just want to top the car up before we leave Surrey." He pulled into a Petro Canada station that was adjacent to a Tim Horton Donut store. When he returned to the car, he had a six pack of donuts and two coffees.

"I believe you take your coffee with cream, right?" he said as he handed her a coffee.

"Yes, I do. Thanks." She took his peace offering and smiled.

Carina held the coffees until they were on Highway Number One heading east. They didn't talk as the radio played, maybe because both knew the radio reception would fade away once they began the climb through the mountains and entered the mountain valley.

As they approached the picturesque town of Hope, Jackson asked Carina if she wanted to go through the Fraser Canyon or through the Coquihalla to get to Kamloops, which would mean an hour off their travel time.

"It doesn't matter," Carina replied.

"I would like to take the Fraser Valley Route because I have to stop at the RCMP headquarters in Boston Bar. Would that be all right? We don't have to go that way if you don't want to."

"No, that's fine. I've always wanted an excuse to stop in Boston Bar again. It has such an unusual name."

"The town is small, but the area is beautiful."

"They sure are isolated, aren't they? It must be very isolated in the wintertime if snow blocks the central highway."

"From what I've heard, that does happen."

It was 10:30 when they arrived in the small town of Boston Bar. Carina sat in the warm car while Jackson went inside. Carina scanned the area. There was a sawmill on one side and the town's post office near the police station. Fifteen minutes passed before Jackson came out of the station. Beside him was another officer whom Carina recognized as Alec Granger.

"You remember Alec?"

"Yes. Hello."

"Hello, Carina. You're looking well."

"Thank you. I am."

"Alec has invited both of us for lunch." They followed Alec's patrol car a few miles down the highway to a family restaurant.

"The food here is quite tasty," Jackson said.

Once they were seated inside, and they had ordered their food, Alec said to Carina, "Jackson mentioned that you have your memories back."

Tensing, she asked, "Oh, and did he mention anything else?"

"I'm sorry to hear that you can't identify the perpetrators. It's a shame the file will be closed and they'll get away with what they did to you."

Carina shot Jackson a grateful look. "It is unfortunate but at least I can get on with my life."

"Indeed. What takes you to Kamloops?"

"I want to do some fishing and while I'm up there," Carina glanced at Jackson, "Jackson can close the file."

"Where do you think you'll go fishing?"

"There is Lac le Jeune, but I prefer Walloper Lake, which is near there."

"Have you ever tried Heffley Lake?"

"No. How is the fishing there?"

"The Rainbow aren't a bad size. You can even rent a boat if you're inclined to do some exploring."

"Carina has her own fishing waders," Jackson said.

Alec was surprised. "Really?"

"She carries her gear in her car all year round."

"Sure, why not? You never know when the opportunity will come up. I used to go fishing after work or early in the morning in Kamloops when the fish were feeding. Walloper is only a twenty, twenty-five-minute drive."

"I wish I could find a woman who felt the same way about fishing."

"No prospects in Boston Bar?" Jackson cajoled.

"Well, you know there's a lot of land here. I'm sure I can find someone who's willing, but I need more than that for stimulation. All anyone does up here is drink, work for the sawmill, or fish. Right now we're watching for illegal fishing because a lot of people who came up for the salmon run never left."

"I don't know why you got posted here. Friends in high places?"

Granger shot him a glare. "Seriously, though, I still have my cabin at Heffley Lake, and you're more than welcome to stay there, if you like."

"That would be wonderful. I used to live in White Croft."

"That place is sure booming now that they're developing it into a ski resort."

Jackson joked around with Alec when he saw how the waitress kept watching him. "Do I hear wedding bells?"

Alec harrumphed in reply. They finished their meals and said their goodbyes. "The key to the cabin is around back in the tool shed under the mat. Help yourself to whatever is there. You might want to buy some groceries before you go up the mountain," Alec offered generously.

The rest of the trip passed quickly. Carina, lulled by a full stomach, fell asleep and didn't wake up until the car slowed for the first red light in Kamloops.

"Your car gives such a comfortable ride. I didn't mean to fall asleep on you."

"That's all right. You mentioned that you were going to stay with friends."

"Yes, you met my friend Katie and her family. She lives on Waddington, not far from the Aberdeen Mall."

Katie, who'd seen Carina get out of the car, came outside to greet her. Carina introduced Jackson.

"We've met before, haven't we?" Jackson asked politely.

"You came over for Carina's grad party."

"Yes, that's true. How are your daughters?"

Katie was pleased that he remembered. "Lorraine and Terry are fine. They were so excited to hear that Carina was coming to visit."

"I just have to grab my bags before I come in," Carina said. It wasn't until that moment that Carina realized that if she wanted to go fishing, she couldn't drive out anytime she wanted.

Jackson saw her expression. "Why don't you leave your gear in my car? I can drive you up to the lake on Saturday."

"Are you sure?"

"I have the late shift on Friday and then I have two days free."

"The weekend will be fine."

"You said the fish start biting around six-thirty? That means if you want to catch breakfast, you'll need to be there by then. How about I pick you up at five?"

"Okay, if it isn't a problem."

"I'll sleep while you fish."

Carina laughed and said goodbye.

Jackson didn't drive off until he saw Carina enter the ranch-styled house. He didn't return to his own home immediately but went directly to the police station and begin to write his closing report. His superior officer, Bruce Dern, walked in and asked Jackson what the results of his trip were.

"Carina Douglas has her memory back from a year ago. She could furnish a few more details but nothing that could lead to identifying or arresting a suspect."

"That's too bad."

"Yes and no."

"How so?" asked Dern, a close friend of Jackson.

"We have a fishing date next Saturday."

"Well, I guess, because she's no longer on your case load then you can see her informally. I didn't know you fished." He sent Jackson a quizzical look.

"I don't."

Bruce burst out laughing. "Good luck, then. Keep me posted."



It was relaxing for Carina to visit with Katie. She was comfortable to be around, and it reminded her of why they were such close friends in the first place. Three relaxing days flew by and Carina decided to phone Brad. "Hello Brad, this is Carina."

"Hello, how are you doing? We must have a good connection because the line is crystal clear right now."

"That and the fact that I'm probably only a few minutes away from your house."

"Really?"

"I'm over at Katie's house. I've been here for three days already."

"That's great. You should stay over here for a few days so you can see our new house. We can have a barbecue."

"Actually, that's a good idea. Katie and her family are planning to drive to Prince Rupert. If you wouldn't mind picking me up sometime tomorrow, that would be great."

"When are they leaving?"

"Around noon I think, but I can just lock the door and leave the key with the neighbor if you can't pick me up until the afternoon."

"That would work much better for me. How about three? Then I can start up the barbecue for us."

"That sounds great, Brad. I'll see you tomorrow. Say hi to Maria for me."



Brad arrived shortly after three the next afternoon. His house was close to the downtown area. He gave Carina a tour of the renovated house, leaving the unfinished basement until last. They were converting it into three rooms, an office, a three-piece bathroom, and a bedroom. There were no finished walls yet. Carina saw the couch and a mattress on the floor.

"I'm sorry about the look but we're still under construction and the tenant has the upper room. Maria suggested you might like the basement because it's cooler to stay in during our sweltering days. Wait 'til you have been here awhile, by the afternoon it's stifling and the upper rooms stay hot all night."

"Yes, I remember Kamloops' scorching summers."

"We plan to get an air conditioner but not until next week."

"This will be perfect, Brad. Thank you."

"Let's go back upstairs, and we can talk while I prepare everything for the barbecue. I've invited Steve and Connie over for supper." He paused, "About the other day, I'm sorry I never got back to you."

"That's all right. I needed to talk to you face-to-face."

He offered her a beer, and they sat outside in the sun to enjoy it. He was proud of the patio he'd rebuilt.

"So, Carina, you have your memory back."

"And then some."

"What do you mean?"

"I have complete memories of two different places as if I have lived here and somewhere else simultaneously."

"You want to elaborate on that?"

"I have memories of when I went missing last year, and they aren't memories of Kamloops or any place that I know about. It was a different place altogether, with different people. I entered Kamloops, or I assumed it was Kamloops, but everything was different. Buildings were being torn down and rebuilt. I met a group of people who were waiting to be assigned jobs by a group called the Leaders. There is another group called the Banished that everyone is afraid of, but it turns out that the Scavengers are the ones who kidnap people and no one believes me that they exist except for the Banished."

Brad was confused. "Who doesn't believe that the Scavengers exist?"

"The Leaders. But the Scavs are the ones who grabbed me and sold me, but I escaped. I don't know how, though."

"Are you absolutely sure about these memories?" Brad asked, trying to follow Carina's words and suspend his disbelief.

"Yes. When you identified me in the hospital, I didn't remember anything. I graduated, et cetera. I was in White Rock last week and I saw a building that must have been from before I lost my memory. It shocked me and then I remembered being abducted. I went home and found the envelope from the Royal Inland Hospital. You know how they take your jewelry and stuff and put it in a safe place? Well, the envelope had my watch, earrings, and an armband. I recognized everything but the armband. However, after my memory returned, I knew where the armband came from. It was given to me when I first entered the other city."

"Did you put it on?"

"No, not right away. That's when I phoned you. Then I talked to Detective Dawes and he came up to see me. We were going to go to White Rock, but we stopped for breakfast at the Pantry first. I tried to tell him about the other place but he was a skeptic and figured that I was suffering from trauma or something. He said I was afraid of the armband and insisted that I put it on."

"What happened then?"

"I disappeared before his eyes."

"You vanished? Wow. I wish I'd seen that."

"I ended up in the other place, but I didn't have my memories of Kamloops and I was there for nineteen days. The armband gave my memories back to me and I remember that I'm going to be given to a man there as his wife, against my will. On the nineteenth day, something happened. I went to a closed room nearby and closed my eyes to think about what to do, but when I opened them, I was in White Rock. Coincidentally, Jackson had come to investigate the building with the painted whales on it and I met him in the restaurant when I came out of the restroom."

"The restroom? How did you get there?"

"Well, in the other reality, I was sitting on the floor of an examining room, with my eyes closed and my head resting on my knees. When I heard water running, I opened my eyes and found myself on the cold bathroom floor in White Rock."

"Weird, how you were both in the same restaurant."

"Too weird," Carina replied.

"What did he say?"

"He accused me of elaborating a hoax. He said that I had only been gone nineteen hours and he doesn't believe me. He denied what he saw, or didn't see, when I disappeared. He closed the police file yesterday. He was going to say that I couldn't provide information that would lead to an arrest."

"You disappeared?" He was grinning.

"One-hundred percent, Brad."

"Wow, I wish I had been there."

"You believe me?"

"Of course I believe you. You're too reserved and conservative to invent such a story for a hoax."

"Is that a compliment?"

"Of course it is. You're consistent, and people can depend on you. Show me this armband."

Carina showed it to him.

"Wow. It is beautiful. What kind of stone is it?"

"I don't know but when it lit up, it was a bright, fiery red."

"Can you take it off so that I can look at it?"

"No, it won't let me take it off." She lowered the armband to her wrist and Brad's eyes widened with surprise as it shrank.

"You must have been unconscious when they took it off at the Royal Inland Hospital."

"I never thought of it, but yes, I think that you're correct."

"You mentioned that you were gone nineteen days and Detective Dawes said you were gone for only nineteen hours. What happens when you return to this other place?"

"It seems to work in reverse. I'm in this world for, say, ten days and when I'm there, it has been ten hours."

"It is pretty wild. Quite an adventure. Tell me more, everything." Brad asked excitedly. "Another beer?"

"Yes, and where is the food?"

"Maria will be here any minute and then we can eat."

"We can't tell her anything."

"Why not?"

"You know she's a reporter and curious as sixty cats. Until I know more about what's going on, I'd like to keep it between you and me."

"And Detective Dawes?"

"There isn't anything that I can do about him."

"Hello, you two," Maria called from the living room.

"Hi, Maria," Carina said as she hugged Maria. "You look great."

"I hope he hasn't been boring you about the house."

"It is a great house. You have a yard, you can put in a garden, and I like the flowers you've already planted."

Maria glanced at the barbecue. "Oh, good, supper is almost ready. I saw Steve and Connie pulling in a second ago."

The barbecue was relaxing and delicious. Carina couldn't remember when she had last tasted barbecued steak and potatoes. She relaxed and enjoyed herself immensely. Steve and Connie lingered until well after midnight.

After they left, Brad asked Carina if she minded waiting until morning to talk some more. He walked with her to the couch and mattress on the floor in the basement.

"The walls will be finished the next time you visit."

"It's great, thanks for everything, Brad."

"Our pleasure. Goodnight, Carina."

"Goodnight, Brad."

Carina went back upstairs to the main floor so that she could use the house's only bathroom and then returned to the basement. Once there, she realized that the only source of light shone directly over the mattress. She pulled the string that was attached to the light fixture and the room went pitch black. She clicked it back on just as quickly. She knew that she couldn't sleep with the light on, and she didn't want to be in utter darkness, either, in case she had to get up in the middle of the night. Carina went to the staircase and turned on the light there. It provided enough light to help her make her way back to the mattress but not too much light that she would be awake all night.

# Brad Discovers The Truth

"C'mon, sleepyhead," Brad called, "it's after twelve already. The day is wasting away."

Brad walked down the wooden stairs to the basement and stood on the bottom step. "Carina? Wake up."

When she didn't answer, he walked carefully around the makeshift bed and pulled the light string. Carina's clothes were on the unmade bed, but it was otherwise empty.

"Where is she?"

He checked the patio upstairs but there were no signs that Carina had been there. He had been awake since seven when Maria left for work, and he hadn't heard anyone in the kitchen. He wondered if she'd gone for a walk. Brad was quick to realize that Carina might have disappeared as she had at the Pantry Restaurant. It was hard to fathom her disappearance as a reality.

"I had better let Detective Dawes know that Carina is missing. He won't be too pleased to hear that."

He searched in the phone book and dialed the number for the local RCMP. Jackson was out on a call, so Brad had to leave a message.

Jackson didn't get that recorded message until after three o'clock. "Damn," he said, when he finished reading it, and kicked the door of his office shut as he grabbed the phone. His hands were shaking; he misdialed. He cussed again, under his breath, thinking no cop with years of hard experience should get so shaken up over a phone message. He forced himself to slow down and punched the numbers a second time.

"Hello, Brad, this is Jackson Dawes."

"Detective Dawes."

"I haven't spoken with you since you and Carina graduated." He asked after Maria and then quickly got down to the purpose of his call. "You called about Carina."

"Yes, she has disappeared. I thought that you might like to know since you were with her the last time it happened."

"Brad, I don't think this is something we can talk about over the phone. How about I come over and talk with you?"

"Sure, here's my address...."

Jackson hurried over to Brad's house once he finished the paperwork that had him champing at the bit. His feet scarcely touched the concrete as he raced up the sidewalk that led to Brad's tidy little house, and as he reached for the doorbell, the door flew open. Obviously, Brad had been just as impatient.

Jackson stuck out his hand, "Hello, Brad."

He nodded and shook Jackson's hand. "Detective Dawes."

"Call me Jackson. I'm off duty."

"Come in."

"Sorry I was late. I had to finish the paperwork."

Brad flashed him a tight smile. His concern for Carina ravaged his face.

"Could you show me," Jackson asked, "where Carina was sleeping?" He followed Brad to the basement and saw Carina's clothing strewn on both the couch and the rumpled bed. "When did you last see her?"

"I think that it was around one in the morning."

"Did you hear anything in the night?"

"No. I assumed she was sleeping late so I didn't go to wake her until after twelve, but she wasn't here when I checked. I've been awake since seven, and I didn't hear any noise at all from down here."

"So we don't know exactly how many hours she's been gone." There was a pregnant pause and Jackson's turmoil roiled across his face until finally, cautiously, Jackson asked, "Did she mention anything about her previous disappearance?"

Brad met Jackson's eyes. "Are you asking about the old case or her more recent restaurant disappearance?"

Both of them were being vague so not to divulge any of Carina's confidences. Jackson sized up Brad, and what he saw must have helped him decide. "Did she say where she disappeared to last time?"

"Are you referring to the other place?" Brad asked.

Jackson sat down on the couch. "What exactly has Carina told you about the other place?"

Brad told everything that Carina had told him, including the fact that she was going to be given to a man as his wife. "She said you believe she's trying to pull off an elaborate hoax of some kind."

Jackson was embarrassed. "Yeah, I wasn't very supportive. I think Carina is under some sort of delusion, and I want her checked out by a doctor."

"You refuse to believe she disappeared right before your eyes? And yet you saw it? You think she waited in that White Rock restaurant's washroom until you showed up so she could stage her entrance?"

"I don't know."

"What if she's actually in this other reality right now?"

"That's impossible."

"Of course it's impossible. Our rational minds can't accept it. Nevertheless, just imagine that it has happened. Imagine how Carina feels living two different lives. Didn't she say that one hour away here is one day there? If she's been gone about ten hours, then she's been there ten days."

243

"I hope she'll reappear soon. Maybe she has multiple personalities."

"You aren't much of a friend."

"So what makes you believe her?"

"Simple. She has no reason to lie. Why would she? She has overcome her divorce, finished her degree, and found a teaching job. I have worked with her on more than one project. We played Dungeons and Dragons with friends. She went to my wedding, for crying out loud. Carina is a very serious and conscientious woman. She isn't an irresponsible person. What does she have to gain by pretending to disappear?"

"You know the state she was in when we found her."

"Yes, I do. I identified her. I knew her well enough to do that. Until she disappeared from my basement, she hasn't been anything but normal."

"No one has said anything to the contrary." Jackson paused before he spoke again. "She did disappear in front of me, and I haven't given any credence to what I suppose I saw. Okay, maybe she has been fine until now. I still want her checked out when she gets back. However, I'll consider the extraordinary possibility that she's in this other reality." He turned to Brad. "Did you say that she's being given to someone as his wife?"

"I don't know more than that except that it's against her will. We had friends over for a barbecue last night, and it got quite late. We were going to talk some more this morning."

"How is she going to get out of that situation?"

"I don't know."

"You just reminded me of something that I've wanted to ask. Did you ever meet her ex-husband?"

"No. Good riddance. Any man who'd abandon his wife like he did is bad news, and at such a vulnerable time, too."

"Don't you suppose her divorce, giving up her home, five years of university, and all of the other stressful events, could explain Carina's delusions?"

"Hmm. I can't agree that Carina is delusional because, when I saw her last night and spoke with her, she was totally rational and normal, as usual. So where does that leave us, Jackson? She's still missing."

"She hasn't been missing twenty-four hours, so we can't put an APB out on her. I think all we can do is to wait for her to come back."

"Will she reappear here?"

"I don't know. I hope so, if she's actually 'disappeared.'"

"Do you believe she'll contact us?" Brad asked.

"I know that her clothing and purse are still here so she'll have to get them eventually. Have you told your wife anything?"

"Carina asked me not to tell her. Probably a good idea, but what if she just reappears and I'm not here? Or what if she's missing for a day or two or more?"

"Tell her that Carina is up at Heffley Lake staying in a cabin. My friend Alec has generously given her permission to stay at his cabin to do some fishing. Meanwhile, both you and I will keep our eyes open. Do you think you can keep this under your hat?"

"Sure, I can do that. The less people who know, the better."

"I'll check in with you later. Here's my card and I've written my home phone number on it. Phone me anytime."

Brad put the card near his computer. "Sure thing. I'll hide her stuff away for when she comes back."

# 28
# Time To Leave

"I've got to stop doing this," Carina said when she saw she was back in the sector early the next morning. It wasn't funny, but the dash of humour helped—and that she had her memories back. Something had triggered them. She didn't know what, but she was grateful to be completely in control again. She rose from the sleeping mat fully clothed. Her skirt had lightened again to fit with the drab colours of the sector. She washed up, and then headed to the cookery to get meals for the patients.

Chenaanah appeared a few minutes later, a little flustered. Carina noticed throughout the day that Malcom and Chenaanah were studiously avoiding each other. The tension between Chenaanah and Malcom hung heavily and Carina didn't know what to do.

Only once had she managed to corner Malcom and the only thing she could wring out of him was, "I told her," and he took off. Carina was immensely relieved that Daric was away so she could go about her days without the added pressure of having to avoid him.

Carina knew Chenaanah had returned to her duties after her short illness, but she was lethargic and reluctant to eat.

One night, Carina, unable to sleep, was thinking about getting up and going to the cookery for tea. She was surprised when Chenaanah walked by her in the darkness. "Can't sleep?" she asked.

Chenaanah jumped. "I thought you were sleeping."

"No, I couldn't sleep, either. Where are you going?"

"Nowhere," she spit out.

Carina lit the candle and looked at her. "You look like you're dressed to go outside. What time is it?"

"Hmm. Late, I guess." She didn't look at her. "I didn't mean to wake you. Why don't you go back to sleep?"

"And leave you pacing the floor? I usually go to the cookery for tea when I can't sleep. We can both go if you like."

"No, that isn't necessary." She held up her hand to stop Carina from getting up.

"No problem, I'll keep you company while you're up," she said as she stood up. "If not, I'll bore you until you fall asleep." When Chenaanah didn't laugh, Carina knew she was holding something back from her. Carina glanced at her suspiciously. "Were you planning on leaving the complex?"

"It isn't your concern."

"I thought you were too ill to go anywhere, or was that just a ruse?"

Chenaanah wouldn't meet her eyes.

"You're going to look for your daughters, aren't you?"

"They have not found them. Maybe I will."

"What makes you believe you can find them after the Banished and the Leaders have failed to?"

"I don't know about the Banished, but I do know the Leaders haven't turned up anything. It is good that Malcom seems to want to keep me as his wife, but I need more than that. I need my daughters and nothing will replace them."

Carina heard how adamantly Chenaanah spoke and knew she wouldn't be able to dissuade her from searching for her daughters without some help.

"And where do you intend to look?" Chenaanah didn't respond. "You have to have a definite plan before you run out of here, otherwise the Defenders will catch you before you accomplish anything. Are you sure you want to go through with this?"

"I'm sure. I have to do this for my own sake."

"Then let's plan how we're going to get away from here."

Startled, she asked, "We?"

"Of course, we." She put her hand gently on Chenaanah's arm, "I'm not going to let you go by yourself."

Chenaanah shook her head and frowned. "We will both get in trouble with the Leaders and possibly be recultivated."

Carina shuddered, but said, "I'll deal with that when the time comes."

Chenaanah smiled and hugged Carina. "Thank you, Carina. You have no idea what this means to me."

"Let me get dressed, and then we can head to the cookery for some supplies. Did you have an escape plan?" she asked as she slipped on her tunic and shoes before Chenaanah could leave the room without her.

"I was going to slip out the side door when the Defenders were absent."

"Have you figured out the timing of their rounds?"

Chenaanah turned red. "No, I did not think it would be too difficult. You mentioned the cookery. I never considered taking supplies."

"You have to consider how long we'll be away; it could be several days. I think we should leave through the back door."

Chenaanah continued her agitated pacing. "Is that the best way out?"

"I think so. They said that when the Scavengers attacked, they came through the main doors. Gath's bondmate came in through the cookery door, found him, and then gave the alarm to the rest of the building."

"But the steel bar will be across it and the Defender will see it."

"Yes, so we must time it for when he lifts the steel bar and just before Gath arrives to begin making breakfast."

Chenaanah stopped pacing and looked at Carina. "How much time will that give us?"

"Before they miss us? We have about three hours, five at the most, before someone starts searching for us. Let's go. Which direction are we going to go once we're out of the sector?"

"West. There is a large expanse of land not far from the western sector. They call it the Wastelands. It's forbidden to travel through there. That is where I am going to go."

"Why is it forbidden? Is it a dangerous path?"

"I have heard it is fraught with perils and only the foolhardy risk it. It has been forbidden for decades."

Carina imagined all kinds of dangerous creatures leaping out at her. "And you want to go there? What makes you believe your daughters are there?"

Chenaanah leveled her gaze at Carina, choosing her words. "Too many weeks have passed. They communicate with horse messengers between the sectors. They have had enough time to deliver the message and do a search in each sector. We're wasting time. We need to leave before it is too late."

"And go where? To the Wastelands?" asked Carina.

"If necessary. Right now we need to get out of the sector."

Now fully dressed, Carina grabbed her cloak from beneath the covers and drew it closely around her. She had more questions that she wanted to ask, but she knew Chenaanah was right, they needed to leave immediately. "I don't know if they'll have anything for us to carry food in, so let's take the pillowcase."

Chenaanah looked at her strangely but removed her pillow; obviously glad the interrogation had stopped.

Carina looked at her. "Let's go." She glanced around the room, feeling like she was forgetting something, and then followed Chenaanah out into the hallway. They went cautiously toward the cookery, jumping at the slightest sound, but did not run into anyone.

They raided Gath's supplies, filling the pillowcases with enough light-weight food and some flasks of water to last for several days. Carina tucked a knife into her pocket and put one into Chenaanah's pillowcase.

Chenaanah gave her a questioning look.

"We might need them," Carina said.

"I found some rope, Carina. Do we need some?" Carina looked at the length of quarter-inch rope. "I'll use some of it to tie the bags and make them easier for carrying." She made a loop that would enable them to carry the bag over one shoulder.

Carina nodded and went to the back door and saw the steel bar lying across the door.

Chenaanah whispered, "What are we going to do? It looks too heavy even for the both of us."

"We can go out the front doors," Carina whispered back.

"I don't know."

"Or we could wait here until the Defender comes back on his rounds; it's usually Elzak. We drink tea together, and sometimes he lets me sit on the steps at the front of the building. He removes the steel bar so that Gath can enter the cookery and bring in supplies and then Elzak continues his rounds."

"You seem to know the routine quite well. But he doesn't know me that well, and he'll get suspicious if he sees me," Chenaanah said.

"I've spent a lot of sleepless nights sitting in this cookery. You can take the bags and hide until I let you know he's gone."

"Where do I hide?"

"It has to be someplace where you can be comfortable enough to stay still for a while. Maybe under the sink or in the cold storage. You choose. There's a handle on the inside the cold storage, so you won't be trapped."

"How long will I have to wait?"

"Ten to fifteen minutes, I'm not sure."

Just then, they heard a door closing.

"Quick, someone is coming."

Chenaanah moved to the cold storage.

"Here, take my cloak to keep you warm."

"Thanks," she said nervously as she glanced at the door.

By the time Elzak entered the dining room, Chenaanah had closed the cold storage door and hidden behind the racks and Carina had lit the stove and placed the kettle on a burner. Elzak heard the clattering and crept into the cookery. Carina was just reaching for a cup that she almost dropped, when Elzak appeared.

The cup clattered as Carina said, "You scared me."

"I'm sorry about that, Carina. I forgot about your penchant for tea in the early hours. Can't sleep again?"

"Uh-huh. Do you have time for tea?"

"Just a quick cup," he said as he sat down at the counter.

She briefly put her hand on his arm and gave him a disarming smile. "How have you been?"

"Busy. They have increased the number of patrols that are checking the perimeter. Now I do my rounds each hour."

"I'm keeping you from your work. It must take all of your time to investigate the entire area."

"Just over forty-five minutes and then I start over again."

She gave him a worried look. "Will the Scavengers—I mean, the Banished, be back?"

He patted her hand comfortingly. "I don't know if those rodents will be back. We have our sentries patrolling also, but it is a large area to check. Usually someone is patrolling an area every fifteen minutes. My job is the inside of the buildings."

"All of them?"

"No, I couldn't do that in an hour. I do the main buildings and alternate with the other buildings."

She smiled at him warmly. "I feel so much better knowing you're out there." He blushed as she flirted with him. Carina feigned a yawn. "Oh, I'm sorry."

Elzak chuckled and stood up. "I have to continue my rounds, and you," his voice dropped as he touched her cheek, "should get back to bed."

She didn't want to encourage or discourage his attentions. She imagined Chenaanah shivering in the cold storage and stood up slowly. "You're a sweet man. I'll just clean up and go to bed so you don't need to worry about me." She saw his eyes and knew it was the right thing to say as he stood proudly at her side.

"Goodnight, Carina."

Carina listened as Elzak went to the back door. She heard the scrape of metal on metal and knew that he was removing the steel bar. She then heard the click-click of the door as it shut. A quick glance confirmed that he'd left out the back door, and she hurried to the cold storage and called for Chenaanah who came out of it shivering.

"Th-th-that was l-l-longer than fifteen minutes." Chenaanah chattered through her teeth.

"I'm sorry, but he wanted to talk. Rub your arms while I rub your legs, and we'll get your circulation moving in no time at all. Here, drink this tea, and it'll warm you up. We need to leave right away and get to the healer's office."

"Why there?"

"We aren't that well-prepared. We ought to bring some medical supplies in case your daughters are injured. They're probably fine," she added when she saw panic rise in Chenaanah's eyes, "but we should be prepared."

"I did not think of that. I am glad that you decided to come with me." Chenaanah didn't say anything for a moment. Instead, she grabbed one of the filled pillowcases and led the way out the back door.

Carina put on her cloak, grabbed the other pillowcase, and threw the makeshift bag over her shoulder. They crept along, hugging the building until they reached the end of the alley. They were just about to make a sprint to the other side of the street when the scraping of boots alerted them to a patrol. It seemed like an eternity before they heard the footsteps moving in another direction.

They ran across the street and made their way slowly to the medical offices. Carina was reaching for the doorknob when Chenaanah pulled her abruptly back. "I saw a light inside."

The flash of light reappeared and they only had time to scramble into a recess before Elzak came out the door. Carina and Chenaanah held their breath until Elzak walked past their hiding spot and turned down a street in the opposite direction. They let out a collective sigh.

"My heart is still pounding," Carina said. "Are you sure, you want to do this? We can still get back to our rooms unnoticed."

"How are we supposed to get back into the cookery?"

"You're right. I guess that means we're committed to this."

Carina used her key to enter the medical building. "I'll slip inside while you stand watch." She stepped inside before Chenaanah could protest.

"I will, but you get the supplies."

*I intend to get the medical supplies. I don't want her there when I go to Ritik's room. I couldn't tell her that I came for a recultivated Banished.* She questioned her motives. *It's my fault he's here. I can't just leave him. It's an absolutely insane thing to do. He doesn't even know me.* Guilt niggled at her. She closed her eyes and saw the sprouted Ritik growing like a plant. She hardened herself and tiptoed on the tiling as she moved towards Ritik's room. It took a moment for her eyes to adjust to the darkness in his room but she didn't dare turn on any lights. She wasn't sure if he was awake or sleeping. If he was awake, he hadn't heard her. Carina moved cautiously until she was within one foot of him, but he still didn't move. A quiet snore emanated from him as she moved to his still body, covered his mouth with one hand, and shook him awake with the other.

She felt him struggle sleepily. "Shh. Get up Ritik, we're leaving this place." She removed her hand.

"You have called me that name before, but my name is Rysh. I think Daric should be informed."

Carina kept talking. "My apologies, I still haven't forgotten your previous name."

"Rysh has always been my name."

"Never mind that. Get up so that we can leave. We'll talk about your name later." She could feel him sit up but was surprised when he grabbed her arms.

She wrestled with him. "Let me go. I can explain everything."

"I think I should call the Defenders. You should not be prowling around at night."

"Rysh," she spoke his name softly. "There's no need. I thought you were interested in me," she lied seductively. She couldn't see his face but she could feel his grip loosen. *God, I've never had to play the temptress so many times in my life.*

"Of course you interest me, but you're spoken for."

Her arms were now loose again. In the dark, she slid her armband down to her wrist while she spoke, "But I'm not interested in Daric. It is you that I want to choose." She brought up her hands and gently pushed away his hair from his forehead. "I'm sorry...."

"What?" Rysh didn't finish his sentence as Carina clenched his head with her arms forcing the armband against him. He struggled briefly as she held the armband in place. The itch in her arm intensified until she could barely maintain her awareness. Rysh no longer struggled against her as his rigid body began to shimmer. She drew blood from biting down on her lip to stop from crying out. Finally, unable to endure the pain, she released him, whimpering in agony, before she stumbled blindly away from him.

She saw stars spinning around the room and ebony shadows threatened to engulf her. Endless moments passed before she became aware that someone was supporting her.

"You did it, Carina. I knew you could do the transformation."

"Ritik?" she asked uncertainly, swallowing breath after breath of air as if it were dissipating.

He heard her rough breathing and rubbed her arms. "Shhh, you'll be all right. Catch your breath."

"E-easy f-or you to say."

"I'm sorry. I didn't know it would hurt you so much."

She looked accusingly at him. "Ritik, you fought me."

"I almost didn't make it." He shuddered, remembering. "I felt like I was wrestling. Rysh's mind was almost impenetrable. A day or two longer and—"

It was her turn to calm him, "You're safe now, and Rysh is gone."

"No, he's not."

Carina's heart hammered in her chest as she stepped away from him.

"Don't be afraid. What I mean is that I realized I couldn't win the struggle with him, so I joined him. I'm me, but I have his memories, too."

She could hear the wonderment in his voice. "So, you're Ritik."

"In the flesh. In the newly made flesh."

"We can talk about this later. It was harrowing enough to witness your transformation. My mind doesn't want to fathom how your essence, as you called it, survived in my armband until I released it." Her feet still felt like jellyfish, but she was relieved that the pain in her arm had receded. "I don't want to think of the armband at all. We need to leave here."

"We?"

"I'll explain as we go."

"Why? What's wrong?"

"Malcom's wife intended to leave and search for her daughters by herself. I happened to wake up before she left."

"Where do I enter into this?"

"We need you to lead us out of here."

"Have you thought this through? You may end up in a cell somewhere."

"I know who I am and where I'm from. My memories are now fully restored. We can find our way without you but it will be riskier by ourselves. Let's go, hurry up, and be quiet. I need to get a few medical supplies."

A few minutes later, they met Chenaanah at the front door where she'd been pacing nervously. She looked at them both curiously. "What took you so long? I thought something happened to you. What is he doing here?"

"He knows how to leave the sector."

"But why would he agree to come with us?"

"We both have reasons."

Chenaanah bit her bottom lip. "This is getting complicated."

Carina patted her arm reassuringly. "It will all work out."


They left the building and Ritik turned right immediately once they reached the corner. It was no longer pitch-black outside and grey shadows loomed as they approached. They walked like cats on the prowl. Twice they fell back into the shadows as patrols passed and Carina held her breath. Chenaanah huddled close to Ritik as they climbed over fallen debris and traversed street after street. Carina felt like they were in a labyrinth.

Ritik wouldn't let them rest for over an hour. He saw Chenaanah's worried look. "You wanted to escape, find your daughters? Well, that means we have to get beyond this sector's boundaries. Having three people escape at once means they're going to be hunting for us." He spoke in a low voice, scanning the dilapidated houses that surrounded them.

Chenaanah was silent; she didn't know what to say.

Carina said, "Of course she wants her daughters back, desperately. There's nothing wrong with that."

"I admire your determination, Bondmate Graer, but you're the wife of a past Leader who is well versed in the laws of the land. I'm sure you're aware that you're breaking them. Do you have any idea what the Leaders will do to us if they find us? You won't remember your daughters once they recultivate you."

Chenaanah looked stricken, and Carina hastened to reassure her. "If we're caught," she said, "we'll make sure they understand that you were distraught. You were trying to protect your children. That's a mother's natural instinct. Surely they will understand that."

Ritik looked at Carina like a recalcitrant child. "That's naïve, Carina. And don't you know what this means for you? You're an outlaw now and you have no such excuses. Even your Daric can't protect you from this and I doubt he'll want to. You haven't been exactly friendly to his overtures. He'll probably still want you as his bondmate, and if re-cultivation makes you a little more compliant to his wishes, I'm sure he won't mind."

"Enough." Chenaanah shrieked at them. "You have said enough. I never meant to get you involved, Carina. I am sorry. Go back before they notice you're gone," she said, pleadingly.

"Calm down, Chenaanah, I can't go back. It's getting light outside. They will see me for sure and I'm not abandoning you."

"You still have the key to the medical office, don't you? You can say you're doing the early rounds."

Carina put her arm around Chenaanah and whispered to her, "Listen, we have come this far and we can't quit. And besides, what about Ritik? How is he supposed to get back into his room with the Defender doing his rounds? I'm going to suggest to him that we separate and create two different trails."

"But we need him."

Carina thought about Ritik, *I've filled my obligations. He's restored to his own memories and he's free to get on with his life. He's still a Banished.* Her resolve strengthened. *It's time to follow a path of my own choosing.* "I agree, he's gotten us this far but he is a Banished, and although he seems to be on our side, I don't trust him completely. I'll divert his attention and I want you to knock him out."

Surprised at her request, Chenaanah blurted out, "Me? I have never hit anyone in my life."

Carina squeezed her arm tightly. "I understand, and you might not have to do it. I just want you to be prepared in case he decides to take us to his Banished friends."

"I hope it does not come to that."

"Will you do it?"

Chewing her lip, Chenaanah nodded. "Where do I hit him?"

"I don't know. Behind the head like in the movies." Seeing Chenaanah's questioning look, she added, "I saw it done once."

They continued walking and Ritik, who'd stopped halfway down the street, returned and told them they had to leave immediately. The time passed quickly as they walked the quiet streets, ever watchful of pursuit.

"Ritik," Carina began, "how much farther?"

"We're halfway through the sector and it's at least an hour before we're out of here completely. There are several places to hide and we'll be safe for a while."

"Are you sure we aren't being followed?"

"No, I'm not sure. We'll have to meet up with some of my men and put them on alert."

"If the Banished and Leaders haven't found Chenaanah's daughters, then where are we going? Are you taking us to the Banished?"

He met her gaze. "I think it's best. It will be better if you stay with the Banished. We'll send some men out to search for the girls."

"That wasn't the plan. How dare you choose without speaking with us first? Have we been going the wrong way? Which direction should we have been going for the last few hours?"

"We're going north—" He never finished his sentence.

Chenaanah came up from behind them and hit him on the side of the head with a huge rock. "Is he all right?" she asked nervously as she dropped the rock.

"Yes, he's breathing." Smiling, Carina complimented her. "You did well, Chenaanah."

"He's going to be furious once he wakes up."

Carina glanced back at Ritik as he lay face down on the ground. "He was taking us to the Banished headquarters and was going to keep us there while he sent men to help find your daughters."

"If Malcom is a Banished like them, then they have already searched."

"That does make sense."

"His head isn't bleeding. He'll recover quickly so we ought to leave before he wakes up. At least he led us out of the sector."

Carina frowned down at Ritik. "Should we hide him? We wouldn't want to repay his help by having the Leaders find him. Let's drag him into that building over there." She indicated a building that was more dilapidated that the others. Chenaanah nodded and helped drag Ritik into the building. They hid him among pieces of the collapsed roof.

# Which Way Should They Go?

"If the Scavengers have your daughters, we need to alter our course."

"Are you sure?" Chenaanah asked.

"When the Banished attacked the sector, the Scavengers intercepted them as we headed out of the sector. They came from the west. That means you were right about going into the Wastelands. Could they be living there? Never mind, full daylight will be on us soon and we'll need to travel fast and far."

They still encountered ruined houses as they walked west, but there were less of them. The land was bereft of plants or animals, completely barren. The two women ran when they could, slowing to a walk when necessary because of rough terrain. Judging as best she could by the movement of the sun, Carina figured they'd been traveling for about two hours; they had almost made up the distance they'd lost following Ritik.

"How are you doing, Chenaanah?"

"Fine."

"Let's rest for a few minutes." They huddled in the shadows of a building while they ate a snack to stave off any hunger pangs. Carina rationed water out sparingly for each of them, and then settled the makeshift bag over her shoulder.

"Chenaanah? How much farther do you think, before we enter the western sector?"

"I'm not exactly sure of the extent of their territory. From now on, we're going to have to watch for Scavengers. They could be anywhere. We could hole up in this building for a bit of a rest."

"How do we know if we are we far enough away from the Central Sector to do that?"

Carina shrugged her shoulders. "I don't know. I do know that it's quite warm right now and in a couple of hours, the sun will be at its hottest. I think that's when we should travel because everyone is afraid of the sun."

"We can't just sit here waiting to be caught. What about my daughters —"

"They have been missing for several weeks," Carina interrupted. "An extra two or three hours isn't going to make much of a difference."

"How will we know if we're in Scavenger territory? How will we know where to look for my daughters? I think they could be scattered all over. How are we supposed to find them?"

"This was your idea, Chenaanah. I thought, with your experience, you'd know more about the sector. But it's not impossible to find them. They have to be in a building. I want to find the one with the cell in it."

"The cell?"

"Yes, when I was grabbed, there was a cell with steel bars. They kept me in it and the men stood around the outside."

"Oh, Carina, you mean Loriia and Liisa were sold?"

"I don't know for sure, Chenaanah, but it's very possible. I want to find a tall building or something else and look around. When I was there, I was forced to work in a shop. I assume there will be more shops around, but we just have to find them. I—"

Carina never finished her sentence. She pushed Chenaanah into the building's shadow as the sound of fallen rock echoed down the street. Carina risked a quick glance.

"There's a man about three hundred yards away. I can see his outline."

"Is he coming this way?" Chenaanah whispered.

"Yes, and he'll be here in a few minutes." Carina could feel her heart racing nervously.

"We could run before he sees us."

"Or we could follow him," Carina suggested.

"But he is going the direction we just came from."

"Move back to the edge of the building."

Chenaanah and Carina slid along the rough wall until they reached the corner of the building. Carina's black cloak had changed colour to a dark brown, the gift from her initial entrance into this reality did what it was meant to, but she hadn't noticed the subtle difference yet. Chenaanah's dark clothing wasn't easily detectable, either.

Once around the corner, they ducked into a doorway and crouched down. Carina held a finger to her lips. She listened to the sounds of footfalls getting closer and then stopping. Carina didn't breathe until she heard the footsteps receding in the distance.

Carina stole a cautious glance around the stone doorway just in time to see the man disappear around a corner. She motioned Chenaanah to follow as she stepped gingerly across the rubble-strewn street. They spotted the man disappearing into a squat, wooden building they'd passed earlier.

Chenaanah's face paled. "We were just there." Her hand clawed into Carina's arm as she tried to hide her terror. "What now?" She managed to choke out.

"My God! How can these buildings have anyone in them? They're practically destroyed. Maybe we overlooked something. You take cover and I'll follow him into the building. If something happens, I'll run into the street and distract him until you clobber him."

"Carina!"

Carina smiled, despite the situation. "You're the expert in that department."

Chenaanah ignored the teasing. "We would do better if we stayed together."

"The idea of going in there alone terrifies me, but I've been here before and, if I get caught, I know what to expect. You don't." Seeing her perplexed look, she added, "I was sold, starved, and beaten. I endured it, but I hope you never have to find out whether you can. For your daughters' sakes, stay here."

"I'll remain here, but you had better be careful." She hugged Carina.

"Watch the sun. You'll know when enough time has passed. If I haven't returned, leave and don't come back." Carina hugged her, and took the knife out of her bag.

She cautiously approached the squat building the man had disappeared into. Its windows were broken and boarded up. When she ducked through the narrow doorway, a long hallway stretched inward and then split at the end. Carina surreptitiously followed the hallway and paused, pondering which way to turn until she heard voices to her left. She decided to go right and investigate what she hoped was an empty room. The door was ajar and a glance around showed that it contained a broken table and scattered pieces of glass on the floor. In the adjoining room, a mattress with a ripped grey sheet lay on the filthy floor. Carina didn't like the vibrations she was picking up from the room. She felt like a dark force was beating mercilessly down on her and forcing her to leave the room without looking back.

She stepped into the hall and leaned against the damaged wall to catch her breath. How can a room feel evil? She shuddered as she moved toward the voices she'd heard a few moments earlier. This time the sounds were clearer and she could identify the voice of a man berating someone.

"You stupid woman. How many times 'ave I told you to keep the merchandise orderly? Be you thinkin' everything is for free?"

"No," a quiet voice murmured.

Carina, upon hearing the man's rough words, knew he was a Scav and moved to peer around the open door. She saw a dark-haired woman on the floor, her arm raised to ward off a blow from a bald-headed man. When the clout came, Carina saw the woman's head swing backward, the man's palm making contact with the woman's left cheek. He never had time to strike again because his body slumped to the floor from a blow to his head. The woman on the dirt floor finally looked up when the expected blow didn't fall. Her blue eyes widened in surprise when she saw Carina standing over the fallen body with a knife in her hand.

"W-who are you? She wiped her tears away.

"Carina. I'm here to help you. Are you all right?"

"I should be used to it by now."

Carina brushed the woman's long black bangs off her face. "You'll have a nice bruise tomorrow."

"It be not the first one that I be havin'. Why did you interfere? You be gettin' us both in trouble. Where be your owner and what be you doin' here by yourself?"

Carina looked fiercely into the unknown woman's eyes, "First of all, no one owns me. Second, no one has the right to abuse anyone the way that brute was abusing you. I couldn't just stand by and watch."

"Then what be you doin' here?"

Carina didn't want to keep Chenaanah waiting. "Looking for someone, new arrivals. Two girls, one eleven and the other nine. Have you seen them?"

"I might 'ave. What be you doin' for me if I help you?"

"You can escape from here."

"What for? I 'ave all I be needin', although it not be much."

"Don't you want more?"

"Like what?"

"Your freedom, for one." Carina saw a faint glimmer of light in the woman's defeated eyes.

"Freedom? There be Scavengers everywhere that we be runnin' into, and we not be havin' a chance to escape in this place."

"And you know how to escape from here, don't you?"

"Yes, but—" Fear spread over her face. "They torture the ones who try to escape."

"Only if you get caught. I escaped; do I look like I've been tortured?"

"They never be catchin' you?"

"Do you know Trator?" She spat out his name in derision. "He owned me."

"So you be the one I be hearin' so much about. He be out for your blood. I heard Axe talking."

"If I can escape, so can you. You can come with me."

The woman got up quickly. "Are you sure? You not be lyin'?"

"I'm dead serious. Get your things. We have to leave before Axe wakes up." Carina watched the woman fly around the room, stuffing food, clothing, and a knife into a bag she grabbed.

"I have to go to tell my friend we're coming."

"There be someone else?"

"Yes, I'll be outside. Be ready to move out quickly."

Carina went outside to talk with Chenaanah about the woman.

The woman waited for Carina to go, then scattered the logs from the fire on the floor. The flames quickly began licking the torn carpet and thirstily spread to the unsteady wooden table and wall. She smiled as she watched the shooting fingers of flame reach the ceiling before locking the door on her way out; this man would never leave his own cremation.

"I found someone inside, a woman. She was getting beaten up by a disgusting man, so I knocked him out."

Chenaanah stepped out of the doorway. "That's terrifying. Weren't you scared?"

"I couldn't let him beat her. I struck out and he fell."

"Did you kill him?"

"No. He's just unconscious. The woman is going to come with us. She knows how to escape from here."

"Will she betray us?"

Carina weighed her words before she spoke. "If she has been a victim for too long, she might feel safer remaining here, but if there is even the smallest spark of hope in her, she won't betray us. Yet."

They saw the woman as she moved toward them. She carried herself timorously as if carrying a great burden on her shoulders. Carina and Chenaanah motioned her into the corner.

"Chenaanah, this is the friend I told you about."

"Hello, I'm glad to meet you, uh…?"

"Tauralee, but you may call me Taura."

"Taura, I'm Carina."

Taura turned to Carina. "I be beholden to you."

Carina looked into her eyes and nodded.

"Shall we continue?" Chenaanah asked.

"Where be you going?"

"We have come looking for her daughters."

"Where did you come from?"

"The Central Sector."

Taura's mouth fell open in surprise. "They let you go?"

"No," Chenaanah replied.

"You ran away?"

"Yes, but we'll return once we have found my daughters."

"Be you afraid of them catching you?"

"Who?" Carina asked. "The Leaders or the Scavengers?"

"If we not be movin', we'll be findin' out soon enough. Your daughters, they not be here."

"How do you know?" Chenaanah asked.

"I was with Axe at the last big sale. There was a whole bunch of people this time, and they be all wearin' their sleeping clothes."

"The Banished grabbed them at night," Chenaanah said.

266

"I not be knowin' about any Banished, but these Scavengers make a regular habit of grabbing people and selling them. I've been here since I was seventeen, and I've been sold and traded a few times since then. The only thing that keeps me going after all these years is the hope I could get even somehow."

"I'm sorry, Taura."

Taura ignored Chenaanah's sympathetic words. She hadn't heard a kind word in so long her first reaction was to scoff. She shrugged off Chenaanah's hand. "Never mind."

"I smell smoke," Carina said.

"We better get out of here then," Taura said. "A fire can spread out of control in no time."

"Are there many others near here?" Carina asked Taura.

"No," Taura said, not meeting Carina's eyes, "we be a fair distance from the main core but, if the fire be spreadin', it will get their attention."

"Then we'd better move."

"I 'ave a sister," Taura said without moving.

"Your sister, is she inside?"

"No, she be somewhere else." She paused before speaking again, "If I go with you, will you be helpin' me find my sister?"

"We don't have time for that," Chenaanah said.

Carina glanced from one woman to the other, wondering why everything had to get so complicated. She wondered why she didn't just didn't leave Tauralee behind, but she could sense her desperation. "Do you have any idea where she is?"

Taura nodded.

"May I speak with you, Carina?" Chenaanah asked as she withdrew a discreet distance away from Taura.

"Sure."

"We should just get out of here. We do not need the added risk; she can stay behind if that is what she wants," Chenaanah whispered.

"Normally, I'd agree with you, but we need information and maybe she can lead us to where we want to go, your daughters."

"But I do not trust her."

"We'll watch her, and at the first sign of betrayal, we'll leave her."

"Are you sure?"

"You have my word."

"I would feel better if you were in charge."

Taura was still standing, shifting from one foot to the other. "So?" she challenged, "what you be goin' to do?" She'd thrown off her timidity and confronted them.

"We'll help you get your sister, but we want information on Chenaanah's daughters. Once we have them, we're heading back into Leader-controlled territory and you'll be safe there. We were going to find the gaol where they held me and then sold me. Do you know the direction?"

"We be havin' to move past several Scavengers' burrows, but I be knowin' how to get past them."

"Lead on."

Taura led them through buildings, around rubble and across crumbled barriers and it was obvious she knew which streets to avoid. Carina saw dark openings beneath a few of the buildings that Taura pointed out were entrances to the underground tunnels.

"You seem to know your way around," Chenaanah said.

"I should, I be here long enough."

"Why haven't you left before?"

"And go where? Until you be showin' up today, I thought that there be no other place near here, that I was going to be here forever and that any salvation be too far away."

"Shhh," Carina said, "someone's coming."

They froze in their tracks, but there was no time to hide. They'd just skirted one cave entrance and were midway to another low-lying building. Fortunately, the two men running past were focused on something farther down another street, the one the three women had just been on.

"That was close," Carina breathed.

Chenaanah sniffed the air. "I can smell the smoke; the fire is spreading."

"That will keep 'em busy for a while," Taura said.

"You started the fire, didn't you?" Carina asked.

"No, I just helped it spread a little."

"But Carina said there was a man in that building," Chenaanah said.

Taura's eyes were chips of blue ice when she replied, "He might 'ave escaped."

"If they discover any clue at all that we were in the building, they'll come for us," Chenaanah said.

"They won't find out," Taura said. "Follow me and stop asking questions. We be goin' to take a shortcut."

Taura zigzagged to the next building, looked furtively around, and ducked into the next building. She pointed to some loose boards that hid a darkened doorway beneath them. She looked back at Chenaanah and Carina and motioned for them to follow her.

"Where does this go?" Carina asked.

"This be where most of us live. It be an underground network leading in every direction for miles around. We be headed for the hub."

"We're going to the center of the complex?" Carina asked.

"Yes, you want information about Shana's daughters, so we 'ave to go to the trading place and see if'n there's a clue to where they be."

"I do not think I like the sound of that and it is pronounced Sh-nay-nah," Chenaanah said.

Taura ignored her and looked at pointedly at Carina. "You probably remember it: The room with the cage for new stock."

Carina's face whitened. "Yeah, I remember. That's where they brought me, put me on display, and then sold me. They had a black hood on my head so that I didn't know how I got there."

"You think my daughters are there?" Chenaanah asked.

"Don't be hopin', Sh-nay-nah. They be sold by now. Children be kept with the women but there be exceptions."

"You mean they're down one of these passages?" Carina asked. She noticed that Taura sometimes spoke like a Scav, but other times she spoke more with more sophistication. *I'll have to ask her about that.*

"Possibly."

Carina looked skeptically at the earthen wall, suddenly feeling claustrophobic. "Is it safe? These walls look like hardened earth and it's pitch black down there. How are we supposed to see where we're going?"

She saw Taura grin at her discomfort. "Do not be fooled. There not be a cave-in for a long time and not all entrances be hard-packed dirt. Once we go down the passage, we be encounterin' entrances like this one which be meant for closing if we be attacked, and others of wood."

That extra bit of information didn't assuage Carina's nervousness. She swallowed hard. "What kind of attacks? I thought the Leaders didn't know about this place."

"They 'ave stumbled across an entrance now and then but, by the time they get equipment to investigate—"

"The cave has conveniently collapsed," Chenaanah finished.

"But do not be worryin', it be a long time since that has occurred. We best be movin'. I know the direction in the dark. Just trail your hand along the wall and keep goin'. This passage breaks off into smaller passageways. The lights be at the breaks."

"This goes on for miles, how can we find them?" Carina asked.

"There be an old woman who belongs to the gaol-keeper. She probably knows where we be findin' your daughters because she lives near the hub and sees who goes in and out of there."

"Why will she help us?"

"I not be knowin' that she will, but I be doin' her a lot of favours over the years and she be the only person who can help find your daughters. We cannot be checkin' every burrow."

"Do you think she'll recognize me?" Carina asked.

Taura shrugged. "Not likely. Hester has seen too many prisoners over the years to make note of one in particular."

"Then how will she recollect my daughters?"

"She remembers children because there be less of them captured." Her answer mollified Chenaanah.

"I agree with you, Taura," Carina said and Chenaanah glanced at her in her surprise. "If this rat's nest goes on for miles in many directions, we'll be caught before we find them. Lead the way."

Taura seemed surprised at Carina's vote of confidence. She brightened, wearing Carina's support like a shielding cloak. She led them through the maze with apparent ease. Twisting and turning, up and down stairways, sometimes ducking through narrow passageways that suddenly appeared around a corner or crevice, it all seemed endless to Carina. She was glad that they had stumbled upon Tauralee, who was confident and at home in this underground labyrinth.

Carina was lulled into a kind of trance as they slipped along through the dark. She closed her eyes briefly, her arm on Chenaanah's shoulder. She tried to recall why she felt so familiar with the surrounding area, as if she'd done this before. Muffled voices reached them; they were just yards away from sound. Carina's eyes flew open. Carina collided into Chenaanah when they came to an abrupt halt.

Taura motioned them to stay where they were as she entered the main hall by herself. The two men, who'd been talking, yelled at her, "You there. What be you doin' here?"

Taura took on a demeaning stance and cowered before them. "Axe be sendin' me. He told me to get help because there be a fire and it be spreadin'. You 'ave got to be helpin'."

"It be not my concern. I be havin' other things to do, girl."

Taura started pleading. "You need to be goin'. Axe' be beatin' me if he be losin' his shop. Please, I not be wantin' to be beaten again," she pled as she groveled on the floor and grabbed the startled man's hand.

271

He laughed as he roughly shoved her backward and kicked at her. "Why should I be carin' for the likes of you?" he asked menacingly.

The shorter man spoke to the other man. "I be in a hurry, you can 'ave fun with her later. Axe be havin' some of my tools and I not be wantin' to lose them."

"Oh, all right," the taller man said as he aimed one final vicious kick at Taura's stomach before he slipped down the nearest passage.

Carina, who'd witnessed the abuse, felt sick inside and Chenaanah was frozen, unable to move, her hand covering her mouth. Carina knelt beside Taura. Taura moaned in pain when Carina tried to move her.

"Taura, speak to me," Carina implored.

"I be sorry," were the only words that Taura managed to croak out.

"You did a brave thing," Carina said, and Taura's eyes brightened. Carina brushed the woman's matted hair away from her pain-clouded eyes, and whispered, "Can you get up?"

"Give me your arm." Taura leaned heavily on Carina.

Carina called Chenaanah over. "Help me. Put her arm around you and I'll get the other. We have to get her to safety."

"Take that corridor"—Taura pointed—"second doorway on the left."

Carina and Chenaanah half-dragged Taura to the doorway.

An old, bent woman heard them and looked up from her knitting as they dragged Taura in, not waiting for an invitation.

"Who be you and what be you doin' here?" she rasped.

"Are you Hester? Taura's been hurt."

"That be me. Did Axe beat you again, girl?" She looked at Taura's face.

"A man kicked her twice in the stomach," Carina offered.

"What did he do that for?"

"Because he's a stupid, vicious man."

"That could be anyone here, my dear," she said dryly. "Bring her to the cot so I be gettin' a good look at her."

There were other doorways connected to the large one they were in and none of them had doors, either. They passed a room that looked like a cookery as they followed Hester down a corridor into one of the two remaining rooms.

"Hester." Taura smiled. "You can help me."

"It not be like you to ask for trouble. Who be these two that you be with them?"

"They freed me from Axe, and they be helpin' me to rescue my sister."

"Did they now? You be helpin' fugitives?"

"We met by accident," Carina explained.

"I be thinkin' you be havin' a broken rib. I can wrap it up for you but you be not travellin' for a bit and Axe be findin' you by then."

"No, he won't," Taura whispered.

"What did you say?"

"He's gone."

"Gone?"

"Carina hit him in the head to stop him from beating me and after she left the building, I spread the embers and locked the door."

Carina overheard Taura's admission. Shocked, she her grabbed her shoulders and shook her. "You mean you trapped him inside the building to die?"

"I be doin' it again," Taura said vehemently. "I could not be takin' it anymore. He had to die so he could not be hurtin' someone else."

"They be after you, girl. They be killin' you now," Hester whispered nervously.

"I not be carin'!" Taura said a little wildly. "Just wrap up my ribs. I be thinkin' about my sister. I aim to free her."

"You be crazy. Girl, you know she be in the Wastelands. You be a fool to be considerin' going out there. You not be knowin' if Sarra's alive."

"What do you mean by that? She has to be alive."

"Old man Darol bought two new girls to work in his mine. Said their size be enablin' them to go where men cannot be goin'. If Sarra grew too big, he might 'ave sold her."

"No!" Taura said fervidly. "Did he sell her?"

"I not be hearin' it. He might 'ave traded her to someone else."

"Two girls?" Chenaanah asked quietly.

Hester turned her rheumy eyes toward Chenaanah. "Yeah, young'uns."

"Were they wearing bedclothes?"

"Mighta been. What be it to you?"

"My daughters—they could have been my daughters."

Hester's face softened. "A redhead and a brunette?"

"Yes, yes, that is them."

"You be better off to forget all about them." She patted Chenaanah's arm. "It not be likely you ever be seein' your brood again."

Chenaanah whipped her arm away. "No, you're wrong. You're just a spiteful old woman." She turned away to hide her tears.

"Is it true, old woman? You know where her daughters were sent?" Carina inquired.

"If Darol has left the territory, then they be as good as dead. No one he be takin' out there comes back. The mine changes them."

"We'll come back," Carina said firmly, "and with your daughters, Chenaanah, and your sister, Taura."

Hester turned to stare at Carina. "And who be you to be makin' such statements?"

Carina met her gaze. "We will do whatever it takes to find them. That's what we can do and that is why Taura endangered herself by coming here. You can tell us what we need to know, if you're willing to share it." Her eyes didn't waver from Hester's as she spoke.

"Sure, dearie," Hester said her voice as soft as tears. "I only wish I be young enough to come with you."

It was Carina's turn to be surprised.

"My man will be here soon. You not be wantin' to meet him or you be findin' yourselves in his cell to be sold." She and Chenaanah finished bandaging Taura's rib and then she started for the door. "Stay here while I be checkin' the main room."

The three of them waited. A clatter in the other room alerted them.

"Old woman. Where be my supper?"

Carina knelt beside Taura. "Can you get up?"

"Sure. The bandage will keep me together." She winced as Carina helped her stand.

"We've got to get out of here. Will Hester help us?"

"I think so."

"Food be ready," Hester's voice carried down the hall to the waiting women.

"Fire be blazin'. I not be stayin' long. I 'ave to get back to the fire. I just came for a bite to eat and my ax. It be under the bed."

"You eat and I be getting' your ax."

"No, woman, I be gettin' it," he said as he pushed past her.

Taura turned and shoved Carina and Chenaanah into the corner between a rough-hewn chest and the wall. She threw a blanket over them and moved to the bed, her choice made. She had just lain down when the burly keeper came in.

"What be this, woman?" he roared at Hester who'd followed him.

"She be Axe's property. She be needin' help after one of the men kicked her for her troubles."

"She not be stayin' here. She should be helpin' with the fire."

He bent and grabbed his ax as Hester said, "She be wounded."

"No excuse," he said as he grabbed Taura by the arm, pulled her upright, and shook her. "How be the fire startin'?"

"I not be knowin'. Axe be usin' special fluids to clean his tools, and I be in the other room when I be hearin' him a yellin'. The room be on fire and the flames be lickin' up the walls. He sent me out."

"I didn't see him."

"He be alive when I left."

The gaoler had been turning to leave when he suddenly froze and spun around. "Alive? I not be askin' you whether he be alive or not. What be you doin' to him, girl?"

He was shaking Taura so hard she couldn't speak. "Nothin'. He be fightin' the fire when I be leavin' for help."

"You not be lyin' to me now?"

"Nnno," she managed to say.

"I not be believin' you, I be lockin' you up until I be checkin' on Axe's condition, and if anything be wrong with him…" He left the threat hanging, grabbed Taura by her shirtfront, hauled her off the bed, and started dragging her by her hair.

Taura began fighting like a berserker, heedless of the danger and the gaoler's strength. He hadn't been expecting the wild attack and found it hard to hang on to her. She left a handful of her hair in his hand when she jerked away from him. As he ducked to avoid everything she was throwing at him, he swung his arm that held the ax.

Carina, who'd lifted the blanket to peek out at the commotion, watched in horror as the ax sliced through Taura's abdomen. Taura fell, as if in slow motion, onto the rough floor, her life's blood flowing like an endless, deep river. Carina's hand flew to her mouth and bit it to stop from crying out.

"You be killin' her!" Hester yelled.

"She be askin' for it." He waved the dripping ax at her. "Clean up this mess before I be gettin' back," he said gruffly as he turned to leave.

Carina didn't wait to see if it was safe to throw off the concealing blanket before running to Taura and trying to stem the flow of blood. "Hester, don't just stand there, give me some cloths, a blanket, we've got to stop the bleeding."

Taura's hand tightened on Carina's wrist, "Carina," her voice wavered unsteadily.

"Taura, Taura, don't die, we're going to help you."

"It be too late for me, Carina but you must save my sister. Please."

"You're not going to die."

"Promise me, Carina, you be gettin' Sarra and free her."

"I-I promise."

Taura smiled. Her eyes went wide and blank as she died.

Chenaanah, who'd run about the room grabbing blankets and cloths to staunch the flow of blood, put her hand on Carina's shoulder, "She's dead, Carina."

Carina had never seen anyone die. An agonized animal sound tore out of her throat. "You can't die. I won't let you die," she proclaimed, her voice going higher with each word. "You're going to live!"

Carina put her right arm over Taura's body as she had cried the last words aloud. A piercing blue light flew down her arm into Taura's lifeless body. The air around them crackled with a life of its own and threw Chenaanah onto the floor and Hester against the hard, cold wall across the room.

Time seemed frozen. The burning blue light engulfed Taura, a light so bright, so intense, that Chenaanah and Hester hid their faces from it. Carina, who was crying softly against Taura, was at first unaware of the power that was flowing from her. The brilliant light caused her to look up.

When the flash faded, Hester and Chenaanah stared in shock as the blood from the dirt floor flowed backward into Taura's abdomen. The blood on Carina's soaked sleeve drained away, leaving the fabric spotlessly white. Then she felt the impossible; Taura's chest moved in an indrawn breath.

Taura's face, as pale as wax only seconds ago, flushed as if a sunbeam lit up her face. Her eyes opened and locked with Carina's. "What happened? I thought I'd been killed."

"What did you do? And you, Tauralee, you be all right. If'n my eyes had not be seein' it, I not be believin' it." Taura stood up and Hester hugged her fiercely. "Oh child, child," Hester repeated over and over.

Chenaanah was too stunned to say anything as she moved to Taura, cloths still in her hands.

"You not be needin' them," Taura said as she lifted her shirt and showed her belly. A fine white line was the only mark left of her terrible injury.

"You did this," Hester began, abruptly pulling Carina to her and holding her until Carina returned the embrace. "I be hearin' the legends, but not believin' them. Never even began to hope, to dream to be seein' the day I be meetin' you." She put Carina's hand on her grey-haired head. "Bless me, please."

"I don't know what you mean," Carina said.

"What do you mean, you not be knowin'? I saw you heal Taura."

"I don't know how I did it."

Hester saw the truth in Carina's eyes. "Bless me anyway, and when you do be knowin' how you did it, remember me."

Carina looked at Hester strangely. She'd never been asked to do such an odd thing. She gingerly put her hand on Hester's head, closed her eyes, and pondered what she should do. She mouthed the words, "Take care of this woman, give her all that she needs, let her be loved." She felt a quick prickle in her hand.

Hester, who'd apparently felt the prickle, looked up. "Thank you."

Chenaanah finally found her voice. "Who are you?"

"I don't know," Carina whispered. She turned away, trying to understand. She was glad when Hester spoke, breaking the hush that had fallen over them.

Hester was smiling brightly. "You cannot be stayin' here, though I never be wantin' you to leave, but my man be back soon enough, and he cannot be findin' you here."

"She be right," Taura said. "We 'ave to be movin' on."

"I 'ave to be tellin' the others," Hester said. "We be saved."

Her words were cryptic, but so was Carina's murmured reply. "Not yet, Hester, but who knows about tomorrow?"

"Remember me," Hester said as she gently placed her hand on Carina's shoulder.

Carina looked at Hester, she seemed to be a different woman, less haggard, less careworn. "I will," she said sincerely.

"What will you tell him when he gets back?"

"Do not be worryin'; he won't be the wiser," Hester said as she pressed a pack of food into Taura's hands.

Taura hugged Hester fondly one more time and then turned to Carina and Chenaanah. "Follow me."

# The Burrows

Carina tried to keep up with Chenaanah and Tauralee as they hurried through the underground corridors. Chenaanah, not sure of Tauralee's recovery, followed her doggedly. Carina felt physically drained and lagged behind the others, but they hadn't noticed, apparently focused only on speed. *God, I'm so tired*, she thought, wiping her eyes with her hand, and even her hand seemed far away.

Chenaanah and Tauralee got far ahead of Carina in the sparsely lit tunnel. The walls were hard-packed dirt in some places and concrete in others. Carina, dragging her hand along the wall, walked a few more steps with her eyes closed. When she opened them, she saw a pale light in the distance and made her way toward it. A flight of stairs led up to the light and a door. Carina listened for any noises while groping for the doorknob. She turned it slowly. Again, she paused long enough to allow her eyes to adjust to the bright light. She entered the room, finally, bone weary and finding it difficult even to focus her eyes.

When a figure suddenly appeared through another doorway a few feet from her, she leapt backward, banging her head against the oven's hood. She realized vaguely she was in Brad's kitchen. He dropped the papers he was holding when Carina leapt back.

"Carina! Where the hell did you come from?"

"You scared me half to death."

"I scared you? What were you doing sneaking in here so quietly?"

"I wasn't sneaking, I was in a tunnel underground and there was a light that I followed that led me here."

Brad was quick to ask. "Were you in the other place?"

"Yeah," she said holding her head.

"Did you bang your head?" He moved closer and could see the blood on her fingers. "Let me see. I think you hit the corner of the stove hood."

Carina nodded.

"Let me clean it up."

Carina sat at the kitchen table while Brad got a wet cloth to clean the injury. Carina winced as he dabbed at the cut. "The bleeding has stopped," he said. "I don't think you'll need stitches, but I'm going to put a bandage on it. I'll get you some ice for the swelling. Just sit here for a second." He left the room but continued talking. "What happened to you? You went downstairs after the barbecue and disappeared." He returned, rummaged through the freezer, and passed an ice pack out to her.

Carina tiredly held onto the proffered ice pack and held it to her head after he secured the bandage.

"Why don't you lie down on the couch? I'll get you a glass of water."

Carina got up and moved slowly to the living room, leaning against the wall as she walked.

Her unsteadiness alarmed him. "Are you all right?"

"Just tired."

"I can help you."

"No, it's okay." She didn't notice that he didn't follow her immediately.

Carina went straight to the inviting green-cushioned couch and lay down on it full length. She fell asleep in seconds.

Brad glanced at Carina and made a beeline to the telephone. He fished the card with Dawes's phone numbers out of the drawer where he'd stashed it and dialed his home phone number. He glanced at his watch, 6:50 AM. He was just about to hang up when he heard Jackson on the other end.

"Hello, Jackson here."

"Jackson, this is Brad Masters, Carina's friend."

"Yeah, sure."

"She's here."

"I'll be right over. Keep your eyes on her."

"Don't worry, I will."

Brad paced the floor, glancing from Carina to the living room window. His lower lip was beginning to show signs of his worried chewing by the time Jackson arrived twenty minutes later at the house he'd left just over an hour before. Brad, who'd been watching for his Mustang, quietly opened the door for him.

Jackson nodded a greeting. "Where is she?"

"Sleeping on the couch."

"When did she show up?"

"Maybe fifteen minutes before I phoned you."

"Where did she come from?"

Brad led the way past Carina's sleeping form into the kitchen. "From out of the basement. We scared each other, that's for sure. I was coming into the kitchen and she'd just come up from the basement. She jumped back and hit her head on the oven hood."

"Did she say anything?"

"She said she'd been in a tunnel and saw a light in the distance that she followed to a door that opened here."

"Are you sure she didn't come through the back door?" Jackson's eyes darted from the door to the basement stairs.

"It's a deadbolt and it needs a key. Carina doesn't have one."

"Could she have been hiding in the basement all this time?"

"No," Brad said, "both you and I checked and I haven't left the house since you did. I've been downstairs several times since then doing the laundry."

He nodded at Carina. "You're sure she's asleep?"

"I think so. The cut on her head wasn't that serious. She passed out by the time I hung up the phone. She looked pretty exhausted."

"I'm going to wake her." Jackson shook her gently. "Carina, Carina," but she didn't respond. He shook her more roughly, and Carina mumbled, "Let me sleep, Chenaanah."

"Did she say anything about where she had been?"

"She said that she was tired, and I saw that she was really wobbly on her feet. She seemed really out of it, too."

"How hard did she hit her head?"

"Not enough to knock her out. Let her sleep."

"Did she mention how long she'd been gone? Did she tell you about her time correlation theory?" Brad sent him a blank look. "How long was she here before she disappeared? She had a theory about the time. She said an hour here was a day there so I want to check the coincidence of her theory."

"What do you mean coincidence?"

"Evidence that it happened. She disappeared somewhere between three in the morning and noon our time, and showed up about sixteen hours later. She figured one hour here was one day there which means she's been gone between twelve to sixteen days there."

"That's assuming she went to the other place," Brad replied.

"I guess we'll have to wait until she wakes up and fills in the blanks for us. Is that coffee? I could sure use a cup."

Brad poured them both a cup. Jackson leaned against the kitchen wall that afforded him a view of Carina while he drank.

"Maria will be here at nine, she's been babysitting her niece. What will I tell her when she shows up?"

"I can carry Carina downstairs into the basement, and we can wait until she wakes up."

"What if she disappears before then? Are you going to stay down there with her?"

"I'm getting awfully tired of the disappearing act."

Brad bristled, recalling Jackson's refusal to believe he'd seen her disappear right in front of him in the restaurant. "I imagine Carina is also tired of it."

Jackson noticed Brad's sudden stiffness, "Let me wake her up." He went to her and shook her, but she didn't rouse. "She's out cold. I can stay with her until she wakes up." His voice softened. "She's my friend, too."

Brad acknowledged Jackson's peace offering. "And what do I tell Maria when she arrives? 'Don't go downstairs'?"

"No, we don't want to get anyone else involved in this. We were supposed to go up to the cabin this weekend. I think I'll take a few days off and go up today with her, that way I can watch Carina until she wakes up."

"Where are you going?"

"Up to Heffley Lake. Alec—you remember him—is lending us the cabin for the weekend. Can you watch her while I gather her things?"

"Sure. He was your partner, wasn't he? Nice of him to lend you his cabin. I've been to Heffley a couple of times."

Jackson nodded as he made his way to the basement stairs. He stuffed Carina's belongings into her duffle bag and carried it out to his car. There was still room in the Mustang's trunk even with Carina's fishing rods and gear.

"You know," he said, entering the house, "I still have to pick up my stuff and buy groceries. How can I do that without leaving Carina alone?"

"I'll go with you so you can run into the store and your place, while I watch her."

"Would you? That would be great."

"You can drop me off when you're done. Just give me a second and I'll lock up."

Jackson lifted Carina gently into his arms and carried her down the three steps to the sidewalk. Brad hurried ahead and opened the car door, pushed the passenger seat forward. He went to the other side of the car and pushed the seat back so that he could help Jackson lay Carina on the backseat of the Mustang and covered her with his jean jacket. Neither spoke until the car reached Jackson's place. "I'll be right out. Keep an eye on her, okay?" He stated the obvious knowing that between his looking in the rear-view mirror and Brad's turning around in his seat that they hadn't taken their eyes off her.

Once in the house, Jackson grabbed his duffle bag and stuffed it with his clothing and shaving gear. He didn't have time to put Casimir, his husky/wolf, in a kennel, so he'd have to bring her with him. The problem was, Casimir wouldn't like the cramped quarters and he didn't want to scare Carina if she woke up and found a wolf staring at her.

"Damn," he muttered, "where's her leash?" It took him a few minutes to find it and coax Casimir out of her hiding spot behind the couch, a languid grin on her face as her tail beat a lazy tattoo on the hardwood floor. Jackson was ready to explode in frustration because Casimir would leap just out of reach each time Jackson made a grab for her. Jackson finally just left her and walked into the kitchen and began grabbing as many cans of dog food as he could find, along with her watering bowl and food dish that he put into a large plastic bag.

Casimir, ever curious, entered the kitchen and stood beside Jackson. He turned and grabbed her collar before she had time to react. "Ha. Gotcha." He snapped the leash onto the collar, knowing he probably couldn't use the same trick for a while.

He fumbled with his keys as he turned off the lights and tried to hold his duffle bag, Casimir's leash, and the plastic bag containing her food and bowls. The Mustang certainly would be tested for its roominess today. He handed Casimir's leash to Brad.

"What's this?" Brad asked in surprise.

"Casimir, my menace."

Brad laughed as he looked at the dog beside Jackson. "What kind of dog is she? She looks like a wolf."

"She is part wolf and part husky. At least that's what the vet said."

"Oh." Brad gulped nervously. "Where should I put her?"

"The seat's far enough back to give you some leg room while she scrunches on the floor. I figured you two would like to become friends."

Brad looked a little unsure of himself until Casimir licked his hand.

Jackson noticed Casimir's action. "Don't worry, she usually doesn't bite. She is just tasting you. She does it to me all the time, runs outside, comes back in, finds me, swipes a lick and vanishes back outside again."

"Usually doesn't bite?"

Jackson laughed at Brad's reaction to Casimir as he put the remaining bags in the trunk of his car. It wasn't every day a wolf dog licked your hand.

The grocery shopping didn't go as quickly as Jackson would have liked but, when he returned to the car, Carina was still asleep. He dropped Brad off at his house, thanked him for his help, and headed down Tranquille Road to the Number 5 Highway heading to Sun Peaks. It was a half-hour drive to the turnoff. The brown rolling hills gave way to trees and ranches.

Jackson angled his rear-view mirror so that he could see Carina's sleeping face. Her forehead was furrowed as if she were in deep concentration. Casimir distracted him when she moved so she could watch both Jackson and the unknown human in the back seat, from the seat Brad had left. Once she was satisfied that nothing would be happening without her knowing it, she curled up and went to sleep.

The road up Sun Peaks was a steady upward climb, all tricky curves, but the biggest danger was the drivers. They pushed their cars to negotiate the tight corners at ludicrous speeds, and frequently strayed to the wrong side of the road. There was at least one fatality every year, usually during the winter ski season and Jackson didn't want to be another statistic. At this time of year, he also had to worry about the cows on the road. There were a lot of ranches along here and cattle guards usually kept them contained, but it wasn't uncommon to round a bend to find several of them loitering on the road.

Fortunately, he didn't need to go all the way to the summit because Heffley Lake was about half way up. He'd just passed the dump and the shooting range, so he knew he had about two minutes to go. He turned off the paved road onto a gravel one that wound around the lake. He'd spent several weekends at Alec's cabin in the past, a two-bedroom log house with running water and electricity.

He parked his car and ran to the shed to retrieve the key from under the mat. The first thing he noticed, upon opening the locked door to the cabin, was the musty locked-up smell. Fortunately, the beds were made. Whoever visited last had the responsibility of leaving everything in ready condition. He figured he'd be better off leaving Casimir in the car until he'd put Carina safely onto one of the beds. When he returned to the car, he saw that Carina hadn't moved a muscle.

As he was carrying Carina in, he decided he wanted to watch her until she woke up. He lay her on a bed and went to the living room to pull out the hide-a-bed, already made up and needing pillows.

Once he felt sure he'd done all he could do for Carina for the moment, he went outside to unload the car, starting with a restless Casimir. He let her run joyously through the trees that covered the acres surrounding the cabin. As he watched, she leapt for a passing butterfly, trying to catch it in her mouth. Casimir was only seven months old and he'd waited weeks before naming her. He'd been fortunate that the logger who found her was a close friend and had allowed him to keep the young pup that had been found with its paw in a leg hold trap, the dead wolf mother in another trap nearby. Chris had told him it looked like the mother had been dead for several days, her paw partly eaten through in her effort to escape.

Something else had killed her while she'd been trapped. Chris and Jackson had speculated that the pup had gone looking for its mother, and been similarly trapped.

Early on, Casimir showed her bold and fearless personality. Jackson had been relieved when the vet had said her markings were more of a husky than a wolf, an unusual crossbreed, but it meant that Jackson could keep her without worrying about the laws against owning a pure wolf. Casimir, of course, won her way into his heart by swishing her tail and flashing her intelligent eyes at him.

Several minutes passed before he finally allowed Casimir into the cabin. She pranced quietly in and began a thorough exploration of the surroundings before settling on the end of the hide-a-bed. Jackson sat in the worn brown-leather recliner across from Carina and Casimir jumped onto his lap and lay half on him and half on the recliner's arm as he stroked her until he fell asleep.

Casimir, licking his fingers and then his face, woke him. He glanced at his watch: 6:00AM. He peered at Carina and it appeared she hadn't moved at all. Jackson went over and listened to her steady breathing. Casimir, wanting to investigate, was getting ready to climb over Carina's head when Jackson scooped her up and carried her outside. It was getting harder and harder to scoop her up as she was leaving puppyhood behind, and turning into a sleek, furry adolescent.

He left her while he opened a can of her favourite dog food in the kitchen, poured some fresh water in her bowl, and set it on the floor. When Casimir came in from the yard, she made a beeline for the food and didn't breathe, it seemed, until every last tidbit was gone.

"For a puppy," Jackson muttered, "you sure are a pig."

He knew that, although she'd just eaten, she would prance around him as he ate his own breakfast expecting him to share, which was why he waited until she was finished and then let her outside again before he poured himself some breakfast cereal and then stood eating it while watching Casimir's antics outside. He placed the empty bowl in the sink when he finished and went to the washroom for his morning ablutions, glancing once more at Carina before he closed the door for some privacy.

# We Have Lost Her

## 31

"Chenaanah," Taura whispered as she scanned the area around them.

"What?"

"I don't see Carina anywhere."

Chenaanah whipped around; there was no sign of Carina. "Carina? Where is Carina? We have to find her."

"When was the last time you saw her?"

"Maybe ten or fifteen minutes after we left the hub's center."

"Chenaanah," Taura began, "it be takin' us over an hour to reach the hub again."

"Even with the shortcuts?"

"We be takin' the shortcuts."

"We cannot leave her behind after all she has done for us."

"If we go back, we be caught and fallin' into their hands. They probably be killin' me if they found Axe, and what about the gaoler? How are we going to explain to him that I be alive when he sliced my stomach open, and," she paused for emphasis, "why I happen to be in the company of a Leaders' wife?"

Chenaanah's face paled. "How did you know?"

"I not be knowin', but your reaction tells me my hunch be correct and your manner of dress and speaking do not be fittin' in here."

"You have been hiding something, too. You keep changing the way you talk. First you speak like one of the Scavs and then you talk normal, like me. What are you hiding?"

"That be—" she corrected herself. "That isn't your concern but if you must know, Axe beat me for talking above him and I learned how to fit in so he would have less to hit me for."

Chenaanah was instantly contrite. "I am sorry, I didn't know. Are you going to tell them about me?"

Taura shrugged. "No, if we do not get caught."

"And if we do?"

"Then, yes, if it means saving my life and my sister's, I'll tell them who you are."

"You're despicable."

"Despite your elevated position, you're no different than me."

"I am nothing like you."

"Yes, you are. If you were in my shoes, intent on saving yourself and your only sister, you would do whatever it took to do it. Wouldn't you do whatever it takes to save your daughters?"

Chenaanah didn't say anything for a few minutes and then nodded. "But I would not kill anybody."

"Depending on the particular circumstances, and the threat of danger to those we cherish, not killing isn't always an option."

"I could not kill anybody," Chenaanah said, but with less force in her voice.

"We're right in the middle of Scavenger territory and I have gotten us through the tunnels, the worst of it. Now we will have to surface. We have about five miles to cover before we reach the Wastelands."

"Is there something we can do to help Carina?"

Taura paused before replying. "I owe her my life and that's a debt I'll repay. I owe it to her to keep you safe until she returns, and if she does not return, I owe it to her to find your daughters."

"When we surface, will there be buildings that we can hide in for a while? We can keep a watch for her and give her time to catch up. You can choose a building somewhere."

"An hour, we will wait one hour and by then it will be much cooler. Then the Scavengers will infest this area and we will have to be very careful to avoid detection." Taura moved forward until they reached a dead end.

"We have to go back—" Chenaanah swallowed the rest of her sentence when she saw Taura turn left, disappearing from sight. She followed her into the darkness.

Taura's head reappeared. "Watch yourself. I'll hold the wood until you slide through."

Chenaanah slid through the narrow opening hidden in the darkness. She could see light shining through from the other side.

The building they were in was nothing more than a pile of decaying lumber and broken cement. "There aren't many places to hide in, and they will be sure to check them inside. We will go over there." She pointed to a decrepit building about five hundred yards away. She didn't wait for Chenaanah's answer as she dashed across the open space.

Chenaanah glanced around furtively before following her. The rundown building was just a skeleton. Most of the outer walls were rotted away and the inner walls had fallen inward. When Taura asked her for a boost onto the roof, she raised her eyebrows in disbelief. "You're not serious. This building looks like it is going to fall down any moment."

"It has looked like that for years and it is our only choice. Help me up to the roof and then I'll pull you up after me."

They crouched in the shadow of the stone chimney for the time being. It didn't offer much shade but it afforded them a view of the surrounding terrain.

Taura flattened herself against the roof. "We can rest for a while, but we will have to keep watching for trouble or Carina. You watch over there, left to right, and I'll watch in the opposite direction."

Chenaanah followed Taura's example and lay flat against the edge of the roof, searching the horizon. There were a few scattered, windowless houses, and endless piles of broken concrete.

"How far have we traveled so far?" Chenaanah asked.

"Underground?"

"From where we found you."

"About three miles; about seven hours underground," Taura explained.

"My goodness, that is incredible; no wonder the Banished have never been found."

"A regular rat's nest." She looked where Chenaanah lay. "What did you call them? The Banished?"

"Sorry, I meant Scavs. I have only known about the Scavengers a short time. I used to believe they were responsible for the crimes and the abductions. My bondmate tried to tell me about them, but I would not listen and now… it's too late for listening."

Taura and Chenaanah waited two hours, talking now and then about Taura's sister and Chenaanah's daughters, before they began to move on. The terrain didn't have much to offer once they abandoned the roof. There was little cover to hide behind, so they needed to be more cautious.

# Where Am I?

Jackson was making supper and his back was to the adjoining living room where, he assumed, Carina was still sleeping. While he was frying onions in butter, Carina woke up. She was groggy at first, so she let her eyes focus and then began scanning the room.

*I'm in someone's living room, but where? Brad's? No, it wasn't the basement, too much light.* She realized that she was wearing her own clothes, but not her nightgown. She felt a weight on her leg and was seized with panic, *Am I tied down?* When she moved her leg, the heavy weight moved also and suddenly something white leaped into view. Startled, Carina jerked back on the bed and screamed.

Jackson immediately dropped the Caesar salad he was making, startling Casimir and Carina even more, and Casmir's barking joined Carina's screaming.

"Casimir!" Jackson called abruptly as he rushed into the room to grab Casimir.

"Carina, it's me Jackson, and this is Casimir."

"It's a wolf! What's a wolf doing here? What are you doing here?" Carina sat bolt upright.

"I should have been watching her. I was hoping you'd never seen a wolf before."

"Is she tame?" The inane conversation belied Carina's underlying shock.

"I've had her since she was a pup. She won't harm you."

"How do I know that? I've seen how wolves react when they smell blood. She may be a pet, but she's still a wolf."

"She's part husky." It was an argument he might face if Casimir's instincts took over one day, but he hadn't expected it quite so soon. "You're right of course, I may have to deal with that some time, but I've never seen it in her. Once you get to know her, you'll see she's just a big softy."

Carina looked at him skeptically. "It's all right, I suppose. She just startled me."

"And waking up in a strange place didn't?"

"I didn't have much time to think about where I was, did I?"

"No, I suppose not, but you hide your feelings well."

"I'm in shock. This isn't the cave." She looked around.

"Are you looking for something?"

*Someone would be a better description.* "No, I just don't recognize this place."

"We're at Alec's cabin. You remember that much, I hope."

She could hear the sarcasm in his voice but ignored it. "How'd I get here?"

"Do you mean, did you just magically get here or did I bring you here?"

"Either version will do, although I'd prefer the latter," she replied flippantly, matching his attitude.

"I drove up last night from Kamloops. You arrived back, according to Brad, around seven, bumped your head and you haven't moved a muscle for about twenty-four hours."

"I've been asleep for twenty-four hours?"

"We tried to wake you, shook you even, but you were out like a light."

"How's Brad? How did he take my reappearance?"

"He's concerned but he handled himself well under the circumstances. Quite a friend you have there."

"Was Maria there when I... appeared?"

"No, and that's why we're here. I didn't know when you were going to wake up and the fewer people who know about your appearances and disappearances, the better."

Carina had maneuvered herself onto the hide-a-bed's edge and stood up, only to have her knees buckle beneath her. Casimir jumped back with a start and let out a yelp.

Jackson was beside her fast, his arm around her, helping her up. "Are you all right?"

"New legs," Carina tried to joke.

He lay her back on the hide-a-bed and propped her up with the pillows.

"Better?"

Carina's stomach let out a huge rumble of hunger. "Wow, I'm hungry. I think it must have been that delicious smell of butter and onions that woke me up."

"Good nose."

"Reminds me of cooking perogies."

"No perogies here. I was frying the butter and onions for the steak and potatoes. Want some?"

"For sure."

"Fifteen more minutes until supper and then we'll talk," he said as he returned to the kitchen; a nook separated by a counter from the living room. When he next looked at Carina, he saw she'd fallen asleep again with Casimir curled up beside her. Jackson ate his meal in silence.

It was after midnight when Jackson decided he had to get some decent sleep and not in the recliner where he'd been dozing. When he got up, Casimir jumped off the hide-a-bed, wanting to be let outside and raced around until Jackson gave in and let her out. When he let her in, she knew exactly where she wanted to go:

Carina's bed. Jackson figured Carina wouldn't disappear; she was too tired. And anyway, where could she go with Casimir beside her?

The light was terribly bright when Carina emerged from a low opening in the hard-packed tunnel. The surrounding area was devoid of buildings, although behind her in the distance she saw a few dark shapes that could have been some. *I must have come out of the tunnels*, she figured, and jumped when something brushed her leg. Casimir's eyes met hers when she looked down. It took her a few moments to register where she'd met Casimir before.

"Casimir. What are you doing here?" Casimir wagged her tail in response. Carina stooped down to pet her. "I don't know if you'll want to be here."

Casimir's tongue whipped out and licked her cheek.

"You're such a sweetie, Casimir. Truth is, it's wonderful having you here with me." Carina talked as she walked. "I wonder how you got here along with me. Jackson will have a bird when he can't find either of us and I'm going to have a hell of a time explaining your presence here."

After ten more minutes, she stopped and knelt down. Casimir turned on her back for a rub, and Carina scratched the exposed tummy. *If only I knew where to go from here. How am I supposed to find Chenaanah and Tauralee?* She looked at the rotted wood that she'd pushed aside to exit the tunnel. *How can I go back in there?* She stood undecided for several moments until Casimir ran outside. *I guess that decides it.*

She glanced around before she stepped outside. Casimir was running toward a distant shape that turned out to be a decrepit house. Carina caught up with her just as she scrabbled up a broken beam onto the roof. "Cas-ih-mir, get down here." Casimir's face appeared at the opening. "Casimir, come here."

"Woof," she barked before disappearing.

"Dumb dog," she muttered as she eyed the beam and began climbing it. She pulled herself onto the roof and spied Casimir sniffing around the chimney. "Dogs don't belong on roofs, don't you know that?" Then she saw what she was sniffing at, a bag—the makeshift pillowcase that Chenaanah had packed. "My God. They were here." She grabbed it and patted Casimir on the head. "Good dog. I wouldn't have found it without you." Casimir barked and dashed back to the beam, leaving Carina to follow.

Carina took a moment to scan the barren distance before she gingerly made her way toward the thick wooden beam. She had to hang over the roof edge, until she was sure she was above the beam, before she let go. Her relief at landing on it was short-lived as it tottered and gave way beneath her. She fell, along with the beam, onto the floor below. She rolled as she fell and avoided the beam but gashed her arm in the process. She lay stupefied for several minutes before she tried to get up, and then she saw the long wooden sliver in her arm. *Damn, it stings like hell.* Blood flowed out when she pulled out the sliver, and she automatically applied pressure as she reached around for the pillowcase. After pouring some water over her wound, she reached for the knife from the pillowcase to cut a strip from the bottom of her blouse. Once it was secured and then, after a swallow of water, she returned the knife to the pillowcase.

"I guess you're more Husky than wolf," she said to Casimir shakily, glad that the smell of blood hadn't brought out any wolfly instincts. She got up weakly but was glad that, despite the bruises she'd have from the fall, nothing else was amiss. "We'd better go. If the racket we caused didn't garner any attention, we'll be fine." She shouldered the pack, grateful for its presence, and stepped outside. Casimir sniffed the ground and set off turning to make sure Carina was following her.

After a half an hour of walking, Carina stopped again to survey her surroundings, the shadows behind her having disappeared. Carina looked up at the cloudy sky. *One good thing: At least it's not too hot. This must be the Wastelands*, Carina assumed.

It was about an hour since they'd last stopped and everywhere she looked, barren, sun-dried land met her brown, worried eyes. *What do I do now? How long do these Wastelands continue?*

The clouds parted and the sun began beating down harshly. She pulled a piece of dried meat out of the pillowcase and gave some to Casimir while chewing on the other piece. "Eat slowly, Casimir, because I'm going to ration the food." She poured a little water into her hand three times for Casimir. Carina, in turn, took two gulps. Water might be a problem, too.

She surveyed the land once again. She'd been following Casimir, hoping she was following a scent, but now Carina wasn't so sure. *I think I'll look for somewhere to stop. We can't go on aimlessly in this heat.* They continued walking in the same direction; the land seemed to be sloping up.

After an hour, she began wondering if she was doing the right thing. She had no idea where she was going or if there was an end to it. The sun beat down fiercely as they trudged along and Carina tried focusing on the distant horizon, and soon became mesmerized, footstep after footstep. It wasn't until Casimir started barking and running off ahead, that Carina saw the fence off the road.

*A road. How long have I been walking on a road and when did the terrain change?*

She had just gone through a gate when she heard, "Where the hell have you been?" and turned to find Jackson standing in front of her. He couldn't conceal his anger. "How can you just disappear like that without telling me?"

"I… I took a Casimir for a walk."

"Then what's the bag in your hand?"

Carina realized that she was holding a pillowcase filled with food. Jackson grabbed it from her, "What's in here? Bread, dried meat, where were you planning on going? I'm talking to you, Carina. You disappear from Brad's house; leave us wondering what happened to you. You disappear from here before six in the morning and show up hours later with my dog and a pillowcase of food. You've got some explaining to do."

Carina tried moving past Jackson but he grabbed her arm causing her to cry out in pain.

"What the hell did you do to your arm?" He pushed up her sleeve and saw the dried blood, his face paling.

"I fell."

His anger dissipated. "Let's get you inside so I can look at it." He pulled her along, more gently than before.

At the kitchen sink, he removed the strip of cloth and held her arm under the water for a few seconds. "Does it hurt?"

"It stopped hurting hours ago." She didn't notice her slip. "There was an abandoned building and your dog figured she could climb onto the roof."

"How'd she manage that?"

"There was a beam she climbed. When she wouldn't come down, I had to go up and get her. Dumb dog," she said softly. "The beam collapsed on the way down."

"Fool thing to do."

"Tell that to your dog."

"Keep talking while I get the first aid kit. Were you carrying her off the roof?" he asked as he went to the bathroom and rummaged for the kit.

"Of course not. She jumped down of her own accord. The good news is, she didn't react wolfishly to the blood."

"That's a relief," Jackson said when he returned moments later. "Where is this building?"

"It wasn't near here, I'm sure."

"Why do I get the feeling that you're not telling the whole truth when you talk to me? I feel like you're omitting some important details."

She watched as he put some Polysporin onto her arm and then bandaged it. His touch was gentle. *He's such a strong man, yet gentle. How can I tell him?* She touched his cheek with her other hand. She moved to kiss his cheek but he turned unexpectedly and their lips met instead. His hand went up behind her head as he prolonged the kiss. For a moment or two, Carina lost herself in his kiss until she finally pulled away.

Reluctantly, she said, "I appreciate what you've done, Jackson. I should never have involved you in all of this, but I need time to think this through and I don't need any romantic complications if this goes south."

He gave her a soul-searching look before releasing her. "You've got to give me more than that."

"I went for a walk around the lake with the dog and that takes time. I found the pillowcase of food on my way."

"You expect me to believe that you conveniently found that pillowcase?"

"I think the last time I told you the absolute truth you called me a liar, so I may as well earn that esteemed title." Her eyes glinted blackly as she spoke to him. "I think the best thing I can do for you is to go home and let you go your way. You can live with your assumption that I'm a schizophrenic nut."

"I never said that," Jackson defended himself.

"Not to me and not in so many words. You've called me a liar. How can I tell you anything?"

"Look, I'm not your ex, and I'm not going to hurt you." He winced. As soon as he said it, he knew that he'd said the wrong thing. He couldn't unsay it, so he bumbled ahead anyway. "I don't want to see you ruining your life this way."

"What way?"

"You can talk to Dr. Montgomery. He can recommend someone to talk to, maybe give you something to prevent your, your—"

"My what? My delusions? My hallucinations? Be specific, please. Which problem will the drugs help?" She pulled her hand away from his and pushed past him, but not before he saw the shine of tears in her eyes.

Carina's hair had escaped her ponytail and loose tendrils touched her cheek, Jackson had been watching how they curled around her ear and was slow to respond to her words. He turned to watch her as she stormed through the living room to the bathroom. A couple of minutes later he heard the shower running, and finally he knew he could relax while she was taking a shower. He tried to figure out why he reacted so rashly when Carina was around. *It's my job*, he thought, but he wondered if there was more to it than that. His thoughts zeroed in on the sound of the water, and he couldn't help but imagine all the lovely places that water was privileged to fall.

Carina was thinking less pleasant thoughts. *Arrogant jerk. Just who does he think he is calling me a liar and treating me like a basket case?* She wiped away her tears and cried under the shower until the hot water ran cold, enough time for the anger to leach out of her pores. Finally, she relaxed. She wrapped her hair in a towel and began to dry herself off.

Jackson heard the bathroom door open and a few minutes later he walked down the hall toward the bedroom. "Carina?" He pushed the door open when she didn't answer. "You know," he began, but his next words stuck in his throat when he saw Carina's bare arm above the bed covers.

*Casimir, you traitor*, he thought when he saw her curled beside Carina. He was about to leave the room when he decided to take a precaution against Carina disappearing. He went to his jacket, took out his handcuffs, and snapped one end on Carina's wrist and the other end to the metal headboard. *I'll have hell to pay for this,* he thought, but I'm tired of her disappearing act.

Jackson woke up to Carina's yells of outrage. "Jackson, you jerk! What's the meaning of this? How dare you handcuff me to the bed! You're violating my rights. I'll report you. Jackson. You get in here and set me free! Jackson! Jackson!" She tried shaking the headboard and then squeezing her wrist through the cuff without success.

"I'll be there in a minute." Jackson figured that he'd be better off facing her once she settled down. *I think I'll make breakfast; that might help.*

He'd cuffed her hand to the middle of the headboard and Carina was unable to get off the bed. When Jackson came in with the tray of steaming food, Carina glowered at him but didn't make a move. *Just you wait until I get my hands on you.*

"Coffee, toast, scrambled eggs, would you like some?" he asked nonchalantly.

Carina didn't reply, just continued glowering at him.

"It's quite tasty," Jackson said with a mouthful of scrambled eggs. "Listen, Carina. I know you're angry with me for cuffing you to the bed. I just wanted you to remain in one place. How can I make it up to you?"

Carina looked at him, then: "You can take them off to begin with." *So I can throttle you.*

Jackson grinned. "Yes, of course."

As soon as the cuff was off, barely containing her anger, Carina shoved him away from her and ran to the bathroom.

"Are you all right?" Carina didn't answer. "Carina, answer me or I'll break down the door."

"Leave me alone, already. Can't I go to the bathroom in peace?"

"Keep talking to me then."

"Go away."

"I'll come in there if you don't keep talking." Carina didn't say anything but quickly got off the toilet.

"Carina, I mean it."

"I'm going to take a shower and if you think I'm able to disappear then that means you believe me. I'm not going anywhere."

"You can't guarantee that and maybe I just think you'd runaway."

"I'm naked, for crying out loud and I didn't run away."

Jackson muttered, "Maybe keeping you naked is the solution for your disappearing."

"What did you say?" Carina asked.

"I said, I'll be out here if you need me."

Carina showered in peace but once she finished, she realized that she had only her nightgown or the towel to wear back to the room. When she saw that her nightgown had fallen onto the wet floor, she decided on the towel with her nightgown draped around her shoulders. As she left the bathroom, she collided with Jackson, who'd been standing outside the door. He automatically put up his hands to prevent the collision, and they ended up resting on her shoulders. Carina's towel fell to the floor, and she quickly crouched to grab the towel against her body.

"Would you mind?" she shrieked. "I don't need you to hover over me like a manic bee." She backed away from him until she was in a bedroom and closed the door.

"I'm sorry, it was an accident."

"So were the cuffs. Just leave me the hell alone for a few minutes. I need some space."

Jackson stood their pensively, not knowing how to make amends until he recalled her love of fishing and knocked quietly on the door.

"Leave me alone." *Damn that man. Isn't it bad enough he cuffed me and then saw me naked? Damn. I'm more upset that he saw me naked.* "What do you want, Jackson?"

He noticed the change in her voice. "Why don't you get dressed for fishing, Carina?"

"Are you going to cuff me to the boat?" she yelled and heard him chuckle.

Carina loved to fish, so she gladly put aside the morning's irritations. She knew she'd be thinking things over throughout the day so she might as well be fishing and get some pleasure out of it. When she came out of the bedroom, she said, "What did I hear about breakfast?"

"I'm afraid it's cold but I can make you something fresh."

"Only if it isn't a problem."

Jackson looked to see if she was still angry with him. "Is everything okay between us?"

"Let's call it a truce."

Jackson took Carina's lead and didn't mention the handcuffs or her disappearance. "I thought we could go fishing."

"If we head out right away, the fish are probably still biting." She raced through breakfast.

# Gone Fishing

The aluminum rowboat rocked gently on the calm lake. Casimir was having a great time going from one side of the boat to the other, worrying her humans, who were expecting her to jump overboard. The continuous rings of feeding fish on the water's surface, and the insects skating like endless dancers, lulled them. Jackson watched the sunrise cast a soft light on the lake, and the trees, and—especially— on Carina's features. He watched her put a dirt-crusted, wriggling worm on her hook. She pulled her arm back and then swung it forward with perfect grace, releasing the line. He saw her satisfied look when the cast flew through the air and her look of chagrin if the worm fell off the hook before it hit the water. He wondered when he'd become the kind of man who could be so fascinated with a woman.

He was so caught up in his thinking that he almost missed a faraway look that came into Carina's eyes. She was staring down into the water as if mesmerized by something beneath the surface.

"What do you see?"

"Oh, uh, nothing. Why?"

"You were staring into the water as if you saw something."

"No, I was just thinking."

"About what?"

"I don't remember, nothing, probably just relaxing. Oh, I've got a bite."

"Really?"

The fish tugged at the line, leaping into the air. Carina kept reeling the line in as smoothly as possible until the fish was near the boat, and then she pulled it in. She quickly freed the hook without tearing the inside of the small rainbow trout's mouth. "Pretty, isn't it?" she asked. "It's undersized so I have to let it go."

His face lit up with a teasing grin. "No supper then?" Casimir barked in response.

"It's still early." Carina grinned back at him.

The sun rose higher as the day progressed, creating sparkling diamonds on the lake's surface. The wind rippled over the glittering shapes, made them dance and shift in constant motion. When Carina closed her eyes, she could still feel the fiery sunlight. Opening them once more, she saw a fish just below the diamonds and leaned forward to look.

Suddenly, Carina let out a scream of pain and clutched at her arm as she stood up in the small boat. Jackson jumped up quickly in response, Casimir scrambled forward barking furiously, and the combined swiftness of their movements caused the boat to tip precariously. When Jackson moved to regain the boat's balance, he lurched into Carina, who then went flying into the water.

Carina felt immediate relief from the burning pain on her arm in the lake's cold water. She quickly pushed her way to the surface and gasped for air. She heard Jackson's voice calling her and turned his way. When she saw Tauralee and Chenaanah instead of Jackson, she thought her eyes were playing tricks on her. She rubbed them and saw Jackson biting his lower lip as he reached to grab and pull her into the boat. She accepted his help silently and didn't speak when he put his jean jacket over her shoulders. Even Casimir kept her distance from soggy Carina.

Carina watched as Jackson rowed back to their private pier. She was grateful he didn't question her endlessly about standing up in the boat partly because, if he hadn't stood up, too, she wouldn't have fallen in the lake and be sitting in front of him looking like a soggy forlorn puppy. She noticed Casimir was studiously avoiding her soaked form.

"Traitor," she heard Jackson mutter, "switching sides again," and briefly wondered who he meant.

Jackson took Carina's arm and helped her out of the boat once they reached the wooden pier. "What happened out there?"

Her feet squelched on the pier. "Can we talk later? I think I'll go change."

He nodded uncertainly as she went by. "I'll grab the gear and put it in the shed."

He stamped his feet on the mat when he returned to the cottage. Carina had just entered the living room after changing her soggy apparel for her dry blue-jean skirt, shirt, and jacket. "I'm going to the shed to look at my tackle box," she said without looking at him directly.

Jackson did a double take. "You want to go fishing again?"

"No, not right away. I'll be back in a minute."

"I'll come with you because I put the box on the top shelf; it'll be too high for you to reach."

She knew it wasn't true, but figured he wasn't letting her go anywhere alone.

Carina took the small grey tackle box from Jackson and opened it to reveal an assortment of fishing flies, hooks, and weights. She moved the first drawer inside and Jackson saw a boning knife, matches, chain, and fishing line. He watched as Carina stuck the matches in a pocket and then, using the wicked-looking knife, cut a length of fishing line which she carefully wound around a nail and stuck in her pocket.

"What's that for?"

"I might need it."

"For what?"

"I'll know when I need it."

"Is something wrong?"

"Have you seen my hiking boots anywhere?" She asked as she scanned the shed.

"They're in the house."

He followed Carina back toward the cabin and tried to grab her arm but she pulled away and hurried toward the cabin without stopping. She found her hiking boots tucked in a corner near the closet and began putting them on.

Jackson came in and, standing with his hands on his hips, demanded, "Where do you think you're going?"

"It doesn't concern you," she replied as she finished lacing up the first boot, wrapping the excess lace around her ankle and tied the ends.

"Damn right it concerns me, especially if you're planning to disappear from here again before I have a chance to do anything."

"For your information, I don't control the disappearing, it just happens. This time I intend to be ready for it on my own terms. I know what I'm in for, and I'd better be prepared." She'd finished tying her second boot.

"So, you're telling me that you're going to disappear again?"

"Whoever started this adventure of mine, I don't imagine they're going to let it end until whatever I'm supposed to do is done."

"Why did you scream in the boat?"

"The armband, it felt like it was burning me."

"Damn, I forgot about that thing. If I'd had any sense, I would have removed it while you were unconscious."

"Too late for that now. It doesn't come off even when I try."

"Let me see it."

Carina took off her jean jacket and tried pulling the armband down her arm but it didn't budge. Turning away from Jackson, she unbuttoned three buttons and then pulled down her shirt over her left shoulder.

He gasped when the armband began shimmering and then disappearing from Carina's arm. In its place was a tattoo of the armband, now a part of her.

Carina went to the bathroom and peered into the mirror at the markings. There were no burn marks or scratches, then she looked up, meeting Jackson's glance. This time concerned eyes met hers.

"Carina," he began, opening up his arms and wrapping Carina in them. "I'm sorry, I've been so hard on you, but what I just saw tells me I've been a complete idiot. Will you forgive me? Let me help you."

"How? I haven't been able to control my disappearances."

"I'm coming with you this time."

Carina looked at him as if he'd suddenly grown horns. "Excuse me?"

"You heard me correctly. I'm coming with you."

"And how do you expect to do that?" she asked as she straightened her blouse and put her jacket back on. "I have no control over it; it just seems to happen. Where's the pillowcase?"

"It's in the laundry, why?"

"I filled it with food, but not here."

"You mean the other place."

"Yes."

"That's not possible."

"Why isn't it possible?"

"It had Heffley Lake stamped on it."

"Really?"

"Seriously," Jackson affirmed.

"I can't explain it. I end up using things there, and then when I'm here my clothes change."

"That's one reason I've had a hard time believing you, but a vanishing solid object that begins glowing and then disappears into thin air convinces me, especially when it leaves a permanent engraving on your arm."

"You mean that disappearing before your eyes in a public restaurant wasn't convincing enough?"

"It was too incredible to believe," he replied sheepishly.

"And a mere tattoo convinced you?"

"I'm sorry, but you have to admit the whole thing's kind of weird."

"Kind of? How about a lot of? I feel like a ping pong ball living in two separate worlds."

"So, tell me what happened the last time you were there in that other place." He took her hand and led her to the couch. He didn't release it as she began speaking.

"Well, when I arrived back, it was the middle of the night and the Leader's wife, whose children were kidnapped, was planning on sneaking out of the women's sleeping quarters to leave the sector and search for her daughters. I said I'd go with her. It was that or stay and be given to Daric."

"Who's Daric?"

"A Leader. He said I was a prime candidate for their breeding program."

"Breeding program?"

"Women are kept for breeding purposes, growing the population. You have to pass some kind of tests and then they match you to someone and you're bred."

"Incredible."

"Then they marry you off to a man who is honour-bound to provide for you until the birth of the child. If you're lucky or unlucky, depending on how you look at it, a Leader picks you as his wife and you get the pleasure of breeding with him."

"You make it sound disgusting, like something out of a science fiction movie." He squeezed her hand comfortingly.

"Tell me about it. I went with Chenaanah because I knew my freedom was running out. The Leaders' scheduled monthly meeting was coming, and when they meet, they assign you to some kind of life position. I've been lucky, I had amnesia there and didn't remember anything, so everyone's been assuming my file would arrive from another sector—where I was supposedly from—and they'd assign me once they received it." She spat out the words.

"The file?"

"They keep track of absolutely everyone. Where they are and what they're doing. But, when my memories of my life here returned, I knew it was only a matter of time before someone discovered I didn't belong. They have this thing called recultivation for anyone who threatens their society."

"Recultivation?"

Carina stood up anxiously and began pacing. Jackson went over to her and turned her to face him, "What's wrong?"

She pulled away and stood looking out the window for several minutes while Jackson watched her. When he saw her shoulders shaking, he went and put his arms around her. "It's okay, I'm here."

Carina wanted to stand there with his arms holding her. She wanted to pretend she'd never participated in the recultivation, but she couldn't.

He felt her stiffen and let go. "Tell me what happened. Don't keep it inside. It will eat away at you."

She turned and faced him, her face ravaged with emotion, and Jackson saw tears and something else, fear. "My God, Carina. What's wrong? What did they do to you?"

She began crying again and Jackson pulled her close and rocked her.

A dam broke inside of her and she cried even harder. The loss of her husband, the struggle to finish university, Ritik's mouth as it opened for the seed....

Jackson held her until her tears subsided, and then led her to a seat at the kitchen table. Carina heard the clink of glasses and watched through bleary eyes as he rummaged in the cupboard until he found a brown bottle that he ceremoniously placed on the table. "My friend Jack Daniels. We rarely get together, but he's a great comfort at times." He poured two shots. "Drink up, it will warm you."

"I don't drink hard stuff."

"Neither do I, but sometimes the soft stuff just doesn't work. You don't have to drink it but if you do, don't sip it." He took the glass and with a fluid motion tossed it drink down his throat.

Carina watched him, then followed suit. She felt the liquid fire hit her mouth and race to her belly before she started coughing. "My God, that's nasty." Then she felt the warmth suffuse her body and sighed, "I guess I needed that."

Jackson poured himself another shot and held the bottle out to her. She nodded and watched him pour. Ritik's mouth opening mindlessly. She downed the second shot before Jackson had even put the bottle down.

"Whoa, there. It's not water."

She nodded. "I'll sip the next one."

"You don't want to get drunk on this stuff. It gives you a nasty hangover."

"Are you speaking from experience?"

His hand wavered and he hesitated to speak. "Y-yes. I lost my last partner when he was shot." He downed his drink for fortitude and poured them both another. Carina gave him a sympathetic look but didn't speak. The anguish in her eyes reflected his own as he recalled his partner falling to the ground from a shot in the chest.

Their eyes met over the table and Jackson's voice came out in a solemn whisper. "This recultivation thing. It's bad, isn't it?" He waited until she was ready to speak and when she did the words poured out relentlessly.

"They made me participate in the Ceremony, that's what they called it. They told me that I'd been specially chosen to participate and that not everyone had that privilege. Privilege. Bastards."

Jackson's eyes widened. He'd never heard her swear before.

"If you don't fit in to their way of thinking, or are contaminated by others, they recondition you. It's like the Russians after the war. Anyone who'd been outside the country, who was exposed to Western influence, was considered contaminated and a risk. They shot a lot of them. I traced my family tree. A distant relative came over to the States hoping to earn enough money to bring over his wife and daughter. He wrote her letters. Finally, he was so homesick he wrote to tell her that he was returning home. The officials were waiting for him when he arrived. They shot him before he had a chance to greet his wife."

"The Leaders are like those officials except they don't shoot you. They recultivate. I wondered for the longest time what planting had to do with recultivation. I found out. They bury you up to your neck in a pit of dirt and then they make you swallow a seed."

"A seed? What kind of seed?"

"I don't know what kind, but I know what it does. I saw it. I still don't believe what I saw. The seed starts growing inside the body. It sends out shooters and another seed forms. Except it's not a seed, it's the person. The original person is the nourishment for the new seed itself. The body is remade, like a clone." Carina paused as she raised the glass to her lips, her shaking hand threatening to spill its contents as she stared into it. "The ultimate punishment. They make you watch yourself reforming while you're dissolving and… and…" she faltered, "you feel everything. You feel yourself dying. The screams. The screaming."

"Did someone die?"

"Yes. No. The seeds make an identical replica but the replica is just an empty husk. Everything you were, every thought, every emotion, every memory is gone. You're a blank slate." She stood up agitatedly and opened the cabin door like a caged animal. Jackson followed her as she started walking through the trees, seeking solace. "The Leaders then re-educate you the way they want you to be, a perfect citizen."

"That's a nightmare. How could you stand to watch?"

"I didn't have a choice. They made me watch. They made me participate, damn it."

"What do you mean?"

She ground the recondite words out, "They made me put the damn seed in his mouth." She drained the glass and screamed, "They made me kill him!" The glass flew out of her hand and shattered against the tree.

Jackson stood in shocked silence. The horrific thing she'd endured ravaged his heart.

"Don't look at me that way, like I'm the devil. I couldn't bear it," she whispered.

"Oh, Carina. I wasn't thinking that at all." He gathered her up in his arms and held her. The trees swished in the breeze, Casimir lay watching them, and the anguish seeped away.

Jackson made sure she'd eaten everything on her plate and watched as she drank her third cup of coffee. They made idle chitchat while they ate, but there were long bouts of silence. He'd put away the remnants of the whiskey, a reminder of her revelations. His mind still reeled from the unreality of it all, and he wondered how she'd managed to keep her sanity. He admitted that he could no longer doubt that she was sane—the armband had denied him that escape. It was real, no matter how he wanted to dismiss it. He found it easier if he just accepted that she had been in another reality even though it was something straight out of a science fiction movie. She deserved that, his belief, his faith in her.

He dragged out a book and tried to read, unsuccessfully. He still had so many questions that he wanted to ask. "Do you want to go for a walk around the lake?"

Carina looked up from her book, she hadn't flipped a page; she'd only been staring at it. She put it aside and stood up. "That's a good idea."

Casimir bounded outside with them and took off down the path. Carina sucked in her breath, remembering how the dog had followed her before. She'd been thinking of the seed and Ritik's screams. That terrifying moment when she believed that the armband had failed, and she was really killing Ritik.

It had been his idea to use the armband. He told her that she could use it to take his memories and hold them until he was remade. She hadn't believed him but had listened to his words and followed his directions. Why he believed in the armband—or in her—she didn't know, but there had been one thing she knew for sure: Once he'd told her what recultivation would do to him, she had had no choice but to try. She'd put her hands on his head, the armband touching his brow, and closed her eyes to concentrate as he spoke. At first nothing happened, and she'd briefly opened her eyes. She'd concentrated again. This time Ritik covered her hands with his, holding them in place as she breathed deeply, at his suggestion. Then giddiness hit her, a lightness-like floating as she freed her mind.

She remembered his warm hands shaking against hers and then falling from hers. She'd looked at him. "Ritik, are you all right? What happened?" He didn't answer, just lay there. A deep sense of defeat had filled her as she tried to rouse him. She'd left him like that to rejoin Chenaanah, not knowing if she'd succeeded.

Much later, when the Defender had taken her to the ceremony, she still wasn't sure. The narcotic smoke in the dimly lit room had made her lethargic, and she'd put the seed in his mouth as his head looked blindly at her from the pit. His screams had ripped through her like defeat and loss.

A smile escaped her lips as she focused on the trees around her. *I brought him back, though. I restored his mind and he escaped with us. I defeated the Leaders.* It was a powerful realization.

Jackson noticed her smile. "I'm glad you're enjoying this walk." They'd already reached the lake and were following a well-worn path around it.

Her smile widened. "Yes, I am. It's just what I needed to clear my head after our friend Jack Daniels had his way with me."

"Where is that abandoned house you saw?" Jackson asked.

"It isn't *here*," she said meaningfully.

"Oh."

"After the ceremony, Chenaanah and I escaped with Ritik."

"The clone?"

"Yes. I didn't want to leave him behind. He was a Banished. I couldn't abandon him because he'd helped me once before. I restored his memories."

"How could you do that?"

"I used the armband. I'd stored his essence, as he called it, before the ceremony and then I gave it back later when he was remade."

"So you escaped with Sh-Sh—"

"Chenaanah and Ritik. He knew how to get out of the sector; he'd been programmed with those memories by the Leaders because they wanted him to have new loyal memories of the Leaders and not of the Banished."

"How?"

"It seems that with the armband and me being a stranger in the land, I have some kind of power."

"That's like science fiction."

"When I first went to that reality, I saw a tapestry." She related the details of it. "I tried doing an online search about dragons and phoenixes, along with legends, but nothing I read sounded similar."

"I did some research too, with no luck," he admitted.

"Really?"

"I wanted to know more and maybe help you if you were delusional. I was wrong and I'm on your side."

She looked at him. "Thank you."

"Weren't you worried he'd betray you?"

"Yes, which is why we ditched him once we were out of the sector. To make it short, there are three groups: Leaders, Banished, and Scavengers. I don't know which one is the lesser evil. The Banished, I assume, oppose the Leaders, and those two factions fight whenever they meet. The Scavengers are the ones who steal, kidnap people, and then sell them. In fact, they're the ones who kidnapped me from the sector and sold me in the beginning. My reappearance in downtown Kamloops was directly after being sold, I think. It's still sketchy, especially with the time thing."

"You remember that?"

"Those Scavengers raided the complex and fourteen people were taken in the middle of the night; two of them were Loriia and Liisa, Chenaanah's daughters. The Leaders and the Banished have been searching for them for at least a month."

"They're working together?"

"No, Chenaanah's bondmate is now a Banished. He became one of them after he spent two years undercover with them for the Leaders. He infiltrated their ranks and ended up joining them. Then he pretended to escape. He was stabbed in the process and I found him. It was a ploy to make the Leaders believe he was still one of them. He's a Banished, but the Leaders don't know it."

"Then how come you know he's a Banished?"

"He was delirious and he talked about the Stranger and the armband. I took care of him and he told me he knew why I was there."

"Did he tell you why you were there?"

"Not enough, but I do know I'm supposed to be saving them, maybe from the Leaders. It has something to do with the tapestry and the legend. That's why Chenaanah and I knew we had to find the place where I was sold."

"I presume you found it."

"Yeah, but we had help."

"Ritik came back?"

Carina stopped walking for a moment and looked at the path. They were over halfway around it and the lake was scarcely visible.

"No, we were searching an area that had some small buildings, and we followed a man who'd showed up. When he entered a particular place, Chenaanah stayed outside and I went in. This man, Axe," Carina paused when she saw Jackson's raised eyebrow, "yes, Axe, was beating a chained-up woman named Tauralee and I hit him from behind. We escaped while he was unconscious. Tauralee took us to the hub where the people are sold—where I'd been sold." Carina said the last words and then was silent. She saw Jackson staring at her. "We couldn't have made it through the underground hub and its maze-like passages without Tauralee's guidance. We left the hub, or tried to, after we found out that there were two girls fitting the description of Chenaanah's daughters, who'd been sold. I lost Chenaanah and Tauralee. I was following them. When I got to a doorway with a light shining beneath it, I opened it and found myself in Brad's kitchen. I was shocked."

Jackson sat up at Carina's words. "You mean you were awake when you went from one reality to another?"

"Yes, I was, but I don't understand what you mean."

"I assumed you were asleep when these things happened."

"Sometimes I am, but not always. I thought I was going crazy when I'd go to sleep in one place and wake up in another. I think my amnesia was a blessing in disguise because it buffered me from experiencing two separate realities. I wonder if I could have handled it had I known all along who I was and I didn't have the answers that I wanted."

"And those are?"

"Why me? How did I get drawn into the other reality in the first place and why was I chosen?"

"I've been wondering the same thing. Why you?" Jackson asked. "I'm sure you could handle anything. But what about you and Casimir?"

"I don't know what to tell you. I'm still wondering how I got to this cabin. I was in Brad's kitchen and then I vaguely remember smelling butter and onions and then I was walking on a rough dirt path."

"What about Casimir? You were in bed sleeping, Casimir was right there beside you, and when I woke up, in the morning, you had both disappeared."

"Oh, is that how it happened? I never made the connection. I seem to be putting on a lot of miles in both places. First I'm in a tunnel, then a kitchen, then I'm whisked off to this cabin, and then I'm walking on dry, sun-baked dirt, and then I'm running into you

319

with a pillowcase in my hand. I don't know how Casimir got there. She was just there, beside me."

"Don't you remember anything?"

"Like I said, so much has happened that I'm lucky I know my name. All I know is that I materialized, for a lack of a better word, beside a tunnel that led outside to open ground. When I came out of the tunnel, Casimir ran off to a building and climbed the roof. She found the pillowcase that Chenaanah had left behind. I saw a few scattered buildings but Chenaanah and Tauralee were gone. I followed Casimir after that. I figured she had some kind of scent. I assumed we were in the Wastelands. It was so hot and I found it difficult to focus on the horizon after so many hours of walking. Casimir started barking and, well, you know the rest."

"That's when you appeared here?"

"Yes. At the lake, when I surfaced, I saw something behind you. I thought it was the water in my eyes and the shock of falling in, but I think I saw an image of Chenaanah and Tauralee, and they were in trouble. Maybe they've been captured."

"By whom?"

"If it's the Scavengers, they'll kill Tauralee for running away and keep Chenaanah. If it's the Leaders, they might weather the storm and survive without the recultivation."

Jackson winced at her words. "And if it's the Banished?"

"I really don't know what would happen then. I don't know anything much about that particular group."

"What are the Wastelands?"

"I don't know. I gather it's a desolate expanse, except for one person and his slaves. He's the one who purchased Loriia and Liisa to work in his mines."

"This Tauralee, why would she help you after her escape, especially if getting caught would mean her death?"

Carina didn't mention the incident in the hub where she'd seen Tauralee's blood flowing backward into her body. Carina thought it was too surrealistic to believe it herself, let alone try to convince someone else it had happened. "The man in the Wastelands has her sister somewhere."

"How'd you get through the tunnels? Who told you where to search for the girls?"

"The gaoler's bondmate."

"There were no men around?"

"They were fighting the fire that Tauralee started as a distraction so we could get inside the tunnels without anyone noticing." Carina stopped talking and then abruptly asked, "Do you have that pillowcase? The Wastelands, from what I've seen, won't provide food and water."

"I'll get it for you."

"What am I going to do? I know I have to help those people. It's just a matter of when."

"I was afraid you'd say that." He came back with Carina's packed pillowcase. Carina reached out her hand to grab it. Jackson snapped a handcuff on her wrist and snapped the other end onto his.

"That's not going to work. I don't decide when to go, it just happens."

"Well, the next time it happens, I'll be there."

"You don't have any right to do this."

"Probably not."

"It could be days or weeks before it happens again."

# 34

# Cabin Fever

As the days passed, tension mounted. The first day was the worst as Carina discovered the awkwardness of being cuffed to someone 24/7.

"I have to use the bathroom," she said after ignoring the fact that she'd had to go for two hours already. Finally, she couldn't stand it any longer. Jackson got up with her and she quickly said, "Alone, if you don't mind."

Jackson went into the bathroom, looking for a place to attach the cuffs. He settled for the pipe beneath the sink and hooked Carina to it.

Is this necessary?" she retorted angrily.

Jackson grinned. "Yup. You are not disappearing without me again."

Carina told him she felt like a child having to say when she had to go to the bathroom and when she was finished. Jackson had it easier because he'd just pick her up and cuff her to the refrigerator door when he had to go. When Jackson put Casimir outside she assumed he wasn't sure how Casimir would react to the constant struggling.

"You're almost as bad as Trator was," she yelled.

He reacted by grabbing her by the shoulders and shaking her. "Not quite. At least I care for you and I doubt you can say that about your previous owner."

"Owner" slipped out accidentally. He hoped she hadn't heard his faux pas but the slap of her hand let him know she had. He stepped backward and tripped, pulling Serena with him. She fell on top of him. She kicked and punched as best as she could until Jackson was able to pin her arms to her sides. She'd cussed and struggled until exhausted. He released her then, and when she curled into a ball on her side, he saw she was shaking. He heard a stifled sob but was unsure of what to do. He wanted to take off the damn cuffs and hold her until she stopped crying. But he had a primal instinct to protect her, and if that meant she had to be cuffed, then so be it.

They fell asleep in that position, on the floor, the fire out long ago. He lay on his back and Carina still curled up in a tight ball. The living room was a shambles. Unconsciously, their bodies moved together for warmth. Jackson awoke first, and he didn't dare move for fear of waking her. Her long hair was fanned out beside her, her face calm and relaxed. He knew the moment she woke up by the sudden tenseness in her body. He felt a momentary sliver of regret about the handcuffs, but composed himself—he was doing it for her own good.

That day passed in studied politeness. Carina treated Jackson like a minor inconvenience. He hated being on the wrong end of her anger but after cuffing her yesterday, he thought he was lucky she wasn't out for his blood.

Getting ready for bed that night, Carina asked for some privacy. Jackson uncuffed himself, gave her five minutes, but didn't leave the room, just turned around. Carina glared at his back and scowled deeper when he told her to keep talking.

"Give me a break."

"Keep talking, or I'll turn around."

"Insufferable...." Carina mumbled.

"I'm sorry, but I didn't make that out."

Carina could tell that Jackson was grinning, teasing her to react. "I'm glad you're enjoying this. Just remember, my time will come."

"Keep talking."

Carina hurried under the covers and turned away from Jackson, who suddenly found himself at a loss for words.

He slipped quietly into bed, grabbed Carina's wrist, and slipped on the cuffs. Perturbed, he asked, "You sleep on that side?"

"Yes, why?"

"I sleep in the opposite direction."

"Sleep on your back, then."

The next moment he was standing by Carina's side of the bed. "Move over," he commanded.

"No."

Jackson picked her up and moved her, and then he attached the cuff to her right hand, then his left. "That way we have two options."

Carina turned to face the opposite direction, her arm behind her back. "You forgot to turn off the light."

He contemplated undoing the cuff. "Get up so I can reach the light switch." He looked at her prone form, picked her up, tried to turn off the light despite Carina's squirming body, stubbed his left baby toe as he made his way around the bed and set her down again.

"Now the covers are all messed up." Carina tried to cover her feet, gave up, and curled on her side. Jackson's arm was pulled over her waist, causing her to hurriedly put her hand behind her back again.

Jackson slipped his arm around Carina once again. "I liked having it there."

"I didn't."

"I thought you said you slept on your side."

"I'll rough it, thanks."

After a while, Carina found herself unable to fall asleep in that uncomfortable position and listened for Jackson's breathing to change. Even then, she wasn't sure if he was sleeping. After fifteen more minutes, she slowly turned so that she was once again on her right side. She could dimly make out Jackson's outline as he slept beside her. The last person she'd shared a bed with had been her ex-husband and it felt odd to hear someone else breathing beside her. She'd been madly in love with her ex-husband and still felt pangs of emptiness at his defection. She'd steered away from dating after his abandonment by taking night classes and working weekends. And now, here she was with Jackson.

Casimir jumped on the rumpled bed in the morning, waking both of them. She licked Carina's face and then Jackson's.

"She likes you," Jackson said.

"What would she do if she didn't?"

"I don't know, lick you to death?"

"Scary fluff ball," Carina said, as she rubbed Casimir's exposed belly.

The rest of the day progressed uneventfully, except for the cuffs. Carina was very frustrated to have her freedom curtailed and harangued Jackson at every opportunity. Jackson alleviated part of the problem by suggesting they go for a walk and then later, fishing, which contributed to the evening meal. At bedtime, Carina didn't even bother protesting. She just rolled onto her side and put out her left wrist for cuffing.

When Jackson woke up the next day and nothing had happened, he had to listen to Carina's pleas for freedom. "Nothing has happened, let me go. Don't you have to work or something?"

"I'm taking some holiday time."

"You can't hold me a prisoner forever."

"You're not a prisoner."

"What do you call it, then?"

"It's for your protection."

"My protection!" Carina's voice was escalating, "I'll tell you what it is: It's called kidnapping. Something usually frowned upon, don't you think?"

Jackson reached out to hold her by her arms. "Carina—" and felt himself falling, the surroundings blurring, distorting, then clarity returned and a strange landscape met his eyes as he looked over Carina's shoulder.

Carina pushed him away. "You've gone and done it now."

"What happened?"

"We're in the other reality. Since we're here, can you undo the cuffs?"

Jackson looked at her uncertainly. "No, I don't want to be stuck here if you should disappear again."

"You could be endangering our lives, my life! You have no right."

"Enough!" Jackson exploded. "I have every right. It's my job to protect you and I'm going to do it with or without your cooperation. It would be a hell of a lot easier if you'd cooperate for a change, instead of fighting me every step of the way."

"This whole thing is none of your business, it doesn't involve you and you should leave well enough alone."

"I won't," and then, eyes glinting like knives, Jackson kissed her. He lost himself in the kiss and felt Carina's body stop struggling. When he pulled back his head, his breathing was harsh and ragged, "You're my business because," he paused for breath, "I'm in love with you."

Carina glanced up into his eyes and saw the truth there. Tears welled up, blurring her vision.

"I know you're probably scared to have a relationship with anyone, especially after your ex-husband left you, but I'm not him. I'll never leave you."

"That's what he said," she murmured, turning away.

# Together In The Wasteland

"Where are we?" Jackson asked.

Carina scanned the area. "From the looks of this place, the barrenness, and the heat, we're in the Wastelands."

Jackson looked around. All he could see was dry, cracked dirt in every direction in the copper-coloured earth. It was devoid of plant life. The heat made the land shimmer in the distance and the dry dust kicked up by their feet made his eyes water.

She didn't give him much time to think. "We have to move on before the night falls while we can still see our surroundings."

"Do you have any idea which direction we should go?"

Carina looked around uncertainly and then, with a flash of inspiration, asked, "Which way is the sun moving?" She stood, shielding her eyes from the hot, glaring sun and until a solitary puff of cloud moved past the sun and Jackson watched their shadows creeping across a rock.

Finally, Jackson pointed. "That way."

Carina squinted. "I think you're right, which means we have to go west. I remember the sun rising and eventually moving off to my right. We'll go this way." Seeing Jackson's unhappy, helpless look, she replied, "Trust me, you're in my territory now."

"I guess I'll have to."

"Do I have a choice about the cuffs?"

"West it is, then."

They headed west, not saying anything for a few miles.

"Do you know what's going to happen now that we're here?"

"I don't know. Maybe we'll find Tauralee and Chenaanah and if we're lucky, Tauralee's sister, and Chenaanah's daughters."

"Plus, whoever has them."

"That'll be your department, taking care of the trouble." Carina hit her head in mock surprise. "Why didn't I think of that before? Get a man to help me."

"Yes, why didn't you think of it?"

Realization sobered Carina. "Because here men treat women like dirt and sell them on a whim, or if you're with a more prestigious group than the Scavengers, you get to be bred like cattle." After a minute or two, she said, "If we run into anyone, they will wonder about the cuffs. I was tied with rope before and I usually don't disappear until I've done something here like helping Chenaanah escape. I just don't appear here and then disappear. Undo the cuffs. I'm not going anywhere."

Jackson gave her a skeptical look. "I'll keep you cuffed until then. Good try, though."

"I'll wait with bells on," Carina retorted.

"I'd like to see that."

"It would be easier to climb it if we weren't cuffed. What if I fall? I'm not going anywhere."

"Okay, I'll let you off for now."

Once freed, Carina rubbed her raw wrist. Jackson looked guiltily at the redness. Carina thought, *You won't be putting those back on me without a fight.*

The landscape didn't change but they'd been gradually climbing. Jackson happened to glance backward, Carina following his gaze and saw nothing but dry, cracked land.

"What happened here to destroy everything?"

"I haven't found out. All I know is that people have been living underground."

"A nuclear holocaust?"

"From what Malcom told me, something ripped through the Earth's atmosphere and, at first there were no effects but then people started dying of the sun's radiation. He said people died by the millions. Those who survived went underground for decades."

"Good God."

"It's a horror that I don't want to imagine for our world."

After Carina's comments, silence fell between them and the hours faded away as they continued walking.

Jackson spotted an outcropping of rocks. "There's our chance to rest."

"I guess we should stop for the night. We might not find any other shelter."

It wasn't much of a shelter. The outcropping was nothing more than a few boulders jutting out of the ground. *At least we aren't totally exposed*, Carina thought as she sat beside one of the boulders. Her stomach growled, reminding her of the pillowcase of food they no longer had. They sat in silence, too exhausted to talk.

The cold came with the blanket of darkness that settled on them. The severe drop in temperature forced them to huddle together. Carina didn't argue when Jackson put his arm around her and drew her closer. They slept.


They'd stretched out on the ground during the night, glued together for warmth. They slept through the early morning as the sun began its trek across the clear sky. Finally, the stiffness of the hard ground registered on Carina. *I don't think I can get up.* She heard Jackson's moan beside her and forced herself into a sitting position.

Jackson woke a few moments later, Carina's eyes watching him.

"Was I snoring?" he asked sheepishly.

"You were moaning."

He moved and moaned again as he stood up.

Carina leaned on a boulder until her protesting muscles let her stand. She let the early morning sun soak through her before she said, "We're going to have to find some food and water."

"Do I have to stand again?"

She chuckled at Jackson's hopefulness. "Yes, unless you want to crawl around looking for food."

The rocks hid a small stream that Jackson stumbled upon, and beside it a patch of thistles.

"Do you know anything about thistles?" he called to Carina.

She came over to look at the low-lying plants. "I have an uncle who adds edible weeds to his salads. You need to strip the green off the leaf and rub off the fuzzy stuff."

"Thank God for your uncle's quirks."

They both drank their fill from the stream and ate as many plant stalks as they could. They gathered the rest to take with them.

They stayed there a little longer before they resumed walking. They walked for several hours, stopping once. The land had flattened out again, and they'd covered a great deal of distance. The scorching sun had long since passed its zenith by the time the land started to slant upward. Carina's aching legs noticed the incline.

"It's getting darker so we'll have to stop in a couple of hours to rest. We won't be able to see anything," Jackson said.

"I haven't seen any shelter, and we don't want to be that exposed to the cold. Let's keep walking. I'd feel better knowing what is over the hill."

Another hour went by and they could scarcely see, but the climb was steeper and Carina and Jackson saved their energy for walking, not talking. Finally, they reached the end of their climb and in the failing light they could make out an endless series of hills that cut into the rocky earth.

Carina shivered. "Walking that at night is out of the question. If it were darker we might have walked right over the edge and into one of those ravines."

The red morning light made Carina's stomach twist uneasily when she saw the numerous rocky crags and crevices that filled the valley below them. A misty layer covered the land in the distance, making it difficult to perceive how far they'd have to travel to get past the hills.

Jackson came up behind her and squeezed her shoulder. "It makes me want to turn around and go back down the other way."

She glanced at him as his words echoed her thoughts. "Back to what? We were in the middle of nowhere and"—her breath whooshed out as she released it—"we're still in the middle of nowhere." She wanted to cry in frustration but forced herself to swallow her tears.

"We can do this, Carina. Think of it as an adventure."

She grimaced. "I prefer having adventures on flat land without any surprises."

"What kind of surprises are you expecting?"

"Snakes, impossible paths, critters...."

Jackson grinned. "Critters? Now there's a word to strike fear in a man's heart."

She saw him smiling. "You know what I mean. Things jumping out of nowhere. And spiders."

He humoured her. "We haven't seen any plants, snakes, or critters so far. What makes you think we will now?"

"I have to believe that something can live out here in this godforsaken place, otherwise I'll genuinely believe the world's gone mad and I'm just an ant crawling across it." She shivered in the sun's rays. "What could have happened to eliminate life here?"

She heard Jackson sigh before he spoke. "It's a mystery just like everything else that has happened to you."

They didn't speak until after they ate a meager meal of thistle stalks. By then the layer of mist had dissipated and the distant horizon spread before them.

"Good God, it's more of the same. How are we supposed to get through that?"

Despair filled her. It wasn't a question that Carina could easily answer. *If Jackson's stymied, we're in big trouble. I wish I knew what path to take through that maze.* She scratched an itch on her arm. Her tattooed armband blazed scarlet under her fingers and flared up over the valley. Too stunned to do anything more than watch the scarlet ribbon, she stood mesmerized as it settled into the valley. *It's a path!*

She heard Jackson's indrawn breath from beside her. "Jackson. Do you see it?"

"What is it?"

"It's a path through this maze. I was wondering how we were going to get through that mess and then my tattoo flared. Did you see it?"

He wasn't looking at her. Instead, his eyes were fixed on the red trail that now lay before them, "Yes, and I see the path is fading."

Startled, Carina looked over the valley and sure enough, the scarlet was less brilliant than it had been only moments before. "We have to memorize it before it fades." She automatically fumbled through her pockets for something to write with and immediately realized the futility. As she withdrew her hand, her fingers touched something soft in her pocket and she pulled it out and gasped.

"What's wrong, Carina?"

She was holding the scrap and eyeing the fading scarlet trail below them. "It matches," she whispered, her hand shaking as she showed it to Jackson.

He recognized it immediately. "This is from the hospital envelope. The last time I saw it was—"

"When you gave it to me in the restaurant," she finished. "I've been holding on to it because Malcom dropped it when he first arrived at the sector. I figured it had to serve a purpose." She absently ran her fingers over its edges, not saying a word for several minutes.

Jackson leaned forward to listen closely as she related how she had found the map, for that was obviously what it was, and shake his head in amazement.

"Do you know what this means?" he asked excitedly as he grabbed her and hugged her.

"Yes." She hugged him back. Her despair had transformed itself into a radiant smile filled with hope and anticipation. She began laughing.

Jackson's laughter soon mingled with her own and it was with lightened hearts they began the trek through the valley.

# A Reunion

Two grueling days later, with a collection of scratches and bruises, dull and aching muscles, the map ended with nothing left but an imposing rock face that loomed in front of them. They were both exhausted and dirty, red dust from the trail coated their hair and clothing but a deep sense of accomplishment had kept them moving forward.

The rock face looked daunting but their desire to see what was beyond it before night fell gave them a burst of energy to scale it. Its edges were sharper than the many crags and crevices they'd already climbed and their breathing was hoarse and ragged as they pulled themselves over the top.

Finally standing on level ground, they moved forward to the opposite edge. They could see a low building in front of them in the failing light; a burning fire pit was in front of it. Before they had a chance to comment on it, a noise behind them spun them around just as a figure loomed out of the gloom. Carina's heart leapt in her chest and a small shriek left her mouth, but then she recognized Tauralee and Chenaanah coming toward them.

"Are you trying to bring unwanted attention to us? Get down." Tauralee demanded as she looked over the precipice and then edged away, turning to speak to Carina. "Who is this?" she asked with a slight tilt of her head.

"Jackson, this is Tauralee and Chenaanah."

Chenaanah, who'd been standing beside Tauralee, came and hugged her. "Thank goodness you're all right."

Tauralee stood up close to Jackson and peered at him curiously. "You do not look familiar, and I do not recognize your clothing."

Although Carina's skirt fit into the women's garb, Jackson's t-shirt and jeans were unlike the tunics and loose pants the men wore.

She turned to Carina. "Is he a Leader?"

"No, but he's from there."

"Where did you find him?"

"Uh. I helped him escape from the Scavs. I was lost in the tunnels and wandered for hours. I tripped over him. He was hiding in the dark. He was a new prisoner."

"You trust him?"

Carina grinned at Jackson. "I'm keeping my eye on him."

Taura looked at her skeptically. "How'd you get past us?"

"I think I came out a different tunnel where there weren't many buildings."

"Hmmm, I didn't know there was a tunnel that far out; must have been an unused one."

"I didn't run into anyone on the way out of the tunnels," Carina said.

Chenaanah spoke up. "We waited for you, but then we had to go because the Scavengers were surfacing."

"I found your pillowcase, so I knew you'd gotten out. We've been searching for you ever since."

"You were lucky to find it. How do you know you can trust this man?" she asked suspiciously.

Tauralee glanced briefly at Carina but kept her eyes trained on Jackson.

"When I told him what we were trying to do, he agreed to help. He used to be a security officer, and he can help us get your daughters back. How did you get here?" She couldn't imagine the two women taking the same complicated route she and Jackson had.

"It wasn't as difficult as your trek, obviously. Why did you go through the ravines? We found a cave after we crossed the red desert and we went through it and ended up here."

Chenaanah said, "It does not matter now, does it? We managed to find each other."

Jackson called for their attention. "Quiet. I see someone down below near the fire."

They lay flat and peered over the edge.

"I cannot tell for sure, but I think that is my sister," Tauralee said excitedly.

"What's directly below us?" Jackson asked.

"It has to be the mine."

A man came out of the structure, followed by another.

"I thought she said Darol, the miner, was the only man out here," Carina exclaimed.

"Who is Darol?" Jackson asked.

"The gaoler's wife said Darol bought two girls recently."

"Chenaanah's daughters?"

"Yes."

Tauralee shot him a glaring look. "You keep quiet until I ask your opinion. Remember you're a man and therefore untrustworthy. I am keeping my eye on you."

"Look," Chenaanah whispered and they all peered over the edge. One man was heading to the cliffs below.

"Didn't Hester say there was a mine, Chenaanah?"

"You could be right, Carina. Do you suppose it could be below us?"

"I don't know, but where else could they be? We covered a lot of Wasteland and didn't see anything resembling a mine. Did the cave you went through look like someone had been mining it?"

"It looked deserted. It reminded me of the Scav's burrows. What should we do now?"

"We need to figure out how to get down there."

The land below them was shaped like a horseshoe. "Why don't we go down over there?" Chenaanah pointed to where the cliffs ended to the left and sloped down.

Carina followed her pointing finger and was surprised to see trees. "There are trees. It's the second sign of plant life in this place."

Taura spoke up. "I noticed them earlier, but I assumed they were a mirage from the intense heat. That means there's water. We've drained our supply." She smiled. "Those trees are the first good sign I've seen."

"First we have to get down there," Chenaanah said.

"We can pair off and each pair can go down one side of the canyon and we can meet somewhere in the middle."

"Or we can go directly down from here."

"It's too dark to scale the rocks, and if it's anything like what we just climbed, it will be too treacherous."

"I can do it," Taura affirmed. "We can use the rope that I picked up in the hub."

"That will come in handy for us to climb down."

"So can I," Jackson spoke up.

"It's dangerous," Carina said. "We've been traveling all day. Wouldn't it be better if we rested and tried tomorrow?"

"We're in the open up here and it's going to get a lot colder. Then we'd have to wait an entire day. We can't go down in the daylight." Jackson pointed out.

"Obviously, if we go down one way, we'll be spotted by whoever is in the cabin, or vice versa."

"We should rest," Chenaanah affirmed.

"I say we move now," Taura said. "You and I"—she pointed to Jackson—"can go down the cliffs, and secure the tunnels. You two can secure the cabin."

"You want us to secure the unknown house?" Chenaanah asked.

"We'll wait 'til it's very dark," Carina said.

"You have experience doing this?" Jackson asked.

"Chenaanah and I have had a lot of practice with rocks lately. Do you still have our knives?" Carina asked Chenaanah.

"I don't like you going down on your own. What if there's more than one person in there?"

"You can't be in two places at once, and we'll have our knives with us."

"It'll take at least an hour to get down these cliffs in one piece. Do you think you can be at the end of the slope by then?" Taura asked Chenaanah and Carina.

"I see my daughter, Loriia." A redheaded figure was leaving the fire carrying something toward the caves.

"You're sure?" Taura asked.

Chenaanah's whispered reply could scarcely be heard. "No doubt."

Carina was exhausted and didn't want to go anywhere but the excitement and the tears in Chenaanah's eyes caused her to turn to Taura and say, "We'll be there in about two hours if the terrain is flat."

Jackson grabbed Carina's arm. "Are you sure about this?"

"No, but it needs to be done."

Jackson spoke so softly that only she could hear him. "You continue to surprise me, Carina. Be careful."

"You, too."

Jackson squeezed her arm and then, turning to Tauralee, said, "I think we should wait for a bit. It won't take us that long to get down the cliffs."

"Let's keep away from the edge, that way we can run upright without being spotted," Carina suggested to Chenaanah.

"Should we run?"

"A quick walk will have to do, Chenaanah. I don't want us to be tripping over something in the dark."

It was farther than they thought, and it took more than two hours to reach the down-sloping point of the cliffs. Carina and Chenaanah paused, scanning the valley floor below. It was dark, except for the dim moonlight. They could just make out the house, which was much smaller than they'd first guessed. Their path was scarcely visible down to the valley floor, but even from there, they still had a long way to cover. They used the trees at first. Carina pressed her nose up to the first tree, like a long-lost friend and inhaled its scent. She didn't linger as they had to leave the cover of the trees and step into the barren valley floor.

Carina glanced back at Chenaanah and noticed how her light hair shone in the moonlight. Carina was thinking how unprepared she was to do all this. If anyone was scared, it was her. *I only hope whoever is in there, is sleeping,* she thought.

Finally, Chenaanah joined Carina in the shadows behind the building. "Maybe we should wait for Jackson and Tauralee."

"I'm scared, too, Chenaanah, but we have to get there before we're discovered. There's a door around the front. Once we're in, we'll have to check each room."

"I think we should go together," Chenaanah whispered.

"So do I."

They crouch-walked around the building until they reached the front door. When they gently stepped onto the wooden floor inside, it creaked—they froze in their tracks. Their eyes adjusted to the dimness of the room as they listened for a response.

There were glowing embers in the fireplace, which Carina stirred. She removed one to use as a torch and looked around. The room contained a rough-looking table and four chairs.

They sneaked slowly past the eating area and farther into the building. There were three other rooms; they inspected the one on the left: It contained two empty beds and assorted items that were decidedly masculine.

As Carina turned to leave, she saw a club leaning against the wall and she motioned for Chenaanah to pick it up, hoping it wouldn't be needed. She stepped out of the room and as she stepped silently toward the door on the right, she heard a soft voice come from within the room, a woman's voice.

"Who's there? It is that you, Loriia? If it's one of you girls, you shouldn't be in here." The woman's voice got louder as she reached the hallway.

Carina backed into Chenaanah, and they shrank into the shadows. Carina snuffed out the torch with her shoe and held it behind her.

"Who are you?" The woman demanded when she saw Carina.

"Are you Sarra?" Carina whispered, pushing Chenaanah farther back so she remained hidden.

"Why?" the woman asked suspiciously.

Carina stepped forward and whispered, "Your sister sent me."

"My sister's dead," Sarra said defiantly.

"What's the noise?" A man's husky voice called out.

"Nothing."

"Your sister's alive and she's here."

"Here?" Sarra asked, looking around.

"She was going to the caves."

Sarra moved to a wall niche, lit a candle, and held it up to peer closely at Carina. "Who are you?" They moved toward the fireplace.

"My name is Carina. We've come to rescue you," she whispered.

"I don't need to be rescued."

"Tauralee said you were being held here against your will."

"Darol!" Sarra yelled. "You'd better come out here."

"No!" Carina blurted as he stepped into the room. She stared at the tall, ruggedly handsome, older man.

"What's going on?" he asked in a low voice.

"This woman says my sister is here."

"After all this time? How do we know they weren't sent by the Scavs? Maybe there are more of them outside."

"She speaks too well to be a Scav," Sarra observed.

The man towered over Carina, well over six feet. "How many of you are there?"

Carina craned her neck. "A few of us."

His arm went protectively around Sarra. "Who are you and where are you from?"

"I was in the sector and was kidnapped by the Scavs. I escaped and that's how I know Taura." She could see Darol digesting the information.

It looked like they were going to have a stalemate; he didn't trust her and she didn't trust him.

*I've come all this way in this reality. Now what will happen?* She kept her eyes fixed on Darol.

They all jumped when the door burst open and Tauralee stepped in. Darol grabbed Carina, his arm around her throat. He pushed Sarra behind him.

"Where's my sister?" Taura demanded, brandishing a metal bar she'd picked up somewhere.

At the sound of the familiar voice, Sarra pushed past Darol, eyes widening in astonishment. "Tauralee!" Sarra burst out and in the next second they were crying and hugging each other wildly.

It took several minutes before Tauralee and Sarra could speak.

"I never thought I'd see you again."

"I never imagined we'd meet again, but I kept hoping it would happen," Tauralee whispered. "It was the only thing that helped me endure the Scavs."

Sarra hugged her again. Holding her hand, she turned to Darol. "Darol, let the woman go and come and meet my sister."

*A woman telling a man what to do,* Carina speculated as he released her. She watched him suspiciously during the reunion. He seemed stunned by Tauralee's miraculous appearance and gingerly held out his hand. "I'm glad my love has found her sister. Welcome. Your appearance here is a miracle. Sarra has always prayed she'd find out what happened to you."

Unable to contain herself, Chenaanah came out of hiding, blurting, "Where are you keeping my daughters?"

Darol pushed Sarra away from her sister. "It's a trick! How many of you are there?"

"It is all right. That is Chenaanah—Hester said you bought her daughters," Taura said.

"And who are they?"

"Loriia and Liisa. Loriia has long, red hair and Liisa has dark-auburn hair."

"And you just happened to be with Sarra's sister. It seems to be a coincidence, but these reunions seem a bit too planned to me," Darol said.

"You have to let me see my daughters. I have risked a lot coming here to find them. If the Leaders ever find me, they will send me for recultivation—"

Carina saw his jaw clench. *He knows about recultivation.*

"But not before you reveal everything about us," Darol finished for Chenaanah.

"I would not tell them anything."

"You wouldn't be able to hide it from them." He paused, looking at Sarra and then Tauralee. Finally, he looked at Carina. "Where do you fit into all of this?"

"She helped me escape and get here," Chenaanah replied as she looked into his face.

"She did the same thing for me," Tauralee explained. "She saved me from Axe as he was beating me. He kept me on a chain and I'll never go back to that," she said vehemently.

"Your daughters are in the mine," Sarra revealed. "Darol buys as many as he can to save them from the Scavs and the Leaders. I'll take you to them."

"Is working in a mine saving them?" Carina asked.

Sarra bristled. "My Darol's a good man. The children don't work at the mines. That's a ruse."

"Do not worry, sister. Carina does not mean to offend. She is just concerned for the others." She paused. "She has risked herself for others, for me."

"And now you have returned my sister to me after seven years. There are so many Scavs and their territory is so vast that Darol couldn't find you. When he purchased me, I didn't trust him because I thought he was a Scav. Had I known sooner that he was such a good man, I could have told him about Tauralee. It was several months before he safely returned to the sales, but by then it was too late." Sarra wiped away her tears and said to Carina. "I am beholden to you."

Chenaanah cleared her throat. "My daughters?"

Grinning, Sarra said, "Yes, let's go see them. They will be elated."

"Wait. There's one more person who came with us. I left him in the mine before I came here," Tauralee mentioned.

Darol yelled, "You were in the mine? Damn. You probably scared the children to death. We don't get strangers here. Wasn't Barot there?" Darol didn't wait for an answer because he was already storming out of the door to protect the children.

Tauralee quickly ran beside him. "He's just fine, just unable to move a bit."

Darol harrumphed angrily. "Fool girl, you could wreck everything we've accomplished here."

Everyone trooped hurriedly after Darol as he strode briskly to the mine's entrance. "Ho in there!" he called. "We're coming in."

"I wouldn't do that if I were you," Jackson called out.

"Jackson, it's us," Carina answered.

Darol ignored Jackson and barreled through the mine's opening. *Here's a man that shouldn't be crossed*, Carina thought.

"Where's Barot?" Darol demanded.

"I'm over here," a deep voice said.

Darol glanced toward the voice and then saw Jackson. "Who are you?"

Jackson sized up the man before him and then replied, "Jackson, Jackson Dawes."

"I haven't heard of you. Who are you with?"

"I'm with them," Jackson said as he pointed at the women.

"Who are you running from?"

Jackson quickly recalled what Carina had told him about the inhabitants of this place. "From the Leaders." Carina shot him a relieved look at his reply.

"What did you do there?"

"I was in security, but I'm not from this area."

"Did you have any run-ins with the Scavengers?"

"I did," Carina said, "I was grabbed right from the sector and sold."

"Who bought you?"

"His name was Trator," she spat out. "I escaped from him twice, once from his quarters and once during the raid on the sector."

"Yes, I'm aware of that raid; that's how I got Loriia and Liisa."

The two girls shrieked as if they'd believed they'd never see their beloved mother again. Everyone watched as Chenaanah knelt, arms wide, and encircled her daughters. Suddenly, other children's voices came from the cave and Darol appeared flustered. He tried to get everyone to leave but Tauralee strode past him, followed by Carina and Jackson.

"Incredible, isn't it?" Jackson breathed the words near Carina's ear.

Children of various ages and sizes were crowded together at one end. When they saw Sarra, they came forward. There was also an older couple that stepped forward.

Carina tried counting but the children kept moving around.

"What are these children doing here?" Tauralee asked. "You own all of them?"

"No, he doesn't own them, not a single one of them," the old lady spoke up. "Darol's my son and he's helped rescue these children over the last several years."

It was an incredible revelation. Carina now saw that there were also young couples who'd come out from their hiding places. The youngest of the children moved to stand by their parents.

"The children are illegals, aren't they?" Chenaanah asked.

"What are illegals?" Carina asked.

"They're children born without the Leaders' matching genetics."

"Only in your world, but not here. They're freeborn. The Leaders will never know," Darol replied.

"You can't hide them forever."

"It's been twenty years now. At first we just subsisted enough to survive on our own but with time and patience, and a lot of hard work, we were able to take on more people."

"How many of you are there?" Jackson asked.

"Before we tell you more, I believe we have a few things that we need to discuss back at the house."

"I'd like to stay with my daughters," Chenaanah said.

"There will be plenty of time for that later. You need to sit in on our discussion."

"I'll be back as soon as I can, sweetling," Chenaanah said as she hugged her youngest.

They walked silently in the dark. When Carina stumbled, it was Jackson who reached out to steady her. Jackson's touch on her arm reminded her that she finally wasn't totally on her own in this strange world.

Once they arrived back at the house, everyone gathered in Darol's cookery. "First of all, let me formally welcome you to our community. People who come here don't leave once they learn what we're doing. We've been fortunate enough to avoid the scrutiny of both the Scavengers and the Leaders. It is rare to have anyone discover us; you're the first in five years. I am concerned that you will jeopardize our entire existence by coming here."

"We won't tell anyone that you're here," Tauralee spoke up.

"You might give us away without intending to, despite your best intentions. What are your plans, Tauralee? Do you intend to stay with your sister, my wife?"

"He doesn't own you?" Chenaanah asked.

"Of course not. We're all free here. Darol and I are husband and wife, not designated bondmates—at least under our law."

Tauralee paused for a moment before speaking. "Yes, I do want to be near my sister," she said as she glanced at Sarra.

"I'm sure Sarra will love having you remain with us."

Jackson spoke up, "What exactly is this community about?"

"We don't belong to any of the other factions. We don't believe our lives should be controlled and decided for us. We want to make our own decisions and be free to control our own lives," Darol explained.

"But you aren't totally independent, are you?" Carina asked.

"What do you mean?"

"Well, you go out among the Scavengers, deal with them. You buy people from them. How do you maintain your secret?"

"I trade with them using what we find in the mine."

"And why don't they just take over your mine?" Jackson asked.

"Because they don't know where it is, and I make sure I don't bring enough resources with me that they think it's a rich venture. I don't always visit the gaols, and I make sure I have a drink with the boys and spread my woes. They all have their own way to survive and working hard isn't one of them. That's why they trade in slaves, more profitable. They steal whatever tools and materials they want from the sectors."

"They've never tried to find out?" Tauralee asked.

"Yes, but unsuccessfully. Whenever anyone wanted to join me, I took them to a different mine. If I'd just bought a person, they'd work the mine, too. After a week or two, the Scav would get tired of the work and the slowness of making a profit, and they'd leave. The woeful stories they spread when they got back helped deter others."

"Who else knows you're here?"

"The Banished leader and a few of his men know we exist and have tried to convince us to join them, but they've respected our independence."

"So far, you mean? Why haven't you joined them? From what I gather, that's the group to be with," Jackson said.

"They're more aggressive, trying to undermine the Leaders and the Scavengers."

"You're pacifists, then?"

"Pacifists?"

"People who won't fight no matter what."

"No, not quite; we'll defend ourselves if need be."

"How will you do that?" Jackson asked. "Four of us have managed to sneak in here unobserved and the only reason you were aware of us was because we wanted you to know we were here."

"We'll get into that later. Right now, there are more immediate problems that need to be resolved. First, I need to know more about the four of you."

They crowded around the cookery table while Sarra boiled water for tea. "We'll start with you, Chenaanah. You've got children, so you've been bred."

Carina winced at his words.

"Won't your bondmate wonder where you are? And since your children were missing, wasn't a search made for them?"

"They've been searching, but I couldn't wait anymore."

Darol spoke harshly. "Why is that? Surely you've been instructed in the strict laws expected to be followed by all women once they've been bred? Why would you go beyond those rules? Don't you realize what they'll do to you once you're caught?"

"I-I thought they'd be less harsh on me because I'm an ex-L-Leader's wife," Chenaanah stuttered.

Sarra and Darol froze, too stunned to speak.

"If I do not have my daughters, Malcom can release me to the sector and I'll be sent somewhere else. I could not let that happen."

"So you were thinking only of yourself when you left?"

"No, I was concerned for my daughters. I love them and I wanted them back, no matter what the cost."

"It certainly will cost you. I cannot allow you to return to the sector," Darol said.

"Why not?"

"You know too much, as do all of you," he said as he waved his hand before them. "Your choices are few. You, Chenaanah, may stay with your daughters but under no circumstances will I allow you to leave. You may be an ex-Leader's wife, but even you'd be recultivated." Chenaanah paled visibly at Darol's words. "And if you weren't, then your daughters would be, and tell everything. We've worked too long to have it all ruined because of one person."

"The last time I talked with my bondmate, he tried to tell me that he was a Banished but I wouldn't believe him."

"Hmmm. I don't know how this miracle came about, but that won't change things for you here. If he is a Banished, and he locates you, or I hear of him looking for you, I'll make some type of arrangement. But in the meantime, this is going to be your new home and the sooner you get used to that idea the easier it will be on you."

"But—" Chenaanah began. "I don't want to be here. I like my life in the sector."

"Then you should have remained in the sector," Darol said bluntly. "Besides," he softened his words, "you and your daughters can have a free life, and they'll be able to choose who they bond with."

"I never gave much thought about being able to choose my own life, but I'm willing to give it a try."

Carina gave Chenaanah's hand a squeeze and Chenaanah returned the gesture before she spoke. "May I go back to my daughters now?"

"I'll take you," Sarra replied as she put down the teapot.

Darol looked at Tauralee. "You never did answer me. Will you be staying with your sister?"

Tauralee looked at Carina.

"It's what you wanted all along, isn't it?" Carina asked.

"Yes, but I owe you."

"For what, Tauralee? You helped us escape and find Chenaanah's daughters in exchange for trying to find your sister."

"I'm grateful and indebted to you for saving my life and I have to make it up to you."

"Tauralee, if you want to make it up to me, then I'd suggest that you stay here with your sister and make a life for yourself and be the happiest you can. That's how you can repay me."

"Oh, Carina." Tauralee's words broke off as she hugged her. "I cannot tell you what you've done for me. You gave me hope when there wasn't any and you helped me start believing in myself."

Darol cut in. "Now that that's settled, let's look at you two," he said, indicating Jackson and Carina. "You said you were involved in security where you came from, and we can always use an extra pair of eyes on patrol. I'll assume that you left and have no plans of returning, or am I wrong? Are you a spy?"

"No, not at all. My being here is totally accidental. I ran into Carina as she was escaping from the Scavenger's area. I've been avoiding being seen, by traveling at night, and that is a lot slower than day travel. When our paths crossed, and we began traveling together, I think. I just got carried away and lost my heart to her." He punctuated his last words with a wink at Carina who responded with a huff.

"Just because we traveled together doesn't mean I owe you anything."

"Carina cannot have anything to do with you. She is going to be a Leader's bondmate; at least that's what Chenaanah said," Taura piped up as if it were a warning.

Darol whirled to face Carina. "Is that true?"

"No. I do not intend to marry anyone, let alone a Leader."

"Which Leader spoke for you?" he demanded as he grabbed her arm.

"What does it matter?"

"It matters like life and death. There are only eight Leaders and it isn't every day that one decides to marry. Who is it?" He demanded again.

"Daric, his name is Daric, but I don't even know the guy."

"Damn!" He grabbed her by the shoulders and shook her. "Don't you know what you've done?"

Jackson intervened. "She's gone through enough without you manhandling her."

Darol glared at him and then turned away angrily. As he stormed out of the house, he met Barot who'd been anxious to know more about the unexpected visitors who'd taken him by surprise and bested him.

"This Daric must be quite important to get that type of reaction," Jackson stated as he glanced at Carina.

"He's just a Leader I tried to avoid every time I encountered him, and for some reason he got it into his head to pick me."

"But here you're free to choose your own mate," Tauralee said.

Carina grimaced.

About twenty-five minutes passed before Darol returned. He apologized for his outburst. "I overreacted. First, you four show up and then I hear the head Leader's name. It was a shock, that's all. I went to the mines and discovered that we were short a few things to make your stay with us comfortable. Tauralee, would you mind carrying these blankets to the mine? Sarra will show you where to put them. Jackson, you look like a strong man. Would you carry that food chest to the mine? We usually keep it there because it's cooler but I wanted to do some repairs on it. That'll have to keep for now."

"Sure, I'll go with Tauralee and then come back."

"That'll be good. I just have a few more questions to ask Carina and then we'll follow you to your new home."

Jackson looked at Darol uncertainly.

"Don't worry, I just need to ask her about Daric."

"I'll be fine, Jackson. The sooner you leave, the sooner you'll get back."

Her words made sense and so Jackson followed Tauralee.

Darol waited several minutes after they had departed. He watched them as they passed the bonfire before he turned back to Carina. His eyes and demeanor were anything but friendly. "I knew you were trouble the instant I saw you."

"What?" Carina responded. "What are you talking about?"

"Yes, it was convenient for you to help Chenaanah and then Tauralee. You're probably helping Daric."

"I can't stand the man. He's an arrogant, pushy man, and I have no intention of being used by him or anyone else here."

"Exactly how long have you known him?"

"A few weeks. He came to our sector when the healer got wounded during the last conflict with the Banished and the Scavengers."

"And just like that he chose you?"

"He looked at my file and then picked me."

"There must have been something pretty tempting in that file to make him choose you so quickly."

"It was just a medical file. The file they've been expecting from my other sector hadn't arrived yet."

"Did you agree to marry him?"

"No. I told him I wouldn't marry anyone I didn't know or love, but he didn't care. I've been avoiding him as much as I could, and I left with Chenaanah so I wouldn't be forced to marry him. I do not intend to go back there."

Darol glared at her. "You obviously don't realize who you offended. Daric isn't just any Leader, everyone knows that. He's the most powerful Leader that has existed and he can crush you or anyone else who gets in his way. I doubt he's *impressed* that not one, but *two* women have escaped. It's a matter of pride now. He'll be coming for you, I assure you. You can't stay here with us."

"But I have nowhere else to go. I don't belong anywhere."

"I'm sorry, but that's the way it is."

Carina sat in stunned silence. She'd begun believing that finding Darol and his community of free men and women was the fundamental reason she was in this reality. She'd already been imagining that by helping Chenaanah find her daughters and freedom was meant to happen.

At the sound of pounding, Darol ran outside. The sky was lightening and he made out his man Pinch riding toward him on a sweat-lathered horse. "What is it Pinch?"

"There are at least twenty men heading this way."

"How far are they from here?"

"Less than five miles."

"Any idea who they might be?"

"They're on horses and wearing blue uniforms."

"Damn. Leaders' men."

The suspicion that had been forming in his head became clear. Something they'd expected for over twenty years: Their worst nightmare was happening. They'd been found. Darol's heart shrank in horror. "It's because of our visitors. They've led them right to us. They have never explored this far away from the sector."

Pinch saw his friend's face harden. "Shall I tell the men to prepare the mine?" he asked immediately.

"Yes, but first make sure our visitors are taken deep into the mine so they don't know what's happening. I'll be sending the woman inside to you on an errand, and I want you to keep her busy until you see me and give the all clear. After that send her back here."

"What for? Isn't she coming with us?"

"No, I strongly believe she's the sole reason we're going to be found out, and she's going to be the offering to throw them off us."

Pinch stared at Darol, evaluating, calculating. "I've known you too long to doubt your decision, Darol, I'll make sure everything goes according to plan."

"Thanks, Pinch."

"Don't thank me until after it's all over," Pinch said, as he rode away.

Carina, who'd been watching the exchange, wondered what had just happened. But, when Darol turned to her with a big smile she assumed something good must have happened to cheer him up. *Maybe he won't be so hard on me now*, she thought, as she watched him approach.

# 37

# The Ruse

"You'll like living with us," Sarra said to Jackson, Taura, and Chenaanah. "Once you settle in and get to know the routine, you'll feel like you've always been here. I'm going to show you the newer accommodations. They're deeper back in the mine, since we've grown over the years. We're all going to be shifting farther back, as we need to expand and make room for the new families. We have two couples who are expecting their first child and this place is getting crowded,"

She paused when Barot came to her and whispered in her ear. She never looked directly at Jackson and Tauralee until Barot left.

"Well, come on, we haven't got as much time as I thought. If you could take the torch, Jackson, I'll be following behind you with Tauralee."

Sarra heard Barot's words and knew she'd follow them to the letter and make sure they moved as slowly as possible through the cave. She knew that Darol had made a hard decision for the welfare of everyone in the community

"I'm sorry, Carina," Darol said. "I know I sounded rather fierce a few moments ago, but that was only because I was concerned about being found out. Pinch just got back from patrolling the area and he says that there is no one in sight."

"Does that mean I may stay?"

"Yes, you may stay and join our community."

"That's wonderful news."

"Why don't you head to the cave with these two baskets and give them to Pinch? He'll know what to do with them. I'll be there as soon as I can. Don't worry if you fall asleep in the meantime, I'm sure you must be exhausted."

"I haven't given it much thought in all the excitement. You're right, though, I'm a bit shaky from being so tired."

Darol passed her two baskets to carry. She headed to the mine. Once there, Pinch showed her to a small wall recess with a blanket. "Why don't you wait here a moment and I'll be right back?"

"Do you know where my friends are?"

"They're back in the cave, but I'll take you to them as soon as I get back." He returned a few moments later with bread and wine. He made sure that she'd eaten a bite and drunk the wine before he left her again.

Carina leaned against the cave wall, waiting for his return, but found herself drifting off. She was so tired. It seemed like only a minute before hands were shaking her awake.

"Carina?" It was Sarra. "Darol wants you back at the house. Your friend Jackson is already there."

"Oh, is everything all right?"

"Everything's fine. He seems to think that there's something more between you and Jackson, and he wants to give you time to work it out."

"What do you mean, there's something between me and Jackson?"

"Well, I've noticed his protectiveness, and he seems enamoured of you."

"I'll have to straighten him out, then."

"I'd love to watch but I'm going to go look for Tauralee." She paused. "Good luck."

"Thanks, but it's him who is going to need the luck."

Carina never stopped to ponder Sarra's sincerity, or the way she wished her good luck. Instead, she stormed out of the mine, fully awake, and ready to confront Mr. Dawes with his wild fantasies.

*How dare he tell them such things! He knows he's not here permanently and he doesn't have to make my life more complex if I have to come back again.*

Carina was halfway to the house when a tremendous explosion threw her to the ground. She turned and saw the entire entrance of the cave disappear as the rock face tumbled down, blocking the mine entrance. She raced to the house as huge boulders tumbled and rolled toward her.

Once the ground stopped shaking and the dust cleared, she turned around to face the catastrophic cave-in "My God! They're gone. Jackson! Oh, my God! What'll I do now?" She ran to the obliterated mine entrance and tried futilely to pull away the rubble, scratching her hands until they bled.

She didn't know how long she was there pulling away rocks. At one point, she looked down at her hands and it vaguely registered that they were bleeding. She tucked them under her arms as she realized that she should be in pain. *Why can't I feel them?* She stumbled to the house. *At least the house is there. I can get my bearings and figure out what to do next.*

She made it to the wooden porch, sat down on the step, and began rocking back and forth.


A man approaching her from a distance saw something moving on the stairs and, as he got closer, he could make out a woman. She must have seen him coming because she jumped up and yelled out, "Jackson? Thank God, you're all right."

He recognized Carina beneath the dishevelled hair and dirty clothing. He grabbed her wrists and held her at a distance.

"Hello, Carina, we meet again."

Carina recognized Daric's voice and numbly searched his face before she fainted.

# Recultivation

Gritty teeth and a parched throat forced Carina to lick her lips before she opened her eyes. Her arm refused to respond when she tried to bring her hand to her mouth. It was then that she realized why the earth floor was only a few inches below her chin; she was buried up to her neck.

With her movements curtailed, she could only move her head slightly. She winced in shock when she saw Daric calmly sitting a few feet away from her, and then the world spun dizzily as panic set in and all rational thought fled. She struggled to break free of the restrictive dirt that kept her in place. It reminded her of Ritik at the Ceremony.

Her eyes flew open.

Daric had moved. He now knelt directly in front of her. He raised her chin with his hand and brought a canteen to her mouth but he only allowed her a swallow before she felt something else drop onto her tongue. Before Carina could react, Daric had passed the canteen to someone standing directly behind her and clamped her mouth shut with both hands. He was speaking rhythmically and Carina recognized the words, the ecstasy in his eyes.

Her eyes bugged in terror. *The seed. He's given me a seed!* She tried to fight him as he stroked her throat until she finally swallowed. Daric let go of her then, but continued his ritualistic chanting.

Carina tasted defeat. The enormity of the situation left her numb with shock and disbelief. *How could it happen to me? How could I have endured so much just to be recultivated?* Oblivion finally claimed her.

The feel of something wet licking her face woke Carina. "Casimir."

She didn't know how long she'd been unconscious but when she saw her partially formed clone lying a few feet away from her she knew it had been several hours. The sky was getting lighter.

"Casimir. Dig. Dig here." When Casimir didn't respond, Carina's brain scrambled to think of a command, until finally, "Where's the bone? Where is it? Where's your bone?"

Casimir let out a joyful yelp and began digging directly in front of Carina. Carina forced herself to remain still as her paws flew up and down in front of her. Casimir's rhythmic digging matched Carina's heart as she struggled to free herself and, when Casimir stopped digging, Carina's eyes flew open. She looked to see why Casimir had stopped and saw the she was holding something long and thin in her mouth and was wrestling and tugging it.

Carina realized that it was one of the tendrils linking her to her clone. She screamed, "Casimir. No."

Her scream alerted Daric and the rest of his men.

"What manner of monster is this?" Daric yelled as he tried to strike Casimir but Casimir was no longer the friendly puppy that Carina knew. Casimir flew at the clone and began tearing it to pieces. Carina screamed in agony as Casimir's teeth separated flesh, bone, and finally the tendrils of the seed were ripped out of Carina.

The pain was all encompassing. Brilliant red and piercing white fiery colours burned through Carina as the pain lashed through her body. The earth moved and shook, throwing everyone to their knees.

Daric's staff of power flew out of his hand and landed beside Carina. *It's the answer*. Another convulsion of earth freed her left arm and Carina reached forward and grabbed the staff.

Electricity jolted through her. The power of the staff, finally joining the powers of the dragon and the phoenix, blazed. Carina was thrown up, spat out of the earth. She landed on her back, momentarily stunned.

It was then that she heard other noises, conflict. She recognized Varun as he grinned at her just before his fist smashed into Daric's face. The fighting grew fiercer and Casimir's frenzied barking spooked the horses and they ran into the forest. The men paused as the stampede of hooves flew past them but then the sound of swords and knives clashing set them to fighting again.

Carina forced herself shakily to her knees and suddenly, before her strength failed, Ritik was beside her, raising her up. Carina cried as he held her against him. She could hear his heart beating as they stood there.

Finally, she spoke. "How did you get here?"

"I ran into Malcom after your friend Chenaanah bashed me on the head. He sent for Banished reinforcements when I told him that I'd had a vision of the Leader's hunting you into a ravine. He knew about Darol's people. We got here as soon as we could. What happened to you, Carina?"

She closed her eyes as tears fell. "Darol's gone, everyone's gone. The mine caved in and then Daric was here. He forced me to swallow the seed of recultivation."

Ritik's face paled.

"Casimir started to dig me up but then she attacked the thing growing from me." Carina started shivering once again and Ritik silently held her until she regained control. Both were oblivious to the clashes going on around them.

He wiped her tears as she continued speaking. "I thought I'd die from the pain when she severed the tendrils. When the earthquake happened, I was able to get free."

"Is that how you got here? What about the staff?"

"It's Daric's. It landed near me and when I touched it, I was thrown here."

Carina was surprised when Ritik moved away from her and bowed. She sent him a confused look. "What's wrong, Ritik?"

"Nothing, Carina, Stranger. You've acquired the three sources of power and now you can stop the fighting. You can get everyone to listen to you."

She stared at him in disbelief. "You're joking."

He didn't respond.

"You're mad."

"It is why you've journeyed here."

"Is it really the reason? Why did the people in the mine have to die? Why did Jackson have to die?" She turned to the men who were fighting. "Why are they killing each other?"

"The people in the mine might not be dead. Malcom told me that the mines go on for miles. There has to be another entrance."

Carina weighed his words. "Who speaks for the Banished here?"

"My brother, Andzej, is here."

"I hope your faith in me is well-placed, Ritik. Let's end this madness or be ended by it," Carina said resolutely.

She turned away from him and positioned herself so that she stood directly opposite the fighters. The cabin had been burned to the ground and Carina surveyed the destruction. She thought of Taura's joyful reunion with her sister, Chenaanah's happiness at finding her lost daughters, and of Jackson.

She brushed away her tears with one hand, raised the staff and drove it into the charred remains. "Enough!" she yelled.

Fire streaked away from the staff where its point touched the ground. The flames flashed, and danced until the fighting men were separated.

Carina waited. "Enough. Put down your weapons."

Daric turned and glared at her. "How dare you interfere! How dare you destroy the seed! Can't you all see? She's evil. She comes from the Upheaval. Look at the monster that helped her."

Ritik spoke up. "No, that's not true. She's the Stranger of the legend. The one we've waited for all these years."

"That means she wears the armband and can prove who she is." Daric taunted.

"Show him, Carina. Show everyone the armband."

Carina looked down. "It's changed, Ritik."

Daric's laughter rang out. "See how she mocks us."

"Is it true, Carina?" Varun called out.

Several of Daric's men jeered at her and Carina saw doubt flit across Varun' face. She let the laughter wash over her and then raised the staff once again. "Enough. I'll tell you what is true. You are all fools."

Stunned silence threatened to overwhelm her. "In the time that I've been at the sector, I've learned that the Leader's fear and despise the Banished while the Banished despise the Leaders. You try to kill each other whenever you meet. Both are blind. You need each other."

"What? We need the Leaders? I'd rather be dead," one voice called out.

"I'd rather starve to death than associate with the Banished."

"You need each other. Daric, you refuse to believe that the Banished are not the ones who are kidnapping and stealing your people. There is a third group who is responsible for all of those crimes and the Banished have been fighting the Scavengers for you. They've been rescuing people. Protecting them from the Scavengers. They've continuously sought to get rid of the Scavengers but they can't because the Leaders are too busy blaming them and attacking them.

"You need to combine forces and flush out the Scavengers from their burrows so that people are safe in the sectors."

"That's not true. They've tricked you into believing their lies," Daric said.

Varun yelled out, "No, you've been tricked by your own blindness to rules and laws that aren't just. You dislike the Banished because we're free to make our own choices."

"That's chaos. We can't have you destroy the world by misleading the people."

Andzej finally spoke up. His deep voice carried easily across the ground. "But it's you and your Leaders who are misleading the people. You control who can have children and what jobs are designated. You punish anyone who challenges your system and recultivate them if you can't control them."

Carina flinched when she heard him say recultivate but she saw Daric unconsciously reach for the pouch at his waist. She turned and saw Casimir with her head on her paws a few feet away. "Come here." Casimir obeyed and sat before Carina as the men continued talking. She patted Casimir and let her smell a piece of tendril that was caught in her fur. "Fetch."

Casimir bounded off and, after a few false starts, made a beeline for Daric, who didn't see Casimir coming from behind him. Casimir leapt up and grabbed the leather pouch and returned it to Carina who praised her so much that Casimir's tail thumped joyously on the hard-packed dirt.

Daric snarled. "Give that back to me, you little monster."

Carina held out the pouch. "She's a dog. I believe your world once had many of them, just like the trees behind us that have been hidden from you. I don't think you'll be needing the seeds anymore." Carina emptied them onto the ground and spat on them. "These are the monsters and you their wielder." She smashed the pile of seeds with the staff and watched as they burst into flame and vanished.

"Ritik?"

"Yes, Carina, Stranger."

"I believe I've done all that I can for the moment." Her words rang loud and clear. "The Banished and the Leaders now have the opportunity to talk with each other and resolve their differences."

"But what if they won't talk anymore?"

"The horses are gone and they'll have to rely on each other to make it back to safety."

"I'm sure we can get the horses back, sir," a Defender told Daric, who smiled slyly.

Carina returned his smile, a little more confidently than before. "That might be a problem if I stop you."

"You," Daric scoffed, "Pretender. You aren't the Stranger because you don't have the armband. Everyone knows that."

Carina looked at Varun, Ritik, Malcom, and Daric. "You're right, I can't take the armband off to show you."

Daric grinned as he saw things turning his way.

"When you saw it, it wouldn't let me take it off." She paused as she rolled up her sleeve. "And now, the armband has carved itself into me and we are one and the same."

Daric's grinned faded and uncertainty flashed across his face.

Flames flickered from the dragon as the feathers of the phoenix flashed brightly. "I'm sorry if this is not the truth that you wanted." The flames streamed down her arm into the staff. The earth trembled beneath the staff. "You need to work together to return to safety. You have the opportunity to get rid of the Scavengers, and you have the chance to build a new society together."

The earth convulsed and split, creating an ever-widening chasm between the Banished and the Leader forces who were nearer to the cliffs, and the charred remains of the cabin where Carina stood. The men could only escape up the cliffs as the way to the forest was no longer available to them.

Ritik ran to the widening chasm. "Let me come with you."

"Your path is with your people, Ritik. Perhaps we'll meet again."

"But where will you go?" he yelled.

"I have some miners to find."

The gap had grown and communication was no longer possible. Carina held up her hand in farewell until she could no longer see the men's faces. Ultimately, the future was up to them.

"Come on, Casimir. Where's Jackson? Find Jackson."

Casimir's tongue lolled out in a happy grin as they set off along the treeline.

# Epilogue

The momentum of the explosion momentarily stunned Jackson when he hit the hard, snow-covered highway. It was the movement beneath him that caused his eyes to widen, especially when two hands tried to push against him.

He pushed himself off the girl as quickly as possible. "Oh, my God. Are you all right? Have I hurt you any more than you already are?"

Carina pushed herself up on her elbows. "Of course, I'm all right. It's only a fall in the snow." She looked up, eyes widening in surprise, "Jackson? How'd you get here? I thought you were dead."

Stunned, Officer Dawes said, "How do you know my name? What do you mean you thought I was dead? I thought you were dead. Your body was all twisted and broken. I was carrying you away from the explosion."

"That's not possible. You were inside the cave when the explosion happened."

Jackson stared at her strangely. "You must have bumped your head very hard. You were hit by a semi and your car was underneath it. I got you out of your car before the truck exploded. Your body? Are you wounded? In pain? I thought you were dead."

Clarity caused Carina to fall back onto the cold snow. "But it was so real. I can't have imagined it."

"Imagined what?"

"You'd never believe me. Just tell me one thing: Do you have a dog named Casimir?"

It was Jackson's turn to be stunned. "You can't possibly know that. I left her in the car." He cussed, "Damn, I left the car door open."

Carina started to rise but when a dark form threw itself on her and started licking her face; she gave into laughter and tears. "Oh, Casimir. My hero."

Jackson finally helped Carina to her feet. Casimir raced joyously around them.

She brushed off the snow as Jackson stood gaping down on her. "Maybe I'm the one who hit my head," he muttered.

Carina smiled. *Maybe one day I can tell him everything that happened. How it had all been... a strange reality.*

Printed in the United States
By Bookmasters